EARTH CHIEF

AN EPIC SCI-FI THRILLER, 2024 SILVER EDITION

JAMES THULIN

ISBN: 979-8-89216-022-3 (Paperback)
979-8-89216-023-0 (Hardback)
979-8-89216-024-7 (E-book)

Library of Congress Control Number: 2024913289

BookmarcAlliance
California, USA
www.bookmarcalliance.com

Contents

CHAPTER I
Emergence

BALMY AND CLEAR WITH an occasional breeze, local conditions in Cape Canaveral, Florida were well adequate for the early August launching of the long-awaited NASA/SPACE FORCE led joint mission to Mars with Space X, the top innovator in design, testing and manufacturing from the private sector. Then watching on the big-screen HD-TV from the North Shore rangers' station at Devils Lake State Park in Wisconsin were two park rangers, Xavier Branion and Jeff Travis, sitting in awed anticipation with a couple other park enforcers for the six-o'clock event. Countdown to lift-off was about to begin, as two unseen announcers are voicing the stage-by-stage action at the launch site and into the celestial sphere above. Cuing off, the towering rocket started spewing the initial smoke cloud while the engines were firing up beneath the piggy-backing vessel. Of winged shuttle/airbus design, its other half awaited at the engineering space station to rendezvous for its addition. Aboard were five astronauts, two men and three women, carefully selected from a diverse pool of champions. Thus, the countdown began with announcers, Don Fielding and Michele Williams of the World News Network. Though their voices sounded a little hoarse from the long build-up show, they reported the event, live, with great enthusiasm.

"Three, two—one! We have lift-off, Don, of the Santa Marsia on its pioneering Mars voyage…first, though, it's to the Space X Engineering Space Facility, where the main ship will be modified and fitted with an all-new, non-disclosed propulsion system and a habitat section, nearly doubling its size," Michele explained with wonderous emphasis, pausing to clear her throat, but then she continued. "And after the forty-eight-hour stopover, it's off to Mars on a three-and-a-half-month journey, a much shorter duration than with conventional systems previously used." In smooth and timely interjection, Don commented further about the highly advanced spaceship, plunging into the sky.

"Yes, Michele, speculation on <u>that</u> is the use of nuclear fission combined with other energy sources, a fusion for enhanced performance. Ha-ha, it's all-too-techno-deep for me, but nonetheless will be installed and implemented for that significantly reduced travel time…Okay, as we're already fifteen-twenty miles up and all is going smoothly, let us again mention our five, most honored astronauts conducting this momentous mission, which includes the activation and testing of the TMFS, the Terra-Mars Forming Station, waiting for them on the Martian surface…" After a few seconds delay, the astronauts' faces were presented corner-screen, as he named them. "Uh, Team Leader, Doctor Barbara De Vida, Chief Engineer, Professor Lee Yeung and…what the hell? Are you seeing that, Michele? Some kind of 'ring cloud' just appeared above it up there, right in front of the rocket!" Following a bursting exhale, Michele responded, also confused by the strange turn-of-events, with a slight flutter in her voice.

"Yeah, Don, what is it—really? It looks like it's intentionally closing inward…Um, it couldn't be a natural weather phenomenon…could it?" Meantime, the televised view displayed three-framed screen shots, close-up, medium and further distanced images of the rocket approaching a bright white circle, five-miles-wide and closing fast, perfectly aligned to intercept its trajectory angle. Then taking notice from the smoke-ring-like anomaly's outer rim, an inverting 'spider web' effect took place, leaving tracers in winding, vapor trails form. Apparently taken aback to a numbing silence, Don resumed his commentary in a wining tone while theorizing about possible causes behind the threat.

"I don't know, but whatever it is…it looks real enough, alright, and not projected…hey! Maybe it's that old 'Star Wars' technology, but drastically updated for 'peaceful' guidance assistance? Or maybe ... we are in the matrix—no joke! Just hope it pokes through before it..." The tragic sight leaves him speechless, as the impact of the bolting rocket into the ring, contracting shut, created a soft boom and a blinding electric-green flash. With final commentary delivered just before an emotionally crushed Xavier commandeered the TV remote and turned it off, Michele Williams sounded angry and started sniffling like she was about to cry.

"Oh, my God, Don, I think this might be some kind of ultra-high-tech sabotage ... Holy fuh—damn! They're gone, blown up ... oh, Dear Lord—help us!" To her closing words, the disastrous, destructive force's aftermath then flickered and expanded out into the spanning matrix, shrouding half the sky in an even circular progression from its sparkling emerald midpoint a glow. In silent rage, the dark-haired olive-skinned Xavier, a tall intimidating quarterback-type, stormed out of the station while Jeff, a lanky ginger, followed, wide-eyed and shoulder-shrugging to the other rangers in somber understanding.

Six-hours later with warm and humid conditions under a crescent moon softly illuminating the Devils Lake's eastward-curving south shoreline, Xavier and Jeff stepped out of their state park SUV, which they parked on the graveled shoulder of the road into the valley. While cursing under their breaths due to the recent tragedy, they began their 'night owl' patrol with their flashlights shining the way past six-full canoe racks near the beach's west side, forging through the cacophonous waves of insects. Along the trek, the odd pairing, so different in most ways, discussed the 'Santa Marsia' mission disaster that occurred earlier that day. First to break his silence, Jeff, with his scrunching slightly elfin face, whined in an annoying high-pitched tone to a somewhat removed Xavier, an exotically handsome guy of a French, English and Iroquois mix. Then bearing Jeff's rant with limited tolerance, Xavier patiently nodded as they slowed their pace to a casual shuffle when they reached the swimming beach's edge.

"Damn it! Now it's gonna be another, what? Ten-years before they give it another shot?" Jeff complained, as he sporadically beheld the starry sky with a nervous jabbing motion and continued. "And those astronauts, getting killed like <u>that</u>? In such an <u>unreal</u>, psychedelic explosion—I've never seen anything like it! Well, what the hell do <u>you</u> think it was? A guidance system malfunction, as they claim … or maybe, aliens?" To the mere suggestion, Xavier suddenly stopped in his tracks and steered his dark deep-set eyes toward Jeff, with a piercing intensity of a most alarming nature. With his non-contemporary, longish-wavy brown hair hanging around his tall, tensed face, he challenged Jeff's certainly relevant questions only to comment in an unnecessarily gruff manner, carrying it out to the extreme. "Yeah, right, blame the 'fall guy' aliens … hell no! That would be <u>way</u> too easy!" Xavier started in usual zealot fashion, with his own rant but much longer, as he got swept away by his 'know-it-all' ego.

"No, no-no—the whole damn thing's gonna boil down to that <u>satanic</u> 'Star Wars' military program started way back in the eighties … with the Challenger space-shuttle disaster, a forewarning? Like, see where I'm going with this? Well, <u>this</u> is so 'Deep State', 'New World Order', the 'ends-justify-the-means' big government, big business and global elitists in cahoots with the twisted, gutless and bought-off mainstream media to keep us, their enslaved peasant masses, weak, fearful and apathetic! This <u>planned</u> tragedy, I tell you, was just their latest, insidious stunt to discourage any kind of hope for 'real' freedom, as in pioneering another world to truly and actually <u>be</u> free, as in—free from them! Nothing would scare them more than losing that parasitic control over us. And might I add, five-dead because of this 'fabricated', guidance-system-failure explanation? <u>So</u>, <u>what</u>—even top-tier astronauts are just a dime-a-dozen to them!" Xavier then peered down to the ground, with his flashlight shining up from his chin to his frowny face and concluded his monologue of dismay. "And thus, well worth it for their heartless cause, crushing our dreams and keeping our expectations low … while so dismally, we trudge on …"

Distancing himself from his 'over acting' comrade, Jeff finger-twirled around his own ear, jokingly questioning Xavier's sanity, and chuckled in response. "Jesus, Xavier! Though I sort of agree, enough with your heavier-than-usual conspiracy theories—you're freaking me out! Besides, I like my 'blame the aliens' idea a lot better! But, if you ever decide to be a 'most depressing monologues in the world' writer someday, you sure have my recommendation." Xavier appeared a bit embarrassed, clutching his forehead and looking about, but then bounced back, well-grounded once again. "Yeah, what got into me? I really went off…this time, but—good one! Oh, my god, look out on the lake—there must be at least a dozen of 'em!" He well noticed, with a rasp in his voice, a human presence that had become routine, as Jeff confirmed the same. "Yep, and their shoes and clothes are right there…God, please let be there some hot chicks!"

Upon closer examination, there were several pairs of shoes, shorts and various shirts set in clumsy array, prompting Jeff to chuckle when he aimed his flashlight upon the lake, revealing the guilty party with their heads just above the water, playing possum. Then giggling amongst themselves, the nocturnal swimmers of a multi-racial, college variety acknowledged the rangers in their tan uniforms and started toward the shore.

"Hey, it's midnight, people, and park curfew's eleven o'clock!" Xavier shouted, suppressing his laughter, which made his tall face, with high cheekbones and a strong cleft chin, very taught. "Please, go back to your campsites or leave the park grounds!" The naked parade, six men and seven women, trudged out of the shallows with embarrassed smiles.

"Jeez! Talking about indecent exposure!" Jeff amused, as he danced the flashlight beam upon their less-than-model bodies. "Please! Put on some goddamn clothes! This is supposed to be a place of beauty." Shaking his head, Xavier was uncomfortable with Jeff's demeaning treatment.

"Cool it, Jeff," he whispered aloud, while crossing his well-tanned and toned arms, only to then pull back his thick brown mop, which had grown well past his collar. "And you wonder why we get such a bad rap…well, well, now the night really picks up! I wonder what's with these kids?" With hands waving in the air to signal for help, three white boys in their early teens, sporting buzz-cuts and the popular phosphorescent yak fringe head band, hurried over to them from the direction of the ancient bird mound, the park's premier archeological attraction. Before reaching the shore, one of them tripped and fell, yet in his panic, barely lost a stride, rejoining the other two.

Genuinely shaken with fear, they all spoke in gibberish until one of them articulated their concerns. "Mister Ranger, Sir," he said, nervous and out of breath, "over there!" He then raised his voice, pointing to the mound. "At the bird mound we saw something so totally bizarre, you're gonna think we're crazy! It was like this big fog patch appeared, but then took the form of some kind of giant gargoyle-looking creature. And there were these other ones, like regular ghosts, that it sucked up into its face. Then after that, the thing fell on its back and sunk into the mound. I tell ya, we heard voices and everything! You must have seen it! It was huge!"

As Xavier and Jeff looked at each other, then back at the boys with sighing, unconvinced smirks, the flustered trio protested. "Aren't you guys gonna make a report, or at least goddamn check it out!" the natural spokesman demanded with marked insolence, while the others grunted words of support. "If we were adults, I bet you'd at least take us half-seriously, and humor us with a little investigation…come on! We know what we saw, and it just about scared us to death!"

In an attempt to calm the aggressively rattled adolescent, Xavier tried putting his psychology education to use. "Easy, kid," he started, turning his flashlight to the ground while speaking in a firm yet non-threatening tone, "I'm sure you're fully convinced of what you saw. However, you must be aware that what you just described would sound rather unbelievable coming from anyone. Besides that, it's also no secret that dropping acid, snacking on shrooms and doing other psychedelics are quite popular with you younglings these days. But you look like fairly straight kids so, therefore, I'll just consider this a simultaneous case of mass hysteria, probably caused by those silly headbands you're wearing—that's what we'll call it! Now, get the hell back to your campsite or wherever else you're supposed to be, and save your weird-ass story for one of those paranormal shows!"

Though disappointed, the three boys meandered, with some hesitance, toward the road out of the valley behind the then-clothed skinny-dippers who were just hanging around beachside, quietly listening to their outrageous report.

"Shit, Xavier, you saw their simultaneous case of red eye! Man, we should have busted 'em or, at the very least, given them a good scare," Jeff berated with his high beam flooding upon their backs in delayed chastisement. "Coming to us with a story like that! They'd have to think us absolute fools to even try. I mean, we're talkin' total insult, and you with your 'mister nice guy' approach! My God, give me a break!" Just as Jeff finished his vented rage, the ground began to vibrate, and a low indistinct hum came to be heard. The haunting baritone seemed to emanate from the direction of the mound where the boys were allegedly spooked. Wavering in pitch and tone, the strange sound had a rather melodic quality, similarly affecting the intensity of the surface vibration. Submersed in near hypnotic intrigue, Xavier assumed a gallant stride toward its source.

"Xavier—don't be a hero, man! This is _too_ weird!" Jeff warned with a holler, as more people with their record-ready phones started to congregate up shore around the three young visionaries, bragging of their sighted prelude to the rumpus. "I'm callin' in! Let the county or the state handle this! Come on, Xavier, I need some crowd control assistance over here!"

Once at the mound, Xavier wandered about in a crouched posture and, within seconds, the ominous audio anomaly abruptly ceased to be felt or heard. "Hey! Sorry, Jeff!" he called to him from roughly fifty-yards-away, forgetting policy use of the shortwave communicator. "Those vibes got me in a trance or something, but, don't worry…I've snapped back since it's gone mellow. Anyway, from here it sounded like someone was playing a 'shit loads' wattage of bass guitar in a cellar beneath the mound! Well, let's put out a report and maybe get some geologists out here to do a sonar study. There's _got_ to be a cavity of some sort," his raised voice then tapered off to a whisper, as he felt an aftershock brewing with a vengeance, "oh God…"

Though his perilous beckoning to a higher being expected no answer, the earth below him rippled and rumbled with a mound-bursting reply that initially tripped up the doomed escapist in its ever-loosening soil. Atop the imminent explosion, Xavier was then catapulted by the surprisingly quiet impact, along with a few torn trees and several tons of sodden dirt in an even spatter. For a moment, he lay motionless and half-buried in his hundred-foot vaulting spot from where Jeff froze back several yards, still at the beach. Meanwhile, the crowd of fifty onlookers promptly ran for cover behind a nearby lavatory building, further inland.

As the cloud of natural dust and debris began to clear before the ground lifting force, the massive silhouette of a towering creature, with banding bon-fire eyes, was revealed, standing like a statuesque monument. Stoic and unmoving, the entity's presence seemed fixed so perfectly just to be cordially absorbed by the world until it soon emerged from obscurity with a sandstone chiseled face that bowed like a tilting mountain peak. Diminished to but a puny crawler for the gargantuan hunter's grasp, the barely conscious Xavier struggled in the mud toward Jeff to only have his banged-up body forcefully turned around, void any physical contact, to face the monstrosity.

The instant that eye contact was established between Xavier and the creature, which was drooping a hood of giant, scarlet-tipped feathers, dual beams of glowing, intertwining red, yellow and blue were emitted from its fiery optical caverns to create a violet sphere that encapsulated his head. Neutralized, the purging of his mind's experience for an unknown purpose left only scarce remnants of himself. He was almost brain-dead, a vacant subject primed to be administered the introjection of another man's life more foreign than he had ever known, and into a time warp nine-centuries-gone and so, indelibly predetermined. Thus, upon the mystical transfer's completion, he was drawn, a will-torn spirit, to this lived life on the cliff's edge, high above the crystal blue waves held common to both of them. There, he became nestled in his host's full sensory array, where he still had no control.

The captive Xavier portion did not yet panic since the man he had become seemed merely on the verge of a sacred ritual, a rite of passage perhaps. An abrupt stammer in his first breath seemed natural enough, as to awe the glorious view before him. The golden orange sun, blurred by the summer haze and near setting beneath the western ridge from across the narrow lake, warmed and almost fused him, content in his new home. However, an increasing sense of dis-assimilation took hold when his sights steered downward. On his scant-of-hair, well-toned legs and bony copper feet, crusts of streaked and spotted blood lay while his perceptions, immersed in chemical distortion, reaped grandiose hallucinations.

All the way down to the lakeside trees, the steep decline of quartzite boulders was morphing into a human congregation. Fully transformed, his adoring audience, with tan round faces and colorful, festive garments of Native American flair, began to chatter in praise of his name, Lone Hawk. Enough of Xavier's former self still lingered to evoke a 'terror dreaming' effect, far removed from the original's delusional state, due to awareness sparked by an intense survival conflict. The situation reeked of ritual sacrifice, and after the 'interpreter' wiring to his yah-dah-dah tongue was fully tuned, he listened, wincing with excruciating dread and embarrassment, to the official statement of his host's intentions. All, for what seemed a fanciful mirage and the wicked one who was savoring it…

"Just as the good chief had told," he raved, spewing an air of confidence in anticipation of the impossible, "the mighty Earth Force has now summoned me!"

Lone Hawk bowed his head of thick, feather-tangled black hair and panned his wide, crazed eyes over his muscular arms. Proud of the rows of freshly sewn-in feathers spanning their lengths, he licked up the blood, which seeped from the hasty self-mutilation. Although his sweeping motions left a generous crimson smear upon his favorite war garment of intricate gray-white stripes, the sight only further enthralled him as did the salty taste of his vein's drink.

Then, feverishly stroking the red tail's beak affixed to his broadly chiseled chin, Lone Hawk peered into the sky with twisted visions of mystic glory. However, his attention was soon demanded by the one who prodded him there, his only true spectator, Stout Raven. A thin, aging man bearing a facial resemblance to his namesake, he was the Warbirds' senior shaman and, as the most powerful advisor to their puppet chief, he was very anxious in his decision.

`I could not possibly allow this madman to continue the spreading of his Earth Force nonsense to our people,' Stout Raven thought to himself, easing his conscience and justifying his administration of the 'daydream' potion, which would seal the radical's fate. 'In but a day, he has spoiled their minds to such dangerous thoughts that they may become as crazy as he. But, fortunately, for the good of the tribe, my magic brew has made him even _more_ insane and so, a slave to my words. Hah! Earth Force, as you now know, the power in the valley is mine! Just as you have taken our premier brave, so shall your impostor follow … to hell!' Self-assured enough, he made frantic gestures from the trail aside and below the towering bluff where the South Shore Village, currently under military arrest, could be seen far off in the distance. Hence, he voiced a sense of urgency with a desperate, shouted rasp:

"The window of time is here and will soon be gone!" the black robed visionary warned, with his left fist raised toward Lone Hawk and his open hand beholding the western sky. "Your words must be brief to coincide with the prophecy. Do _not_ stray your eyes from me, for I will show the talon symbol at the latest juncture. Then, you know what to do!"

"Thanks to the Earth Force, the Wind God and the Avenging Hawk," he started again, but in a different tone that would escalate from a loud whisper to the summit of his vocal ability; "thanks to _all_ the forces that have combined within me, it will be done. By my actions so divinely instilled, a common enemy will be vanquished, allowing the Warbird, Earth Force and all great nations of good intent to flourish without worry." As he could tell that Stout Raven was about to signal, he hurriedly pulled his prized Toltec sword from its holster and raised the silver bladed keepsake to reflect the solar submergence.

"Beware, Owlmen!" he shouted amid fearlessness, midrange of his total, vocal's projectional climb; "your worst nemesis has been born in me, Lone Hawk, with the fury of a thousand braves. By the power of the Earth Force, I will seek out your sky-bound domain and remove your threat from _all_ reality! On behalf of the _entire_ world, triumph by my magical hand is _destined_ to prevail!"

Following his bold and faithful declaration, Lone Hawk began to oblige his cue. Thus, Stout Raven gave him the talon sign by clenching his index and middle fingers to his thumb, to which he nodded with affirmation to the sun's less-than-profound setting behind the ridge across the lake. His heart was pounding with an anxious, yet eager, rapidity when 'what he thought' was the Hawk Spirit encouraged him through a shrilling voice inside his head, "Yes, Lone Hawk, let there be no doubt that you <u>are</u> The One, so worry not! The Wind God will catch and deliver us as my flight is reborn in you. And with that, the Owlmen will be but sand flies to our power, which shall <u>crush</u> them out of existence to complete our sacred revenge. Proceed now, good brave, savior and friend. Carve your glorious path into history!"

Upon the winged warrior's faithful guarantee, Lone Hawk extended his arms and with a three-step running start, thrust himself forward with all his strength, and for a moment felt as though he were swooping. Yet, in an instant, he was all too aware that the Wind God was not there. He only plummeted, catching a glimpse of the smug-faced Stout Raven, who tossed his Earth Force amulet of turquoise disc to join his fall, the most thorough of insults to them, the fool and his hapless god. To follow, in a flash of torturous disbelief, he could swear that the taunting bevy of boulders, awaiting him below, engaged in uproarious laughter just before he met them.

'How can this be?' His thoughts raced by during his quickly receding moments. 'The magical sphere of the Earth Force spoke only to me as the savior,' he gasped his last breath of life-giving air to press against his heart; 'I am <u>not</u> crazy! The Chief confirmed my victory by prophecy, but Stout Raven only <u>pretended</u> to believe in me. Betrayed by one of my own people, and I was their only hope. <u>None</u> of them can stop the Owlmen! Oh! That didn't hurt at all!'

With a loud clang of his sword, Lone Hawk's blood splattering impact against the jagged rocks was physically painless. His passing of death's doorway was complete, and only darkness followed, leaving a vultures' feast behind. And thus, fully 'spirit' transitioned, he continued to speed on a downward path inside the nevermore to nowhere.

'Falling and falling, but to where?' he wondered, while his emotions had traversed in so few moments from prideful exhilaration to panicked disbelief. 'It does not change. Only a path of darkness and I have no choice! I'm as powerless as I was in the womb, void even of a nurturer. This is simply unbearable.' "Stop!" he commanded in desperation, then to his immense relief, his descent slowed to near suspension, where he could at least see himself, arms, legs and torso taking on a multi-colored glow. And once convinced the falling sensation had truly ceased, he assumed it was an answer of profound accommodation. "Earth Force, thank you!" he shouted out loud. "I suppose Stout Raven's meddling has changed everything. Please, reveal to me our new plan of attack, which will eliminate the Owlmen ..."

Even after repeating the request a few more times, there was no sign of acknowledgment and soon, a cold and lonely fear poured into his soul. His words seemed to have been swallowed by the surrounding silence. Hovering in burning stillness, Lone Hawk's broken heart took over and turned to the love of his life, and how the tragic aftermath would affect her. "And what about my dear, ever-sweet Rainbow?" he posed with deep concern for the new bride he left behind to a questionable fate, as she was deemed by Stout Raven to be the Earth Force's tool of deception that sealed his fate. "She hasn't rejoined me ... so, since only I could be her soulmate, she must still be alive. I hope ... or better, I must believe that Stout Raven would at the very least have the decency to let her go back home to her father, the venerable Chief, who seemed to know that something horrible would ... well, what is done ... Whatever stage this quest is in now, I am for some reason unheard, or even worse—ignored?

"Why have I been banished?" his detached spirit howled with burgeoning anger. "Earth Force do not desert me to this! You have put me through much too much pain already! I want my reward, the chance for glory, the glory which I have earned! Earth Force!"

No one answered him, as his shrieking words echoed in the vast, unforgiving darkness.

"You know I'm their only hope, who else?" he challenged. "No one! The world to them is but an orphaned fawn to the hungry wolf, without me!"

Lone Hawk's fury dissipated, giving way to a qualified acceptance. "This is not the end," he reconsidered, his faith glowing anew. "Though I have not a body, I think and feel. I have a purpose yet in this life. I am not dead; I'm merely cocooned. Sooner-or-later, the day will come when I bear my sabered wings, shred my way out of this nowhere and fly to my sacred destiny."

Set in his commitment, he did not care that his life's flashing-in-its-closing-moments experience had been denied since past reflections, anyway, were upstaged by explosive yearnings for the future. However, the review of a mortal existence so wound toward the extraordinary could not be long ignored. Lone Hawk soon surrendered to a look back on his days of flesh and blood. And with no shortage of time, he sifted through their every aspect, from the point of childish innocence to the unsavory period of bestowal and possession by the forces he did not yet understand.

CHAPTER II

Lone Hawk

'**H**OW VERY FORTUNATE THEY were to conceive me,' Lone Hawk's thoughts drifted to his absolute beginning, though, unlike the last days of his righteous reign, they were of selfless reminiscence. Void the smug air of destiny roots, only extreme happiness was wallowed for his parents, Timbers Earth and Solarain, since their life together may have never been. Trying for years to reap offspring without any luck, they were thought an infertile match. From what he was told, they were then repeatedly coerced to seek suitable, fruitful mates, because the old 'replenishing and expanding of the tribe's numbers' was preached a sacred duty. However, being of such splendid compatibility, to separate them would have been a crime. Just by the mere sight of their mutual stares and open kisses, anyone could tell that this love mustn't be denied.

Thus, it was to the tribe and his parents' great relief when he was born during the first autumn's snow, a healthy bundle of boy initially named Timber Seed for his father's sake. Though, due to his mother's slight pelvis and his hefty size, it was a very difficult birth, and so she would not risk another. He would remain an only child. And how fortunate for them to have no more, since this one was quite a handful, very curious and tempting death as a constant from the start.

From the time he was very small, young Timber Seed took this energy to the trees. In pursuit of birds and squirrels, he climbed as a predator and called himself the Bobcat. Soon, with his insistence, he was known as such, and a little later became the avid Tree Stalker. While only a child's game, the exercise was excellent strength and coordination training, leading quite naturally to his superior physical condition. As a bonus, a mind-enriching benefit was gained by this activity. For once he could climb the highest treetops, especially those atop the towering bluffs, their majestic views captured his wonderment and made him ever want more. He was insatiable!

At seven-years-old, Tree Stalker was already helping his father, the Warbirds' chief builder and designer, to put up lodges.

Working stone, wood and earth just right was very hard work, but he did well, so that his father would treat him like a man. In turn, by age-eleven he was almost as strong as an average man and, with his father's approval, ambitious enough to pursue his dream. Compiling all his hopes, he planned to build a massive watchtower of twelve-men-tall on the highest bluff, his Warbird landmark to gleam upon the territory and beyond. A giant conglomerate on a four-pronged base with multi-level structuring, all of thick timbers and quartzite supports, it certainly would have been the Warbird jewel, but it was not to be.

Once he thought the project had adequate political support to get past the preliminaries, Tree Stalker's dream was shattered. By the orders of Chief Howling Wind and nameless opposition, mostly just humoring the lad, Timbers Earth's over-zealous son's grand tower project was cancelled, only moments before they started construction. He was devastated and, as some kind of appeasement, was taken into the army, a scout. Though with honors of 'so young, yet so qualified', he felt so utterly betrayed, with no choice but to pout and bear it. Fortunately, however, his outlook improved immensely as to be nothing but the best. And soon after this declaration when mock battle practice commenced, the fear in his opponent's eyes, intimidated by his unrelenting ferocity, further fed a will that seemed boundless.

Thus, since he also knew the territory better than anyone else, the thriving Tree Stalker was inducted most aptly, the supreme knower of the forest, cliffs and animal calls. The animals…he always loved the animals. They did not bother him with wasteful chatter like, so often, the human folk would. Refreshing in their way, they gave him an extra sense with unassuming rapport of the invisible, vital things that they knew, and that he, otherwise, would so naturally have overlooked.

By his second winter of military service, the champion-scout rapidly reached physical maturity and, through his regimen conditioning, was as strong and nimble as any warrior or brave. It was then that recognition of his efforts began. For, with his outstanding performance being well noticed, he was unexpectedly exempt from the traditional rites of passage into manhood. A grueling winter survival task, it was as but an unfounded formality with its host of unpleasantries, which he 'personally' found needless anyway for one so fit as he and happily avoided. While such an exclusion was unheard of until then, he was also promoted to warrior status, the youngest Warbird ever to achieve the intermediate post.

Though officially a member of the warrior camp, Tree Stalker, exuding with ambition, was considered unreasonably favored in his rapid advancement by the others, who were at least a few years his elder. Indeed, they respected his fierceness and raw physical ability, as well they could not deny the obvious. Even so, they were not required to accept him socially and did not. Besides the barrier of jealousy, he was considered an arrogant 'brat boy' in a hard man's body. With that, he had no peers. Anyone of his age was, by responsibility level, too immature, and the older warriors, of course, despised the warrior pet. Rendered a serious loner, his misfortunes of friendship did not finally turn until late that spring.

During the brisk forest survey when this fateful transition occurred, erratic strips of midday sunlight seeped through the tall, wind torn treetops to the dense undergrowth, which he slashed with a crude moose-horn sword to clear a new trail. In forming the virgin passage, he etched the mark of the Warbird, an upright arrow with horizontal zigzagged wings, into every big tree of twenty paces. Proceeding as he was in the low priority Warbird territorial expansion project of the desolate western fringe, he stumbled upon quite a gem of a tawny and white-speckled bird, with tiny tail feathers streaked red as blood.

Unable to fly, the red-tailed hawk chick, barely taller than his hand, approached him with an impressive display of valor. With its high-pitched shrill and underdeveloped wings at full spread, the brave chick tried to be as big and loud as possible, an aggressive attempt to intimidate the intruder and survive. Tree Stalker was very impressed and confronted the little hellion as gently as he could. He knelt before it and laughed. But when he put his hand out, as only a calming gesture, it lunged forward and bit his finger.

"You are a <u>brave</u> little screecher, but you draw no blood. Or did you not even try?" He spoke softly to the riled creature, still in its survival stance. "Where is your nest from which you fell? Oh, worry not! I know the trees, so just wait here. I will seek out your nest, and then return you, somehow, to your grief-stricken mother." In a systematic search for the chick's felled treetop abode, the concerned Tree Stalker patrolled forty paces from the midpoint to form a circular route, returning every quarter span. There was no hawk's nest in sight, leaving him befuddled as to how the abandonment occurred. He decided then to conduct a broader search, yet this time he would bring the chick for its safety's sake. It was quite a surprising struggle subduing the flapping, pecking and scratching handful. But once he had a good grip around its wings, he pinned them to its back, gaining submission.

The second round revealed not a clue to the mystery, until he found a scattered nest with two dead hawk chicks nearby. Hence, Tree Stalker felt very sorry for the noisy little imp for which he had developed a paternal fondness. He would save this one from sure starvation and adopt him, allowing a unique friendship to bloom.

"Alright, you little screecher, I'm taking you home where you'll eat like a chief," he reassured the exhausted little hawk that was reduced to peeps. "Ah yes, Screecher! By the Wind God's will on this blustery day, <u>that</u> will be your name." In kind to his divine words, Tree Stalker peered up to the flailing branches in the wind with a worshipping gaze, then spied a bobcat on the prowl cautiously coming towards them to where he left the dead chicks. He sighed with a strong exhale of relief.

"Feast well, warrior cat, but not on this one!" he called out to the hungry feline, already chomping away. And while cradling the near silent Screecher against his chest, Tree Stalker backtracked his trail to the Valley of the Warbirds, running most of the way with a sense of urgency. Once he bounded down the steep path just inside the valley, the winged orphan was in a state of shock and was fast-losing body heat. "You grow cold, brave Screecher—just hang on a <u>little</u> longer till we get home!" He burst into a full gallop, yet further down the trail about halfway to the Warbird village's edge, he encountered a few 'cannabis-smoking' warrior acquaintances, one of whom blocked his way.

"Hah, ha-ha—what's your hurry, Tree Stalker? And <u>what</u> are you hiding in your hand?" the outspoken, brutish Jaded Fist teasingly queried, while he took a smoke-spewing drag off a leaf-rolled, disparagingly called 'wander weed' stick and grabbed his wrist for a peek. "Awe, the loner found himself a baby hawk to fill that maternal void in his life—hah! I know…we'll call you 'Lone Hawk' from now on—it fits you <u>perfectly</u>!" They laughed with taunting eyes, while Tree Stalker batted Jaded Fist's intrusive hand away.

"If this chick dies, <u>you</u> are next, Jaded Fist," he warned with hateful eyes, as the fully animated Jaded Fist stood wide-eyed, feigning deep fright to his threat. "Or at the very least, when I become chief, you'll be demoted and die the oldest scout in Warbird history!"

"Chief? A freak like you!" Jaded Fist retorted and wallowed in more sadistic laughter with his friends, then added, piously looking up to the racing clouds in the sky, "Oh, dear Wind God, <u>please</u> save us…if <u>that</u> shit ever happens!" Insulting as they were, Tree Stalker did not hear them for long, as he quickly left their 'smoke induced' mirth far behind. And, even though he hated the man with his blatant disrespect, the name 'Lone Hawk', clumsily meant as an insult, rather appealed to the young Tree Stalker. Thus, he adopted the regal identity to proudly be his own.

Decidedly so, Lone Hawk's full attention returned to the chick in hand when he soon arrived, panicked, in the village's south end, where he made a stop-over at the first of dozens earth homes, sodden-soil-insulated, wood and stone structures with quartzite chimneys jutting out of each. Without hesitation, he slid open the wooden door on the dilapidated little shack, went inside and instantly emerged with an animal trap about hip-high held sideways. From there, he darted home up the mulch-laden main path, past the market and ruling class village center, to their much larger, finely appointed lodge at the forest's edge on the other side of the residential row, northeast near the lake.

Pleasantly temperate and a little breezy, Lone Hawk surveyed the crowded beach in the distance, glad that most everyone else was there instead. Therefore, he had time to prepare an adequate environment for the young Screecher, undisturbed. Thus, he ducked into the relatively lavish abode, facing southwest, with Screecher and the trap-turned-cage in tow. Inside, Lone Hawk quickly found a folded blanket in his parents' bedroom, partitioned left from the front room with deerskin curtains hanging as a privacy doorway. He slid the blanket into the cage and gingerly placed Screecher onto it and swirled a nearby wash cloth around his almost motionless body. In the back of the lodge-center, he discovered some fresh bass in a ceramic pail on a beautifully crafted, quartzite hearth beneath an elaborate, three-fireplace chimney system. He cut up one of the fish into several small, meaty chunks. Just as he served the fleshy heap on a little wooden tray, Screecher's state of shock turned into a ravenous attack while he gobbled down the entire lot.

Lone Hawk smiled in relief and praised the stuffed, sleepy bird. "Good boy, Screecher, now that was some good wing-growing, full-feeding you just did—I think you're going to make it! Uh, that is, I <u>know</u> you will…and 'high in the sky, as a Warbird can fly'—<u>that</u> will be you!"

Just as he finished his avian pep-talk, his mother, Solarain, a petite pretty-faced woman of thirty-four, snuck up behind him, not immediately noticing the cage wedged in the lodge-front, under the hemp-screened window. She looked around for an instant in her beige, somewhat revealing swimwear, tapped him on the shoulder and whispered loudly in his ear. "What's going on in here? Are you talking to ghosts again, Tree Stalker, my haunted warrior son?" she half-joked, referring to his comical reputation for spirit-speak, as Lone Hawk, a bit startled, turned with a smirk and playfully nudged her on the shoulder.

"No, Mother, but I do want you to meet someone…tah-dah!" He stepped aside, took a knee on the colorful rug over their pine wood floor and beheld his hand to the sleeping Screecher, for an introduction to which she endearingly shook her head. "I present to you, Screecher, the orphaned hawk-refugee I saved from a hungry bobcat. And, through the Wind God's good favor as well, I too have a new name…" He tapped himself on the chest, grinning proudly. "Lone Hawk!" he announced, as if heaven-sent, and thus sought his mother's approval. "Has a nice, regal ring to it—don't you think?"

In turn, Solarain reminisced, with a typical motherly smile. "Oh, my 'little Bobcat', as you first were, brings home a hawk chick he saved from a bobcat, and re-names himself as the bird, hmm…" She stood there, perusing his abundant artwork on the maple wood walls and grazed her fingers on one of his best hawk etchings on the front wall, right next to her. "Lone…Hawk—why am I not surprised? Even as a small boy, hawks were on your mind, here in your artwork and watching them up there, wishing you could fly. But, this 'Wind God' stuff, I don't know, that remains to be seen…Meantime, however, you better have a plan ready for your 'Screecher' by tonight, because I'm sure your father will not let him stay here for long!" Lone Hawk paced back-and-forth for a bit then walked in-and-out of his bedroom, partitioned right-side from the front with its own little fireplace like his parents'. He scratched his head deep in thought, while she tapped her foot, cross-armed in expectation. Then finally onto something, he snapped his fingers and pointed over his shoulder with a plan.

"Oh, I know—your brother's…Wonders Eye's crummy little shack, where I got the trap!" the jubilant Lone Hawk expounded on it with great enthusiasm. "It will be perfect! Since he left for Big River City the other day and won't be back till later this summer, I'll convert it into a luxury birdcage. Just give me a week for Screecher to grow strong enough, and for me to get it ready—sound good?" With her hips a shift, Solarain nodded and stood at ease, placing her hand onto his forearm for reassurance.

"Yes, good idea, I'm sure your father will be agreeable and, in fact, will probably insist on helping you," she said, with a giggle to state the obvious. "As you well know—that guy can never turn down a new project! Speaking of which, he started construction on those new barracks today and so, I'll just wait at the beach for him while you do your thing." She kissed him on the cheek then while walking out the door, Solarain looked back and left him with a proud, loving smile.

Upon the good luck that his uncle Wonders Eye, a roving barterer, had unknowingly provided his rarely inhabited, broken-down shack at the far south end of the village, it became the perfect place to keep and raise young Screecher. With his father's occasional assistance, Lone Hawk spent every spare moment at the remodeling site, which was ready by the week's deadline. Through the following summer, that was Screecher's home, with Lone Hawk staying there whenever he could. But most of the time, military life kept him away and busy, so the young hawk was kept locked up alone in the sweltering heat. Too proud to ask anyone for help, the culpably conscious warrior was then forced to leave Screecher for many a duration, by himself pent-up in the forsaken bird-shack. However, the squawking feathered one could no longer tolerate the confinement, and soon broke free.

Lone Hawk was on duty that mid summer's day when Screecher took his first test-flight. Initially, upon returning from his regular warrior day, he found that his precocious companion had partially dismantled the crisscross pattern of sticks and earthen stone, his long tempting prison's window to the outside. Though his being there, inside, was obviously not the case, the bereaved Lone Hawk still searched the crippled lodge in frantic desperation and, most depressed, turned up nothing. Then, after gathering a mildly willing task force to recover his friend, all was not lost. For everyone in the vicinity was treated to a most precious sight, seeing the newly airborne-capable Screecher suddenly soar down from the southern sky and land on his shoulder. From that point on, they were inseparable, as the lovable raptor became his gray, all knowing eyes in the sky.

Before long, Screecher was retrieving small game for them to share. And so, after hauling in prey of varied sorts, Lone Hawk would skin and split them for two, leaving the raw flesh for the hunter and the rest to cook for himself. However, as generous as he was, Screecher was no fool and always seemed to choose the larger half! That bird … how Lone Hawk so enjoyed watching him grow. Thus, with a fortunate mild winter to follow, they made great strides since their training never ceased. During that time, they also developed a dance purely by accident. Just by his spinning and deflecting Screecher's tenacious attempts at landing on him, the 'hawk dance' was born.

By the next summer, they were the unstoppable tandem that carried out autonomous duties. And a very special unit they were, as even Screecher was honored for his achievements, deservedly being named the official Warbird mascot. Very large for his species, this wonder hawk, with plumage darkened mostly brown and tail feathers fully red, grew to be three-hands-tall and with the wingspan of a man's arms. He was big as an eagle and had talons so strong, Lone Hawk usually wore dear skin pads strapped to his forearms and shoulders, to prevent puncture wounds from his frequent perching points.

Considered celebrities, and constantly exploring and expanding the Warbird territories to their outer reaches like a growing fan, they outshined the entire Warbird army in this time of peace. Most logically then, Lone Hawk was promoted to 'brave' when at his official ceremony, after receiving his custom-copper Warbird pendant before the sacred bird mound, he and Screecher performed a more well-refined version of the hawk dance. For the first time in front of a large crowd, they rocked the audience with a wild yet graceful display that had the drummers and flutists joining in and the young ladies swooning to his virginal blush. While though he was no smoothy with the women quite yet, and was by duty still no more than a glorified scout, Lone Hawk sincerely believed that his achieving chiefdom status was not far off and 'there' would lie the cure for his social shortcomings. However, more than anything, his yearning to become chief was much more ambitious, if only to make the ever-growing Warbird Nation the greatest in the known world. But it would not be until two summers later when he would realize what his ultimate aspirations were. And much thanks went to his uncle, the enemy of convention, Wonders Eye, by whom he was launched to learn more about himself and his destiny than in all his preceding life. With a sled of stacked furs and various leather sacks of merchandise next to Wonders Eye's high ground shack, the merchant's mission to Big River City would begin:

"Hello, Screecher! You're sure looking good and ready for a great journey," Wonders Eye, a tall, lean and slightly wrinkled man of thirty-five, told the hawk, in shouldered transport with an affectionate knuckle trill to his feathered throat which made him gurgle. "I see you brought your military friend, anyway...well, all right, he can come along." While Lone Hawk only shook his head, Wonders Eye laughed with a rattle of his bamboo, turquoise laden chest-plate and a wave of his well-tied, nearly waist-long hair laced with colorful feathers from the tropics. His flamboyance was excessive, yet with large, deep-set eyes on a strong, high-cheek-boned face and masculine physique, he carried it well.

"Oh, Lone Hawk, my sister's all-too-serious son," he added in a jolly tone while scratching the breast of the serenely poised Screecher, who hopped down to the young brave's forearm; "you look ready to conquer the world...or, maybe just eager to try and deal some of your creations which she's told me about. So, may I see them?" Apprehensive, Lone Hawk shooed Screecher away to perch elsewhere and loosened the drawstring atop the big, waist high deerskin bag that held all of his trip belongings. From inside, he pulled out a burlap sack that was then jingling with metal stuff.

"They are but child's toys and other things that I have made these past few years," he said with near embarrassment, while emptying a dozen tactical adaptations of wooden handles and leather straps with stone, bone and copper blades, spikes and ornamentation. There was also a smaller sack of charcoal black that his uncle curiously snatched up and poured out to reveal the rest. "These aren't serious trade items like yours. I merely want to feel as though I'm going for a purpose...that's all."

"Shush with your humility! These are toys that can slice, batter, shred and kill," Wonders Eye expressed with a careful appraisal of the lot. "You have become quite the expert, working the copper...and, in the secret black bag...Lone Hawk, these are exceptional!" One-by-one, he removed the thumb-to-fist-sized figurines of stone and wood, eighteen in all, and placed them on the grass beside them. In rowed formations of four-by-four, plus two favorites which he held in his hand, the ensemble brought a genuine smile to his face.

"Very nice detail, Lone Hawk. The time you must have put into such, I would have never believed!" he continued to compliment, leaving Lone Hawk to feel somewhat patronized, yet enthused. "Mostly hawks, of course, an owl and what is this? A <u>birdman</u> with big arms and a mean face—how frightening! Bear, buffalo, deer, wolf and bobcat, the standards.

"All of those are quite fine, but <u>these</u> two, which I would wager you never showed your mother, are excellent!" Wonders Eye declared of two wooden figurines of a curvaceous naked woman, true to human form, in erotic poses. "You put the most time into these visual delights, ha-ha, even when you weren't making them. Copper painted lips, nipples and, well…so you <u>do</u> know where the erogenous zones are! Great effect, this type of artwork will produce a most favorable response in the city. I wish you had made more, though I am glad to see a clear indication that you are interested in the pleasures of the woman. I was beginning to worry about you, but the final solution lies ahead. A common Warbird woman cannot entice one as rigid as you. So, when we arrive in Big River City, I will introduce you to 'Night Owl', the lady of the night who will transform you. After a couple of nights with her, you will be shy no more!" Wonders Eye's intuitive assessment brought about an uncontrollable case of blushing upon the virginal face of the well-overdue Lone Hawk.

"I have been much too busy with my military duties to make it with the women," he defended to the unbelieving, yet respectful, smile of his seasoned uncle. "Perhaps, when I am chief, I'll have a whole bevy of brides and concubines. But, meantime…sure, training with this 'Night Owl' woman will be excellent experience for future female conquests. I will do my best <u>not</u> to disappoint you, Good Uncle." Lone Hawk's attitude sent Wonders Eye into a fit of uproarious laughter that could have awakened the whole village in the dawning haze. In turn, Lone Hawk covered his uncle's mouth to quiet the ruckus, while further sustaining his embarrassment to the point that his crimson face was about to burst.

"Disappoint me?" Wonders Eye continued to laugh, yet controlled it to a moderate level. "This is about enjoying yourself with an attractive woman and <u>not</u> about disappointing her, yourself, or especially your uncle." He then shifted to a serious tone mid-sentence: "You are <u>always</u> trying to prove something, or impress people like Timbers Earth, Chief Howling Wind and even me. Well, the only thing that would impress me is a Lone Hawk who can forget the army; enjoy a trip just for the pleasure of going somewhere new; and becomes the one who frees himself. If your demeanor was not so <u>controlled</u> and <u>distant</u>, people would know what a fascinating man you are. Oh, but you will <u>definitely</u> be forced to open up in Big River City. When they set their sights on you, the mysterious, muscled birdman from the North, Night Owl will have to get in line with all of the <u>other</u> intrigued women!"

Wonders Eye's words of encouragement were very effective, as seen in the fact Lone Hawk's blush retreated and a broad grin of confidence flooded his face. Thus, the mood became jovial and all they needed to do was secure the canvas tarp over the cargo, piled waist high on the low friction, copper-tracked sled, which measured roughly one-by-three-paces. Avoiding any morning delays, goodbyes were already said to his parents and Wonders Eye's old friend, Stout Raven, the previous night. And, fortunately so, since Screecher was growing impatient. With prodding calls prompting them to hurry the last preparations, they started up the trail toward the southwest corner of the valley's rim. By a roped poll in the front and a fixed one on the back, the pushing and dragging of the bulky sled load was quite laborious for the two of them up the gravel incline until it soon leveled off to a smooth-sanded path through rolling, wooded countryside. As their efforts eased, they switched sides on occasion, with Lone Hawk voluntarily pulling solo a few times to give his uncle of less strength and stamina some much needed rest.

On the way to the Wise Crow River where their long water journey would begin, Wonders Eye talked about his recent trapping and hunting expedition in the North. Telling of the bountiful marten, beaver and muskrat stock of his easy plunder, he referred to such exploits as the noble role they played in tempering the overpopulation crisis. Also, and most especially, he elaborated to excess about the big, wildly insatiable women of the Wolverine tribe at the far north reaches of civilization on the massive Superior

Lake. Throughout his bold tales, Lone Hawk was a perfect audience, only commenting with praise.

Toward the end of the hike, the stagnant, late morning heat began to take its toll in toiling sweat. By that time, Screecher, who had been following them very loosely between the treetops, perched on Lone Hawk's shoulder with chirps of greeting and news of their river's nearing. Though they were aware of this, the visit gave them a morale boost and quickened their pace to the palisade's edge, overlooking Otter's riverside cabin of canoes for borrow and trade. A slight breeze arose from the slow waters as they took an effortless slide down the smooth, sloping eastbound trail, which gradually sideswiped to the Wise Crow's north shore. And there he was—Otter, a short and stocky older man with incredible spryness, awaiting them at the adjoining docks by their reserved canoes.

At the riverfront, his many children of three wives gathered around Lone Hawk to pet Screecher, their endearing mascot. While Wonders Eye and Otter dragged the sled of merchandise to the docks for loading, the famous tandem did a show for the young people, who were wide eyed, smiling and laughing. It was, of course, the hawk dance at play, the trick show in which Lone Hawk would keep calling Screecher to land on him with various shrills while dodging every attempt. His bouncing body and swaying arms, combined with Screecher's frantic wing-flapping and missed talon grabs were dizzying. Mesmerized, the children were clapping and cheering, yet there was one uncharacteristic curmudgeon nearby to spoil their fun.

"Get over here, you fool!" Wonders Eye hollered with severe annoyance in his tone. "The Wise Crow calls us and you show off to the children with your _silly_ hawk dance! Come now, it's time to launch these water bugs!"

Lone Hawk was suddenly angered by his mild shouts of abuse and whisked Screecher away into flight. Thus, trotting over to the loading dock in an obvious cloud of red aura, the children scattered in fear, witnessing his violent change to a rippling mass of flexing muscle that looked ready to tear out of its skin.

"_No_ _one_ calls me a fool, not even you, Wonders Eye—and gets away with it!" he barked with an unusual wrath, which left his uncle speechless. "Never even a whisper of that word pertaining to me! Now, that we are clear on that…yes, I agree! There is no time for such needless delay. Let us skim this tiny river to the Big One!"

As Otter backed away with his collateral furs, Wonders Eye offered only a meek grin and a shake of his head, in surprise at Lone Hawk's overacted display of the warrior's drawing of the proverbial mind blood.

"Oh, you are really something—I am well intimidated, my 'Nephew of Fury'! Should I walk on the autumn's fallen leaves so quietly around you that I not make a sound?" he responded, trying to keep a whisper of authority. "I was just getting your attention like I would any other brave, but I forgot about your regal pride and infernal temper. So, don't you worry, your eminence…I vow to be much more careful in the future to preserve my own life before the great future chief, Lone Hawk…may I bow to you, Great One?"

"Stop, with that tone! Making me fall into that deep pit of guilt, just like my mother!" he accused, hoping to then make peace. "Very well! I will be one of levity, who only laughs when he's angry. I will be your ideal traveling companion, as I respect you, Wonders Eye, my elder. Now, let us be painted and forget this moment of senseless conflict, or else we'll never even begin to enjoy ourselves…agreed, Good Uncle?"

Wonders Eye tapped a knuckled backhand with Lone Hawk to signal a clean start with no animosity. Receiving the all-clear with previous tensions resolved, Otter then applied the white balm on their upper arms in the horizontal, four striped merchant's pattern and brought additional tarps, wrapping and other provisions to bolster what they had. Finally, they boarded the canoe with its trailer loaded with the trade merchandise, while the rest lay between them in the rider, Lone Hawk affront and Wonders Eye astern.

When they shoved off the dock to make the most of the Wise Crow's gentle westward flow, Otter had some last moment requests. "Bring me back some sapphire, turquoise and ruby jewelry in gold, for my wives and daughters!" he shouted, before they had gone too far. "You know what I mean, Wonders Eye…from the South Sea merchants, those exquisite pieces from the Great Southwest Empire! Do so and I will make it well worth your trouble! Please, try!" Otter seemed anxious, as though he were being ignored, yet Wonders Eye glanced back to him in reassurance. "We'll do what we can, Otter!" he yelled back to his distant form with a wave of his hand, while Lone Hawk diligently powered foreword. "In twelve to fourteen days, upon our return, you <u>may</u> be surprised!"

Voyaging on, the current grew weaker, and the river's depth sank lower. The lingering dry spell had taken its toll and was so alarmingly severe, the canoes began bottoming out in spots, late afternoon that first day. Trudging through the river's sludge, on occasion, was an unfortunate side effect of the drought, a drudgery that would last until the third day at high sun. It was then that the river opened to a greater width, depth and flow where, ever-increasingly, the foliage became greener the further west they traveled, due to the better rains generated by the Big River. They spanked the wild waters with their hefty paddles, warmly exuberant and freshly empowered, as their abilities were enhanced by the momentum of the suddenly awakened Wise Crow. Screecher expressed his enthusiasm as well. For when the canoes became free-flowing and their exhilarated hoots and hollers came to follow, he surprise-swooped down to join them at the same level in parallel flight, close to the water. Yet, seemingly conscious of non-interference etiquette, he did not try to land on Lone Hawk or the canoes.

"Keep powering the vessel on this center current, Lone Hawk!" Wonders Eye advised, trying to project his voice over the roaring river while receiving occasional backsplash to the face by Lone Hawk's rapid side-to-side strokes. "If we stay with this one till dusk, we'll celebrate at our next camp for making up the lost time of the past two days!" The river flushed behind them with whitewater fury and, while they held their bladders, full and delirious advantage was taken of the magical driver. Being lost in the excitement, the long and speedy ride seemed to pass in half the time, as the orange sun had come down so soon on the slowing river, cutting through a maze of cross-slashed palisades. Big River was less than a day away and, therefore, Wonders Eye's festive promise would be fulfilled that night at a good flat site nestled on the north bank.

They dined very well with a surprise donation of a nice plump rabbit from Screecher who was immediately divvied his share, the head and front legs, saving the fleshy rear portions for themselves. Cutting the rodent meat into fire-pit ready chunks on a small cutting board, Wonders Eye, a bit of a spice expert, sprinkled the pieces with a special mix from a little pouch. He skewered them on some sticks that he collected, and they both held the meat-bound wood over the fire, which also gave them appreciated light while all remnants of the sun had faded. The feast was a carnivore's paradise and, after they finished with some sweet corn patties for a stomach base, Wonders Eye revealed the celebratory treat.

"Lone Hawk, we must salute our day's record travel time and the 'great hunter' Screecher, for this devoured gift of fresh rabbit, which we never would have gone hunting for in the dark," he told in a low, boisterous voice while offering him a sizable deerskin flask of intoxicating sour mash of corn. "So here, have a cup of this with some water, Lone Hawk. It's Stout Raven's strongest brew!"

Lone Hawk took the flask and drank a gulp. After following with an immediate dose of water, as Wonders Eye suggested, his voice became low and raspy. "It burns so good in my throat, stomach, and now, my mind," he described to his uncle who poured a more generous splash down his own gullet. "Let me try some more, so I can experience the 'shaman' visions!"

"Oh, this is not _that_ mix!" he corrected with a warning sweep of his hand. "There is no _dreaming_ mushroom in here, no—that would be disastrous! Only a true shaman in a controlled situation can use such without harm. Even this straight sour corn mash is prohibited, as you probably well know, by the tribe for casual enjoyment like _we_ are doing this night. So, do _not_ mention to anyone that Stout Raven allows me these things, because he wouldn't do so unless I was deemed one of responsibility."

Lone Hawk took a second gulp of the brew and smiled, rolling his eyes. "_Everyone_ knows that _you_, Wonders Eye, are Stout Raven's best friend and that you tout yourself as an honorary shaman," he stammered, his speech beginning to slur while he tossed another log on the fire. "They _all_ know what privileges go with that! But don't you worry about me. I talk of nothing with any of them, except for vital military reports and strategies. Your words are safe with me!" He guzzled a third intake of the brew and with his emerging openness, Wonders Eye seized the moment to better know his sister's unique son.

"Speaking of friends, why is this Screecher your only one, and a hawk no less?" he asked, pulling the flask away from Lone Hawk's guarding clutches. "Are the other braves and warriors really so bad?"

Lone Hawk called Screecher from his perch in the tree next to them. With gliding ease, he was upon his forearm, watching the two in expectation. "This hawk has more personality, bravery and intelligence than all of them, combined!" he hailed in thick-tongued fashion, while the full-bellied Screecher began to look bored. "Perhaps, if these times were not so peaceful, the others would not be so lazy and complaisant. Yet, as it is, most of them are mere prey for an opposing tribe. They are content to live and die with nothing of valor to show. I cannot associate with such, for fear that I may become like them and never reach my goals. We need a good battle in our expansion to awaken their brave and warrior spirits. Only then, could I possibly ever befriend … but, forget it—I just want to be Chief, and make the Warbirds a proud nation!"

"I understand quite well, Lone Hawk," Wonders Eye said in an agreeable tone, which took the effects of the sour mash well into account. "While I choose to walk the outer rim of the system to have my way, you would choose to be in the center, changing it to suit yours. In fact, you are the better man, looking also for the good of many. But I do bring them good stories, because it's so easy—they never go anywhere!" He laughed, backhanding Lone Hawk on the shoulder for meager credit, prompting a swift peck from Screecher on the wrist. "Sorry, Screecher, we are acting strange tonight with the drink. Would you like some? No, we need your clear mind, standing guard when the deep sleep takes us. And, before it does, Lone Hawk, you talk about needing a battle or conquest? Well, not far down the river are a weird, arrogant and very rude people who call themselves the Earth Force.

"Two summers ago, I stopped there upon my return from Big River City," Wonders Eye continued. "While I hoped to sow the seeds of trade and learn more about them, I mostly just wanted to see the fabled magic orb in their sacred cave. From a reliable source, I heard that it is big, bright and powerful! They guard and worship it as the entire Earth's spirit, and I found out how much—too much!

"No matter what I offered, they refused me even a peek. The Chief, a very, very big and old man, told me that only Earth Force and 'The One', whoever that was supposed to be, could gaze upon this magnificent object…and I was neither. Their attitude angered me so, and you know I'm not that way! Finally, as you probably have guessed, they drove me out of their village at spear point. So, if you want to start a battle and take something of worth without conscience, the Earth Force would be a worthy prize, which I believe the Warbirds could win. Bring that back to the valley and you, Chief Lone Hawk, have the beginnings of an empire!"

"This is your best story ever, Wonders Eye!" the intrigued Lone Hawk cheered, un-slurred, and then, with a strange squeaking sound and a pat on the winged one's breast, he made Screecher roost back where he was and started another series with the drink. "You certainly know how to swell my ambition—you, tricky man! Come tomorrow, you must point out the Earth Force shoreline and describe to me the approximate depth to the village, and anything else that you can remember. And now, let us forget such serious talk…for now, I just want to laugh myself to sleep!"

Wonders Eye rubbed his eyes twice with his typical theatrics, to emphasize the shock of seeing the hidden, jovial side of his nephew. "Do I know this man? Laugh myself to sleep?" he beheld the impostor with open palms and a genuinely impressed, goofy grin of disbelief. "Well, if you want to laugh, Lone 'Sour Mash' Hawk, I propose that you learn to be more humorous. For instance, tell me about the braves, especially the ones you despise most, and focus on their peculiarities. Exaggerate them as much as possible and build on it. I'll do the same with the worst people in Big River City and then, we will laugh ourselves to death!" And the merriment pervaded deep into the night until they were arrested by a dead slumber, a sprinkling of the future, which was too soon to come.

CHAPTER III

The Serpent's Blade

T HE NEXT MORNING, THEY arose well past dawn in a regretful state of wooziness that affected Lone Hawk most severely. For just as he stumbled to a nearby tree to urinate, he felt his stomach jump and, hence, projected a sour-mouth geyser beyond his control. "I'm truly paying with misery this morn for such a fun night, but the Stout Raven brew sure let me say many things that needed saying. And while I _am_ a brave who can endure this 'okay' through its full term, I was hoping that, perhaps, there was a counter brew to cure my pain. Have you a remedy, Wonders Eye?" he asked most pleadingly with his hand clamping his forehead to keep it from splitting, while he hid in the shade of the trees to avoid the piercing sun.

"Yeah, I'm in a sad way, too, yet fortunately, for the miseries that Stout Raven's magic brew leaves the day after its joyous run, there's also his magic 'spunk leaf' powder," he groggily answered, upon the desperate request by advising the intake of a fine white powder, which he carefully sprinkled into both of their cupped palms from a small leather pouch. "This will revitalize us! Bring it to your nose and sniff, with all-your-might, like this..." He demonstrated the technique and Lone Hawk followed the same, then held his hand out for more. "One should be enough, but you look much worse than I," Wonders Eye assessed and so, considering how inexperienced he was with such indulgences, gave him a second dose. "Also, drink plenty of water and try to eat some corn patties, even if your appetite rejects them. Soon, you will return to your former, robust self."

As instructed, Lone Hawk ate two of the corn staples that tasted awful compared to the night before. He came close to another vomiting spell, yet with frequent sips of water and many deep breaths, he paced the inclination away. While he proceeded to break down their camp in pure drudgery, Screecher arrived from across the river and called out in greeting, no less than a torturous sound to his ears. The magic powder's effect, however delayed, suddenly lifted the cloud of persecution and in appreciation of the alleviation, he loaded and readied the grounded canoes with no demands on Wonders Eye, who wandered into the forest and returned, pleasantly surprised.

"You should have called me, Lone Hawk!" he shouted, upon his approach, first noticing the cleared sight and then the water-bound canoes. "Oh, but you look <u>much</u> better. I suppose you had to do something with all the energy of <u>two</u> 'spunk leaf' powder sniffs!"

Lone Hawk stood, smiling and waving him over to the shore where he held the ropes, eager to resume their trek to the Big River. "The magic powder has worked its miracle. I feel better, lighter on my feet than normal. This is fantastic!" he expressed, fully satisfied. "When I become Chief, you will be a full shaman and my personal medicine man. Yes, and finally, you will be a <u>true</u> Warbird!"

"No, no-no! Please, do <u>not</u> drag me into the official fold," he quickly denounced, as they boarded the canoe. "When you become Chief, leave me as I am—free! Besides, Stout Raven, who far out-qualifies me, still has many good years left to serve. And there are his two subordinates, dedicated to the army on the north shore. You know them, Falling Cloud and Mound Talker. Both are very fine, as Stout Raven has told."

Lone Hawk chuckled and glanced back at his defending uncle in a jocular way, as he started to power the bow toward the calm river's center. "Worry not, Free Spirit Uncle," he said with pride of his foolery; "I would never appoint <u>you</u> to <u>any</u> post! I merely need to be more careful with the 'happy' drink. Though, I must say, it is <u>certainly</u> a nice change to make you, the gullible one!"

In good-natured retort, the fake-laughed Wonders Eye gently poked the witty one's back with his paddle. "That was good, too good!" he complimented, while yanking the rope to the canoe in tow. "I must have taught you well last night, but I think you forgot about the Earth Force. You wanted me to point out their main shore. Well, just past this snaking, triple-ridged bend, we'll hug the south bank and you'll see their landing. I <u>will</u> tell you more when we pass it." They cut through upon the scenic river's path that wormed in a tight double bend between lush, straddled hills along the north and south shores.

On the other side of the third ridge, the river widened two-fold and not far off on the northern bank, the backside of a curvaceous, statuesque woman came into clear view. Bathing at the edge of the sunlight's reach just before the water hill's morning shade, her light tan skin glistened while she gracefully stood and bent over to reach for a white cloth on a nearby rock. Her sleek naked form captivated Lone Hawk's attention so much that he stopped paddling. However, an untimely Screecher disrupted his fancied stare and captured her notice when he released a sustained shrill upon descent to his shoulder. Alarmed, she turned to face them, swinging her long braids in a whiplash motion about her 'goddess' face to her unwavering breasts of perfect dimension and form. She crossed one arm and draped the cloth on her crotch for modesty's sake. With big, squinting eyes casting a unique shimmer, she stood as a regal guard, making sure they were on their way.

"If I am not mistaken, that is the Princess Rainbow of the Earth Force," Wonders Eye quietly told, as he seemed to become nervous. "And, as you can <u>plainly</u> see, she has blossomed into a full-grown woman."

"Plainly, nothing! She is the most <u>beautiful</u> woman I have <u>ever</u> seen!" Lone Hawk declared, with frequent glances toward her between strokes. "Tell me more about her!"

"Forget her, Lone Hawk," he warned. "Do <u>not</u> fall in love with the enemy, or you will become soft and vulnerable. In fact, let us hurry past this place. See the warriors by the landing? We need no trouble here!" Wonders Eye paddled with a fury, carrying the load for Lone Hawk, whose paddle barely touched the water while he gazed at the enchanting woman. And though she became increasingly indistinct with the growing distance, there was a connection between them. They watched each other until the Wise Crow eventually curved to block their view and break the spell. Before he could ponder the blood-burning attraction, there was a sudden headwind, which brought the coldest air they had felt since middle Spring.

They battled a near constant west, northwest wind with gale force gusts, which transformed the lazy river into a choppy bed of defiance. Even so, the brute strength of Lone Hawk's feverish, side-to-side double strokes and the crafty current catching of Wonders Eye were an unstoppable combination. Though it was so unseasonably cool, the determined duo generated their own, more-than-adequate heat by the sweaty labor of propulsion. Through this most arduous leg of the journey, Screecher was mostly absent, flying by only three-times, as the partly cloudy skies built, in threatening progression, to massive thunderheads at the Wise Crow-Big River junction. Rapidly, the late afternoon's sky darkened and when they graduated to the Big River, totally exhausted, they were 'oh, so' relieved to be swept southward by a strong, swift current. There, Lone Hawk became completely astonished by its scale.

"Wow! This is just like our lake and valley, but stretched as-far-as the eyes can see," he remarked with a euphoric glow to the wooded bluffs lining the shores, and the Big River's wide opened girth, both dwarfing the Wise Crow's three-fold. "By far, the most fascinating sight I've seen in all my life! Oh, no! Feel that warm breeze?" Lone Hawk's tone then took an abrupt change to dread, as he warned, "we are at the two fronts…this is really bad! The Wind God's about to get very angry—Look! It's coming down on us! We must go to shore—now!" A funnel cloud was descending from the ash gray cluster above them, with a gentle swirl that was gaining momentum.

Soon, it reached the water close behind them and started churning a white foamed path, which followed in their direction toward the west bank. As they fled with all their energy in full rebound and reached the muddy shore, the dipping cloud spin had developed into a full-fledged tornado, creating a huge roving whirlpool at its base. After running the canoes aground, Wonders Eye motioned to an overhang at the foot of the sandstone bluff when Lone Hawk, with a great surge of adrenaline, dragged both canoes, arms tucked on the inside bows, up into the squatting cave. The moment he dove into the natural refuge, the forge of the Wind God came ashore and ripped the trees from the ground before them. The roar of its destruction was deafening as they covered their ears, curled bodies braced behind the canoes.

Though covered with the dirt kicked up by the twister, they were unharmed and, thanks to Lone Hawk's valiant, yet foolish life-risking effort, the canoes and the cargo were saved. They watched the black and brown body of doom roam down the river, bouncing off the east bank and back off the west. Before it reached the east shore again, it lost its concentration and rose from the water, a harmless funnel cloud as it was, to dissipate into the cumulus sea from whence it came.

"You could have been killed, trying to save those canoes, Lone Hawk!" Wonders Eye scolded, as they carefully walked the slippery, freshly polished dip into the river for a much-needed rinse. "Though I _am_ thankful to have not lost my furs, I could _never_ fathom your life for such things … oh, but there's no use telling you, the hero at any cost!" Surveying the severed timber strewn upon the sight before their chin-level cave, Lone Hawk was proud of his feat.

"Even if it caught me, I would have turned around inside of it, holding the canoes like two spin seeds," he fantasized, peering into the sky with a cockiness that raised his uncle's eyebrow. "Then, when the tornado released me, I would have floated by my own momentum and once it eased, I'd gently fall to the river. From there, I would merely have paddled back to you, safely waiting there in the cave."

"You would have been ripped to shreds!" Wonders Eye firmly corrected while climbing back to the cave. "Please tell me that I'm not responsible for the craziness you spout, which I hope is an attempt at humor. That said, let's have a drink of the sour mash— ha-ha!" he suddenly laughed to the sight of the diving Screecher, appearing from nowhere, high above his unsuspecting nephew. "And here comes your winged warrior to join us!"

After Screecher recaptured his shoulder perch, Lone Hawk brought him to the cave amidst the sharing of some spirits with

Wonders Eye, who had already gathered some kindling for the fire that would be vital for the cool night ahead. Between tiny sips of the sour mash, they started the dry wood with flint sticks and meticulously arranged the much more abundant fresh branches around the center blaze for later use. Being that the cave was shallow and wide to near open ends, they placed the canoes perpendicular to the back wall on either side of their camp as a wind block. They were famished, and soon the fire was ready to cook.

"This will suit us quite well for the night," Wonders Eye commented with a sense of security, as he began to clean some river bass, which he had caught a couple nights before. "Now, just take it easy and do nothing more. I'll take care of everything and reward you with a very special meal for saving the cargo." While Screecher took off as-soon-as Lone Hawk brought him inside the cave, he returned to shore with a catch that was almost too much to handle. Dragging the ugly, gray flip-flopping mass in river-skimming flight, the tireless hunter brought them a strange, scaleless fish of over three-hands-long. Wonders Eye was pleased and rubbed Screecher's breast in appreciation of yet another hefty contribution.

In contrast, however, Lone Hawk only glared at it with disgust. "Screecher truly hauled in a bad choice this time!" he fervently disapproved, with his upper lip scrunched against his nose. "That thing is probably poisonous to eat! I'll put it back."

When he started for its tail to be rid of it, Wonders Eye grabbed his wrist to avert his action of ignorance. "Do not be a fool! I mean, don't judge by its unsavory appearance," he explained, fast covering his near insult. "The whisker fish is excellent for the skewer on the open fire. It's a very fleshy fish and is also a staple in Big River City, where it is prepared in the market oh-so many different ways—you just wouldn't believe! The secret is that it has very little flavor, but great texture. You can make it taste like anything! So, I will cut this up as well, and give Screecher the tail fin and the head." The pieces from the river bass were puny compared to the generous cubes which he was able to slice out of the thick, meaty belly and tail of the odd fish. Then, snacking on smoked deer strips while waiting, Lone Hawk watched in hungered anticipation, as Wonders Eye sliced mushrooms and squash to be pressed between the fish. Topped off with a sprinkle of spices, he handed his apprehensive nephew a stick of the bass and another with that of the whiskered one.

They cooked them and compared. "The whisker fish is juicier, looks better and carries the flavor of the mushroom and squash so well," Lone Hawk offered his praise of the new delicacy, which he rapidly devoured while taking only a few bites of the bass. "Mm-mm, please make me another…I must admit, I prefer most any other game to fish. But this is different—I like it <u>very</u> much!" They cooked several more of the lanced fish combinations and drank the sour mash at a moderate rate with plenty of water.

The sun began to set and, as its red shadow was cast upon the bluffs across the river, they grew very drowsy yet could not fall asleep because of Screecher's unusual, obnoxious behavior. Hobbling around the fire, he pecked at them in passing and hyper-actively peeped a weird trill. Then, after bolting out of the cave, he almost immediately swooped back inside, exhibiting the same dance.

"Cursed bird! Let us sleep!" the tired Wonders Eye complained and whisked him away, forcing his retreat. "Why is he acting like this? Is it a game?"

"I think he's merely restless and a bit insecure, being so far from his own territory," Lone Hawk rationalized, with no clear label for the display that Screecher repeated a third time with his immediate return as before. "What's wrong, Screecher? Do you miss the valley, where <u>you</u> are the Sky Chief? Ha-ha—now that's good! Peck at my uncle, if it makes you feel better…"

"It doesn't even hurt, really," Wonders Eye surrendered to the gentle attack, with a spell of uncontrollable laughter coming over him. "In fact, he's pretty cute when feisty, but <u>that</u> is enough…Get him away from me, Lone Hawk!"

Lone Hawk, caught up in the humorous situation, started to giggle, as he bodily removed Screecher from his pesky posturing and tossed him into flight toward the river. Uproarious laughter in a contagious loop then followed with a couple gulps of sour mash. However, the mood took an abrupt turn to alarmed silence, when their sounds of mirth were hauntingly mimicked from just outside the cave. Immediately, Lone Hawk realized that Screecher was warning them of a new danger. A cue that he would have taken more seriously, he regretfully thought, if he had not indulged in the drink.

Afterward, they showed themselves by dropping into view, two from either side of the overhang, which sheltered their camp. And in an instant, four, short and stocky mahogany-skinned men who were stalking their camp had them cornered. Their shaven heads, hairline painted with red, yellow and black stripes, narrowly cleared the low ceiling, as they closed in on them. Though puny, their stature, barely that of a Warbird woman, was well-balanced by the long exquisite swords, which they proudly reeled with intimidating swipes. Like the extravagant gold and silver ornamentation about the chest plates of their black warrior's garb, the double edged, silvery blades had intricate gold patterns of a spiraling serpent design, which grew thicker and more prominent in the woven, texture-grip handles.

To Wonders Eye, their appearance and obnoxious, sing-song tongue identified these ones as virtual demons. "They're Toltec bandits, and they want more than our cargo," he whispered, with the warning of doom in his eyes. "They would _love_ to have our primitive, long-haired heads as souvenirs from their safari, but I will try to convince them to take the merchandise and spare our lives." Wonders Eye pleaded to them in broken Toltec, reaping only vile snickering behind wicked, bloodthirsty smiles.

All the short while, they were much too near for Lone Hawk's tolerance, as he was fully flexed with an adrenaline surge on the verge of eruption. "When I say 'go', hurdle the canoe and run," he told Wonders Eye in a quiet rasp while his confidence brimmed toward, what he considered, inferior competition. "They will get _nothing_ from us, but their own deaths!" He put his plan into motion by initially grabbing two good-sized branches, which were smoldering into hot coals at their dry ends. With an ample piece in each hand, he scooped the entire fire up into the air off a swift, back handed jerks of his wrists. "Go!" he shouted aloud, to follow with incessant howling and barking that he hoped would add a measure of fright and confusion to the spattering of red-hot embers.

Then as the primary result, his ultimate desired effect of a substantial flying-ash-induced smokescreen was created, and thus allowed Lone Hawk to invisibly charge the intruders and topple two of them into a struggling slide toward the river's edge. With the sturdy tree limbs smoldering ends, he guarded himself well against their swinging swords, using one of them, like a burning buffalo horn, to gore the heart of his first kill. Though the other captive aptly slipped away and sprang to his feet, the sword of the dead man became Lone Hawk's to overpower the second. With his superior strength and reach, he made short work of the little man by instantly slashing his wrist and tendons to a resulting limp hand. So, unable to man his weapon, the wounded one fell prey to the swinging blade of his deceased comrade's sword across his throat. Blood spouted from the wound upon the felled body's impact against the rocks, painting Lone Hawk in full-frontal red, as he leaned over the open-throated carcass to snatch a second sword for Wonders Eye.

"Wonders Eye! _Here_—A _real_ weapon!" he shouted, frantic, as he ran to assist his uncle chased by the other two down the river shore, well beyond the cave. Even though Wonders Eye seemed to adequately hold them at bay with a couple of guarding branches of his own, the remaining Toltec were a furious and swarming pair. "Keep them in front of you, Wonders Eye!" Lone Hawk yelled, as he was halfway there in a double sword-wielding sprint. "Do _not_ let them get behind you! No-oh!"

While one of them climbed a boulder next to him for a height advantage, Wonders Eye looked up and took his eyes off the other, who chopped his left arm near the shoulder with a swift double whack. Thus, when he turned to see his blood-drenched arm hacked to the bone, the elevated man saw the opportunity for a perfect strike so driving the sharply-thick saber deep into his unguarded neck with a toothy smile of victorious delight. At that unavoidable point, Wonders Eye was reduced to a kneeling, quivering gush of blood that would drain and collapse, splashing into a puddle of crimson demise. Just a sliver of time was the difference between rescue and death. Yet, with the reality being the latter, Lone Hawk was embroiled in failure, sorrow and incomparable rage, as he bore close range witness to his beloved uncle's brutal execution.

Fuming, he pounced with lunging fury, utilizing all his momentum and strength to mount his most devastating attack.

Then, even though the assailants were stunned on their heels, they attempted a last ditch, simultaneous swipe of their swords to catch and kill the hulking primitive by his own slamming force. However, the cross-armed Lone Hawk reigned superior, as he flung his deadly pair outward upon impact and foiled their plan by blade-to-blade deflection. Following the resonating crash of silver, the created gap served to host an inward backswing, which landed the swords in a scissoring strike upon their short fleshy necks. Together, in perfect proximity, he scored a double gash-and-slice from which he pulled away, their blood spewing into Wonders Eye's to form a generous pool of death stain. Three lifeless heaps before him and two more back at the cave, Lone Hawk felt empty and only stared up to the twilight sky, hoping for a vision of his uncle's forgiving spirit in the faint stars a twinkle.

"Sorry I failed you, Wonders Eye," he squeaked, steeped in guilt, since his bold course of action resulted in the sacrifice of the one who so loved life. "It just seemed the only way we could...but I took too long with the other two and now, just like _that_—you're gone! What the hell am I to do now? I can't stay here, and neither can you. Well, there's only one choice for any _true_ brave, and that is to finish what he starts. We _are_ going to Big River City, just as _you_ would have wanted! I _know_ you, and only _there_ would you have your body lie." Upon his declaration to complete the journey, Screecher landed next to Wonders Eye and rubbed his beak on his mane of long bloody locks, nudging and gurgling to revive him. The sight prompted reluctant tears to break the dam of Lone Hawk's brave but loving heart. And though he made not a sound, his eyes became waterfalls of sorrow.

"Come, Screecher," his fluttered voice called the faithful yet confused hawk to rest on his shoulder; "you cannot wake him anymore, but if _only_ I had heeded to your warning—Stop that!" he scolded himself, trying to avoid the self-destructive pattern of harboring all the blame. "You did what you could and, at least, _you_ are alive! Yes, but now, you must live _twice_ the life, for his sake and more!" He dragged Wonder Eye's body to the cave, and made a new fire with two torches spiked into the ground outside of it to provide light for his task in the blackening sky.

First emptying the trailer of its merchandise, Lone Hawk brought the hollow vessel down to the river's edge, and there he wrapped his uncle's corpse in his 'most valuable' trade item, a full-length buffalo-maned pelt. With plenty of leaves for stench control, he loaded the body and put most of the cargo on top. Saving the rest to be carried in the riding canoe, he pulled the lead craft from the cave-to-shore, both ready to launch. Finally, he stripped the Toltec of their marvelous swords, chest plates and holsters, thus leaving them as they were to rot where they lay. Before his departure, he took a gulp of the sour mash. In disgust, he spit out the intoxicant and dumped the rest of the half-filled flask into the gaping throat of his second kill.

"Drink to your victor, Toltec demon!" he deplored, finding no comfort in the desecration of even one so despicable. "What's the use? Your deaths pay <u>nothing</u> for my uncle's…I have only your swords as my trophies to show. But perhaps, fate gave them to me so that I could keep my own life. Indeed! The rites of passage, with a vengeance? Let's just see if there's more to this, Good Uncle, as I hope your spirit guides my way…" he tearfully concluded the dialogue with himself and Wonders Eye's forgiving spirit. Yet, to fill the lingering emptiness, Lone Hawk boarded the canoe and called Screecher over, from his perch on the overhang. "Come on, Screecher, let's lose this death abode and get out of here—that's right! Rest on my shoulder and keep me awake—never know <u>what</u> to expect till we hit Big River City!" Then going solo, Lone Hawk paddled canoe-centered down the slow river, seeming as still as the death they left behind. While the torches there burned brightly, they only but faded off in the distance, as he and Screecher slipped into the darkness.

Lone Hawk tried to think only of the positive points, the many interesting experiences his uncle had been graced to live and enjoy. Maybe for some good reason, a higher purpose, he had been called upon to another realm. Nonetheless, deep sadness wiped away such wishful thinking, as he was angry at the forces for taking him so soon. His heart then agonized like a cancerous tumor growing in his chest. The only bright spot in the world seemed to be the company of Screecher. Purring and chirping into his ear through the all-night trek, he was the perfect, commiserative friend, so necessary during this ever-creeping state of mourning.

The first full day of his lone voyage was blustery to his advantage, as the strong northerly winds at his back and the conforming current gave him some well-appreciated vibrancy, with the ideal conditions allowing his covering a vast distance. However, by the middle of the next day, Lone Hawk's insomnia had worn off and to no surprise, he began to lose consciousness. Then to offset this, he was saved by a gentle rain that came like a prodding spirit to spur him on into a third night's lonely, southward forge at an ever-slowing pace. While he shored-up only briefly the morning before, he found himself pre-dawn drowsily a beach, soaked and chilled, not remembering his nocturnal rest stop. Even so, the deprivation's relief was only marginal, as he was shrouded and tangled in seaweed and riverside overgrowth, with the dead body in tow beginning to emanate the unmistakable odor of decay. In desperation, he peeled the canoes out of the web of greenery and was soon greeted by the morning sun, which would eventually bake him to his survival's limit on a day marked by its relentlessly scorching presence.

Lone Hawk mumbled, dosed and drifted into near dreams, seeing frequent mirages while steadily working the heavy load down the Big, which saw an increasing number of riverside settlements. People pointed and hollered to him in their friendly foreign tongues that morning, but at high sun and beyond, the vultures began to circle above him. The hawk-shouldered curiosity then became the traveling embodiment of death. Stirring reactions of fear and avoidance, the cringing natives saw the bold buzzards starting to perch on the trailer, seeking the carrion lure. Fortunate to everyone's relief and entertainment, Screecher then lived up to the burdensome task of chasing off the plague of scavengers, faithfully protecting the sacred haul. Even so, the sleep deprived, malnourished and dehydrated brave of destiny was already in much more serious trouble than heat exhaustion. For once the brewing sun took its full toll, it caused him to keel over and hit his forehead with the paddle. Though almost totally unconscious, he fought the debility by flipping himself backward. Yet, the motion was too forceful and, consequently, threw him out of the canoe.

In a fleeting moment of acceptance, Lone Hawk allowed his submergence and flowed with it, spread eagle, under the mighty current. Its all-encompassing cool-down was wonderfully refreshing, but when he saw his uncle a glow in the aquaworld ahead, Lone Hawk was convinced that he was facing his own mortality. In contrast, Wonders Eye, wearing a headdress and ornate chiefly apparel, shook his head and offered his hand in greeting.

"Ahoy, Lone Hawk, good ole nephew of mine—come on, chin up!" Wonders Eye's cheerful spirit encouraged with heart-warming gusto. "You <u>can't</u> die, now—your destiny calls! So, when you get to the city, you've <u>got</u> to find Night Owl—she'll know what to do!" Lone Hawk trustingly took his hand then found himself resurfaced, clutching the trailer-canoe from astern with Screecher still waiting there. Peering down at him, not surprised, he merely thought his human pal had decided to go for a swim. Nonetheless, after coughing the water out of his lungs, Lone Hawk was still able to maneuver the two vessels to shore. In a west bank out-cropping of trees, he found a good shady spot to recover and regroup.

He dragged himself ashore and drank plenty of water, along with a snack of corn flats and smoked deer. His head was pounding, and his knotted stomach was not taking well to the forced food. Undeterred, despite his poor overall state of health and near demise, he was back on the river just after he caught his breath and worked the cramps out of his limbs. This determination was finally rewarded when at dusk he sighted Big River City's vast stretch of heavily trafficked docks. Well-lit in the multi-torched distance on the east side, he then began to pass the central waterway and landings to the south.

When he heard the festive sounds of the city echo across the river, Lone Hawk felt the resurgence of life within himself. However, because of the putrefied body of his entrainment, he could not park conventionally and explore as he would have liked. So, to avoid any problems, he continued down the river's west side past the city lights, and came about in a wide arc to a patch of thick foliage on the east bank. While there were no outward observers, he quickly grounded the canoes and slipped them into the brush, well-hidden as could be, so close to civilization. His first impulse was to strap one of the Toltec's holsters around his waist and, for the first time, pack one of the fabulous swords. In so doing, his natural propensity toward balance led him to wear a second on the left side as well. All seemed in its proper place for his readiness to go until the impatiently squawking Screecher, on the branch above him, suddenly jostled his mind to an obvious problem.

"Shush!" he barked in a whisper, quieting the riled bird to figure a solution. "I must have a way to communicate is _so_ right. No one here will speak Warbird, I'm sure, except perhaps the one named Night Owl. But this is _far_ more crowded than any place I've ever seen, so how will I find her? Of course!" Reaching into his bag of arts and crafts, he snatched the sack of figurines and extracted the two pieces that would serve his purpose. "_These_ will be worth a hundred words," he remarked, thinking himself brilliant, as he looked upon the owl and the provocatively posed woman statuette in the crescent moon's light. "And, from what Wonders Eye said, she is quite popular. Now, finding her will be easy! However, telling her about you, my uncle, will be so very hard. Oh, and how your body reeks so! I _must_ bury you tonight. Hopefully, she'll help me find a good mound for you…Come Screecher! Let us seek out this Night Owl!"

He strolled up the shoreline to the south end landings and continued up the wide, sloping path of gravel smoothly set in sand. While his entrance was initially unnoticed, Lone Hawk, with the shoulder-riding Screecher and double hipped swords glimmering in the torch's light, soon attracted curious stares and a canine following. Dogs of varieties he had never seen before excitedly ran circles around them, as he strutted boldly across the main canal's bridge, north to the city's bazaar. Screecher was not amused by the onslaught of frisky mongrels and shrilled at them accordingly, unshaken from his perch. The crowds, put off by their presence, were increasingly concentrated around the many rows of trading tables under four, big sprawling canopies. Thus, the mostly small people of varied exotic appearances cleared their path.

He moved about void encroachment, which was fine enough until he wished to approach anyone, with his impromptu method of communication. So intimidating was his savage presence, they feared him insane as well when he showed the figurines to them and pointed at the night's sky. After so many had shunned him, he almost lost faith in his clever search tactic. Yet, there was one brave merchant with an interest in his swords that followed and knew who he was after, by repeated observation. So, with a nod and an agreeable smile, the big man led the thankful Lone Hawk a short distance to a leggy, somewhat voluptuous woman with cute up-slanted eyes of painted violet, who stood surrounded by throngs of eager men.

"Could this be the nephew of Wonders Eye's boast, the <u>truest</u> of the Warbird braves, Lone Hawk?" the bubbly Night Owl called out to him in the Warbird tongue, with an arm-raising gesture that jiggled her generous breasts so-as-to poke through her long, tight-fitting garment of sheer, white and red pinstripes. "He told me to expect the muscled man with the hawk this summer and <u>here</u> you are, but where is he?" Instantly, she knew something was wrong and, therefore, dispersed the circle of admirers with a wave of her hand, sporting long, pink-polished fingernails that she flung ever so gracefully. While Lone Hawk stood speechless, with his Adam's apple in suspicious flux, she approached him and put her hand to his forehead. "You do <u>not</u> look well…Hmm, something <u>terrible</u> has happened and <u>that</u> is why you are alone! Now, tell me—<u>where</u> is your uncle?" With concerned eyes that demanded the truth, she anxiously awaited his response that did not come easily from the bearer of horrible news.

"Night Owl, I presume…oh, I am <u>so</u> glad to have found you!" he started, nervously scratching his brow. "But…sorry to say, indeed your suspicions are true," he added in all lameness, due to his extreme state of exhaustion. "Only, the <u>very</u> worst has happened. When we were camping up the Big River near the Wise Crow, we were attacked by Toltec warriors. Then to counter, I became a killing beast and slain two-of-four from the start. After I took their swords…" he demonstrated with the pair, which he had brought; "I charged down the river to supply Wonders Eye with a worthy weapon, but it was too late. They executed him, right there in front of me, and so I <u>killed</u> them the same. Dead by their own swords, those Toltec demons! Well, though I won the spoils of victory in their great things, their deaths cannot replace my good uncle…who, by the way, still needs to be buried. Um, so…Night Owl, could you <u>please</u> guide me to the mound here that would best suit Wonders Eye?"

Night Owl was shocked to a bowing silence, which prompted Lone Hawk to comfort her with a hug, driving Screecher to roost on the nearby market canopy. After a moment's consoling, he released his hold, yet she remained arm locked around his waist with her face against his chest, tears trickling down his sectioned stomach like raindrops over etched stone. She peered up to him with watering eyes to the tragedy he just told. And, although it was inappropriate, there was a mutual stir of the desire that they initially pretended to overlook. She released her embrace and backed off slightly.

"Wonders Eye was my very good friend for seven glorious summers," Night Owl said while she wiped her eyes and regained the city-wise composure, she so aptly exuded. "Unlike the other men, he talked to me with respect and sincerity. Oh, I will miss him so. Those <u>cursed</u> Toltec and their safaris! Well, at least I can be glad you prevented them from killing more, but at <u>such</u> a cost? Anyway, about the body—where have you put it? Maybe bringing a rotting body into 'Warbird Land' is acceptable, but here in the city there are strict codes of conduct, especially with unlawful burials. He <u>cannot</u> be buried in the mounds! Violations are punishable by a very painful death, and the Great King Cahokia has many eyes to enforce rules. Well, perhaps there <u>is</u> another place which is not of the official mounds, yet…is of sentimental reverence, as I'm sure his spirit would agree. Okay, now that I've calmed down, tell me, Lone Hawk—<u>where</u>, exactly, is his body?"

"He's in the thicket just south of the landings," Lone Hawk finally revealed, as his attentions strayed amidst the bartering paradise, accented by a singing and dancing commotion that was becoming a blur. "We better get over there before someone discovers him, along with the other swords and the cargo that could be stolen, if we don't hurry!" Wasting no time, Night Owl waved him to follow in a determined gate southward over the bridge from the marketplace straight onto the city's westside main street. While Screecher rejoined his shoulder in his trailing of the thankful contact, the dogs came back. But this time, they dared to jump against his legs and butt, barking in hopes of nabbing the infuriated hawk.

"Go! You, wretched strays!" she shouted at the frenzied pack, sending them away with a barrage of swats to their behinds. "I <u>am</u> sorry about their … how would you say, enthusiasm? But your hawk draws them like nothing I have ever seen."

"Oh, I don't mind … I like the dogs, and how they challenge my flustered Screecher, ha-ha," he laughed, unfazed by the incident, yet eager to remedy the burial situation when they paused at an intersection on the cobblestone street, well past the canal. "Now, why do you stop here?" he wondered, looking around. "For someone else to help us?"

Due east from the main stretch in a mostly residential area, she suddenly darted onto the side street toward one of the many lodges of long rectangular depth, set in close multitudes. With trees and bushes in perfect conformity, Lone Hawk wondered how they could tell the virtually identical dwellings of steeply pitched, thickly thatched roofs apart.

Curious of her diversion, he went after Night Owl and tried to enter what turned out to be her singular abode. As she opened the sliding wood door, she pushed him away, forbidding his passage. "Wait by the street while I must change into more appropriate attire," she explained in a loud whisper, as she held the hem of her flowing gown to state the obvious. "I will be brief, but, on second thought, do <u>not</u> loiter here—it will only arouse suspicion! Instead, start down the first trail veering off to the right from my street, heading toward the river. I will intercept you shortly…" Lone Hawk abided by her instructions and, as an inconspicuous measure, he shooed Screecher off to follow from the branches, both avoiding the curious pairing and the dogs.

Despite the effort, the swords still drew the attention of the people from their trailside homes, but, fortunately, the lodges thinned from few to none at the path's dead end. At the edge of the wooded slope, he could see the moonlight glistening on the river and figured the canoes to be just slightly to the north from the bank before him. Impatient, he began to turn back until a waving black figure approached in the distance, whence he came. He met her halfway to see that she had decided to wear a short black garment, similar to the Toltecs'.

"I think I know where everything is," Lone Hawk said, speaking softly into her slightly pointed ear, which was now exposed since she had put her long mane up in a tight roll; "a mere stone's throw upriver from here!" He raised his voice to compete with the increasing volume of the crickets, frogs and cicadas, which had reached a delirious level as they trotted down the hill. In a diagonal northwest jaunt, the deathly stench was soon detected, thus guiding them to the proper destination.

"Ewe, the moist heat carries that odor <u>so</u>—oh!" she declared, holding her nose and stomach, as Lone Hawk dragged the canoes to buoyancy. "I think I'm going to be sick, but maybe on the open river it won't be so bad. So, once out there, I'll steer us to the other side and then go south, crossing back to Sunset Palisade. Laden with a maze of trails and crevices, it will be ideal for what we must do."

Soon after their launch, just halfway across the river, they were caught off guard by fast-approaching vessels, which were suddenly a burst with drumming war chants. Lone Hawk froze in shock, as the clamorous assault made him play possum, to Night Owl's disappointment.

"Keep your pace, man! They are military vessels, and you only look suspicious!" she warned in a stern whisper, to which he obeyed and resumed powering their puny craft before the armada of ten big seven-man canoes with a torch-bearing drummer at each bow. "Just as I suspected, they'll turn into the Kings Inlet for their usual stopover…" There was relief in her voice as the fleet accommodated their secrecy by ducking into the royal canal to dock, allowing them to dare a more direct route. "Let's just go straight down the center, right past them. They're so eager to hang out at the market and get drunk that they won't even care to notice us!" Thus, just as she said, the warriors began securing their mammoth canoes in pre-carousal mode and paid little notice of them, inviting the hopeful body stashers undaunted passage to the foot of the great conglomerate of wooded bluffs known as Sunset Palisade.

Grounding the canoes with much more difficulty than his arrival, Lone Hawk grew worried that his declining strength would deny him the task. Yet, when he struggled to remove Wonders Eye's post-rigor mortis frame from the tipped holding cell, Night Owl volunteered her services. With surprising strength, she then hoisted the furry bison-wrapped body from the front while he pushed from the rear. There, the treacherous climb began upward amidst their breathy chorus on the landmark's winding trail.

"We must go well above the flood-line," she gasped, clearly nauseous from the fumes of decay. "Up there, I know of some small caves that will serve well as natural tombs." Just above the highest riverside treetops, Night Owl located a generous indentation beneath a small ledge, just as Lone Hawk fell to his knees, unable to climb another step. And so, he slid the corpse into the deep-set sunken slot from where he knelt, finding it a more than adequate fit. Hence, plenty of room remained for ground cover, which they foraged in the form of loose earth and shrubs packed as the first layer, then rocks and stones to form the face.

Upon completion of the makeshift grave, the muddied Lone Hawk lay on his stomach in a sweaty pool, positioned to pay homage to his only true human friend. "Wonders Eye, you've been free of this body for a few days now, and I am _so_ thankful that your chiefly spirit saved me from drowning, seeing me through to complete my voyage, and again I thank you," he began his impromptu eulogy in a soft, choked voice while Night Owl knelt beside him, rubbing his back in communal support. "Well, I have safely arrived, as you can see, and I found your good friend Night Owl, who has made it possible for you to have your own great mound—and with a riverfront view! Now that this is done, you need not watch over me anymore. You must expand your travels to the moon, the stars and all the realms where spirits may go. You will show the others, I am sure, the _true_ meaning of adventure…just like you did for me, before you had to go.

"As my mother's brother, a part of you now lives on through me, and in the common blood I will continue to make you proud. Slaughtering those Toltecs to avenge you was only the start. For now, as I cherish this life evermore, I know I mustn't waste time and do great things at the moment. But don't worry, Good Uncle, I also learned the importance of enjoying oneself. And there, in that balance, is the secret to happiness, uh…" He yawned, barely staying awake thus concluding, "So, goodbye, Wonders Eye…may we meet again, and journey to the Big River Cities in the sky."

"Parting words, so nice. You are a good man, Lone Hawk…" Night Owl wept, as she helped him to his feet. "He was fortunate to have such a loyal and loving nephew, but if we don't go back soon, I will have to bury you as well…Come, lean on my shoulders. I will help you to the canoes and get us a proper spot at the launch." She held his wrists, tight, as he draped his arms around her from behind and practically rode her in a sleep-walk down to the canoes. Boarding the craft, he almost capsized it and, while Night Owl supplied the propulsion to the landings at a snail's pace, Lone Hawk fell asleep. By the time she had awakened him with the trailer already shored, his reaction to which was quite ornery in his concern for the cargo, as he struggled out of the rider canoe onto the beach.

"We cannot leave these things here!" he chided, with a fleeting cry of conscious vigor while he put the swords, which were kept in the canoe during the climb, back into their holsters. "Wonders Eye's furs, the canoes, the other swords and the chest plates, they will all be stolen! We must take everything to your lodge for safe keeping!" To these demands of such gall, she put her foot behind his ankle and easily pushed him, in his frailty, tripping him to fall on his back to the sanded riverbank. Amused by the commotion, people looming nearby began to laugh and gather around them.

"The furs stink of death and must be aired! And these canoes are so heavy and primitive, no one would ever want them!" she shouted with a fury, confident that nobody could understand the Warbird tongue, as she dragged the other one ashore. "Nonetheless, I will have someone take care of them while I allow the swords and the chest plates, only, to be stored in my home. In the meantime, let's just bring these things to my place, and then I <u>must</u> take care of you! Your health is failing, and I will <u>not</u> let you die!" They gathered the Toltec valuables while Night Owl, Queen of the Whores, boasted to the whispering onlookers that she was to obtain quite a boodle from the drunken merchant for her services.

The crowd chimed into uproarious laughter toward the primitive fool, who was apparently drunk and being bamboozled by the popular lady of the night. Yet, of course, she had no such intention, as she only wished to create a believable scenario to diffuse the ruckus. Soon, after they burrowed through the countless droves of nighttime revelers, Lone Hawk caught a glimpse of Screecher, the spy in the sky all along, chirping from his roost atop her lodge. And though he was so glad to see his loyal companion again, the stumbling brave blacked out when Night Owl walked him inside, on his last legs to tumble into her big, soft bed for a long, deep slumber.

CHAPTER IV
Cahokian Queen

LONE HAWK SLEPT SOUNDLY through the night yet went into a thrashing fit of delirium early the next morning, as he dreamed a perfect replay of the Toltec tragedy. Night Owl calmed his feverish rage with cooling damp cloths applied to his head and chest, and water, which she nursed him to drink for his dehydration. Eventually, with his temperature reduced, she was able to rock him back to a quiet sleep that lasted into the early evening. By that time, he was fully rested but weak. However, since he had awakened in his nakedness beside Night Owl, who was sitting with her bare peach-tan back to him on the edge of her black and white, zigzag-quilted bedspread, he felt new energy stir amidst the waning daylight. Unable to resist her softly curved silhouette, his groping hand reached over and stroked her side, if only just to make sure it was not a dream.

"Finally, you wake, and the day is almost done!" the twisting Night Owl surprised in joyful relief, as she leaned over to feel his forehead, with her bare breasts suddenly around his arm. While her other hand held a polished rose quartz pipe, burning with pungent cannabis, Lone Hawk raised an eyebrow to the familiar odor. "Have some smoke of love. It will take your fever down, make your appetite strong and your endurance long!" she offered with a giggle, as he drew on the beautifully-crafted notched stem a few times, inhaling the harsh smoke into his virgin lungs. He then squinted and coughed repeatedly. To his rescue, she snatched the pipe away and poured a cup-full of fermented 'sour grape' drink for him, which he guzzled in one gulp. While it soothed his throat, he felt a serene wave going through his mind and a surging sensation growing in his groin. He then peered into her seductive eyes and tingled to the start of his carnal initiation, as she crossed her knee over his hips and mounted him.

With the sweet essence of flowers and honey, she leaned forward and planted a kiss of passionate exploration, tonguing beyond his lips, to which he clumsily responded. He grasped her full, pressing breasts and pinched them a little too hard, prompting Night Owl to squeeze his wrists for release. "Gently, Lone Hawk," she cautioned his unseasoned roughness. "These are fragile. Soft, circular motions, like this, are good," she half-whispered while demonstrating the desired technique by manipulating his hands as such. "Save the pinches for this pair down here." She then pulled his comfortably roving fingers away from their new frontier and whisked them down along her soft narrow waist and well-curved hips. Thus, with a naughty smirk, she slapped his hands against her pertly extended buttocks, the 'pair' to which she referred. Just as he applied the pinches to the supple flesh of her direction, she slid backwards with a raised eyebrow of her own and artfully guided him, no hands, into the luscious warmth of her window's pleasure.

Plunging up-and-down then to-and-fro interchangeably, she created trilling vibrations throughout her entire body in a love-making frenzy that had his dreamily distant eyes and ear-to-ear smile reflecting his fascination as if in an other-dimensional paradise. And to further heighten the experience, the full-rocking, half-acting Night Owl gasped in delight as she reveled in cliche. "Oh! How you fill me so deeply, Lone Hawk," she rasped, as she licked his ear. "You should be very proud!" Naively falling for it with an 'awe shucks' grin, Lone Hawk triumphantly pulled her quivering rump down upon his base for a most glorious smacking of mutual climaxes in an almost spiritual communion that he was so honored to finally share. After such riveting intensity, pleasant pulsations, bonding their softly fused parts, still lingered as she affectionately celebrated the long-overdue fulfillment of his manhood.

"You were…a virgin before this, yes? Awe, come on—tell me true!" she teased, playful, as she smothered him with congratulatory kisses. "Whatever, it doesn't matter…for now, you are my prized pupil as you pass, so far, with flying colors. Well, you needn't be ashamed anymore, Lone Hawk." Flushed of face, he was quick to reply in a slick unfazed way.

"No shame here, at least, not anymore—uh-oh! He's back!" Lone Hawk declared, instilling with confidence his first success in taming, as he thought, a new territory of the greatest riches. Thus, it was a place where he found himself quite insatiable.

"Oh, my goodness! Your snake stirs again, and so soon!" she praised, noticing his prompt revival. "We will appease him, of course, but now it's my turn to lie down. So, time to learn from the top side…" Though thoroughly aroused, he worried that the rest of his body was barely up to the task. Yet, when she rolled off her mount and lay with wantonly spread legs beside him, he tapped reserve strength just by the sight of her willing pose in the dwindling, hemp-screened daylight. Then after a second round's slower and sweeter completion in the reverse, Night Owl's expert use of her strong-drawing pouty lips and swirling-pressing tongue trained the well-apt Lone Hawk to kissing perfection. So, as they came to a tender close in the approaching darkness, they exchanged their last moment's tongue-bathing kisses and adoring gazes until then, spoiling the moment, his stomach began to growl like a bear. Thus, with his remaining strength depleted, he laid on top of her as dead weight.

"I would have made it last, but I need food, badly," he gasped in a muffled tone, face buried in her pillow. "The smoke of love, which back home we call 'wander weed,' made my appetite very good as you said it would. Now, please let us eat, so I can be my true self, the strong man who you have yet to meet." Immediately, she pushed him off to the side and stood, holding her fuzzy crotch with a red cloth she had nearby.

"What more can you prove, a stronger man? You've already turned me into a waterfall, Lone Hawk the weaker!" she raved, revealing the well-dampened cloth with an awed expression that made him giggle. "Such a deposit, I have never had! Yes, back to your request, I will go to the market and fetch us the finest food in the city." Night Owl put on a simple tan robe, which she lifted from a three-prong wall hook beside a variety of others, and then lit a few scented, honey wax wicks in little bowls around the room. While she was readying to go on the food-run, he watched her with concern and pried a little too deep.

"Night Owl, don't you worry that I could make you with child," he asked as an after-thought, just as she was walking toward the door in the front room. "I have planted my seed and you seem to give it no thought, but you <u>must</u> know better." She turned to him and crossed her arms, as though he had struck a nerve.

"That would be impossible," she admitted with saddened eyes; "I am barren and can give no man a child. That is why I'm so old and without a mate. They only want to keep a woman, if she can help bolster their immortality with a son. That said, I am only good for play…. While I do want a child, I have been considering taking in one of the unfortunate strays that nobody wants. I may not have a working womb, but I can give one of these poor children a home."

"You are not so old, but you <u>are</u> so beautiful," Lone Hawk praised, with the perfect complement and a contagious smile. "Let me see these children tomorrow, and I'll help pick one out for you." She shook her head, smitten by his endearing silly grin, and walked out the door to the market in good spirits. While she left him alone to his own device, he then took a tour of her not-so-humble abode in search of his swords.

Before her expansive framed bed piled high with several layers of woven feathers, there were thick colorfully striped rugs, completely covering the floor into the front room. The only divider, besides some sliding units, was a wide semi-opened fireplace of stacked, clay-mortared sandstone. All around, the smooth wooden walls were peppered with exotic artwork, leaving the only sizable gaps to the door and two windows. East, to greet the sunrise, and West, to bid its farewell, the square pair of half his height held sturdy hemp and bamboo screens of translucent shading. Though he was very impressed with the decor, his seemingly endless search had him mystified in worry. Then, when in his anxiousness he was tapping on a big kettledrum in the front corner of the lodge, the tension became unbearable until a glimmer from above caught his eye. In a small loft right over the bed, his swords and chest plates were safely kept, as-well-as his shabby clothes which he immediately slipped over his naked flesh. As he laid the fine weapons on her bed and marveled at them with a much greater sense of their value, he suddenly heard the call of his faithful friend. Delighted, he lumbered outside to greet him.

"Oh, thank you, good Screecher! But you don't have to share your squirrel with me," Lone Hawk told the ready-perched Screecher with heartfelt appreciation for his generous offering. Yet, his attention soon turned to Night Owl, crossing the busy street with a big basket of local delicacies. "I already have my feast…Sweet Night Owl, would you care to cook us up some squirrel as well? My first warrior here, Screecher, caught it for us." Night Owl walked toward the door and kicked the dead rodent to the side.

"Come! Leave your Screecher to his vermin meal, for you shall now eat as only fit for a king!" She shooed Screecher from his shoulder and dragged him through the doorway by the breach cloth for some well-deserved gluttony. Onto a large wooden tray, she laid out the items from the basket. Buffalo stew based in corn, red and green vegetables with a thick hot sauce was the main course, while pheasant breasts and whisker fish filets, basted with a sour honey glaze served as appetizers. In addition, an after-meal treat was provided for his sweet palate, as she packed some raspberry corn pastries of which Lone Hawk was especially fond. He gorged on the scrumptious edibles in a lunging fashion, leaving the snatching Night Owl to pick an occasional tidbit at her own risk.

"Oh, Night Owl, this is a tremendous feast!" he proclaimed, with a hearty belch and a yawn after he gulped a cup of gullet-washing, sour grape drink. "However, I have become very sleepy and cannot go into the city tonight, as I had wished. Let me just thank you for all this, and promise to be the strong man tomorrow." He reclined on her bed and slipped into a snoring slumber almost immediately. His feet still on the floor, Night Owl removed his moccasins and swung his legs onto the bed, allowing him to sleep undisturbed until the morning's dawn.

Starting his 'big' Cahokian day, Lone Hawk woke up extremely thirsty and in dire need of bowel release. Sufficing with several guzzles of water and, fortunately, not waking Night Owl, he took a quick trip to the river, arriving just in time. While Screecher kept watch from an overhanging branch, he took care of business in the bushes and washed in the river with a chunk of scented soap, which he scooped from a jar he saw her using the night before. Thus, he wasted no time in his cleansing ritual because the river's traffic had already begun to flow, with many glares of disapproval. Though sopping wet, he clothed himself, feeling almost full strength, and invited good Screecher to his leather-pad-strapped shoulder.

"Sorry I was so short with you yesterday, ole pal, but I was <u>still</u> too weak," he apologized, with knuckle trills to the lonely hawk's breast when they neared the main street. "Well, I am a Warbird once again, and we will scout this city together! Oh, she looks perturbed…Screecher, I think we better bring her along…" As his 'once again' determined strut carried him back to her luxurious lodgings, Lone Hawk found his intimate hostess outside the door in a purple robe, shaking her head.

"Please, do <u>not</u> venture off without me like that!" she scolded in peeved rasp. "Though <u>I</u> know better, you look to others like a dangerous criminal. I will <u>have</u> to soften your image today. Uh, did you, by chance, see your canoes grounded near the launch house?"

"Well, since I trust you, I didn't even think about them, but as you mention that, did the furs get aired?" She nodded with a subtle affirmation, then took his hand. "Let's go for a walk and then a ride," she cheerfully suggested, as the three of them started down the street. "There is something <u>quite</u> wonderful, which I would love to share with you. And, of course, your precious Screecher is invited as well!" After he insisted on holstering the swords, much to her chagrin, she guided them down the street a few hundred paces to a southside clearing, where the army canoes had docked a couple nights before.

Among the three-dozen canoes parked at the double-slipped docks at the Kings Inlet, the manmade waterway just off the Big River, four such craft of the canopied type awaited, each manned by two oarsmen in flashy orange and purple-striped garments of scant fit. When they approached one of the vessels readied on the canal, Night Owl reached into her pocket, extracting a rectangular wooden swatch with a sun brand, and handed it to the stocky man astern. While they dawdled a little before stepping into the wide canoe, the lanky oarsman at the bow waved them aboard as though he was in a hurry. Quickly seating themselves, they started along the virtually traffic-free aqua-route to some special place of her promise while Lone Hawk was already quite impressed by the novel start.

"Fancy canoe! And these, with their strange 'feminine' outfits bring us to wherever for just a piece of wood? What sort of exchange is <u>that</u> for them?" he asked, quite perplexed over the strange barter, while Screecher leaped off his shoulder to glide above them in their facing, sitting position. "Oh, but <u>what</u> a stretch of corn fields, and the soil! It's so <u>red</u>—could it be fertilized with blood?" Night Owl released some adoring laughter to the naive one, who blankly gazed southward at the seemingly endless rows of pallid stalks, protruding from the maroon post-harvest plain. Then, with a turn of his head to the north, she chuckled again at his awe, trying to see where the continuous blocks of residential lodgings might end.

After a moment's amusement, she redirected his sights southward while pointing to the ravaged fields. "Indeed, the earth bleeds for 'the Sun' to reap our abundance…" She spoke as the all-knower, with her hand caressing his knee. "But it is blood from within, not without. Also, you asked about the wood pieces. Well, they are Sun tokens made by the King's holy men. We use <u>them</u> as-well-as regular trade like symbols of value. They're especially useful for army personnel, since they are paid only with these. Though of course, the token is only good here in Cahokia's realm, and so, but wood chips elsewhere." She further explained to him the structure of the city in which the canal, further east, was the divider between the business and residential districts to the north, and the King's 'solar theocratic' governance and military bases to the south.

"And over there, you can see, is our great Bird's Eye Lake of the Sun. The beak is the narrow meeting the canal; the head and breast are the lake's body; and the island is its eye," she described of their great lake to the northeast with a prideful beholding hand, as they neared the main treat on the opposite side. "That is the source of most of our fish and game, as its vast waters and woodlands are well-stocked. Oh! Now, <u>look</u> at the enlightened center of our kingdom, right toward the Sun where it rises!" There, in the distance next to the Kings Launch of multiple docks half-filled mainly with military vessels, the architectural wonder of Wonders Eye's most lacking description came into view further inland.

Just upon sighting the massive pyramid with its glorious red and white stone palace atop, Lone Hawk was hurled into an explosion of intrigue as its four squarely aligned satellite structures, also of pyramidal design, added to its perfect symmetry. Meantime, however, their attention was stolen away for just a moment with some harmless laughs at the dockside guards in passing. Passed-out with cradled spears in hand, the golden-clad dozen actually insulted Lone Hawk's warrior sense, though Night Owl would explain their laxness soon enough with another surprise for a later visit to her city's park of worship.

"Oh, Mother Earth! It must be at <u>least</u> thirty-men-tall, just at the base!" Lone Hawk enthusiastically estimated in exaggeration of the gargantuan stacked structure, still a fair distance away, as they strolled onto its public grounds, which were perfectly blanketed with evenly cut grass. "And it must be <u>another</u> ten to the top of that beautiful palace. It looks so strong, so regal! What do you call this magnificent place?"

"This is the Great Temple of the Sun," she praised, with a proud and beholding sweep of her hand. "And it is also the home of our 'supreme' leader King Cahokia, for whom this land is named. While he and his family live there, closest to the Sun, the ultimate life source, the four high priests inhabit the lesser temples of the Moon, Mars, Venus and Jupiter, which surround his. And, of course, there are the time poles," she added, pointing to a great circle of wooden shafts coming into view, set on the other side of the King's pyramid; "that also serve as the playing field for the games. We owe <u>so</u> much to his making this city, with its fertile fields, the thriving metropolis it is today. In fact, 'lucky' you, Lone Hawk, have come at a very special time…for tonight, there'll be a 'wowing good' festival in celebration of his hundredth summer to grace this world with his divine presence. Usually, this place is dizzy with activity, but, for his earthbound anniversary, no one must work, and I'm afraid that the guards you scoffed at earlier feel much the same. Because, with the record harvest this summer, who cares? <u>This</u> will be the happiest night one could ever imagine!"

Lone Hawk began to veer their roundabout path toward the temple for closer inspection. "I love the way the three platforms are so elegantly placed, to rise above the square mound for the sky," he raved with increasing fascination while, much to Night Owl's disapproval, he shuffled toward the entrancing structure. "And with such a wide-stepped path leading to its splendid palace, it's as if it were the <u>top</u> of the world! Oh, I could never say enough to adequately praise this perfect continuation of stone. Stone … hmm," he repeated, with great thoughts beginning to churn in his mind. "The Valley of the Warbirds is laced with bloodstone rocks and boulders of every size for such a project. However, I would need to go up there and have a closer look, so I can accurately recreate this marvel for the new glory age of the Warbirds."

Night Owl weighed anchor on his arm and brought him to a halt. "Silly, naive Lone Hawk—you can't go <u>trampling</u> around up there, that is, unless you want to lie on the altar for your body's sacrifice!" she warned with a gentle slap to his face. "Do you not <u>see</u> the guards along the steps?" she questioned his selective sense of observation while pointing to the gold-plated guards that were posted at all three levels, up to where the altar and palace blossomed. "I <u>assure</u> you they are awake, and would kill a hulking primitive like you, on sight, with their poisoned arrows!

"That is why I urge that we admire from afar, so you can stay alive for your dealings with Swarming Sands, the merchant who brought you to me. He's watching over your goods in hopes that you will include a sword or two for a sweet 'surprise' deal that he will propose. I told him you have two more and he nearly jumped into the sky. This could mean a very lucrative exchange, if you include the chest plates, as well. You will leave this place a young, strong, cultured and, possibly, very rich man … Lone Hawk! Did you hear me?"

While he nodded unconvincingly, his mind was in an adulated whirlwind, dedicated to some ambitious planning for the Warbirds' new destiny. He surmised that the Big River City's worship of the sun, as opposed to the Warbirds' four forces of earth, wind, fire and water, lay as the fundamental reason for their building of such great things. Then, in his sifting for a way, he realized that, besides an obscure heightened spirituality sparked by Wonders Eye's death, he personally had never taken any such beliefs, besides that of the Wind God, to heart. So, as he would seek approval for future works, he could feign and incorporate the solar worship aspect, a great edge over his failed tower project that still bothered him. This time they would not laugh but believe in the monument that would bestow good fortune and spread enlightenment upon their stale society of the primitive North.

"Have you gone deaf?" Night Owl asked, rather annoyed, as she hated being ignored, "Walking in a trance with that peculiar grin, you act as though I'm not even here. What are you thinking about that could remove you so?"

Lone Hawk looked at her with the eyes of the happy dreamer, which he had become, envisioning such grandeur. "With this model, I have great plans for my people and as the awe of it takes me away, so shall I bring it back to them!" he vowed while he drew his swords to a crossed pattern before the rising sun, where the post-harvest corn fields stretched past the horizon. "I salute you, Good Sun, and the Great King Cahokia upon whom you bestowed such ambition and good fortune to create such a beautiful city," he announced as a sudden claim of faith, driving Screecher off his shoulder and Night Owl to suspect him of mockery. "May you shine your preferential light upon me, Lone Hawk, in the same for the sake of the Warbirds, so we too can taste the fruits of your glory. And, in your honor, I shall build the Great City of the Sunbirds, Paradise of the North!"

"Though no one understands your tongue, you plainly used King Cahokia's name in vain!" she sternly warned while she pulled his sword-reeling hands downward. "People are starting to arrive for worship, and they're talking about you, I'm sure. Even the guards, though far away, can very well see your stance as intimidating, and be alerted to investigate. I can see that teaching you city etiquette will take some time, but your appearance is another matter. Let's go back and refine your image for tonight's celebration." Removing his spectacle with a sense of urgency, Night Owl ushered him out of the park and back into the taxi-canoe, which brought them back to the westside docks, whence they came. With Screecher rejoining his shoulder at the walk back's start, word of the whore and her birdman was well-circulated, as they were to only find rows of onlookers, whispering their gossip, for an uncomfortable return to her lodge.

Once inside, Lone Hawk reluctantly submitted to her time-consuming modification of his thick, somewhat matted hair, which he tied into a frizzed tail, extending well past his shoulders. With plenty of corn oil, she was able to comb out his lumpy locks and cut the ends, barely changing their actual length yet making it appear notably shorter with her multi-layer braiding technique. To finish, she tied the many uniform braids behind his ears and laced them with blue and yellow feathers imported from the tropics, arranging them in cascading rows which conformed to his hairline.

"Now, all you need are some civilized clothes of exceptional style," she said, still admiring his new hair but dismaying to his plain, worn and sparse warrior's garb of dirty tan. "You are <u>such</u> a good-looking man. It is no less than a terrible waste for you to wear such pitiful things…onward! To the bazaar with your bargaining swords. We shall find Swarming Sands and meet your riches' full potential. Your transformation has only just begun, my <u>dear</u> primitive!" They arrived at the busy marketplace for a late morning's meeting with Swarming Sands at his sizable stand of general goods. For an initial agreement, Night Owl persuaded the exchange of the late Wonders Eye's furs for a lavish wardrobe with accessories, which she helped him select. He spent a good portion of the day parading before her in a variety of clothing and accumulated twelve outfits, eight of summer's wear and four for winter. Generally, he chose gray, red and tan combinations, which met her kiss of stunning approval.

Set with his heaping array of smart attire, Lone Hawk had plenty of time to think of the primary trade and presented a rather shrewd proposal. First and foremost, he wanted a pair of the incredibly lightweight, pine-layered canoes of their most streamlined design on display in exchange for Otter's sturdy but heavy craft, plus one sword. As the merchant demanded both swords and their holsters for the same deal, Lone Hawk wanted to see turquoise, ruby and sapphire jewelry. When he was shown a generous assortment, he teased Swarming Sands with the swords, waving them before his face. He was blatant in his intentions for the entire lot, or nothing.

After much pacing and haggling, the desperate merchant finally agreed to the terms and upon receipt, he kissed the swords as if he would have died without them. Thus, in a show of good faith, Lone Hawk offered him the four chest plates for a mere pine bow-and-arrow set that was an obvious mis-trade. Then matching the hard bargaining brave, Swarming Sands proudly wore his double-holstered Toltec treasure blades while he made the canoe exchange, with a boasting demonstration and a test-ride of the superior craft. In all, the transaction was amicable and, as the beaming merchant faithfully agreed to protect his merchandise until his departure, Lone Hawk and Night Owl happily skipped off and laughed all the way back to her lodge.

"You did very well, Lone Hawk…with the nice new canoes, beautiful wardrobe, jewels and everything," she congratulated with a powerful kiss that had him touching his lips to make sure they were still there. "I _am_ sorry that there was no interest in your weapon works and figurines. May I keep them?"

"Indeed, they're all yours, but especially note the owl and the crawling woman," he mentioned, suggestive in his shy, indirect way. "They helped me find you the other night, with Swarming Sand's immediate recognition."

She poured the sack of whittle works out onto the pinewood counter, just inside her entry, and held the erotic statuette to his face. "_Crawling_ woman? Oh, Lone Hawk, so cute as you describe! I know how you want it!" she tempted while removing his new, red and gray beaded war garb with careful admiration. "Like animals we shall be!" Then In a swaying stroll to the bed, she climbed onto it and assumed the position on her knees and elbows, gyrating at full extension yet still wearing her robe. Instantly aroused by the inviting pose, Lone Hawk followed her lead and knelt behind her. With some gentle bumping action from behind and between her draping garment, he massaged her, hips-to-breasts, as she began to hike the 'barrier robe' up past her thighs. Meanwhile, from outside of Night Owl's lodge, the neighbors and passers-byes paused in curiosity, as Lone Hawk made cat-like yowling sounds to which his 'cat woman' temptress chimed in with meows and giggles amid loud, rhythmic slapping noises. Soon, a small crowd gathered when they got even louder, with the wildly vocal Lone Hawk beginning to growl. Deep into their frenzied, prolonged climaxing pulsations, they spouted off in a chorus so obnoxious, the people outside, once cheering and laughing, ended up yelling at them to quiet down.

In embarrassed response, Night Owl quickly disengaged, turned around onto her back and cupped her hands over both of their mouths. Then taking her releasing hands away from their lips, Lone Hawk leaned over and pressed his chest upon hers. Much to her surprise, he launched a smattering of the most affectionate kisses she had ever had, so planted all about her pretty face made romantically a glow. Thus, with her thoroughly enchanted, he described their feline role-playing almost boastfully. "I imagined we were a couple of <u>horny</u> bobcats, in reckless coitus! You <u>heard</u> me—I was yowling just like they do!" he quietly rasped, feeling that people might still be listening while Black Moon, uncaring of their possible lingering, spoke at a normal volume. "<u>I</u> would say that you were more like an impassioned cougar, fully satisfying his mate … and <u>you</u> were growling—you, Wildman! So, after so much excitement <u>already</u> today, I think we could use a little rest and then, I'll show you a few more techniques and 'behold,' a complete and excellent lover you shall be—extraordinary!"

Through her masterful instruction, Lone Hawk performed his final training in the fine points of female pleasuring playfully well, and completed with kiss-laden honors. Furthermore, not only did he achieve expert status in the lovers' realm, he unlocked his soul to feel free in expressing himself in the deepest ways toward a woman, without the stifling childish games. Then so completely satisfied and with a bit of supper to follow, they grew drowsy and took a nap in a loving embrace. Come evening, they awakened rejuvenated and so, headed back to the canal, hailed the taxi craft and went back to Sun Park to feast at King Cahokia's hundredth summer celebration. While the nearby market by the river was practically deserted, it was plain to see that most everyone had amassed to partake in the festivities, which included a symphony of various flutes, drums and cymbals played in perfect harmony, along with singers of a wide vocal range. Thankfully, Lone Hawk arrived much too late to witness the brutal sacrifice of the ball game's losing team, which took place that afternoon on the altar of the Sun's Temple. Thus, with all the bloody evidence cleaned and disposed, he only saw the godly King up there in his golden crown, viewing from a colorful, feathered throne.

After they visited a few of the many canopied eatery stands lining the perimeter of the park, Lone Hawk became boisterous with his sampling of the full array of alcohol drinks, which flowed most freely. Void of inhibitions and rejoined by the feisty Screecher to his shoulder, he took his mood of exhibitionism to the foot of the temple and performed the hawk dance. There, accompanied by the intrigued symphony, he moved well to the music and with Screecher's unyielding cooperation, the primitive dance became an elaborate display he carried all-the-way-around the central bonfire with a fiery display of artistic athleticism. Upon his finish, the crowd roared and, as he stood and bowed before King Cahokia with the proud Warbird mascot perched on his forearm, the old man clapped, bowing in return. For the rest of the night, much fun was had in his short-lived, 'big city' gauge celebrity. And while he savored the attention, Night Owl showed him off to everyone, her prize of passion. At the end of the festival by the moon of the late night, they took the last taxi ride back to the Big River sector and stumbled back to her lodge, the most enduring revelers, where pleasant dreams of each other produced the most satisfying sleep.

Early the next morning, Screecher soured to extreme impatience and called from outside Night Owl's lodge with such intensity that most everyone in the neighborhood had been awakened, grumpy, to curse the obnoxious bird. He seemed to know that it was time to go, as Lone Hawk had told Swarming Sands the day before to tentatively have the canoes ready for an early start. So, in a somber mood, Night Owl walked him, swords-to-hips and hawk-shouldered, to the launch where the faithful merchant had his sharp new canoes in the river, with his goods and full provisions loaded as well.

"I will plant flowers at Wonders Eye's grave, and tell him about his unbelievably bold nephew who wooed the Big River City and its King," she venerated, standing beside him with watering eyes to their farewell. "Of the living and the dead, you two are most dear to me. I wish you could stay longer, but I know you have big plans and your Screecher grows sick of the city life. In the short time we had together, though, I am _so_ glad that I could help you know the woman so well. They are sure to flock around you wherever you go, and now—you know what to do!" she giggled then sighed, as Screecher took off. "Oh, but _please_ do not forget me, Lone Hawk, for I pray to see you next summer as your 'special' woman once again. Does that appeal to you, my _savage_ prince?" Lone Hawk hugged and kissed her, as she rose to an invulnerable role only to fall against his chest, weeping.

"My 'wonderful' Night Owl, I am forever indebted to you for enlightening me from my boyish ways to complete manhood," he praised, with a stroke of her long luscious mane. "_Oh_, how I _thank_ you!" he gushed to a roar, immersed in an appreciation that perked her up to a smile, as he wiped away her tears. "I will never forget you, and of course I will return to you next summer. By then, hopefully, I'll have big news of my Warbird renovation project. I just _know_ that there's something _great_ in these plans, and I'm sure that my uncle's spirit will be cheering for me upon their completion. Yes indeed, Night Owl, what a _great_ future it is to be!" After a final embrace, he boarded his canoe and paddled away, with trailer in tow.

While his heart was welling and his throat was constricting, he watched the thankful Screecher bolt upriver, and embraced the moment. However, after he looked back one last time to savor the sight of her lusty figure, waving from the dock where he left her, a lonesome chill engulfed him. Too soon, she vanished in the haze, never to see him again, as his journey would take a fateful turn upon fulfillment of his late uncle's bidding.

CHAPTER V
Earth Force

THE NORTHWARD JOURNEY AGAINST the more formidable southbound currents was bearable only because of the light, water-cutting canoes and the strength of his body, mind and soul, all of which seemed born again through his city experience. And most of that Lone Hawk owed to the much-revered Night Owl, helping him shed his naivety and thus realize in his lonely thoughts up-river, what Wonders Eye meant by his reference 'lady of the night.' She was, in fact, the city's 'queen' prostitute. Yet, he was not of pious judgment. She would always be held in highest regard, as a warm and caring savior of sorts. And so, her absence was only felt more the worse by his untimely awakenings at the various riverside camps. Tenderly erotic dreams about her were to only sadly end, without her sweet 'real' kisses and warm, loving embrace.

Such nocturnal disappointments continued for three nights, as he sought no invitations by the sporadic settlements of the small river tribes, where he easily could have had a woman. Thus, his determination was one of solitude, and his onward trek to the point of destiny became a sole obsession, intensifying with the wind on his back as he neared the Wise Crow River.

"We're getting close, good Screecher, to a strange place of hostile people and a <u>magical</u> sphere…I hope," the spirited Lone Hawk told his un-interrupting audience of one winged warrior who was busily chomping on his braids from his shoulder perch, as they glided toward the turn-off. "A scouting mission will reveal whatever secrets these Earth Force people hold. We <u>must</u> find the cave past the village and force a diversion, depending on the guard situation. <u>Nothing</u> is to deny us this uncovering because I have had a premonition of the Warbird Empire, stretching the whole north side of the Wise Crow, with our valley as its eastern city and the Earth Force as our western jewel. We will have the northeast trade center to do business with King Cahokia's land and beyond, so our nation will grow ten-fold. Then, with our superior military might, Big River City can be taken as the southern jewel and, perhaps, the Wolverines for the Warbirds' northern claim. Oh, how my dreams <u>fly</u> like the wind, yet I can think no less—hah! If I were a sensible man, I'd only hope I don't get myself killed!"

Lone Hawk then veered off the Big River and headed east on the near placid Wise Crow toward the domain of the elusive Earth Force sphere. His heart started beating at a sharply increased tempo, in anticipation of mystic discovery and adventure.

In the early evening with strong steady strokes, he paddled in a timely fashion and passed the Earth Force shoreline, posing no threat by displaying the merchant stripes on his arms. Therefore, he was challenged by none of the posted military. Though only a half-dozen spear-toting guards, he also observed among them several civilians conducting peaceful exchange. Nonetheless, Lone Hawk inconspicuously kept his course tightly to the south bank, keeping his sights set forward toward the river. To further his anonymity, the renegade Screecher left him alone for most of the Wise Crow's route. Yet, he rejoined his company at the same campsite of the drunken night with Wonders Eye, from where the land route would not be far.

Safely beyond but conveniently close to the Earth Force territory of curiously small river boundaries, Lone Hawk grounded the canoes into some particularly dense brush. Uprooting several shrubs, he then concealed them completely. In preparation for his predawn raid, he and Screecher went on a moonlit scouting run to the west over thickly wooded, rolling hills. During his investigation, he discovered a northbound trail from the river, leading to the faint torch lights of the village in the distance. He could hear some loud foreign chants, which he could not understand yet could surmise that a ceremony was in progress. Uneasy with the escalating activity, he quickly turned back, noting the location.

Upon returning to his makeshift camp, he wished his investigation had probed further, to at least have seen the cave's entrance. In hindsight, his apprehension was most disappointing, as he lay down beneath the stars and dozed to a lucid vision. In dream-state, his scouting mission was quite different from the previous one of actuality. For, in its rather bold rounding of the noisy village to a remarkable climb of a giant oak tree, he could see the mouth of the magic cave from beyond the dwarfed treetops. While Screecher joined him on a nearby branch, they were startled when a curious gap jutting into the shrubby knoll turned bright red and began to rumble. Suddenly, after the red light began to ooze like lava out of the cave, a giant purple hand with an expansive fiery green arm burst out of it. Reaching upward to the treetop, the marauding digits snatched Lone Hawk and even Screecher, who was caught in mid-flight, trying to escape. They were crushed together into its palm and pulled into the flaming cave to be burnt to cinders, the eternal punishment for intruders, so it seemed. He struggled through the end of the nightmare with the intense pain of being burned to death and was ever-thankful to awaken in a cold sweat, with the concerned Screecher peeping from above.

After a brief chill of worried reconsideration, Lone Hawk dismissed the fearful dream as an obsession side effect, knowing only one cure. The mystery of the cave now had to be solved, if just for his sanity's sake. But the quite possibly lethal mission needed more careful planning to prepare him for any possible situation. So, while he thought of a lengthy series of action-reaction, proper response and willingness to dare compromises, he exhausted his mind to sleep. The quest was nearly sabotaged by his unintentional slumber until Screecher pecked at his shoulder when the darkness of night was soon to lift. In response, he bounded into the forest with sudden alertness, and an extreme sense of urgency.

In the fullest of war garb, he followed the same general path as before, while his trusty first warrior tagged along through the treetops above his winding route. Donning dark gray attire and a charcoal bamboo chest plate, he was a shadowy figure with holstered swords, a hunting knife, a bow and a full quiver of arrows, all of which he deemed adequate for any unfortunate encounters.

When he finally neared the village trail of his earlier reconnaissance, he detected a person lurking about in the dim light of the predawn sky. Fearing he had been discovered, Lone Hawk stopped in his tracks and tried to filter the hiding one out from the many tree trunks nestled in the lush foliage. Slowly, he leaned his body from side-to-side to get a wider angle's view and to possibly provoke some movement. Thus, his animated lure was only to find a drawn bow releasing an arrow from a well-camouflaged, olive hued figure next to a tree of fifteen paces away. With no more perfect a reflex, he drew his sword and incredibly deflected it, from what would have put out his eye.

As the failed arrow was launched from close range, Lone Hawk decided to charge the attacker with shielding cross swords. Hence, he deflected another arrow, which haplessly clanged against the mighty blades. Before a third arrow could be readied for flight, he lunged upon his assailant, dashing the threatening bow and arrow with a backhanded swing of his left-reeled sword, which he spiked into the earth. Once the four-long-and-lean limbs were firmly pinned beneath him, his freed hand clasped a thatch of bountifully soft hair while he pulled the back of the defeated one's neck to the remaining wielded sword's throat-pressing blade.

Though tall and dressed like a typical male warrior, the curve of the waist-to-hips and suppleness of compacted breasts, well noticed upon takedown, were unmistakably feminine. Consequently, Lone Hawk realized to his surprise that he had viciously tackled a lone 'woman' instead, but still stalking with the intent of killing him. Yet, in the heat of the muggy prelude to dawn, they gasped and gazed into each other's eyes, as their sweat dripped together. Her face was fine of feature, with full lips and large teardrop eyes of a unique brown, gold and blue-rimmed color expansion, which slanted down into her cheekbones most attractively. And even though her life was being compromised by the blade at his control, she fearlessly stared back at him with raw curiosity. It was a wonderful lock of sights until Screecher soon landed on his shoulder, causing her eyes to flare with contempt while she began to thrash.

"Screecher—go!" he barked in a whisper, nudging him away with a swing of his head. "Do not be frightened, warrior woman. I merely wish to see your fabled magic sphere. You? <u>You</u> were the one bathing at the shore ten or so days ago. The Earth Force Princess! <u>Princess</u> Rainbow, as my good uncle told!" Her eyes widened with interest, yet she remained silent. "I'm sorry, but I can only speak Warbird. You probably can't even understand me at all," he continued, with notice of her eyes suspiciously following his words. "Wonders Eye might have known your Earth Force tongue, but he was murdered by Toltec warriors on our way to Big River City. I <u>killed</u> them for that! And with using these, their own bloody swords. <u>Please</u>, say something, anything, my beautiful hostage!"

To his plea, her tensed muscles relaxed, as she cleared her voice. "I remember <u>you</u>, Birdman," she broke her silence with a palatably low voice in surprisingly well pronounced Warbird. "Yes, I was the one bathing at the river that morning, and I <u>am</u> the Princess Rainbow. Your uncle's death is a shame. However, <u>yours</u> will result as well, if you do not release me. Your <u>only</u> hope may lie in those swords for what you seek!" Considering the grave alternative and his immediate attraction, Lone Hawk lifted the blade from her throat and re-holstered his sword, hoping a peaceful maneuver would succeed.

"I could tell that you understood me, Princess Rainbow, and so, you <u>know</u> what I want," he gently inferred, perplexed as to how she could know his spoken tongue so well, considering Wonders Eye's all but too brief visit. While thoughts of such were consuming, Lone Hawk refocused on the possible deal. "Do you suggest a trade for a visit to this magic sphere? And, if such an exchange were made, tell me—what can this great thing do?" His query was excitedly delivered with the wonderment of a child, which sparked a smile that the Princess tried, unconvincing, to control by pursing her lips.

"Though you are <u>not</u> worthy of such an honor as even a glimpse of our sacred sphere, my father, the Chief of Earth Force Center, is a collector of fine weaponry. And <u>nothing</u> of his compares to those, I am certain," the Princess told, as she daintily slid her fingertip down the side of the intricate Toltec blade, and seemed less than uncomfortable lying beneath him. "However, he _is_ very selective as to which strangers can see this, for there is only _one_ who is truly justified. You may very well be rejected, Birdman, but, by my honor, I promise to forget our clash and promote your obsession, _if_ you release me now."

Lone Hawk sensed an aura of sincerity in her voice and so, gently helped her up by the hand. She was as tall as he and athletically light on her feet, with a gracefully provocative hip sway walk. Leering, he watched with a lick of his lips, as she wiped the dirt from her backside. Then catching her notice, he quickly re-holstered his spiked sword and retrieved her dashed bow, trustingly giving it back to her. With a warm look, she led him by her tugging hand up the trail to the village.

"Rather than _Birdman_, please call me by my proper name, Lone Hawk, top brave and 'future' chief of the Warbirds," he boasted, spewing his ambition to win her heart, and then he pointed for an introduction to Screecher, flying above them. "And, of course, you've met my red-tailed companion, Screecher ... first warrior, and one of the saving graces I owe to my survival on this long journey. This, the first pleasure trip of my seventeen summers, and it carried such tragedy. Good Princess, I am _sure_ that to see your magical sphere would heal my great loss, and bring me the strength of mind I so require to return to my homeland."

Screecher joined them to shoulder-perch along on their short trek up the graveled trail. While she was momentarily put off by his presence, she cautiously scratched his breast, but soon pulled her hand away to tend to Lone Hawk's appearance. Straightening his braids, chest plate and vest, she fussed all over him to prepare for his presentation to the Chief. Confidently pleased by her attentiveness, he was especially encouraged when she slowly swept her hand down his face, neck, shoulder and arm. Finally finished prepping him, she clasped his hand between both of hers, and pressed it to her breast as they entered the village.

"You are a foolish brave, Lone Hawk, but ... I _will_ make your chances good," she affectionately reassured, slight of smile and a twinkle in her eye. "You shall have your wish, if my daughterly charms don't fail me ... You are _so_ different from the others! I believe you may be…well, <u>that</u> is for my father and the sphere to decide.

"Oh, and I prefer that you simply call me Rainbow," she continued. "I mean, since you are, as you claim, a 'future' chief, there's no demand of you to use my formal title."

"<u>Rainbow</u>, yes, that stands alone quite well." He offered, with slyest of flattery while they strolled through her sleeping village on the widened path that forged past six-curved-rows of duplicate lodges, similar to those in Big River City. Nestled in the center of the innermost circle, consisting of six lodges, a huge, mossy cone-domed structure of hexahedron design lay like an axis, with only a small back-dropped hill to break the symmetry. Built up on a circular, elevated incline, its height was six times that of the two guards posted at its widely arched doorway. While their garments were of simple, tan warrior stock, the large, round turquoise amulets worn on their chest plates were noticeably impressive.

As dawn lit the sky to blue, the guards began to snuff the six, big standing torches, surrounding the structure at each angle. When Rainbow and Lone Hawk arrived at its perimeter, they dropped their polled snuffers near the entrance. Quickly, they retrieved their spears, leaning against the doorway. Then in urgent approach, they forbade her and the hawked stranger from passing, even though she led him there. They crossed their spears at the bottom of the walkway and stood at attention, facing them with forced frowns of disapproval.

"Stand aside!" she commanded in the flowing Earth Force tongue. "The Warbird brings an offering for the Chief." The guards, a hand taller than them, immediately eased off their blockade and allowed them to pass while Screecher, setting his sights on the marvelous structure, suddenly transcended the ever-strange company to roost on its summit. They entered the geometric-domed mass, with Lone Hawk commenting that the building looked like a giant deformed squash. She only rolled her eyes to the comparison.

Once inside, he found the interior to be larger than its outer skin would suggest, due to a deeply sunken, semi-open room of six walls surrounded by a ledge of common living sections above, at the entry level. In the center of the gouged basement was a stacked sandstone chimney much like Night Owl's, but much taller and thicker. In its enormity, it resembled a giant tree trunk that pierced through the domed ceiling, high above its black stone floor. Down twelve big steps, they walked along the submerged walls where, all around, a vast array of weaponry was hung for display. True to Rainbow's words, none of these were as beautiful as his Toltec swords.

Affront the wall opposite their first steps upon the sunken room's floor of ten-paces diameter, just one incredible piece of furniture stood. Turned away from them, an elaborate, buffalo-pelted throne laced with blue jay feathers with a horn-sculled crown then regally greeted them upon a full-faced, grizzly bearskin rug. Lying before it, a wide, funneled fireplace lay with smoldering embers. As ominous as the big dark chamber was illuminated by only a few torches, a huge old man suddenly rose from the extravagant chair that with its high back, initially hid him so well. More than a head taller and of proportionate width, the tan-and-black-robed giant turned and fixed his big bold eyes upon Lone Hawk, who was then feeling quite puny. With long gray hair and a well-wrinkled, broad yet tall face, the big chief, he figured to be at least sixty years old.

"Father, this Warbird brave named Lone Hawk would like to exchange a genuine Toltec sword for a visit to our sacred sphere," Rainbow proposed to the Chief, again using the Warbird tongue while the emanator of authority stood cross-armed, maintaining a penetrating stare into his vulnerable eyes. "You _must_ agree that one of _these_ would be the star of your collection!" The Chief waved them over and, once in proximity, his downward staring presence was especially uncomfortable for the dwarfed Lone Hawk.

"A Warbird, indeed!" he started in the lowest, most gruff voice that Lone Hawk ever had heard, however, his use of Warbird-speak was rather comforting and explained the mystery of Rainbow's adaptation. "Yes, I had the pleasure of visiting your remote valley long ago … before you were even born. I must say, it's a _beautiful_ area, and your people are quite friendly and most honorable … Except for one …" he trailed off.

"Summer before last, there was a Warbird merchant whose name, I believe, was Thunder Sky. He was so obnoxious and intrusive a sort that his welcome was doomed from the start. Therefore, I wouldn't let him see the sphere for any trade he could offer, and that would be that I hoped. But he was unbelievably relentless, and began to grow very angry as well. This <u>hot</u> head, oh! We had to force him out of the village and into his canoe at spear point." Lone Hawk gave him one of the swords to examine and cleared his throat, well knowing of whom he spoke.

"I believe the Warbird to which you refer was my uncle, Wonders Eye," he obliged in correction while the Chief's eyes flared with disbelief. "He was the one who told me of the great orb in your possession. I would never have considered this visit, if he was not murdered by the Toltec. But their ambush on the Big River just south of the Wise Crow took us by surprise, and so, brought his execution. However, I swiftly avenged his death, as I <u>slaughtered</u> all four of them and retained two of their swords, dealing the other pair in Big River City. Now, I carry his solemn wish, as well as my own, to see this wonder and offer a worthy gift to make it so."

"Yes, Wonders Eye, that was he," the Chief acknowledged, regretful, while he marveled at the coiled serpents handle on his shiny new toy. "Though I did not like the man, I <u>am</u> sorry for his death and your loss of an uncle you 'so obviously' loved very much. But I'm also very alarmed that the Toltec would venture so close to my peoples' home of the Earth Force. I salute you for freeing the world of such devils who wield, as you can see, the executioner's sword with the feather snake inlaid handle. Among their many prescribed tortures, these are used to behead those who are enslaved and then sacrificed atop their sun temples. I will cherish this sword, not so much for its exquisite gold and silver craftsmanship, but as a tribute to <u>Lone Hawk</u>, the <u>Toltec</u> Slayer!" As the Chief praised him, Rainbow clutched his upper arm and leaned her head on his shoulder in admiration. Lone Hawk was amazed at the way they so readily embraced him and felt that a major streak of good fortune had just begun.

"I am honored by your flattering words and very pleased that you like the sword, good Chief of the Earth Force," he expressed most politely, expecting fulfillment of his just reward to follow. "Now, will you bring me to your magic sphere, so I may witness this that is the wonder of the world?"

"You are <u>not</u> like your late uncle, for you seek higher things," the Chief assessed with a glowing smile of approval. "You are drawn and impassioned. This seems a sacred quest of your own, to which I feel the Earth Force's undeniable welcome. I grant you your simple wish and, perhaps before the sphere, there will be more. Come with me into its sacred home." He led them through a tapestry-concealed doorway below the top of the stairway, which they had just tread. Crudely framed with oak timbers, the space inside was of rough sandstone walls and a smooth bedrock floor that declined to stretch as a tunnel of about fifty-paces. At the other side, Lone Hawk was astonished to find that the Chief's impressive lodge was connected to an even more grand, subterranean enclosure.

Known to them as Earth Force Temple Cavern, it was a long, narrow and very tall stalactite hollow with a torch lit perimeter and a sizable hexagonal pit near its front end. There, a cool damp draft swirled in the air, producing goose bumps on Lone Hawk's skin, as they approached the soft-blue-lit crater. Once at the edge, the secret of the sphere began to unfold.

"It's so <u>beautiful</u>! How does it make and hold the wandering, colored lights?" he shouted in query with wild-eyed fascination. "Is it safe to touch?" The Chief nodded with affirmation, inviting him by his beholding hand to quench his attraction to the orb. Unstifled, Lone Hawk trotted down the seven steps to a larger bottom one, like a small platform. There, he turned to the middle of the pit where 'it' was set like a great jewel surrounded by six black boulders, which served as ceremonial seats for the shamans. At a diameter half-more his arm span and a height same as his own, the slightly sunken sphere illuminated swirls of blue, tan, yellow and green. Without hesitation, Lone Hawk draped his arms around the top of its glowing curvature.

"It's spreading <u>wonderful</u> warmth throughout my body!" he reported, smiling in pure glee while Rainbow and the Chief came down into the worship pit, glancing to each other with utter amazement. "I am upon a miracle well, well-well worth the sword. <u>What</u> did you say?" They said nothing and surmised that the voice they could not hear was of the sphere. "I <u>must</u> be imagining things. What's it doing? Hey, <u>hey</u>! I'm being pushed up!" Separated from the sphere, he was flung into suspension just above it and had a vision.

In an astral-projective state, he was launched through the ceiling of the cave into the clear blue sky above it. Granted the phenomenal power of flight, he shared Screecher's avian exuberance of viewing the wooded hills and the river in pleasant passing below him. Soon, as his speed over the terrain became too great, utter nausea set in while the chants became more audible. Ever encompassing, the demanding voices that seemed only a variation of one filled his head to its limit. Combined with the blinding rate of his aerial advance, the vision showed him great mountains and waters of such magnitude, his senses were over-loaded and praying for some intervention on his behalf.

"No! Not me!" He screamed at the loudest level of angst a human could muster, as fingers of lightning danced beneath his body from the churning sphere.

Amidst his refusal to the rumbling, blaring Earth Force, Screecher swooped down from the vast ceiling and talon-clutched his scalp-yanked braids, pulling him away from the menacing orb to drop him, motionless, before Rainbow's feet.

"Oh, my brave Lone Hawk…please, don't be dead," Rainbow tearfully pleaded with a gasping flutter in her voice, as she instantly knelt to him and put her ear to his chest, hearing not a beat. "Earth Force, please let him live!" Immediately following her words, Screecher landed on his chest beside her, wings flapping like the hawk dance, and butted his little head against his chin. Lone Hawk coughed and shook his head and body with a chill while Screecher hopped into flight. "Father! It listens through the bird. He is reborn! Lone Hawk, relax. You are now safe," she comforted with his face to her bosom, and so his tremors were calmed. "Do you remember any of the Earth Force words to you? Are you 'The One', as I am sure you are?"

Lips pursed, he rose to his feet and stretched his limbs while a daze kept his troubled mind at temporary bay. "Where's my little hero? Screecher?" Lone Hawk inquired with a shout while he peered up at the ceiling with hopeful eyes. "I want to thank him for saving me from your merciless ball of torture!" He turned and pointed at the sphere, which retained its same amiable glow from upon his arrival. "It hurled me over the land at such a rate that I, the bravest of braves, was helplessly frightened. I had no control while it chanted into my head, over and over, faster and faster! I wanted to die! Could you hear nothing?" Extremely interested, the Chief held Lone Hawk's right hand with both of his big mitts, while his daughter clung to his left arm, her expecting eyes convinced of the profound.

"There was nothing for our ears, but a message for The One," the Chief explained in a calm, yet intense tone, suggesting far more than for what Lone Hawk had bargained. "What did the chant say? It is very important that you tell me, for what you now know reflects upon the fate of all that is to be … now, tell me!" The Chief's insistence became an interrogation, and so Lone Hawk's secret was flushed out by the big man's impetuous turn.

"I was told, 'Beware! The evil will come! Powers bestowed … Protector of all to be—You, my Earth Force Son," he recited, reluctant, to their ecstatic grins. "I do not need this! It asks far too much!"

Establishing a three-way embrace, the Chief declared the end of the search, as other hopefuls produced nothing compared to the lone Warbird. "My daughter, we are blessed to have witnessed the reckoning of the Chosen One, the Earth Force Son!" he celebrated with words and proximity that made him anxious and faint. "Yes, it is you, Lone Hawk. Your true quest has only just begun!"

Lone Hawk immediately broke the triangle and backed away in a fit of nervous rage. "I need some fresh air!" he shouted, hyperventilating, as he bounded out of the pit, blindly following another tunnel beyond the Temple Cavern, which led to its outlet where Screecher entered. He ran through the upward winding passage, as fast as his feet could carry him. Soon, he reached the mouth of the cave and slowed to a trot. The pressure in his face began to subside and with his easing demeanor, he emerged from the rocky opening to a couple of standing guards who were just out of view on the other side.

As was their duty, they alerted to the situation and tried to jab the trespasser with their spears, but Lone Hawk's lightning-swift reflexes denied their attack. Snatching their not-so-trusty spears, he spun his body and wrestled them away. He discarded one of the crude weapons and reeled the other while drawing his remaining sword to end the fight. With their backs against a stone wall on the side of a grassy hill arched around the cave, Lone Hawk held the stunned guards by masterful intimidation with their pointing spear tip and his readied blade. Rainbow and the Chief soon caught up to their chosen brave, and were not surprised to find him in a conquering posture.

"Bow to him and tell the villagers that 'The One' has been chosen!" the Chief boomed in command, prompting the hapless guards to meekly tip their heads to Lone Hawk and nervously retrieve their spears. "Relish this honor, as <u>you</u> are among the <u>first</u> to be in the presence of The Earth Force Son! Now, go and spread the word that the celebration of The One's arrival will be at high sun in the Shaman's Circle!"

Their neutral expressions were suddenly transformed to giddy smiles, as they obediently scurried off over the hill to awake the masses with the good news.

Though uncomfortable with the title of such profundity, Lone Hawk managed to stash the religious, supernatural aspects of the experience into a remote section of his mind and concentrate on the great opportunities it presented. Then, with but another brief survey of the beautiful Princess Rainbow with her worshipping eyes, the decision was made. Amidst their obvious attraction ta boot, she would be his wife. It would be the first step in his plan to join the Warbird and Earth Force territories as one nation under his eventual rule.

"Uh, Rainbow, I would be most delighted if you would join me for a walk to your 'fine' nation's east end by the river," he requested in a tone so calm and cool, it emanated but boundless confidence. "As I have many valuables in my canoes there, I would like to relocate them to your official landing for proper care. Also, I would like to discuss our future plans, with your father's consent, of course."

The Chief whisked his hand to the early morning sun, peeking through the forest, and smiled with wide-eyed exuberance. "Go with him, my little Rainbow," he approved with a nod while shuffling backwards toward the cave. "But remember to return by high sun when <u>all</u> will be present for the most joyous celebration the Earth Force tribe has <u>ever</u> known!" A moment after he disappeared into the cave, they heard the Chief's husky laughter echoing to Screecher in passing, who then flew out of the cherished underworld with a bat clutched in his talons. He dropped it at Lone Hawk's feet and perched on his shoulder, expecting gratitude.

"Oh, Screecher! You save my life, and <u>then</u> you grant me a meal," he praised with a smile that was ready to burst into at least a chuckle. "You are <u>too</u> good to me, my feathered warrior! Now, do you have any tasty ways to prepare bat, my little Rainbow?" She blushed to his fatherly reference and laughed a nervous titter, sparking his uproarious laughter, which sent the angered Screecher into flight as he sensed an insult to his gift.

After the pair managed to calm such mirth, they began to hike toward a perimeter trail of her steering where, upon impulse, she kissed his shoulder and excitedly peered into his eyes, her heart beating wildly. "Did you mean our future plans, as in you and me being together … husband and wife?" the bubbly Rainbow asked, as she played with his braids upon her taking him on a different trail that swung, unbeknownst to him, right to his secret camp. "Now, that's a true brave! Wanting a woman who tried to kill him! Yet, <u>you</u> know that <u>I</u> know you are no mere brave, nor a powerful chief. You are <u>much</u> greater, the greatest … the One, and you want me?" Lone Hawk took her hand in his and admired her tenacity, as she interlocked their fingers.

"When I first saw your shadowed figure in the predawn haze, I thought you were a man, a warrior scout doing his rightful duty." Lone Hawk spoke of their first encounter like it was long ago. "However, as I took the advantage and put my blade to your throat, your enchanting eyes stopped me cold, warm and then carried us into a most heated passage. We ventured into each other's souls and love had no choice but to grow. Do you see? To me, Rainbow, <u>you</u> are The One! And, since I am now Warbird <u>and</u> Earth Force, will you be my wife?"

She leaped in front of him like a barricade and confronted his lips with a long, wet kiss, while she wrapped her arms around his back with a strong jerking motion. "You <u>knew</u> my acceptance before, as my father was so <u>blatantly</u> hopeful. Yet, you feel the need to say such sweet things and, well, it is even <u>more</u> enriching," Rainbow told him, welling eyes of pure joy and trembling with infatuation. "I love you as a man, and a god…my 'wonderful' Lone Hawk, and I would be <u>more</u> than honored to be your wife." With her spirited willingness to his intentions, he kissed her back in deep tongue-bathing fashion and felt himself the mightiest man of the world in the making.

During their short jaunt down the trail over a forested hill to the river-site with the canoes, Lone Hawk dared to stroke her pertly firm buttocks, which made her gasp and smile in coquettish profile to him. While thinking her compacted breasts must be the only measurable 'fat deposits' of her svelte body, he was impressed to the touch that so strong and lean a woman could also be shaped so feminine. And to even return such roving as did he, the time was ripe for some sweet engagement. Thus, when they arrived at the camp area where he pointed out the hidden canoes, Rainbow quite overtly expressed her desire to pre-consummate their marriage.

In delicate fashion, she removed her clothing with a graceful flow, slinking out of her faded green garb and tiny peach-hued breechcloth with her backside to him. She then placed them upon a thick solid log nearby. Seeming a little apprehensive, she turned around and sat down, arms forward, on the natural sitting bench. She slipped out of her black moccasins and revealed her pristine, almost fully exposed form. Beneath fuller than expected breasts pressed together by her elbows, she crossed and draped her hands and wrists between her legs over her nether region with an Earth Force turquoise disc waist-lace, dangling above it. As Lone Hawk beheld her near-willing pose like a precious work of art, Rainbow blushed with bashful hesitance while she continued to cover the view between her wavering thighs a half-spread. With a nervous flutter in her voice, she peered up to him and explained her reluctance. "Even though I started out so bold, you can <u>probably</u> tell I have never done this before…Could you then just take it slow and easy, so I can get comfortable with it? I am <u>such</u> a child!" she squeaked, being too hard on herself, and then recomposed herself to a still-forced wiliness. "Alright, I'm over it…and more than ready now. But just so you know, Lone Hawk, you'll be the first and <u>forever</u> my only one…"

Though eager to plunge in right away, Lone Hawk reconsidered her 'slow and easy' request and thus decided to take the gradual approach by first kneeling before her well-arched feet and softly kissing each one. Then with a barrage of licking kisses, he forged a zigzagged path foot-to-foot, ankles, calves and knees until he reached the crucial point when she could truly be put at ease. There, he gently pulled only her left hand to his lips and planted a smacking kiss, then cradled her trusting face jaw-to-temple with his soothing right hand, erasing all her ill ease. "Hey, I'm pretty new to this too, but sure…let's just take our time and know that when you're totally in love, it can only be all-the-more-sweeter!" he whimsically charmed, melting her heart ever further with his encouraging words. "And <u>you</u> are not alone, as I <u>too</u> am yet to know that special feeling…till now…" With her blush fully retreated, Rainbow smiled and giggled, then slowly slid her hand just halfway from her crotch while Lone Hawk quickly disrobed. Smoothly, he positioned himself between her trembling thighs and slipped his massaging hand under hers for full release.

As he primed her with roving circular motions, she pulled him close to her hardened breasts and nodded with a sumptuous kiss of impassioned urgency. "That's <u>more</u> than well enough, Lone Hawk, wonderful and perfect, but <u>now</u> I need you inside me more than ever!" Lone Hawk happily obliged her wish, then after their first and ever-so-joyous round of lovemaking had gloriously climaxed, upright on the sitting log, the newly delved Rainbow wept and tittered to the fleeting burst of pain that quickly subsided to the filling caress of ecstasy. Then gently massaging her shiny sweated backside, writhing and flexing, Lone Hawk kissed all about her beautiful face a glow and whispered into her cute, swept back ear with concern. "Are those happy tears, I hope?" he calmly asked, well-knowing that to be the case, as confirmed by her slit-eyed seductive stare and breathy tone, expecting more. "Happy? Oh, yes! If I could <u>possibly</u> be any happier, dear lover, <u>please</u> show me the way—mm, hmm!" she tempted, wide-eyed with a naughty smirk while grinding her pelvis against his for the intended response. "Whoa-yeah! 'Happier, indeed'…coming right up! Now, let us really make love…"

So well familiarized their bodies had become, they slipped back into their pleasure zones of merging delights as naturally as breathing. Then after a second round's writhing engagement ended up migrating off the log and onto the ground, they lay to sweetly climax yet again, uncaring to be muddied by their rolling romp of lusted fusion. There, upon completion, the rapturous Rainbow lost control and started to scream in such a terrorized manner, Lone Hawk promptly covered her mouth to muffle the unexpected response. And so, he playfully cautioned, "Okay, being vocal is one thing, but those, my stars, sounded like cries of torture! And now look what you've done, your whole army's been alerted and here they come, over the ridge!"

She broke into a titter and released a flurry of strong pecking kisses upon his lips, chin and even his nose in appreciation. Thus, she explained in her cutesy voice, "It's because you make me feel so good inside, outside and all around me…that I become crazy! With that, and so much more that I love about you, it will be easy for me to be a good-and-willing wife. For every spare moment we'll have, I can just tell…ours will never grow dull."

Lone Hawk kissed her long and affectionately, as he certainly liked her mind-set. A frigid woman could by no means make him happy, and so, a vow of such willingness was a thankful sign. And though his god-like status was the spark that procured his wish, their explosive physical compatibility and good promise in attitudes were the vital qualities, which allowed true love to take root and grow.

Then rising from the cuddling stage to their feet, they embraced to wavering imbalance, as dizziness followed the heated passion with laughter and soft kisses. They were surprised by the generous amount of dirt which stuck to their bodies and, in turn, rinsed each other clean in the river shallows. Since her garment had been stained while sitting on the log, Lone Hawk uncovered the canoes and selected two of his new outfits, light gray with rust trim and dirty blue with red pinstripes. She chose the latter and they dressed in complimentary talk of the limb-exposing apparel.

Satisfied in their appearance, she helped him drag the canoes into the water, boarded the lead and insisted on her powering from the front. He was impressed by her paddling strength and technique, which could be compared with many a male warrior. In a short while, they were around the river bends and upon the Earth Force landing. With their arrival, she instructed a couple of the dozen warriors standing guard to mind his craft with special attention. In their compliance, they looked to Lone Hawk with worshipping awe and flinched in fear when he reached into his canoe for some jewelry to adorn his future bride. The word of his bestowal obviously had reached the riverfront.

"Rainbow, please tell them <u>not</u> to act like that," Lone Hawk pleaded, looking perturbed, as he pulled a small brown sack from his grounded trailer and added, "they're making me uncomfortable…just urge them to treat me like any other approved guest…" To his wish, she told them the same in Earth Force speak and thus, they smiled and nodded with understanding then glared at Lone Hawk, smirking in brave-face. He was amused to a titter, yet nonetheless satisfied. "Ha-ha, thanks for that, sort of…anyway, have these, my precious, as small tokens of my love," he offered to her delighted inspection. "Turquoise, opals, sapphires and more laden with silver and gold. Let them decorate you today with your most beautiful dress for our union, which will be declared before all your tribe to see."

She was ecstatic, and so, dragged him by the hand, skipping like a happy little girl up the trail to the village. However, along the way, her mood was compromised when she noticed that Screecher was following and spying from the treetops. She was intuitive of a looming bit of animosity. "I believe your Screecher is jealous of me," she surmised, with a touch of concern in her tone. "Though it seems he is quite tame, I don't need to worry about him…do I?"

"Don't be silly! That's <u>Screecher</u>, my self-appointed guardian, of whom I raised from a chick," Lone Hawk reassured without a care, as he kissed her hand. "He just thinks he's human, like a concerned friend. I sure wish he would find a nice female hawk to remind him of his wild side. <u>That</u> would cure his over-watchful eye upon us!" Though he tempered her own immediate concerns, in the back of her mind she remained wearied of what she considered a spooky bird.

With Screecher bolting from the branches above them to his favorite roost atop her father's lodge, the Earth Force palace, the Chief called out to the huge assemblage at its foot to announce the return of the most honored one and their princess. There, he stood out in his bold presence among the chattering crowd and the six black-robed shamans, as he waved to them in a festive manner with smiling eagerness.

When they neared the celebration scene, Lone Hawk tried to be humorous with a rather inappropriate, crude observation. "Before, I said your father's lodge looked like a giant squash or something, but now I see that it more resembles a giant ground-breast," he laughed with an impish grin, causing Rainbow to roll her eyes and shake her head, somewhat annoyed. "But, since I was just all around and about worshipping those beauties of yours, I guess even the most innocent of rounded things like that will remind me of them…"

"Shush!" she rasped, having none of it while approaching the religious ceremony ahead. "Enough with the palace design and now, my breasts…my father's right there!" Her firm retort demanded his respect and silenced any further comments, as they rejoined the Chief at the Shamans' Circle around his thought-provoking palace. Amidst the gawking and whispering natives of several hundred, Lone Hawk was uneasy. And, upon surveying the Earth Force people, he found that the women were generally big-boned and homely, rendering the beautiful Rainbow quite an anomaly, he thought, and fortunately so.

"I would like you to know, good Chief, that your daughter has agreed to be my wife," Lone Hawk proudly told in confidence of his approval. "Now, I ask you for your blessing, and that you make our sacred union official on this historic day."

"Of course, it will be done, Lone Hawk, as you probably already knew that one cannot deny the Earth Force Son his daughter's vow of marriage," the Chief agreed, glassy-eyed and with a hug of his daughter, well prepared for their intentions, as he was then ready to share the good news with the villagers. "Yes, as I can see, most everyone is here, besides our perimeter military. Well, you all undoubtedly have heard that a brave of the Warbird tribe came to us this dawn with a bold proposition: This magnificent sword, in exchange for a visit to our sacred sphere," he told, with a twirl of the Toltec sword above his head while the people marveled with wide-eyed, droning awe. "I had a profound feeling about this man and gladly agreed to his terms. Then, true to my inkling, the sphere immediately embraced him as The One in the final proof by his receiving its word, as <u>no</u> stranger could <u>ever</u> know. So, here I behold to you, my good people, the Warbird, Lone Hawk…and bestowed savior, The One—the Earth Force Son!

"And, to further this wondrous event, you will all be honored to witness the joining of this, the most precious woman in the world, my <u>only</u> living offspring…the <u>beautiful</u> Princess Rainbow and Lone Hawk, who needs no further introduction, in the sacred union of marriage. As these two prepare in the palace for the ceremony, follow the shamans to Temple Cavern for this miraculous joining. Vows will be brief, and a long celebration shall follow!" Emanating thought waves of conformity, the long parade led by the six shamans passed by Lone Hawk, with turning heads of haunting, sensationalized eyes that disappeared in a thankful hurry over the hill. Yet, while he did not understand the Earth Force custom, his ignorance would only serve as temporary relief since there would be yet a second bout with the sphere but in full concentration.

"Lone Hawk, though you hide your feelings well, like a good brave should, I sense your apprehension and discomfort to attentions of such intensity," the Chief lovingly acknowledged, remaining behind the rest of the tribe, as he patted him on the back like a father figure would. "The good word has spread, and they are overjoyed. So, excuse their stares. They gaze upon you as an extension of the Earth Force, one whose presence commands much more veneration than me, the shamans, or any man who lives. You and your bestowal will take <u>much</u> getting used to! Let us merely agree on that fact for now.

"In the meantime, I am pleased to see that you've changed into a more festive garment. It will enhance the occasion quite well. Perhaps you would like to help Rainbow pick out an appropriate garment of her own as well, since I'm sure she is eager to show you her vast wardrobe. And, while I leave you to your privacy in my home, there is a special prenuptial feast inside which the shamans' wives have prepared. Enjoy and, please, do not be too long." He kissed Rainbow on the forehead and thus, started over the hill to join the others in worship.

"Where are they all going?" Lone Hawk asked in a mild state of confusion, as they entered the lodge. "Are they marching in our honor, only to return when we're ready?" She evaded the question and guided him to her canopied bed on a well-girthed loft above the Chief's weapons display area. There, with the draw of a sky-blue drape, Rainbow revealed a voluminous chamber where several wooden racks of clothing were hung in an impressive array of designs and colors. Immediately, his eyes were drawn to a spiraled, multicolored beaded gown of ankle length. He held it before her and nodded in fervent approval, playing along with her evasiveness, just for the moment. "This one will be _perfectly_ exquisite for this, our most formal day," he declared, as his lent garb dropped to her ankles and she slipped into the colorful gown with breathtaking results. "Wow! _Look_ at you…it's like a rainbow wrap, my love— your namesake! Nature's most _beautiful_ creation—how you _so_ complement each other!" He hugged her in cherishing fashion, then whispered in her ear, "they wait for us at the sphere, true?"

She nodded, meekly, well knowing his reluctance to rejoin the orb of his near fatality. "Please, do not fear it; your bestowal is already done," Rainbow said, sadly looking to the floor, but then she swung her chin up and straight ahead with firm persuasion. "To stand before the sphere is the most vital part of declaring matrimonial union, so we must! I'll throw myself between you and the sphere, if it _dares_ to try and take you again—I promise!" She held his hands with pleading eyes, but he tensed up and threw them down.

"The One! The Earth Force Son? This is crazy!" Lone Hawk denounced, forgetting all that would be gained in his grand scheme. "That mystic ball has a morbid power beyond anything else, and I admit…well, if I can't confide in you, then who? Yes, I _am_ afraid of it and…I _cannot_ accept this feeling. And now you think less of me."

She clasped her hands behind his neck and cracked an adoring smile. "No, _not_ true! My love for you only grows more when you allow that brave's rigid wall to fall, so letting me to contribute in a strong way," she encouraged in a soothing tone while stroking his broad clefted chin. "Your reaction is not surprising. In fact, it is to be expected, since you <u>were</u> a Warbird pagan. Enlightenment does not come easily to one of such. And so, to quell your denial, you chose <u>me</u> as your spouse. At this time, my faith must be strong enough for both of us. For soon, you shall realize that every day and every night <u>must</u> be enjoyed as though they were our last. We just don't know how or when you will be summoned, but destiny has been served and to worry about it like that can only be futile. Lone Hawk, come. Let us live this glorious moment undaunted by the other future." Her brave words were ever inspiring and convinced him to proceed with the tradition.

"Very well, I'll put the other future aside and concentrate on the here and now with you, that is, after we have eaten," he agreed, suddenly so easy going, with his conditional finger pointing at two covered baskets on a counter in the eatery near the entrance. "Whatever the shamans' wives have prepared, it smells delicious, and I am starving!" They brought the baskets to her bed and lay side-by-side while he feasted and she snacked on a prenuptial meal of poached pheasant eggs on corn cakes with maple syrup, delicate filets of smoked bass, honey-wheat pastries and mixed berry juice. During the quiet of the intimate meal, they were able to become acquainted, revealing their regimen pasts to each other.

Though as a princess, a spoiled child, Lone Hawk learned that Rainbow's life was by no means an easy one. By her father's insistence, she was constantly tutored in the ways of the world, and well so, as the Chief was very well traveled. From the Big River East to the Great Mountains of the West and the Salted Gulf of the South, he knew much of the other cultures and languages in existence, funneling all the knowledge he could to his ever-curious little girl. Her only friends were the shamans, exhausting her with religious instruction, and the top braves, athletically training her as a warrior since she was eight years old, nearly half-her-life. She filled the role of son and daughter, trying to be everything to him.

Along with the numbing death of her mother during childbirth, the Chief had lost two wives and seven children who were inflicted by untimely deaths of unusual circumstances. The Chief's fifty-nine well-seasoned years were flooded with triumph and tragedy, though more notably the latter. Rainbow was so glad that, for the first time in all of her life, her father carried the carefree, loving glow of true happiness. He was free of the bitter past because she was chosen by 'The One', the highest honor. He could not possibly ask for more, in her lifelong quest to gain his approval.

"You brought an unmatched joy to my father, the Earth Force people and someday, the whole world. And, of course, to myself most of all!" Rainbow showered him with flattery and affection while he, staring off to the side, began to convert his fear of the orb into the gall of harnessing its power. His thoughts drifted toward tactics of defiance and intimidation, which could unlock its mystery and expose its weak points. Even though his ever-returning attitude of military domination was, for once, well out of its league, the grandiose schemes spinning through his head restored his confidence.

"What are you thinking about, Lone Hawk?" the curious Rainbow asked, gently backhanding his shoulder. "I know, I praise you too much and you become uncomfortable…Well, in so little time, I am the proudest and most in-love woman of the entire world. There! That's all you must bear…Lone Hawk?"

"Oh, sorry, but…I don't want to sound shallow or anything, but…it's about your exotic beauty, and not having any resemblance to your father nor anyone I have ever seen…was your mother so foreign? Like, from a faraway tribe?" Her eyes instantly welled to the all-too-sensitive question, as she gave him an emotionally charged account of her sordid roots that she told with a flutter in her voice. In thoughtful support, Lone Hawk held her hands and hung onto her every word.

"Well, it's a long story, but the short of it is she was a half-breed…Wolverine tribe on her mother's side and on her father's, a strange pale-skinned, red-bearded type of man from far-far away," Rainbow tearfully explained, with a tight-lipped frown just mentioning the man. "Part of a marauding naval army, he raped her mother as they pillaged her village, up north on the Great Superior Lake. A product tainted by half-enemy blood, she was shunned by the tribe and never really loved by my cold and heartless grandmother. Eventually, she was taken in by the chief as a concubine for her 'novelty' good looks. Luckily though, my father, in his many travels, rescued her from a life of servitude and so, bartered for her freedom. He often said that once she set her listless, dull blue eyes on our ever-loving sphere, she smiled for the first time and then her eyes miraculously transformed…to a vibrant fiery violet! Thus, called only half-breed until then, her name became 'Violet', a 'real' name that she utterly cherished. I so regret her death while bearing me, but…at least, she could know love and acceptance, without cruel judgement, in her last days…"

Her voice became too choked-up to speak any further. And while he wiped her tears, Lone Hawk felt their connection grow even stronger just hearing about the healing-power of the Earth Force for the good bestowed upon her unjustly abused mother. "I am so glad you told me her story…and I'm sure her loving spirit lives on in you," he sweetly encouraged, with a kiss to her hand and renewed bravery in his heart. "And now that my fear of the sphere has totally passed, I look forward to meeting its magnificence once again, but only to join us—husband and most uniquely rooted wife!" he declared to her with an adoring kiss to the lips and roll off the bed to then suddenly stand beside her, still lying there but cracking a smile. Thus, Lone Hawk beheld the room and beyond in grand style with a self-touting pirouette. "I suddenly feel a great vitality from this and, as I was thinking about you and me together anywhere and everywhere, I have concluded that there exists not a place on this Great Earth that can shy us away. Come now, my sweet Rainbow, let us go to the sphere and wed. They have waited long enough!" He lifted her off the bed and gazed into the sincere, dampened eyes of pure joy upon her pretty face. His heart swelled like never before, as he kissed her for the last time before their vows.

CHAPTER VI

Till Summons Parts

EAGER TO PUBLICLY DECLARE his loving commitment, Lone Hawk carried Rainbow down the stairs into the weapons display area and pulled aside the secret tapestry. Then, leading her by the hand, they trotted through the tunnel to the dimly lit end, where the people echoed praise to the Earth Force for its deliverance of The One. When they entered the Temple Cavern, the packed floor of witnesses abruptly ceased in their song and cleared a path to the sphere pit. Muffled cheers began to break as they slowly strolled through the crowd, exchanging smiling glances and lame hand-waving. Front and center at the pit's edge, the Chief awaited and raised his hands when the couple came before him, signaling the congregation to silence. Only the nuptial chants sung by the six shamans sitting around the mighty orb could be heard. And with a mere glimpse at the divine object of their worship, ice cold chills shot up Lone Hawk's spine and seemed to shatter in the back of his head. He quickly redirected his attention to the Chief, who began to speak in the native tongue to open the ceremony:

"Just as the Earth Force was once a wandering entity until its union with the Life Source Sun made it prosper as this fertile plain of life, so did the Earth Force Son wander until one brought him to enlightenment. Hence forth, I present to you, Lone Hawk and Princess Rainbow, a match as perfect as the Earth Force and the Sun. The stranger has come to be bestowed, as the ancients told so long ago, yet the marriage to the tribe is of no prophecy and only comes with the surprise of true love…With that in its rightful place, let us now go to the sphere for your matrimonial blessing."

With his hands clasped to their shoulders, the Chief guided them down into the pit to face the sphere. When he joined the shamans, his baritone singing of the traditional song filled the bottom range and as he sung, Lone Hawk noticed an obscure face behind the swirling clouds inside the sphere. Soon, it developed to clarity and was recognized as Rainbow's anguished face, her swollen eyes streaming with tears.

`*Spare this good woman, my son,*' the tranquil, mystic voice commanded from the disturbing image in the sphere, flooding his mind even worse than before. '*You must go alone to your homeland. There, the end will show you the beginning of your true purpose.*'

`Interfere in my life no more! You are a <u>wicked</u> ball of pain and deception!' Lone Hawk vehemently directed his thoughts of defiance to the sphere, well knowing that no one else could hear the profound interaction. 'I'm marrying this woman who I <u>dearly</u> love, and your treachery <u>cannot</u> stop me. Together, Rainbow and I shall stay and rule this land, with or without you, while you may seek another to fulfill your 'dead-end' prophecy!' The pained image of Rainbow faded just as the singing subsided. Yet, as he thought, the Chief, Rainbow and the shamans took no apparent notice of his lashing out at their god.

"Earth Force, please bless these two, my daughter and your son, and allow them the full rights of marriage," the Chief continued with a roar, spanning his hands onto the crowns of their heads as the merging of souls. "Lone Hawk," he said, shifting to the Warbird tongue while the people peering overhead seemed ready to fall inside the sacred crevice; "do you promise in honor of the Earth Force to love, respect and support this woman, Rainbow, regardless of misfortune, until you die?"

"Yes, I do, and I will until I die, and beyond…" he answered with gusto, glaring at the sphere, which remained neutral in a blue and white streaked haze.

"Rainbow, do you promise in honor of the Earth Force to love, respect and support this man, Lone Hawk, regardless of misfortune, until you die?"

"Yes, I do and will," she calmly vowed with a smile and joyous eyes, rolling a tear apiece. The Chief kissed the sphere, as did the shamans, then Rainbow put her hand to her mouth, signaling that they must do the same. The hesitant Lone Hawk followed her instruction and put his lips to her anguished double, who reappeared inside the sphere. He felt so dreadfully sorry, but was overwhelmingly relieved when, afterward, he turned his head and saw the happy face of his newly wed bride.

"The union of marriage is complete!" the Chief happily announced as he backed away from the sphere and turned, raising his hands to the crowd above them. "Lone Hawk and Rainbow, you are now husband and wife. So, as my lodge is your domain until tomorrow's high sun, hurry and make me some healthy grandchildren," he added, well knowing by her earlier change of clothes that they had already started. "Also, be aware that food, drink and whatever you wish will be catered to your door amidst the sounds of celebration." In procession, the Chief led them out of the Temple Cavern, followed by the shamans and the villagers, taking the long way over the hill back to the Shamans' Circle. Breaking away from the congregation, the eager couple waved their goodbyes and went back into the then deemed 'pleasure palace' of her father's generosity.

Immediately, Rainbow ran into the display pit and motioned to Lone Hawk, most suggestive, with a swing of her head and wave of tongue. After he promptly complied to her invitation, she pushed him into her father's buffalo chair, seating his attentions for a private show. As she seductively danced to the rhythm of the drummers playing outside, she wiggled free of her ravishing gown. Gracefully stripped to her splendid nakedness, she aggressively pulled the intrigued Lone Hawk out of the chair by his hands, guiding them crotch-to-breasts while forcefully disrobing him.

"Remember what I said," Rainbow reminded, ever-enthused, as she writhed against his libido-stirred body; "every spare moment!" She then added, with a dash of humor, "what say you, bear—mind if we come aboard?" Chiming in on cue, Lone Hawk replied for the bear rug in a funny growling voice, "please do, I need a back-massage, anyway…" Thus, after some giggles, their passionate, somewhat savage lovemaking began on the soft furry, grizzly bear rug with him on top, only to turn-and-switch to her domination, wildly rocking and plunging up-and-down, to-and-fro toward their most impactive, surging climaxes thus far, which merely whetted their appetites. Insatiably wanting for more but in a less open setting, they migrated to the upper level, finding an array of surfaces to posture against. By midday, they had exhausted themselves to the merging delights, ending up on her bed and deciding to venture outside. After cleaning up a bit, they joined the celebration still raging in their honor. There, in the Shamans' Circle, Lone Hawk managed to coax Screecher down from his mighty roost atop the palace and perform the hawk dance. As was the case in Big River City, the Earth Force musicians played to enhance the tandem's vibrant expression, proving once again to be an absolute crowd pleaser. After much feast, frolic and various sour berry, honey and corn alcohol drinks, they wandered back inside the palace at twilight, and fell asleep in each other's arms. Late that night, Rainbow awakened the groggy Lone Hawk to tell him about a glorious dream from which she had just emerged.

"I had a dream <u>so</u> fantastic, Lone, I just <u>couldn't</u> fall back to sleep for fear that I would forget it!" she told, trimming his name to the familiar, while he was a bit annoyed by her untimely excitement. "We were naked, floating through the tunnel to the Temple Cavern, and you were riding me from behind but not yet inside. From there, we flew like magic to the sphere, blushing a most brilliant pink, and landed on its softly curved side. Brought to a smooth stop, we were draped around it and then you came into me, <u>oh</u> so deeply. With every thrust, you pushed me more and more into the sphere until I was inside, with you to follow. We became at one with the sphere and bolted through the ceiling into the sky toward the moon. Unfortunately, then, I woke up from our wondrous ride, cut short, and <u>now</u> I am obsessed! Let us be daring, my Love. The sphere has blessed our union and so, it should gladly want to share in our earthly pleasures…Please, Lone…please!" Her insistence of such naughty exploration twisted and tore his conscience to guilt, as only he knew of the Earth Force's objection to their marriage. But then reasoning that even amidst the seemingly forbidden act, certainly no harm could come to Rainbow, the Earth Force's darling, and so he caved to her wishes.

"Alright..." Lone Hawk half-heartily agreed while remembering his declaration said back in her bedroom, right before their wedding vows; "sounds risky, but I _did_ say we'd shy away from nothing..." So, being a good sport but against his better judgement, Lone Hawk went along with her naughty sex dare.

Naked and vulnerable in the dim torch light, his conscience churned with guilt all the way to the sphere pit with her pulling him along, rubbing his hands on her flexing buttocks. There, its glow only intensified with every step down the stairway, where Rainbow bounded ahead of him and pressed her warm body against the cool orb. She curved her spine, backside in dark silhouette at full extension, and offered a faint glistening view from the soft blue glow between her thighs. She looked back at him in thrilled anticipation, as he smiled with hidden dread. Playfully, she then invited him inside for a dip.

"Well, come on, dive in—the water's _oh_, so fine!" Unable to resist the sumptuous pose, the very conflicted Lone Hawk rushed over, plunged into her luscious pool and combined their writhing silhouettes to climax with his almost immediate release. However, the unromantic ramming did not end as soon as he had wished. For once he withdrew to a spill, the Earth Force's booming voice shouted out to him, furious.

"Alas, you refuse your sacred role, marry against my advice and now, insult me with your flaunted lust!" the Earth Force lashed, then calmed a bit with cryptically vague instructions. _"Come this morn, leave this place; go to your homeland; and, most important of all... know your enemy well!"_

Expecting the worst, Lone Hawk grabbed Rainbow by the elbows from behind and pulled her off the sphere, burning a deep syrupy red with escalating heat. Startled and terrified, she looked back at him in utter shock to the hot sticky goo stretching between her and the sphere, as he saw the giant purple hand from his nightmare then rising and palming her from behind like a tiny doll into its grasp. In an overpowering sweep, he too was captured by its all-surrounding digits while it squeezed them together and lifted their pressed bodies well above the pit's edge. Then from its vascular, searing-green arm's forward whipping motion, it tossed them like a pair of dice and sent them flying to impact the bedrock floor, halfway to the palace tunnel. They rolled to halt, emotionally and physically scored, with cascading guilt but only minor scrapes. After they soon gathered themselves to their feet, Rainbow took the blame in tears.

"My crazy dream made us desecrate the sphere!" she cried with an expression like the face he had seen in the sphere earlier, sending chills of regret throughout his being. "Did it speak to you, Lone? Are we forgiven?"

"Indeed, the Earth Force did <u>not</u> appreciate our flaunting of the carnal union, for it cannot partake in such pleasures," he explained with vague deception, packing away more sadness to seem strong and in control. "The punishment's been served. We <u>are</u> forgiven. However, there was also a message unrelated to this that requires my immediate attention. Come morning, we <u>must</u> go to the Valley of the Warbirds. Though without a reason, the mighty orb commands it. Have you any thoughts on this?"

"It is further punishment for my wicked deed, I just know it!" she shrilled as she apologetically backed away from him, covering her crotch and breasts while her soppy eyes reflected the purple sphere. "It's only <u>fitting</u> that I go. I am no longer worthy to be with the Earth Force. So, why <u>not</u> banish me to the Warbirds' domain?" She ran through the temple to the mouth of the palace's tunnel and stopped, dropping to her knees, weeping.

"Don't torture yourself, Rainbow. You are <u>not</u> unworthy, and you are <u>not</u> being banished," the valiant Lone Hawk told, as he lifted Rainbow to her feet and hugged her limp body of apathy. "I love you <u>so</u> much that, and, when I see you hurting this way, my heart starts to crush itself. You <u>know</u> you did not marry an ordinary man. Your dream could very well have been the means by which the sphere could wake me for my first instructions. Besides, the Valley of the Warbirds is not so bad. In fact, it will be paradise when I am through with it! That's what this must be … the enlightenment of the Warbirds to the Earth Force. And I'm 'The One' to show them, and you have become my wife to teach me how. See how it all makes perfect sense?" He said all the right things and to attest was the strength returning to her limbs in a leaping, arm-wrapping kiss. Then, content to his charms, Lone Hawk carried her back to the palace, falling fast asleep while he only lay the rest of the night in sleepless worry.

Early the next morning, after he assisted Rainbow with her packing for the journey home, they went to the shaman's lodge where the Chief had spent the night, to tell him of their abrupt plans.

"Last night we were drawn to the sphere and there, burning bright red, it demanded that I go to my homeland, immediately," Lone Hawk told with a forced calm demeanor, rendering the Chief to hold his own forehead with shocked concern. "I wish I could stay for a few days, but I do <u>not</u> want to defy the Earth Force's will. So, this morning we shall leave for the Valley of the Warbirds."

"What is the nature of this urgent deliverance?" the Chief queried with an air of suspicion in his glare. "Will you need a war party? Or do you sense, perhaps, that this <u>is</u> your ultimate summons against the great evil one of the ancient prophecies?" His words created a rash of goose bumps on Lone Hawk's skin, which made the Chief nod mildly to his hunch.

"No, no, no, I don't sense any danger…I believe it's merely a mission of enlightenment for my people to the Earth Force way," he defended to the Chief's unconvinced sigh and Rainbow's worried eyes, as they strolled back to the palace. "Also, my mother <u>should</u> know of her brother's death…Please, <u>don't</u> look so worried. We'll return in about ten-day's time."

"Regardless of this mission's exact purpose, I will appoint escorts for your safe journey," the Chief said, abandoning his pursuit of the truth as he patted them on their backs, reassured, upon entering the palace. "They'll be your servants, and as well, make your trip easier. Now, let's be sure that you have all of your needs, and I will see you off at the launch." After he was sure that they had adequate provisions, especially for his daughter's comfort, the Chief immediately arranged for two of his two-hundred-men army to accompany the worshipped couple. One of the Earth Force's top braves, Running Blood, and his first warrior, Snapper, also his younger brother, were big and most able-bodied for the task the

Chief had assigned. When they were ready by mid-morn to depart, a hundred villagers followed them to the river for a regal send-off.

"Do not rush this journey on my behalf," the Chief recommended with an assertive stare, as the canoes were put into the water by the river guards. "Just take good care of my daughter, and do well by the Earth Force in this joining of nations. I, too, would like to visit the Warbirds' valley again and make our relations official. Perhaps by the autumn's sun, I will do so. But as for you and your rushed promise, return in twenty days if so needed. However, if it's any longer than that, I _will_ be coming up the Wise Crow with reinforcements, looking for you." His emphasis toward a worst-case scenario had shaken Lone Hawk's self-reliance, spawning an urge to invite the Chief, a perceived pillar of wisdom and bravery, along for the voyage. But he could not diminish his own reputation to the big man, so he continued with his mounting worries to feign fearless delight to the suspiciously forced return home.

"That would be _wonderful_ if you came to the valley then, for the weather's still good and the leaves will begin to change. A _beautiful_ time of year—indeed!" he gleefully told him while he waved Screecher from his canoe shack perch, prompting his first warrior to eagerly bolt to his shoulder. "I think _this_ one, wants to go home, anyway. Now, let me just stay with my promise of ten days because, as you may know, we Warbirds are a more rustic people. Rainbow will miss her fancy palace soon enough and so; I'm sure even _my_ plan will be testing her tolerance. Just give me a couple years, and I'll have the valley up to _your_ standards. And by that time, our distances will close, and our nations will flourish!"

"Such ambition, yes, and it is best to believe as such," the Chief agreed with an annoying tinge of doubt in his voice while Rainbow, mostly oblivious to their underlying dialogue, boarded their canoe. "What I said before still stands, though, I will be very glad if you are back in ten. So, good journey to you. And good journey to you as well, Screecher. You _are_ a very special hawk, _so_ smart and loyal. May the Earth Force bless you to keep protecting this one." He gently scratched Screecher's breast, reaping gurgles of appreciation as Running Blood and Snapper were ready in their canoe.

"You do not need to tell him that," Lone Hawk laughed while he threw a friendly backhand to the Chief's shoulder; "Brave Screecher already thinks he's, my mother. In fact, Rainbow has even mentioned that he spies too much. We have plans to somehow get him a mate, so he doesn't get jealous of her."

"Do not chase him off too soon!" The Chief warned his last words to him and, while Screecher flapped off to a glide over the river, he strutted to their canoe for a last moment's chat with his daughter. After they finished, he kissed her farewell from a leaning posture over the canoe. Thus, he moved aside and invited Lone Hawk to board while placing a perfect, turquoise disc amulet around his neck. The Chief then left with only a stern smile and, without even looking back, waved as he walked up the trail toward the village, leaving the many well-wishers to wonder why he could not wait until the actual launch.

Watching the man, he so admired disappear up the forested path, Lone Hawk appreciated the gift, but was saddened to abandonment. Yet, to look back at Rainbow, smiling with an 'air kiss' to him, his apprehension was eased to pleasantry, just like the weather losing its heated humidity of the preceding day to a most comfortable spell of dry warmth.

CHAPTER VII
Wind God Warrior

IRST TO SHOVE OFF and already forging ahead for their savior's sacred journey home were the Earth Force brothers, Snapper powering the bow and Running Blood manning the rear. In their big deep canoe with a same-sized trailer in tow, they carried most of the load. To follow in their wake, Rainbow took the rear as a switch from the day before while Lone Hawk supplied the main propulsion forward. But, of course, as they left the Earth Force's little river bay, the many tribe members present shouted cheers of good fortune with a quaintness so precious, he felt obliged to salute them with a hearty, jabbing brave's fist. Then, paddling away with a winner's grin over his shoulder, he left them with the everlasting impression of a most righteous Earth Force Son, departing on a holy mission to spread the good light of the sphere.

For two days and nights, their travels and camps were swift and effortless, due to the high river, strong west winds and the graciously accommodating Running Blood and Snapper, who consistently did all the work ashore. During that time, Screecher occasionally rode on Lone Hawk's shoulder, but sensed Rainbow's ill ease, so tended to mostly glide nearby or duck out of sight ahead of them. Though all was going as smoothly as could be expected, the situation was not conducive to arousal for the preoccupied brave even though his new wife was so willing. Fortunately, she was understanding and reassured him that it was merely a 'post-chosen' side effect that would pass, at the very latest, by the time he was home.

On the third day not so far from Otter's place at the Warbird trail, the sky burst just past noon with black clouds of torrential rains that forced them to immediately seek the highest ground for refuge. Finding an ideal spot on the wooded crest of a dwarf palisade, they settled there under a fire-dried canopy, which was efficiently set up by their exceptional escorts. Additionally, they hauled the canoes up to a nearby well-protected overhang for safe keeping. It was only then during the near-tragic circumstances that Lone Hawk came to know the Earth Force brothers, who were entertaining and of good humor. Thus, when they took a liking to Screecher, the taunting centerpiece of their water-pelted yet resistant over-world, Lone Hawk taught them some basic Warbird words and phrases so they would not seem so big-and-dumb in his Warbird realm.

While they readily learned the language basics, the attention starved Screecher also taught well-liked Snapper the hawk dance. They achieved nothing as exquisite as the original tandem, but they were good. To that, Lone Hawk had to intercede thus lured the happy hawk to tread his body in an explosive barrage of extended ankle-to-wrist and head-to-rear jerking motions of communal energy. While they danced with a fervor, Rainbow, Running Blood and the defeated Snapper clapped to a rhythm that gained momentum with every approving thrust. To end his superior demonstration, he snatched the enthralled hawk and kissed him on the beak, receiving a pecking of disapproval to his neck.

"Come now, Screecher, our captured audience wants <u>none</u> of this cast member bickering," he joked, with the quarrelsome bird yapping on his forearm. "Well, and so ends 'the show.' Snapper, you were good. But I <u>never</u> thought my first warrior would go off, 'cheat dancing' with another. Oh well, with his regrets—Thank you!" Lone Hawk amused, with their understanding only fundamental, laughing in place of words, and so he taught them more with Rainbow assisting in translation. They learned quickly and seemed only interested in the nature of the Warbird women. Consequently, being the rather inexperienced with such, he told them in a way the womanizing Wonders Eye might describe.

During the following night, Lone Hawk's worries culminated in a nightmare of proportions so grotesque that Rainbow had to slap his face a few times to bring him out of his torturous imagination. In the bizarre dream, the sphere's warning of the enemy manifested itself in his people, which began once they returned to the valley, happy and unassuming. However, in this twisted version, the five of them came into the Warbird village and saw what appeared to be every tribe member standing along the main path. Packed on both sides, their presence stretched all the way through to the bird mound by the lake. Like statues they stood, with no signs of life besides the sounds of clicking and scratching emanating from within them. As they dared to walk the morbid path toward his parent's lodge, the people remained in the same motionless state, possessed, with the dreaded noise of something trapped inside them.

Suddenly, there was a shattering racket from the back of the trail while the overcast sky turned pitched black. To follow, many sets of red eyes were quickly approaching from the rear, with his parents' heads exploding before them to reveal the hideous faces of serpentine possums that spit burning blood onto their sizzling skin. In frantic response, he grabbed Rainbow's hand and sprinted to the mound where Screecher was heading, with his most personified wing waving them there. As they looked back, Snapper and Running Blood were swarmed for dead, and all the other human enclosures opened up to release the rest of the monstrous brood. When they arrived at the mound, Screecher dove inside of it. Though he gained refuge, their attempt to follow was denied by the solid ground. Hence, with all its terror, the creatures proceeded to eat them alive in an inescapable struggle that seemed of reality; yet, in his explanation to Rainbow upon awaking from such a hell, he merely told her it was just 'your typical falling dream,' so as not to spread his worry.

The rain diminished to a sprinkle by dawn and was finished by mid-morn, as a clear blue front came to the rescue from the northwest sky. They took to the very high river then and, with its favorable current, were swiftly brought to Otter's launch by high sun. With a special pouch of jewelry for his wives and daughters plus the trade-in of the modern canoes with no conditions, Otter was overwhelmed. And as he promised a worthy gift for his new bride upon their return to the Earth Force, he welcomed her with the utmost warmth and grace. Yet when he was told of his good friend Wonders Eye's murder, the heart-broken Otter gave his condolences and insisted on being added to the valley trek, along with his eldest daughter 'Sun Fish.'

Soon after they began to tread the Warbird trail, Running Blood and Snapper tried their charms with their new-found language in competition for the pretty woman while they pulled the heavily loaded cargo sled. And so, Lone Hawk and Rainbow strolled unencumbered but in relative silence. During the last leg of the journey as they neared the valley, Rainbow intuitively sensed enormous tension seething from within her new mate, even though he behaved in a carefree, stable manner.

"Lone, you act with the calm and cool of the most admirable brave," she said, twisting his jaw toward her for eye contact; "yet, you carry all the sadness and worry in the world. I realize your confidentiality with the Earth Force, and I respect that. So, look…even if the sphere did tell you more than you can reveal, do not forget me! Please, whatever may be, let us not be strangers. Our love must be honest and strong to the end!"

Lone Hawk put his arm around her waist, tight, and quickened their pace well ahead of the others to further insure their privacy. "You already know me too well and I'm very sorry, about the distance that I've put between us," he apologized with a single tear escaping his eye, which he promptly wiped away; "well, I suppose I can tell you that the Earth Force did say more, and it was disturbing. I do not know what we will find here…even so, I must simply face the situation, trust my best judgment and hope I prove worthy. You are so right. This brooding that curses me must go. And, thanks to your prodding words, I will make it so. Now, let us act like the newly married, deeply in love, beautiful people like we were in the beginning." They stopped and shared a long, heartfelt kiss of which they had not shared since their wedding night, allowing the others to pass by with their approving smiles.

With much improved spirits, they reached the trail's decline into the valley late afternoon, where the village was not far beyond; however, Lone Hawk became alarmed as they had yet to see a warrior on patrol. At the same time, Screecher, once monitoring from the treetops, suddenly took to direct flight toward the village with all his attentions drawn by a commotion, which they began to hear. On full alert, Lone Hawk insisted that the others wait at the valley's edge until he returned from a quick safety check of the area.

He bounded down the trail and soon reached the start of the village path at Wonders Eye's lonely lodge. However, the sounds he came to recognize were those of celebration, and to further confirm this was the distant sight of the entire congregation gathered around a huge bonfire, billowing a massive cloud of smoke by the lake. He felt silly when he returned to the group where Otter laughed, already knowing what was happening.

"It's the Wind God Festival! Am I right?" Otter told with a smirk while Sun Fish covered her mouth to snuff her incessant giggling, the others following suit. "I was about to tell you, but you got <u>so</u> serious and ran off so fast, I didn't want to spoil your investigation." Lone Hawk made an arrow-shooting gesture toward the good-humored Otter and joined their boisterousness into the village. Then passing the rowed and scattered lodges of relative primitive-squatting design, he sighed in embarrassment as Rainbow looked about, unpretentious. At least, he thought, Chief Howling Wind's prominent lakeside abode looked modern enough. Along with the blazing bonfire before it, the bold two-story structure was a quite regal centerpiece bound to impress her amidst the crowded celebration.

"Yes, it seems that there's nothing unusual to see here besides the party of all parties," Lone Hawk, then unworried by impressions, commented in joyous relief, as Screecher had already started mingling with the people and their strutting approach was finally taking notice. "The Wind God Festival, Howling Wind's favorite—how could I forget? Well, I see my parents over there near the beach, so let me introduce you, my beautiful wife…Oh!" Suddenly stopping and backing up, he cautioned with pointing finger at them; "there's to be <u>no</u> mention of Wonders Eye's death tonight," he whispered aloud in command mode, wishing not to ruin the atmosphere of joyous levity abounding before them. "He is <u>still</u> in Big River City, and that is all…until tomorrow. For now, let them enjoy as we should too…" They nodded in agreement and followed as he led Rainbow by the hand, with a somewhat arrogant air about him.

Soon, they broke the perimeter of the huge celebrating crowd, which all together was well over five-hundred singing, dancing and laughing Warbirds of all ages. While their eyes were bulging at the sight of the towering Earth Force brothers and their ravishing princess in her form-fitting deerskin vest-suit studded with countless colored beads, a barrage of questions came from curious onlookers. In response, Lone Hawk only smiled and waved to them, as his entourage sifted through the noisy mass to where his parents were situated, watching Screecher play with the children on the beach.

"Mother, Father! I have a wonderful surprise for you!" he shouted from behind them in their tawny summer's wear, backs to the bonfire crowd, as they turned around to him and the beaming Rainbow with startled yet pleased faces. "May I introduce to you my new wife, Princess Rainbow of the Earth Force tribe, the good people of the magic sphere of enlightenment." In silent awe, they looked at each other and then to their son who had no previous female involvement, as far as they knew. Still speechless, they cleared their throats, thinking of a response.

"Rainbow, it seems that my parents, Timbers Earth and Solarain, are completely shocked to see me with a woman...and to be <u>married</u> to one?!" he emphasized with a respectful laugh while both seemed to expect the other to handle the matter. "But I assure you, they <u>do</u> speak."

"Oh, Lone Hawk, we're just very surprised because you seem <u>so</u> different...so worldly and mature," his mother, the chattier of the two, explained as she sprung to her feet and came tiptoeing to them, offering hugs of congratulations. "I am <u>so</u> happy for you...and how did you happen upon such a <u>beautiful</u> princess, no less to marry in so short a time? And <u>where</u> has my brother been during all of this? I thought, for sure, he would return with you. At least, that's what he told Stout Raven." The dreaded question arose, and his answer was essentially true.

"Naturally, with the attentions of a woman friend named Night Owl, Wonders Eye stayed in Big River City. Yet, with Screecher being so nervous from all the people and the dogs, I decided, after some quick business, to come back earlier than he," Lone Hawk answered in slick fashion, sending Otter and Sun Fish who had followed only to wander away while Running Blood and Snapper stood loyally by their princess, a few steps back. "Then, on the way home, it was the calling of their sacred Earth Force sphere that led me to this wonderful woman. So, as I was chosen, we fell in love and got married…it's as simple as that!" For the moment, Lone Hawk had effectively shifted their minds away from Wonders Eye, who was sometimes gone for whole seasons and more. However, there was an eavesdropping shaman nearby who had heard enough to pounce on the situation in a more probing light.

"You are now 'Earth Force,' Lone Hawk? I <u>know</u> your uncle would never approve of this!" Stout Raven interrupted with terse, eye-piercing conviction, as he stood in a bold, finger-pointing stance. "They <u>threw</u> him out of their village merely because he wished to see the magic sphere…yet <u>you</u> were granted its viewing, the princess, the amulet <u>and</u> the sword? When you passed their river port on the way, Wonders Eye said nothing of their vile treatment? I find <u>that</u> hard to believe! There's 'something' very wrong here. We must speak about this in my lodge at once!" A gaunt-faced man of forty-two-years, he had large eyes and a jutting nose like the beak of a raven, thus reflecting his namesake. And though he could hardly hide his slight frame behind his black shaman's robe, his power of intimidation was astounding.

Yet, not to be taken lightly, the Earth Force brothers took notice as the shaman's verbal attack was visibly upsetting to the shaken Rainbow, who began to look about nervously. And so, they crossed their formidable arms with brawling on their minds, only glaring at Stout Raven, demanding his restraint.

Fortunately, when things looked about to come to a volatile head, Timbers Earth, bearing an obvious resemblance to his son, mediated the hostile climate with surprising ease. "There will be no such discussion until tomorrow, Stout Raven!" he declared with a hearty laugh, smile and a tension-subsiding spread of his arms that also swept the mood to further celebration. "For as this evening belongs to my son and his new wife, we'll talk of only happy things. And for tonight, I insist that 'these two' shall enjoy the sacred Warbird matrimonial tradition. Of course, meaning the <u>love</u>-rafting! Now, let us prepare their blissful float to ride the water spirits and savor this wonderful 'surprise addition' to our usual festival."

"Yes, Timbers Earth, that is an <u>excellent</u> idea!" Stout Raven agreed with a devilish simper that looked to nearly crack his face in half. "Let them share a <u>Warbird</u> tradition, that is—if he can remember anything of such? In fact, Lone Hawk and Princess Rainbow, is it? I congratulate you for your tribe-bounding union. And, as my contribution to this, I will prepare you a batch of my 'special' lovers' brew, a sweet fiery drink of passion. It will be ready for your love-rafting tonight, which shall have you 'the romance' of the stars and the moon on this clear night as well. So, I will see you off just after dusk with the rest." Turnabout amicable, the shaman walked off to his cross-shaped homestead and medical facility called the 'Four-Corners' on the southwestern shore. Then in his absence, a unanimous sigh of relief was quick to follow.

"Stout Raven is a man of great responsibility and much suspicion. But as you can see, he <u>really</u> only wishes both of you the best," Timbers Earth told while he patted the newlyweds' shoulders, suddenly realizing an oversight. "I'm sorry if all this talk confuses your beautifully exotic wife, my <u>suddenly</u> aged son. But even though you introduced her in the Warbird tongue, I didn't know how far along..."

"I've understood everything, Timbers Earth...you need not apologize," Rainbow firmly interceded while much to his surprise, she sandwiched his hand between hers with a gentile caress. "The shaman is only acting as would be expected. He <u>knows</u> that Lone Hawk is 'special' to the Earth Force, in a way however to which he can only show ignorance. Soon, he'll learn about us as will you...but for tonight, I only wish to ride the love raft which you have so graciously promised." She hugged Timbers Earth with the affection of an only daughter and made him blush, looking at wife and son with his shoulders shrugged.

"Beautiful <u>and</u> smart...<u>very</u> smart, Lone Hawk," he gushed, to their adoring laughter as his eyes wandered to Lone Hawk's holstered Toltec treasure. "And now that we know there's no language barrier here, tell us about that <u>marvelous</u> sword, glistening from your side."

"It's my <u>prized</u> Big River City souvenir, a Toltec executioner's sword which came all the way from the Great Empire of the Salted Gulf. Let me show you my masterful technique!" he shouted amidst the crowd noise and drew his eye-catching sword while attracting half of the village to see him swing the deadly weapon in a tight-circled dance. "I also happened upon some jewelry of sapphire, ruby and turquoise when I was there," Lone Hawk added while directing his attention to his mother during his elaborate display. "From the City of Cahokia, the Sun God…like your name, Mother—Solarain! I will get them for you after this little show, so you can wear them tonight…"

Before he finished his sword-reeling demonstration to which Rainbow clapped and coaxed the drummers to join with a well-timed rumble, Screecher tried to do the hawk dance. But Lone Hawk batted him away with a solid backhand and thus abruptly ended the show. "<u>Not</u> when I am with the sword, Screecher!" he scolded the startled bird who perched on a low branch of a nearby oak tree, never feeling such a reprimand before. "I could have <u>killed</u> you, my friend." Screecher then flew off to the north shore and the party resumed while Lone Hawk fetched the jewels for his mother who was overjoyed, as she adorned herself like a princess.

Once twilight had come to the valley, the festival's most popular couple had feasted on the various delights of the Warbird's modest corn harvest and satisfied their carnivorous needs with broiled duck, possum, varied fish and deer. And of course, they obliged themselves to circulate and exchange greetings throughout the celebration site, including a special visit to Chief Howling Wind. There, sitting on his elevated platform before the crowded bonfire, Lone Hawk introduced Rainbow to their 'stale' mumbling leader and became angrily embarrassment. Without congratulations nor acknowledgment of any kind, the old man merely proclaimed his wish to have his army stocked with big warriors like the Earth Force brothers. Though polite, Rainbow had only to roll her eyes with a smile to Lone Hawk's blushing squint of disgust. Seeking relief, they promptly left the chief's side and while Running Blood and Snapper began to mingle with the many single women, the eager lovers went lakeside to check on the love raft.

When there was no more hint of the sun, they boarded the sizable craft, which was nothing more than a well-padded row of tied logs, with two paddles and waist-high wooden side panels for privacy's sake. Then calling from behind throngs of shoreline well-wishers to halt their departure, Stout Raven burrowed through the crowd toward them, waving a big deerskin flask. There just in time, he gave Rainbow the promised drink with a surprising kiss of her hand and so, allowed a group of young boys to provide a swimmer's boost to the raft well past the shallows. Thus, heading toward the center of the placid sky-mirroring lake with brisk unified strokes of their paddles, they shared a passionate gaze as their desires swelled. Certain to be a love raft speed record, they reached the midway of the Warbirds' watery gem and took a drink of the special brew while they kissed and caressed each other to a flood of surging vibrations.

"I admit that, at first…I thought this to be quite a 'silly' custom," Rainbow half-whispered, panting a bit while shedding her clothes with a moon-gleam smile and a gentle rocking of the raft; "but now, I praise your 'sweet' father's suggestion. Oh, to be out here alone with you, the stars and the moon, it's so perfect. Now, we can truly be ourselves again…'all the way' again—just as you like it!" She soon had his clothing removed and as well proceeded with the dominant position, a choice of which she proved innately adept.

Aggressive as she mounted him, Rainbow plunged and slid back till he nearly slipped out, yet recaptured his rider and repeated the same, kissing and moaning in a passion-crazed frenzy. Thus, while her rapid, all surrounding motions brought him to an early release of his lusting flow, Lone Hawk opened his pleasured eyes to only flare to the terror of the ominous Screecher in a fast-descending dive upon them. Sighting Rainbow as his comrade's attacker, the overly protective hawk sank his puncturing talons into her upper buttocks before Lone Hawk's double-backhanded swatting could block his way.

"That cursed bird!" she screamed in bloody anger, echoing over the lake to everyone's attention. "It was stalking me the whole time!

You <u>must</u> be rid of that crazy hawk! He's become too wild for 'us,' Lone…it's high time he joined his own kind!" She wiped the blood from her backside and wept while Lone Hawk paddled promptly back to shore, spewing apologizes but in vain.

"I am <u>so</u> sorry, Rainbow! He must have thought you were killing me or something," he reasoned in pleading, though offering no appeasement. "If only I had opened my eyes a bit sooner, I could have blocked his attack. Again, I'm <u>so</u> sorry! Screecher will need to be disciplined for this act of terror."

"Listen! This is <u>unforgivable</u> and requires much more than mere discipline," she demanded in a low, harsh tone which he had never heard before. "<u>You</u> had better figure out…<u>something</u> to drive that <u>menace</u> away—permanently! <u>Do</u> we have an understanding?"

Regretful, Lone Hawk agreed to her terms with a reluctant affirming nod when they reached the crowded beach. Then while Rainbow held her skirt-vest to her chest, he wore only his breach cloth and shrouded her blood-streaked buttocks with his vested garment, as they hurried to Stout Raven's lodge for medical attention. Amidst the whispers of the gossiping onlookers, theirs was of undignified embarrassment and a far too questionable start in the Warbird commoners' bloody assessment of their mysterious union.

And there he was, Stout Raven, as much the same demeanor and beyond, readily ushering them inside his crossed complex to an elevated wooden-slab type of examination table, on which he instructed her to lie down on her stomach. He drew the draped skins over the doorway and the windows for privacy's sake and treated the talon wounds with a stinging alcohol solution. After they were cleaned and the bleeding had subsided, he secured a bandage, which was tied around her waist and between her legs to stable perfection. With that part completed, he then revealed his forecast of doom. "Could <u>this</u> be a sign that Earth Force and Warbird don't mix?" he asked as the all-knowing one, weaving a hopeful web of doubt, guilt and suspicion. Rainbow quickly sat up and jumped off the examination table but did not speak.

"Is this the beginning of one way's destruction of another…or two, to befall each other? And <u>what</u> really happened to Wonders

Eye, Lone Hawk?" Stout Raven insinuated while throwing his head back for effect. "There is absolutely <u>no</u> doubt in my mind that he <u>fully</u> intended to return with you. But maybe he can never return. That is, if he <u>is</u> dead because he was on to them…then murdered by their worship of the Earth Force who spared you, tainting your mind as the enemy in perfect disguise. Well, at <u>least</u> admit that your uncle is now with the spirits…admit it, Lone Hawk—<u>admit</u> it!"

Lone Hawk guarded Rainbow with his cradling arms about her, as he launched his defense of her honor:

"I came to the Earth Force long after Wonders Eye's brutal death by the hand of Toltec warriors who ambushed us on the way to Big River City. See? I've kept one of their swords, which had found their deaths by my avenging hand!" he told with a searing display of the evidence right next to the shaman's scowling face for closer examination. "I only wished not to ruin the festival, so I was saving the terrible news for tomorrow…but you have caught me, Stout Raven. And so, I now tell you tonight: Wonders Eye is dead and buried in Big River City where I hauled his body, to my <u>own</u> near demise. That is the truth of the matter, and it was to <u>his</u> bidding that I came to the Earth Force upon my return. He told me the same story as he did you, so I only wished to see the magic sphere because of his denied opportunity.

"There, I came into the village a marauding intruder and almost killed my guide, who then kindly led me to the sphere," Lone Hawk squeezed Rainbow with a kiss on her cheek, and continued. "Glowing with all the splendor of the world, the mighty, cave bound orb adopted me and soon sent me home for my first mission. During that time, of course, I fell in love with my guide and married her, this magnificent woman whose wounds you just tended. And so, to sum this up, I believe the Earth Force intends the allegiance of our lands against a common enemy. And, as the Earth Force Son, my role is absolutely vital for this to succeed. With my great heroism, which I'm to learn, know and execute…for the good of us all, it will be done!"

Stout Raven exhaled loudly and exaggerated while he paced, shaking his head at Lone Hawk's ludicrous words. "Lone Hawk, you are a Warbird brave and should be proud of that fact. Yet, you now talk like a self-deified traitor! Come to your senses, boy, and let us remove this spell of treachery before it's <u>too</u> late!" he accused with a vigor that could be heard by the people outside as he hammered the brave fist gesture at him. "It's bad enough that you shroud the death of your uncle and marry to another tribe, but do <u>not</u> abandon or compare yourself to the Warbird Gods of Fire, Water, Earth and Wind. That's what you suggest with this 'Earth Force Son' nonsense, uh, really? Well, I promise that such an attitude can only be the precursor to catastrophe! So, please reconsider and realize that you were misled. By my sacred honor, I will forgive you and make no moves against your marriage. Lone Hawk? Can I expect you to rejoin the Warbirds?"

"Stout Raven, you are of the old way, and I understand your position, so I forgive you your ignorance," Lone Hawk calmly lashed in a tone of descension. "You <u>must</u> realize that there are other ways that hold no threat to the old. They're merely enhancements to what we already know. In Big River City, as you must know, they worship the sun, which they also believe harbors its power in their King Cahokia. And while the Warbirds worship the four-forces, we <u>certainly</u> don't believe that old Howling Wind is bestowed as such. Then to close the gap on all of these, the Earth Force worship the one sphere, the conscience of everyone and all we have, including our invaluable relationship with the Life Source Sun. You, see? They're all meant to work together in harmony and complete the balance, a process I've been chosen to protect, so that its goodness can flourish to maturity. I beset this new age of enlightenment for you and all the tribe. Warbird isolation is soon to be of nothing but of the dark past!"

As Rainbow beamed with renewed pride and admiration for her husband's worthy stand, Stout Raven sneered in disgust. "You are of <u>far</u> too many words to even resemble the 'good ole' Lone Hawk anymore—<u>impostor</u>! However, I <u>will</u> be telling your mother, Solarain, of her brother's death, if someone else hasn't done so, already," he threatened in a whimsical manner. "And as for you, young temptress, apply this ointment liberally to the wounds three times a day. Since they are not terribly deep, healing should be complete in week or so with little scarring. Good night!" After

Stout Raven pushed them in a huff out of his four-corners lookout lodge, the righteous couple of his cursing were relieved to find that the festival had resumed with no one's leering attention to suffer. Yet, he knew that the people were listening before and so, they hurriedly headed to the bonfire to find his mother, hoping to deliver the dreaded news before the gossip web had reached her.

While they began to search for his parents, Lone Hawk pondered his irreverent retort against the powerful Stout Raven and surmised that the sphere had captured a part of him to his gradual acceptance. He had become a volunteer to its will and the denial phase had faded. However, his infernal ambition was fully retained as he watched the chief on his pedestal above the playful crowd, dancing and singing around the fire. Anxious, he prayed there would be enough time bestowed him to replace the old man, who he considered so disgracefully ineffective. Thus, after the wishing trance had lifted, his thoughts returned to the task of locating his mother. Then as the participants of the celebration thinned and the drumming subsided, the obvious told them that she and his father must have gone home. Otter, being one of the remaining revelers, confirmed their deduction and further informed him that his parents retired to their lodge soon after the love-rafting's launch. There, Lone Hawk told his mother about the Wonders Eye-Toltec tragedy in all its truth, as Rainbow lent her loving support.

"I knew that someday with such daring tendencies, my brother would not return from his travels," she cried in a discreet manner while Lone Hawk and Rainbow sat beside her on the edge of the bed, holding her hands as his father lay rubbing her back from behind. "He lived a full life, but I will miss him <u>so</u> much…yet, I'm also so very glad that you defied the same fate and were able to give him the burial he would have wanted. I hope to visit his grave…someday, before I die…Oh, Lone Hawk, I <u>must</u> believe that his sacrifice was vital to your return as one so strong and purposeful—as its <u>only</u> consolation." Suddenly Bursting into tears, she still took the news rather well, so allowing Lone Hawk to retire with a clearer conscience as Rainbow cuddled against him on the bed in his semi-private room.

"I really like your mother, Lone. She is so nice and accepting toward me, and has so much faith in you," she said, with some friskiness brewing in her touch. "She should have <u>seen</u> the way you stood up to that nasty shaman. Oh, how you put <u>him</u> to shame! You are <u>fearlessly</u> coming into your 'Earth Force' self, and now there remains but one obstacle. Once that's hurdled…ours will be perfection!" She slowly removed his breach cloth, after her sad reminder of the `Screecher' solution had him obliging to comment.

"Indeed, dawn's first shimmer will start his rejection for the better," he reaffirmed, depressed, but with his gradual arousal by her hand. "Already, he's feeling quite alienated, and I assure you that my plan will not fail…it will be the final blow towards our complete separation." She rolled to her side and carefully guided him through the bandage ties, into her from behind. Lone Hawk lovingly complied to a very slow and gradual session of passionate yet somber love making. And thus, every thrust became evermore precious by a sudden and obscure premonition of death; hence, he feared this loving merge to be their last.

CHAPTER VIII
Mark of the Owlmen

AFTER A FAR FROM restful night's sleep, Lone Hawk set out just before the sun rose past the jagged eastern ridge to perform the brutal task which he had promised. He gathered a sack full of good throwing stones and started rounding the shore eastward, with self-reproach building in his heart. When he soon reached the northeast side of the lake, well away from the village, the faithful Screecher came soaring toward him from the west. While the excited hawk expected to land on his shoulder or forearm and be cuddled, Lone Hawk greeted him with a barrage of stones to the breastplate and wings.

Even with the painful assault, Screecher hovered and tried to land with a puzzled tenacity. The stone-pummeled hawk finally retreated when Lone Hawk threw a rigid fist-sized stone squarely between the base of his right wing and breastplate. Almost falling into the lake's shallows, the sturdy one regained flight and flew away in an erratic fashion. Fortunately, he was able to gain enough altitude in his crippled state to glide above the lake to the trees on the other side.

As a result, Lone Hawk felt for the first time in his life to be cruel and unjust. His conscience, desperately seeking amends, pictured Screecher finding a mate, nesting and hatching some healthy chicks. Optimistic as he was convinced, his thoughts were then twisted to depression once he arrived at his parents' lodge. For as he intended to go for a spiritual walk after just passing there, Rainbow and his mother emerged from the doorway, calling him.

"It is done?" Rainbow asked as non-confrontational as she could be, with sorry eyes and hands to her cheeks. "I hope you didn't hurt him _too_ badly…Lone! Will you not talk to me?"

"I need to go for a walk!" he shouted in a guilt-ridden grumble, with tears running from his eyes. "I was _never_ so cruel in my life as I was this morn!" He ran to his speed's zenith and disappeared down the path and up the trail, from whence they had come the day before.

`Why did I let her make me do it…that princess-bitch! She plays me like a drum!' Lone Hawk lashed in his thoughts until he stumbled upon a distraction of a very curious sort; then he spoke out loud and roared, "_Who_ or _What_ could have made these?"

Meantime, Rainbow wished she had just forgiven the poor bird, for fear that there may now be an impassable rift between them. "I am so _wicked_ for how I made him reject his best friend, even if just a hawk…but not to him. Solarain, my good Warbird Mother—what can I do?" she pleaded to the prime nurturer of the one she so loved. "He was so sad during our journey, and then he was becoming happy again when we arrived here…but now, he's worse than _ever_ because of me!"

"Oh, don't worry, Rainbow, my good 'not wicked' Earth Force daughter," Solarain comforted in a warm mothering tone, never heard before by the paternally raised Rainbow whose distress was softly eased while her new mother, truly feeling as though she gained a daughter, wiped her streaming tears. "Whenever Lone Hawk was angry or disappointed, he would always run into the forest to be with his _true_ best friend, 'nature' and all its life…I think it's out there, away from all the people, with the animals and trees where he learns _who_ he must be, and _what_ he must do. It has always been his sanctuary. But, trust me…when his stomach starts growling, he'll return, let's say, no later than at high sun, mm-hmm—I know this boy!" Much to Rainbow's elated surprise, Solarain's prediction proved much sooner than expected as Lone Hawk returned just moments later.

"Wow! I saw something so weird—there's got to be an investigation!" he told them, wide-eyed and breathing heavily to his profound discovery. "In the corn fields of the recent harvest, I saw big burned rings of a most peculiar design. They're sure not from kids, playing with torches—too perfect! They must have been made during the festival with our lax patrols. I'm only just now, beginning to understand the Earth Force's warning. This is the first sign!" In pure military function which he was supremely adept, Lone Hawk then consulted Stout Raven and Chief Howling Wind to acquire a dozen braves with four-dozen able warriors from the north shore base.

By a flurry of smoke signals, drumming and the waving a big red flag, they drew the contingent across the lake in their waking canoes, assuming there was an attack. As the message was clarified upon their prompt arrival, Lone Hawk led the troops to the sight of the strange markings, only to verify that they were an intrusion of unknown origin. For a temporary measure, all of them, including Earth Force volunteers Running Blood and Snapper, were designated to the area in shifts of constant guard and patrol. By the time Lone Hawk felt the situation was well-secured, there was still much of the day left for his energies to be diverted elsewhere.

"Well, the men are posted and perhaps tomorrow, we'll call on some more warriors to expand the perimeter," Lone Hawk, still sounding a bit militant, updated Rainbow and his parents at their lodge after he reported to the chief. "In the meantime, Father," he added, softening his tone, "I would appreciate your help today, as I would like to renovate Wonders Eye's lodge. Rainbow and I need a private love nest, and I'm in the mood for building. So…my 'ever-so-sweet' Rainbow, if you could just stay with my mother for the rest of the day, I will have a very nice surprise for you this evening, assuming my father is willing." Timbers Earth was more than happy to assist him in the renovation project, and assured the rapid conversion of the old shack that had been neglected for several seasons.

Since Lone Hawk seemed so well recovered from the Screecher incident, Rainbow was completely relieved of her previous worry, as he merrily marched off with his father to survey the structure for a materials list. And with their initial inspection, the entire roof needed replacing due to termites and wood rot, so they began its removal. After accumulating a quite pile of rubble, they measured the dimensions and gathered the necessary timbers along with some quartzite and sandstone to repair the chimney. By midday, the roof's frame was laid to merge around the reinforced chimney with a slight crest, which they then sealed with a generous topping of sap-saturated hemp and branchy leaves. With the roof's completion concluding the most laborious portion of the project, they pondered the Spartan interior at their leisure. Thus, to Lone Hawk's three-point plan, the refurbishing would merely require a storage loft, an improved cookery and a big framed bed. By the dwindling light of the setting sun, they finished the charmingly cozy abode and showed it to their approaching spouses with sweaty pride.

"How did just the two of you do this? And in only half-day, no more!" Rainbow wowed with astonished congratulations while peeking inside the doorway at Lone Hawk, lighting a bundle of sticks in the full-hearth fireplace. "Before you started, it wasn't even fit for a raccoon! But now, it actually looks quite stately in a small way. Thank you, my generous Warbird Father—for this most wonderful wedding gift!" Intensely appreciative, she hugged and kissed the blushing Timbers Earth to a shrugging ear-to-ear smile, then turned her attentions to his son who was still coaxing the fire. "And as for you, my overzealous husband, I will thank you later tonight…After a good meal, that is, which you'll definitely need to keep your strength!"

As the villagers came to see the transformed shack sporting an attractive rock garden Lone Hawk had arranged around its perimeter, Rainbow encouraged them to take a look. She took charge, allowing the curious to see the showplace for themselves. Leaving them to peruse, she then led the way for the four of them to feast on some Earth Force culinary delights she had prepared at his parents' lodge.

"I don't want to seem rude, my Warbird father and mother, but I think the time is well ripe for us to chase the tourists away." Rainbow laughed, over their brief meal of little talk and her obvious eagerness to get busy in the bedroom. "I believe we would like to be the <u>first</u> to use that nice big bed that these two dear men set up for us today!" Wide eyed and smiling, Lone Hawk let her drag him out of his parents' home while all of them shared the humor of the situation with departing chuckles.

When they soon returned to their virgin love nest, a dozen villagers still lingered and so they shooed them away. The moment they were gone, Rainbow dropped her simple tan garment and stood nude, back against the bedside wall with expectant eyes. She raised her knee and pulled it to her breast while Lone Hawk shed his clothes, appreciating her form in the fire's soft light. He braced her raised knee to his chest and eased his way into her moist spread, following with gentle thrusts. They maintained the upright position with lunging kisses and made love to lasting completion, her knee to his armpit in full quiver. Then falling sideways onto the new bed, they giggled over the fact their pleasures did not even require it.

"We have never laughed and been <u>so</u> happy as we've been this night," Lone Hawk declared with a loud, smacking kiss to her lips in their joyful embrace. "The scourge of unpleasantries have passed for now, so let us lap up these good times before they finish their run!" They tossed and tumbled, with her sore rump of no hindrance to their lovemaking that took a sporting twist into a 'positions' marathon. Engaging every which way, they completed an incredible, three more fun-filled sessions. Then during their panting sweet kisses that followed, they fell into quiet slumber.

His first bit of tranquil sleep in a long while lasted deep into the night. Yet, it came to an abrupt end with a peeping of tragic familiarity from outside the lodge. Undeniably so, Screecher was alarming him to the presence of intruders, using the identical call of warning that he had used for the Toltec ambush. Lone Hawk woke up with an innate grasp of his deadly sword, as he rolled off the bed ready to fight.

"Oh, no…no, do <u>not</u> go out there, Lone…<u>please</u>, don't go," Rainbow pleaded in a dreamy whisper, as the light of the moon shone on her frowny face through the coarse hemp shade. "Shh, the bird will go away…" Oddly, she drifted back to sleep, as if her will had been swept away by the moon glow.

"Don't worry, my Sweet," he reassured his unconscious beauty with a stroke of her cheek; "though there <u>are</u> the reinforcements from the north shore on patrol, I <u>cannot</u> ignore Screecher's warning like the last time. Once I see that all is well, I will return to your arms…" He kissed her unresponsive lips and went into the 'night of the peeping Screecher,' perched in a nearby tree with a most disturbing demeanor.

"Hi Screecher, sorry about that 'stone pummeling' yesterday, but…with that attack of yours, well…" the adjusting Lone Hawk clumsily apologized with what first came to mind, but then he absorbed the squawking hawk's intensity and cleared to the chase. "This <u>is</u> serious! Show me, Screecher. Lead me to the intruders!" Reunited for a most suspenseful investigation, Lone Hawk followed 'trusty' Screecher's tree to tree flight which drew him out of the valley, southeast to the cornfield of the markings. With the confidence of the reinforcements directed there the day before, he approached the area and soon lost all sense of security. A plague of deep sleep had befallen the entire military unit.

"Screecher! You've done well alerting me to this. But why do their torches burn bright while they're all lying around, sleeping? Or do they lie dead?!" he panicked while backhanding the nearest guard's face to the relief that his was warm and with an active pulse, yet the sleeper remained un-rectifiable. "<u>What</u> is wrong with them? Are we the only two who can defy this? Hey, who was <u>that</u>?" The chirp of the crickets suddenly fell to an eerie silence when he caught a glimpse of someone in the forest. Out of the corner of his eye to the right and then left, there were at least two intruders. Thus, Lone Hawk held his sword in a defensive stance, fully focused, sighting nothing astir. His perplexity over the sleeping guards and the presence of others who seemed to appear then disappear, gnawed at his tactical decisiveness. And though sure that an elaborate trap had been set for him, he also felt his Earth Force bestowal would provide the victorious edge.

"Show yourself, cowards!" the re-ignited Lone Hawk shouted into the forest, as he began to pace the field's perimeter past another guard, snoring like the wind. "I was told you would be here and, though you've taken the guards, <u>I</u> the 'Chosen One' Lone Hawk am

<u>ready</u> for you. Through me, the mighty Earth Force will unleash its powers! So, come out of the woods and <u>face</u> me, if you dare..." Amidst the silent treachery, the nondescript human figures flashed in the brush, side-to-side in an erratic fashion. And once again, his scouring eyes could not firmly locate the ghostly opposition.

However, something of the tangible finally did present itself in an object that seemed the hatchling of the Earth Force sphere. From out of the forest in a careening pattern, a glowing red ball about the size of his fist came to him with the finessed flight of a dragon fly and hovered well out of reach above his head. After a moment's stationary posturing, the floating orb descended and circled while he tried to slash it with his heavy sword, every swing well dodged with impeccable agility. His savage, vain attempts were not only discouraging but tired him immensely. So as to conserve and hopefully allow his energy to rejuvenate, Lone Hawk merely kept the impetuous ball at sword's length, with its brilliant lava light reflecting on the blade.

After going round and about with his matching its every move, the spherical one he sensed as an anti-Earth Force demon messenger returned to its original position. Too high to touch, he could only watch with his guarding blade extended, as it grew brighter and began to hum like a mosquito. The high pitch of its emanation grew steadily more intense and soon became ear-piercing. He dropped his sword and covered his ears; hence, stifling his resistance. Only then did the intruders come out of hiding. In their float-gated approach like walking on air, the strangest of the strange were revealed as they neared. Despite his body being numbed by the sound effect then fading, his vision remained functional. Hence, standing before him, he could see four, gray manlike beings with big, owl-like eyes of shimmering black. Willowy thin and short as well, the pumpkin-headed warriors wore silver one-piece garments with a red seven-circled insignia. Ogled to mere specimen status, the immobilized Lone Hawk dropped defenselessly to his knees in frustrated shock.

While they surrounded his forced vulnerability into adequate posture, one of them snatched and concealed the floating red ball with its finely scaled, reptilian hand. Thus, with their little scarlet scout retrieved, its keeper directed a couple of the others to commence the first of two painful procedures. In simultaneous conjunction, they inserted sharp probing instruments into each nostril with a grinding effect that crossed behind his brow into his frontal lobe. Even though his perceptions were in dreamscape, the pain was excruciating as he felt the burrowing devices ruthlessly venture into his brain. Task one completed, the operators backed away and gave their small rectangular tools with their metallic spikes retracting to the keeper of the ball, who began to fiddle with the tiny lights displayed on their bases.

With an apparent adjustment needed to prepare the devices for their second and final phase operation, the keeper, obvious leader of the deviled band, handed one of the instruments to the other when they were soon properly set. As the pair then began to close in on his head with another systematic infliction of pain, there was a distraction. 'Alas, for them!' Lone Hawk thought in cheering for his winged hero, swooping out of the star-lit sky upon his perpetrators. "That'll teach 'em!" Undaunted by their unworldly presence, the fearless Screecher latched his talons onto the bubbled head of the busily unaware assistant. He flapped his wings and lunged with pecking fury while shrieking the call of attack. The flimsy alien so caught by surprise, nonetheless, provided a comical spark to the bizarre experience with its bony arms waving haplessly during an unusual dance of imbalance.

However, despite Screecher's valiant effort, the alien's head was protected by a virtually indistinguishable outer casing, so no harm came to that one. Though, the harm would be fatal by the rescuing hand of the team leader who drew a copperish flat-coned device and pointed it at the unrelenting hawk. Emitted a single purple beam, the weapon struck Screecher dead-center in the breast, instantly falling him to the ground.

As his heart sank to a depth he could have never imagined, Lone Hawk cried in his thoughts for his ever-loyal first warrior he had raised from a chick, murdered right in front of his disabled witness. Then with no care for his thoughts and the nuisance eliminated, theirs was only to proceed with the invasion of his head, focusing their attention to the rear. Behind each ear at the base of the scull, they placed the modified instruments without any immediate pain. But with his jaw being held up by nauseating cold and clammy hands, his stomach felt to jump into his throat. Suddenly, they paused while the other two watched and nodded to the position that was to be the calm before the storm. For the pressing of their devices in chorused unison, just so, injected a burning wave and something far more sinister coursing throughout his entire being. Like the all-consuming flames from his nightmares, Lone Hawk prayed for death's release but to only be denied as their evil deed was soon done, with him still helplessly aware.

To close their mission, the alien abductors, he silently cursed and deemed 'the Owlmen,' were almost accommodating. They turned his stiff body over from his kneeling slump to a more comfortable face up, lying down position. And there, the Owlmen graciously put his sword at his right side and Screecher's smoldering carcass to his left then stood at his feet, peering into the sky. Then materializing before his unblinking eyes, a silver oval-shaped vessel of massive proportions filled the entire view, hovering in absolute silence. With an underbelly of six red lights around a larger one of blue at center, the three Owlmen subordinates floated up into the blue passageway of the magic ship. Lagging behind, the leader stayed to gloat his last, and thus projected a simple message without a voice, *'You shall serve well, chosen one!'*. That eerily said, the remaining Owlman pointed the same weapon used to kill Screecher at him and released a blinding white light.

Lone Hawk felt his spirit rise thankfully from the pained body. Yet, as joyous a float it was into a kind light that removed all worry, someone pushed him back down into his hellish embodiment. Thus, in the dawn's pink sky, he awoke to Rainbow's warm hands cradling his sore head and face. As her eyes streaming with tears lit up amidst her smothering posture over him, his parents and the many others who had gathered around him shared sighs and gazes of relief.

"Oh Lone, <u>again</u> you come back to me from the dead!" Rainbow rejoiced, as witness to a miracle while she wiped the dried blood from his upper lip with a damp cloth. "We came as soon as we could, but the 'deep sleep' took everyone! Your sudden patrol last night was like a dream. So, when I awoke and you were gone, I thought of the cornfield. And there you were, cold as ice, with the guards all asleep and Screecher…well, <u>what</u> in Earth Force's name does this mean, Lone!" With no immediate reply, he turned his head away from her and, in confirmation, made the dreaded discovery at arm's length to his other side.

Grasping it by the back of the neck, Lone Hawk curled Screecher's stiff, lifeless body to his chest and pouted with a tormented glare as Rainbow backed away from him. He leaned forward and began to pull himself upward with his sword, which was beside him as he last remembered. Though his legs were very weak, he rose to his feet unassisted and stood, beholding the carcass of his ever-loyal hawk for all to see.

"This, my deceased first warrior who we all knew as 'Screecher,' died in his attempt to rescue me from the Owlmen, a strange, spirit-like breed of men who made the 'big sleep' to capture me!" the ominous Lone Hawk told with his eyes ever gaining in intensity while his strength quickly regenerated to his shuffling feet. "Yes, I was <u>their</u> chosen one as well, and there was <u>nothing</u> I could do, but endure their magic torture and watch the fearless Screecher take a fatal shot from their lightning box. Let his heroic sacrifice be <u>forever</u> remembered and <u>not</u> be in vain, as the soul of the avenging hawk shall have his revenge!

"These Owlmen are the enemy of which the Earth Force had forewarned me and now…the war has only just begun! Oh, the pain they put me through, and my head still hurts <u>so</u> much! I <u>must</u> go to Stout Raven for a remedy before I can prepare for battle." He started back to the village in a determined gate, and the others followed while Rainbow took notice of his cranial inflictions.

"Your bloodied nose was not so unusual, but these <u>gruesome</u> black circles behind your ears are like the burn marks in the field, with six-swirls and a big one in the center—weird!" Rainbow gasped while she slowed his pace with a close but gentle inspection of each side; the others encroached and spewed sighs of astonishment. "Indeed, let your Stout Raven explain these! <u>Now</u>, he will know that it was the Earth Force's prophecy that revealed the threat of these 'Owl people' to his tribe!" She led him by the hand with a mission of her own to convince 'the shaman of insults' that the calculated purpose of all that he had condemned was merely destined to save his precious valley.

Thus, Rainbow wasted no time as she guided him with her forceful arm held out, sweeping to disperse the curious villagers obstructing the path to the lake. Like a parade, they marched through the valley town that was abustle incredibly early due to the strange events. And most notable to cause was the news about the mysterious death of their mascot, who hung in tow by his wild-eyed comrade. When the morbid procession arrived at Stout Raven's facility, village center was amassed by the same numbers as the Wind God festival of two nights before. The people were demanding answers, but the warriors held them at bay as the shaman allowed only Lone Hawk, Rainbow and his parents to enter his externally mobbed abode.

"Oh yes, the messenger told me that you had been revived, but your hawk friend…well, I can see he was not so fortunate. I am <u>very</u> sorry, Lone Hawk," Stout Raven consoled his loss while he wiped the blood that began once again to trickle from his nose. "Let us first clot this nosebleed, then discuss the details of what must have been a <u>harrowing</u> night." After Lone Hawk blew out whatever blood he could, the shaman dipped from a small jar a fine, white powder like the stock his uncle shared with him at the river-camp. Holding the tiny spoonful to his nostril, he instructed him to briskly sniff and repeated the process with the other. Instantly, he could feel his sinuses dry and thus the drip of blood had ceased. As he tested his nose with an appreciation for the easy airflow, Rainbow pointed to the alien marks behind his ears and, upon their examination, the shaman exhibited a sudden rash of goose bumps.

"They appear to be identical brandings done with a circular smelter's tool, yet there is no inflammation," Stout Raven deduced with an intrigued tone to the miraculously well-healed scars. "These tribesmen of the field markings claimed you with this conversion tactic as a symbol of their strength. Were you asleep like the others during this raid?"

With a resurgence of his throbbing headache, Lone Hawk clasped his free hand over his crown of agony and explained the experience in shocking detail. "No, I was fully awake and able-bodied when I first came upon the field with sleeping guards. But, as I started to search the area for clues, I saw the enemy sneaking about in the forest and I began to stalk them until their flying red ball of torture subdued me," he described the situation, spinning about with his swinging fist as the portrayed ball of menace. "Without the use of my body, I could only watch as these skinny gray Owlmen shoved sharp things deep, deep-deep up my nose then into the sides of my head to <u>burn</u>, so that I only wished to die. And with all that going on, I had to watch Screecher take a strike from their lightning box. In fact, the lightning that killed him was the <u>same</u> as what went into my head, I am sure. So, <u>please</u>, please-please, Stout Raven…give me <u>something</u> that will prevent my scull from splitting open! And <u>please</u> hurry!"

Stout Raven went over to a shelf of many flasks upon the suffering brave's request and brought one of them back with a squint of confidence. He poured the brown liquid into a small cup, which Lone Hawk eagerly snatched when it neared the rim. Following its immediate consumption and praying for alleviation, his tight lips loosened to a thankful smile.

"Now, that's some magic brew!" Lone Hawk happily proclaimed as his mind found sanctuary from the throbbing pain, and started its trek to a manic state. "It tastes like the sour mash of corn I had before, but there's <u>something</u> more…something <u>absolutely</u> wonderful!"

"Yes, it <u>is</u> a refined version of the sour corn mash, and I'm glad to your response, but these Owlmen…" Stout Raven said with a delving pause as he filled another cup of his special brew; "are they men like you and me, or something different? What I mean is, your account of this strange encounter does seem to suggest the latter."

Lone Hawk guzzled the second cup-full and seemed to look the enlightened. "Of course, they're not like you and me or the Toltec, Earth Force, or anyone human! The Owlmen are more like spirits with their powers not in muscle but in magic and, I assure you, they have <u>no</u> respect for 'our' kind!" he vehemently told as his lunging hand twisted the shaman's collar, much to Stout Raven's discomfort but the others' admiration. "Your brew sparks my memory even further, Stout Raven, for now I remember the end, just before the white light. There was, best as I can describe, a round raft with lights on its belly that seemed to just appear into the sky like it was always there. I know that makes no sense, but neither does the fact that its lake was in the sky above me! And I saw them float into its bright blue center, the tunnel to their home inside…or beyond, perhaps? I don't even <u>begin</u> to know of such! Yet, I do know that the one with the flying ball and the tools of pain told me in the end, without a real voice, that I would serve well as <u>their</u> chosen one. Serve <u>them</u> well? As soon as the Earth Force activates my powers, the Owlmen will not even exist to serve as anything—much less <u>be</u> served!" he staunchly proclaimed then unexpectedly giggled as he twirled Screecher's corpse around by the tail feathers just above the floor. Considering the strangely brutal assault of his claim, his mood had in so short a time become quite oddly chipper. Thus, he requested a mere half-cup's drink to which Stout Raven graciously obliged when suddenly, Solarain boasted and proposed, on Lone Hawk's behalf, a brilliant 'artisan's approach' idea.

"Hey, why not let Lone Hawk <u>best</u> describe them, these Owlmen, with some ash-stick drawings…he's a <u>very</u> fine sketch artist!" While Lone Hawk shrugged his shoulders and looked to Stout Raven with the others nodding in support, the shaman seemed a bit dismissive but then agreeable.

"Sure, Solarain, I've got some…just let me explain something to your son before I lose my plain of thought," Stout Raven said while stroking his jutting chin, and continued. "Lone Hawk, this may surprise you, but <u>I</u> am the one who must admit fault as my mind was slow before, so trapped in the old ways…I was blind to your quest," the turnabout shaman emphasized with a slap to his own forehead, feigning shameful regret while Rainbow, Solarain and Timbers Earth looked at each other in communal disbelief. "The Four Forces of the Warbirds now tell me that there <u>is</u> another, pleading allegiance. I must commune with these so that I can understand the new way…In the meantime, Lone Hawk, I'll get you some ash-sticks and a sketch board, but I <u>do</u> suggest you bury the valiant Screecher soon, so that his avenging spirit will be free to help us obliterate these <u>evil</u> Owlmen."

"Clutching my dear-departed, feathered brave heart all along and it took <u>you</u> only to say his name…so I heed to your advice, and it will be done!" Lone Hawk announced in blatant feeding on the shaman's all-too-good words that made the three disillusioned bystanders raise their eyebrows and shake their heads, ever anxious. "The only one who didn't fear them, even in their glory. Yes! His sacrifice shall be honored to its absolute pinnacle in myself, the Earth Force Son!" Stout Raven patted him on the back and handed him the sketch tools. In just a moment's scribbling, he drew and thus presented to them a very accurate rendering of the Owlmen' mission leader. They gasped, clasping their foreheads to the sight of the creature he had drawn. With big, creepy black eyes piercing back at them from its bulbous face, they cringed as Lone Hawk went on, and in a hurry, "Oh, and just now, a ritual has come to mind, perhaps divinely inspired, that I must perform with the utmost privacy. So, do respect me now as my wish is to be alone. I am sorry, Rainbow, but I must ask you not to disturb me … it is time to mark the 'New Age,' so it may come!"

After his forbidding words, Rainbow began to weep in the arms of his parents who glared at Stout Raven with distrust. Mockingly, he only returned a fiercer stare with his smirking face a swivel, as Lone Hawk darted out of the doorway with a maniacal grin.

Trying to trail his footsteps in a rush behind him, they only saw the dead Screecher in his fist like a figurehead above the blur of his charging form, smashing through the restless multitudes. Then, outside of the 'questionable' healer's facility, they could see at the very edge of the village the hauntingly affected Lone Hawk, ducking into his inherited abode from a full gallop with the carcass in straight-armed extension. Theirs was to worry even more while the shaman's contrary demeanor only soared with confidence.

"What have you done to him?" Rainbow fervently demanded of his supposed cure. "Your special corn drink has made him crazy! Now, there's no telling what he has planned … or what you have planned—pretender!"

Stout Raven patted her on the back like a reassuring father figure, then attempted to quell any disbelief. "Now listen—I've known Lone Hawk since he could barely speak, good Princess," he told while softly re-establishing their natural opposition, with a smile and beholding hand toward their distant lodge of recent renovation. "Lone Hawk is a warrior and brave of the first division. For this type of person to be in a situation void of defense is <u>pure</u> trauma! His wounds run ever so deep, especially to his pride, and the special brew I administered is only that of hope, not craziness. First and foremost, on his mind is the loss of his dear companion, the dear departed Screecher who swallows him in a grief comparable to the death of a brother. If there is <u>any</u> blame for insanity, it is <u>not</u> due to my potions, for they are prescribed with the utmost care. His problems only began because he met you, and you <u>cannot</u> argue that point!"

Rainbow delivered him the evil eye while Timbers Earth stood before them with hands waving like their initial meeting, trying to mediate the underlying conflict. "Well, I propose that we leave Lone Hawk to his privacy until high sun," he volunteered his plan, stressing with a cautionary finger pointing that way, to which the others were agreeable. "He's in a <u>very</u> fragile state of mind that could go to <u>any</u> extreme! If we were to pester him too soon, only anger would result. Give him time for this 'Screecher' ritual, but let's keep watch and make sure he doesn't wander off…Mother Earth! Look at the thunderheads rolling in from the East! We'll have only to estimate the high sun check…"

They then alternated in monitoring shifts at an unobtrusive distance from the lodge, where the secretive Lone Hawk was preparing an outrageous surprise. And all the while, Stout Raven tried to maintain control outside his mobbed facility, but was unsuccessful in his attempts to disperse the confused congregation.

Meanwhile, out of sight within his sanctuary, Lone Hawk was performing a gruesome bit of taxidermy with a bizarre twist, applying it to his own. To join the hawk's avenging spirit to live on within him, he split the top of its scull with his hunting knife. Savagely, he scooped out the meager portion of gray matter and he swallowed it like a raw clam to then immediately follow with the eyes, which were assumed integral to the other. He suppressed his urge to vomit and proceeded to remove its mighty beak with a razor-sharp filet knife. He cleaned it well and tied a thin deerskin strap about the base, with plenty of slack. Pressing it to his chin, he was well pleased the fit.

After chin-strapping Screecher's beak, Lone Hawk plucked all his feathers to construct a headdress. He wove them together with hemp thread and created a handsome flow with a red-tail-centered trailer, which hung to his lower back. With the remaining feathers, he imagined their transposition to his arms and so looked at his copper needle, deciding to fulfill the vision. Using the finest hemp-wound thread, he then hastily sewed them into his forearms and triceps, with Stout Raven's brew allowing his resistance to the pain. Lastly, he removed the talons, the symbol of the hawk's clutching strength, and wore them as a necklace wrapped above his chest-bound Earth Force amulet.

When he proudly emerged from the lodge in the late morn donning feathered arms and a beaked chin, Lone Hawk dug a shallow grave in its mostly hidden southside yard and buried Screecher's stripped carcass. After finishing the remaining task, he then came around into clear view and started back to the village center. There, during Solarain's watch, she spied his newly embellished form and, henceforth, hurried back to prime the others, awaiting by the welling crowd. While she offered a preview, the rains held off amidst the thundering dark clouds veined with lightning flashes, bursting to the north.

"Hey, I just want you all to prepare yourselves because he's mutilated himself with the feathers and such, as I saw him bury the hawk's bare corpse!" Solarain warned, weeping, while she rubbed Rainbow's shoulder, trying to soften the shock of his altered appearance. "I am so sorry, my Earth Force daughter, but it seems Lone Hawk has now truly assumed the birdman role!"

Just after Solarain had briefed them where they were closer to the lake, Rainbow could barely see her modified mate because of the huge following he drew by mere shock of design. In a panic, she tried to squirm through the gawking throngs yet made little progress, as they were so well-packed. Unable to reach him with any ease, she delayed her efforts of approach to allow his announcement without a spousal scene.

"Warbirds, these are strange times, indeed, and I intend to explain them. However, I would first like to pay tribute to Screecher, the fearless and faithful hawk whose avenging spirit now lives on in me!" Lone Hawk began with untethered charisma, which with the rumblings of the looming storm brewing from above took on a magical quality. "For as you all can see, I have adorned myself with the symbols of our great mascot's strength. With these, I will remind the evil intruders from the sky, of whom by their eyes I call the Owlmen, that the victim of their <u>unforgivable</u> acts returns with a vengeance.

"When I am soon summoned by the Great Earth Force of the magic sphere that has so chosen me, I will <u>retaliate</u> against these master foes with all the powers of the Earth Force Son as well as the Warbirds' avenging spirit. This double-edged sword will ground these <u>soulless</u> demons and quell their threat to our kind. Then, once I have eliminated the Owlmen and have fulfilled the Earth Force' quest, I promise that the <u>true</u> age of enlightenment will begin. Warbird, Earth Force and all peoples of honor shall soon know and enjoy this new and most giving world of <u>ceaseless</u> miracles!" Upon the finish of his words so enticing and profound, there were some adolescent boys chanting praise to Lone Hawk who nodded to them with approval. Thus, shortly after its start, they began to clap their hands in rhythm to the compelling slogan for victory, and nearly everyone joined in to what Stout Raven considered a dangerous state of mass hysteria. While the volume of their frenzied shouts grew with the thunderous background, the shaman rushed into the grand lodge to see the 'still sleeping' Chief Howling Wind for some urgent consultation.

"Lone Hawk, Earth Force Son! Owlmen, your days are done!" the captive audience of hundreds continued the encouraging 'praise to Lone Hawk' chant whose hand-raising and sword-reeling gestures seemed to command the entire sky to be filled with their voices. Even Rainbow, who was initially appalled by his ghastly appearance, was overcome by his eloquence and its effect on the tribe. Proudly mesmerized, she was glad to be joined by his parents, Running Blood and Snapper to witness the joyous rally in her husband's honor.

Unfortunately, the one with the immediate power had arranged a solution to the perceived mayhem and so, just as the black clouds billowed overhead and began to pour, no one could escape the force of skepticism. Without notice of the tactical formation assembling behind them, the entranced congregation was suddenly shocked into submission when the hundred warriors and braves of Stout Raven's direction stormed their party with jabbing spears that punctured some of those in the front line. The screaming masses were swiftly chased off and removed from the outraged Lone Hawk, who then slashed and sliced a few of his former comrades before a dozen of them had swarmed and subdued him.

During the siege while his parents and the Earth Force brothers were corralled with the others, Rainbow had dodged the military wave and slipped through to him by rounding the violent concentration. "Lone! Do <u>not</u> let them take you away from me!" she screamed, trying to join him, in vain, as the warriors soon aware of this converged upon her amidst the pounding rain. "Unhand me, you mindless savages! Lone—I love you—forever! But <u>please</u> don't leave me! By the Earth Force's bestowal, <u>find</u> the power within you—make them stop!" She called her last words to him, and with the face of utter anguish that included the missing detail. Beaded with raindrops, her expression and conditions—'exactly' as he so hauntingly remembered from the sphere's projection with its plea to spare her. Drained of his strength, he only whispered her name with a dying heart and tears of guilt to the saddest of prophecies fulfilled by his defying the sphere, well knowing the consequence in her pain.

And so, in parting like the mighty oak to the all-powerful lightning bolt, Rainbow and Lone Hawk were dragged off in opposite directions, he to Stout Raven's heavily guarded facility and she to his parents' lodge, which like all the others was placed under military arrest. Once confident that the hostile removal was a success in quelling the 'Earth Force' uprising, the beaming Stout Raven called off the guards from restraining the prisoner, yet he was prudent in keeping his back-tied wrists intact.

Alone with the pacing shaman in his initial detention, Lone Hawk cooled to a simmer and awaited his keeper's explanation, which would prove a perfect dose of deception. "Lone Hawk, I <u>am</u> sorry that we were forced to hinder your 'open' revelation, but I received a most urgent message from a source that <u>you</u> know only all too well! And I must say, this one is <u>very</u> angry with you because of your <u>careless</u> blabbering manner in regards to this mission which demands absolute secrecy," Stout Raven told with shaming eyes as the table-seated Lone Hawk was seeded with a trusting interest by the well-performed charade that personified the Earth Force he knew. "As I said before…I was of the old way, so very stubborn, until the voice of the Wind God relayed to me the warning of the newly allied Earth Force.

"Quite simply, your summoning is to come very soon, but there was an immediate danger, unbeknownst to you, in the crowds with all their consuming attention," Stout Raven continued. "There, the frenzied droves were beginning to absorb and deplete your necessary energies, which now can thankfully develop a thousand-fold, according to plan. So, along with the strict order of a covert launching, we <u>had</u> to take action and protect you from the masses. In doing so, we have insured that you will reach the level of power necessary to save us all from these <u>evil</u> Owlmen who were, as you know, divinely made known to <u>only</u> you, the Earth Force Son.

"Well, in the meantime, I have been instructed to prepare you for the summoning—an honor I will forever cherish! So, until then, you will feast on the finest of foods and enjoy the enhancement of a 'magical' drink only fit for a god. <u>You</u>, Lone Hawk, will be invincible! However, I must first start this conditioning by cleaning your feather-stitched work with some burning water."

Though Lone Hawk was impressed then enthralled by the shaman's glorious news, there was just one detail of reassurance he needed before his confidence could rise to its summit. "After my quest is completed, of course, I <u>will</u> be able to return to my wife and parents—right? I <u>so</u> want to shower them with the <u>best</u> that life has to offer." He presented the scenario as a 'test' precondition while Stout Raven soaked a washcloth in a bowl of alcohol solution and proceeded with the cleaning of the bleeding arms, stinging of a pain to which he was not phased. "Speak, shaman! Since you <u>know</u> so much—tell me! Is this part of the plan, or have the forces not yet told?"

Furthering their trust, Stout Raven cut the ties behind Lone Hawk's back, freeing his hands which he stretched toward the ceiling with a growl of relief.

"Oh, <u>absolutely</u>, Lone Hawk," the clever shaman assured as though he had communed with the gods at great length, hence, tying the final fate-sealing knot. "As 'godly' as can be, you will do whatever comes to whim, feasting on the pleasures of both worlds. Knowing <u>no</u> boundaries, you will come and go in this reality, with them, then to another and back again as you please. Yours shall be a never-ending adventure through space and time. With all this…I plead you, Lone Hawk, as a fellow tribesman of the Warbirds, <u>please</u> do not forget us. For, we will seem so puny when you become one so great, so infinitely grand. So, once you've crushed those dreaded Owlmen, you <u>will</u> remember us…won't you?"

Lone Hawk patted Stout Raven on the shoulder, and looked at him with renewed respect. "Stout Raven, I must apologize for my anger and suspicion of before, but now I feel your sincerity is most genuine," he trusted, so gullible, with a firm nodding smile while falling into the role that Stout Raven, the seasoned master of persuasion, had ingeniously planned. "Though I found the handling of this matter disturbing and abrupt, what's necessary for so <u>great</u> a task, despite hurt feelings, must be done. I am <u>sure</u> that Rainbow will be most forgiving upon my victorious return. So, let's begin the sacred preparations needed for my back-lash assault and ultimate defeat of our common enemy, Good Messenger of the Gods!"

Swimming in quiet jubilation to Lone Hawk's naive concurrence, Stout Raven presented a toast with the strong sour corn drink, offering his victim a cup-full laced with an extra dose of the very finely-ground dreaming mushrooms. While the mixture of earlier that day held only half the hallucinogenic properties of that which he had just readily ingested, Lone Hawk experienced its adulating effects as the shamans would for spiritual clairvoyance. In turn, he became increasingly susceptible to the befriended shaman's wild suggestions, including the enhancement of his sword. Hearing of the lightning box of the Owlmen, Stout Raven convinced him that his sword was blessed with the power to absorb the fatal bolts and return them with twice the force. The chosen brave's intrigue hailed the notion with a hearty upward thrust of his magic blade to its imagined abilities, and was infected beyond repair. Henceforth, his only remaining concern became that of his challenged patience, awaiting his summons for the relying world.

———

"I want more details…I'm sure your contacts with the Earth Force and the Wind God have told you, so when and where, <u>tell</u> me—the <u>precise</u> time and place for my launching to triumph?" Lone Hawk demanded in a raspy voice as he started to devour the many Warbird delicacies, forcefully catered by the tribe's most beautiful women. "And it had <u>better</u> be soon because I just can't wait much longer, with all these bursting thoughts dancing in my head. And this is <u>not</u> the mere wonderment of a fool…I'm telling you, and <u>all</u> the forces that I'm now ready! So, tell me, my good shaman—<u>when</u> and <u>where</u>?"

"At the sun's setting behind the western ridge from atop the sacred Mammoth Bluff, quite appropriately, from its highest point towering above our eastern shore," Stout Raven answered, so incredibly, with remarkable improvisation as he created the moment of destiny in vague yet pleasing terms. "Did you not hear me before?" he added, as the lying host of doom; "perhaps you don't remember because of my ever-rambling talk and the magic drink—whatever! Just thank the gods that I can serve you during this crucial time…I am <u>sworn</u> to deliver you, Lone Hawk. You need only to focus on the primary goal!" Once again, Lone Hawk's expectations were met by the deceiver and by mid-afternoon, the shaman had effectively lulled him to sleep. So firmly under the spell of the 'extra' magic brew, he met slumber with opened eyes. Pleased and amused, Stout Raven took a drink of the same in near celebration of his own personal triumph and closed the eyelids of his target, the neutralized brave of tribal instability.

"Soon, I shall wake you, Earth Force Son, or rather the problem child, the wayward Warbird," he laughed in congratulations for his crafty techniques, surely leading to the defeat of this intolerable subversive behavior. "Oh, and then I will deliver you…yes, but <u>certainly</u> not the direction you will expect!" Stout Raven paced back and forth before the inoculated Lone Hawk, slumped over in the shaman's moose-horned throne and with no temptation toward a nap he himself could use, Stout Raven watched over him through to near sunset. Amidst the security contingent issued for the homebound arrests enforced throughout the village, he peered out to the 'ghost town' from his well-guarded door and noticed that the sky had begun to dim. From there, he instructed the nearby military personnel to form a torch-lit corridor to the foot of Mammoth Bluff, creating a send-off atmosphere of absolute glory.

"Lone Hawk, wake yourself! It is time!" he woke the groggy Lone Hawk with a shoulder shake that activated Lone Hawk's strained lifting hand-to-forehead from the slouched position. "I can see that you need more of the Fire God's brew so that you are lighter than air for the Wind God. Everything in proper measure, my good friend, is to fuse with the assurance of your victory…isn't this wonderful? Yes, drink and rise to your feet!" he commanded so amiably but with a firm hand to help him up, as he spilled the wicked corn drink in their haste. "Oh, worry not about that. You've had the perfect dose. And now that you have had the necessary sleep, your energies will build to their full magical potential…just as I promised!"

Finally free of the shaman's 'Four Corners' facility, Lone Hawk followed the shaman on the warrior-torched eastbound path around the bird mound onto the forest trail to the bluff, where it narrowed. They were then alone, hiking the winding upward trail through the boulders.

Though he first walked in a stumbling gate, the sight of the military route ablaze in his honor gave him an immense sense of pride which made him break into a powerful strut of determination. Stout Raven being a much older man, however, had great difficulty matching the stride of the eager brave. But he kept the vigorous pace only to race the setting sun, the prescribed window of time in his fabrication. Due to the heavy rains earlier in the day, the rocky path was very slippery. Yet, the journey began to lose its hazard as the clear sky started to brighten and adequately light the rugged incline.

While Lone Hawk's muscles tensed in throttled anticipation, the puncture wounds in his arms that had just started healing were reopened. Thus, the fresh blood trickled off his elbows onto his knees, feet and to the quartzite steps, where his vital fluid of crimson dripped. Splashing upon the red hued rock in near perfect camouflage, it would not be long before the rest would follow.

"Lone Hawk, I ask you for just one more thing," Stout Raven requested as an afterthought for the insult-topping sake of his hideous plan; "may I keep your Earth Force amulet as a beacon for your return home? I will place it on the stump at village center for you to see upon your glorious return. Oh, I can see you now, plunging out of the sky and wearing it again to mark your victory!"

"Of course, Stout Raven, here you go…have the amulet ready on the ole stump for that or, better yet, give it to my wife and let her put it there," Lone Hawk suggested while lifting the leather-strung amulet over his head and trustingly giving it to the unscrupulous shaman. "The less weight the better, I suppose…and it would be a good reminder for all. Well, I think the sun's about to sink…have you any more advice?"

"No, all is in perfect order, and I want you to continue to the launch site without me," Stout Raven told with a gasp as to establish his distance from the travesty about to unfold. "Indeed, the setting sun will soon call the Wind God, who will await you with opened arms. But be sure to watch for my signal, a simple nod with a talon sign, alerting you to the precise time. Then, and only then is the moment that you must lunge and throw yourself toward the sun with all-your-might into magical flight, chasing behind it. Though a fledgling, you will quickly soar, receiving further instruction and infinite wisdom on your way to destiny…now, do as you were chosen. Save our land from the evil ones and return for a victory celebration the world has never known!"

Lone Hawk savored his words and marched up to the 'Mammoth' summit, the bastion of quartzite stone, overseeing all to meet his demise by the shaman's scandalous prod.

The archived reliving Xavier had endured faded while he perched, once again, upon the cliff of death. But then, sparked by some kind of 'Lazarus' effect, he found himself lying on a hospital examination table for an autopsy. At that moment, he pondered in a dismal, confused state, 'it's all over now, end to beginning to end…but whatever it was—epic! Damn—and forgot it right away! How typical…and, what's this?' Xavier paused while receiving a telepathic communique he could not quite make out, and thus dismissed. 'Go where—west? Chosen…battle—who <u>is</u> this? Ah, just dream-lingering, I guess…' From his squinting eyes, the fuzzy bleached light then dissipated to invite human forms that hovered around him as his vision began to clear. '<u>Who</u> the <u>hell</u> are these people? And <u>what</u> are they doing with <u>that</u> thing over my head? My god, where am I?…I?' Xavier panicked to the anxious chill of amnesia that had set in while he began to struggle, strapped onto an examination table presumed dead.

CHAPTER IX
Evermore Awakening

AFTER INNUMERABLE SESSIONS OF analysis, sorting through his long-departed life in the physical realm, Lone Hawk's insomniac soul continued its 'phantom-form' float in the dimensionless hollow of the alter-universe. There, his five mortal senses of reference did not exist, besides the dim glow of his multi-colored translucence. Though otherwise, he was without sight, sound, smell, taste and touch yet his memories of such lingered. With such a fertile imagination to merciful rescue, it filled the generous gaps of time. How much time or how long had it been? He did not know. His ability to quantify duration had for the most part slipped away. Yet, he could still surmise that several generations, even centuries worth must have passed. And as his term became evermore convincingly eternal, he only worried more and more about the fate of the present world.

`What have the Owlmen done, with their only threat presumed dead and probably forgotten? Perhaps they have enslaved our Warbird descendants and maybe my own, if Rainbow had conceived before I left her. <u>Oh</u>, how I miss her!' Lone Hawk envisioned a dismal Earth and held chronic thoughts of longing guilt for his wife's tragic fate being left behind, yet he remained strangely faithful in one respect. `Well, she is long dead by now and hasn't joined me as a soul mate. Oh, <u>what</u> has become of her in this spirit world?…<u>Must</u> stop thinking about her! The quest! Think <u>only</u> of the quest and nothing else!

`Am I to return to a world of their complete domination? So be it! My victory shall then taste even sweeter! But if they've killed all the people, what is there to come back to? No! The prophecy would <u>never</u> have that! Soon, yes, very soon, when I finally wake the others.'

In his isolation, other senses within him began to emerge and tear down invisible walls. By these, he knew he was not alone. Shadings, impressions of others nearby in a kinder place touched his soul, but they could not feel his presence as he did theirs. They were peacefully sleeping and he needed to wake them, lest madness consume him, as he was convinced that they were the vital link to his destiny.

Lone Hawk forced a countless regimen of communiqués to his listless companions. He humbly begged them to awaken; he commanded that they hear him as their threatful chief; he played the soothsayer and promised them the glory of victory; he warned them that the world, which gave them life, was in peril; and if they did not transcend the life-robbing slumber about them, their people would be embroiled toward certain doom. Clever as his verbal tactics were, not even the faintest response was reaped by these. Yet, there was another who could listen, though it was one of no allegiance.

All the while he could feel the presence of evil lurking near him, hiding in the nowhere. It was the chief of the Owlmen, spying on his only true nemesis, he was sure.

"I know it is you, Evil One!" Lone Hawk shouted with incurable zest. "The time is near, and you worry as well you should. I promise you, there will be others in my great army who will <u>slaughter</u> your frail, pumpkin head warriors while you <u>torturously</u> await my wrath, which burns like the sun. Watch and so sink, evermore depressed, for my powers are burgeoning, outgrowing this hellish place. I will soon emerge in massive scope and fulfill the prophecy as deemed by the great Earth Force. Bide your time, Evil One, for despite <u>all</u> you have done to me, I'll soon awaken, and the dawn of your destruction will be at hand…Oh!" he yawned, feeling a lulling wave all about him. "How very strange…<u>all</u> of the <u>sudden</u>, I'm so tired and sleepy—I <u>never</u> felt tired as for the want to sleep since

I've been here! <u>What</u> is going on? Ah, unless…could it finally be?" Lone Hawk wondered aloud and suspected perhaps it was not a false calling meant to fool him like before. Thus, for the first time in his Evermore detention, his insomniac soul yawned but with a throat-clearing howl and could see his hands transform from an unfeeling, phantom-like translucence to a solid, very human form with full-range tactile sensations.

Ecstatic, Lone Hawk so delighted to a clap of his hands, without them passing through each other. The hyper-impacting sound of just one palm-to-palm collision sent him off into a dream world, not of the imagined sort but anew with full perception like he was truly alive. However fantastic though the change had been, his levitation out of the nowhere grew quite disturbing and beyond his control. With his guarding hands at full extension before his face, he soared into the dark lightening-veined clouds above him. He plunged into the all-encompassing, flashing grayness and started to suffocate with a terror-dreaming effect, taking hold. Thankfully brief, Lone Hawk then sailed above the morbid layer and saw to his astonishment the lonely sun…but with a face, <u>her</u> beautiful face. At long last and blazing before him, it was Rainbow whose fond memory most certainly helped him survive his 'Evermore' near-eternity, with his last grain of sanity still intact. Like a sky goddess, Rainbow's sunshine spirit became facially more discernible while her ever-perfect body from before filled in to complete her form. Impressed as he was by her golden tan skin's glistening glow, Lone Hawk marveled at the beaming, crystal blue round swirling into view beneath her navel.

With the clouds harmlessly rolling below them like a herd of roving hills, his heart welled to the glorious sight of her divinity and was soothingly charmed by the sound of her warm sultry voice. "Your time has finally come, 'Lone ma Love'—your true quest only <u>now</u> begins…and <u>so</u> far in the future, I know! <u>Much</u> further than either of us could ever have predicted!" Then exhausting the time lapse dimension, Rainbow cut to the chase. "I also had no idea that I would have such the honor as a sacred role in all of this, way back then…Yet, I <u>was</u> chosen as well, but only to instruct you and help blanket the sky…when that time soon comes…" she hinted while

Lone Hawk gushed in dreamy reply. "My <u>dear</u>, sweet Rainbow…it <u>really</u> is you! Oh, how I've missed you, thinking about you always and all, but well I know there's very little time. And, how I've longed to be pressured to do <u>anything</u>, with no time to spare. So, tell me…what do I need to know now to then get on with this!" She nodded to him with an adoring smile, blew him a kiss and answered quite simply, soon to reveal a most welcomed surprise. "Eager as ever, and just one of the many reasons I love you <u>so</u> much! Well, all sweetness aside…first, you must wake the others whose chosen presence you have been sensing and create an allegiance with them. Then later, there will also be another to let you know this future world and third, the sphere awaits to complete you. Once these are done, you <u>will</u> know what to do!"

Upon her finish of his concisely delivered instructions, the then leg-spreading 'Sky Goddess' Rainbow began another delivery. Painlessly giving birth from her crystal blue pool that had migrated further down between her legs, a head emerged out of the sparkling round. Expecting a baby to come forth, Lone Hawk laughed with an inviting wave of his hand when the newly reborn Screecher showed himself to rejoin him. Once fully free and flapping his wings, the lovable raptor lived up to his name and called out to him with the most endearing, screeching shrill he had ever heard. Thus, as Screecher glided and flapped his way over to him, Rainbow sent them off with a beholding hand-fling towards the ungulated cloud cover below them, but with words of warning to follow. "My father was so right about you and Screecher, your 'hawk spirit' guide—you <u>so</u> belong together! Oh, what a <u>precious</u> sight and what an honor, so…farewell for now, My Love. For as you say, 'get on with this'—the change has begun! Oh wait, there are just a couple more things I was told to tell you: Beware the <u>false</u> promises to your 'feeding' ego; and listen for the <u>true</u> voice calling inside you. Hmm, turns out the Earth Force <u>does</u> know you all too well, so heed its advice—love you!"

Then while fading off into her original sunshine form, Lone Hawk puzzled for an instant over her closing words. Yet, so overjoyed as he was being reunited with Screecher, his distracted mind gave them little more immediate thought. And so, he waved fond farewell, unfazed, and blew her sugar kisses while grunting, "uh, sure will, and so love you too, my 'forever' Love...," as Screecher perched on his shoulder and nuzzled against the side of his head. Their hearts, minds and spirits as one, he patted his most ever-vibrant, winged warrior on the breast and assured him with unmatched gusto in echoed rejoice, "Good Screecher, we're going home!" While they descended into the clouds, Screecher flapped his wings then began to playfully hop and shriek, as if wanting some 'hawk dance' action. Obliging his request, Lone Hawk broke a move and thus they did their signature dance, mid-air, until they disappeared into the swirling cumulus thundering below.

Just moments later while they spun so tight as to implode, he spiraled out of the clouds, nakedly alone, and plummeted back to the solid ground below him. Upon impact, it felt so different from his lethal jump nine-centuries earlier as to only but stop with a resonating jolt. Immediately frustrated, trying to remember what had transpired up there with Rainbow and Screecher, Lone Hawk rose to his feet and rubbed his eyes. It was apparent that he had returned to his previous yet depleted physical form. Feeling heavy, weak and off balance, he wavered as he cracked a squint. Although he only saw a purplish blur, the sensation of light and solid footing sent ecstatic shivers throughout his body. Once focused, he turned his head back and forth, and all about, finding himself in a familiar yet disturbing world. "This is no dream," Lone Hawk declared, relishing the sound of his own voice. "I have finally crossed over, well, at least halfway. And this is 'their' world, the sleepers of my calling? Hmm, how peculiar..."

With a piercing red sun in a purple sky of midday, the compliments on this alter-earth were like an illustration of dissonance. An encampment of black rocks, dusted with reflective shavings, surrounded him. The jagged boulders glittered with his changing perspective as he gingerly moved through a pink haze in a downward path. There he would go, for beyond and below was undoubtedly Lake of the Warbirds, even though the water of its unliving body was hot violet.

Since he was lost no more, Lone Hawk adapted to the weird color scheme with surprising ease. Then while testing his footing, he stumbled and fell. To stifle his resulting slide, he was fortunate to take hold of a well-anchored boulder as his quick-reflex arms embraced it for safety. He had once been so agile a man, yet his death had caused him to atrophy in the physical ways. Aware of his disability, he decided to crawl backwards down the treacherous rockslide.

By the time he neared the bottom of the rocky expanse, he found that his legs were sturdy and his balance true. More than just sure-footed, he effortlessly bounded from boulder to remaining boulder, and reached a full sprint when he met the old sloping trail that was then bordered by chromium-barked trees with crystal royal blue leaves. He was elated by his incredible swiftness. Thus, through the still and ominous shadows of the branches, he darted around the bend and instantly reached a familiar clearing yet with turquoise grass and a soft, red-sanded beach behind it. Where once he thought his village stood, there was nothing manmade, though not to his surprise.

Drawn to the water, Lone Hawk stopped at the shoreline's edge to wet his feet. He indulged himself in the cool sensation, delighting in his return to the earthbound pleasures. During that self-exploratory moment, his attention was drawn to his arms, head and neck. Upon the first observations with his lakeside reflection's assistance, the feathers he stitched into his forearms so long ago had taken root. Intrigued to a handclap, he turned around to check out his scalp, nape and back, finding them in a similar condition. Along with his ancient headdress, feathery but scant crotch cover was also planted like a hawk, giving him his first laugh there to its well-intended modesty. Overall, he was pleased. And once finished his 'vanity' phase, Lone Hawk peered through the strawberry vapors rising from the water's surface and noticed in the distance the floating body of a woman.

Eagerly, he dove into the deep magenta pool. Once submerged, he could see no aquatic game, only bountiful beds of fluorescent blue seaweed. And while he held his breath like normal cutting through the water on the way, the speedy swimmer found he could inhale water and air the same. The reborn Lone Hawk felt vibrant and invulnerable as he arrived beneath the silhouette of the woman.

He extended his cupped hands upward to her perfectly formed buttocks yet resisted his urge to touch them. Instead, he backed away and rose from the water, breaking the surface at eye level at the span of her feet. She lay with her arms and legs spread as if awaiting the sky's indulgence. Lone Hawk moved nearer, inching toward her, and salivated to the luscious sight. He further broke the surface up to his waist and, aroused, inserted himself between her knees, but then suddenly was forced back by an unexpected kick to the forehead.

Lone Hawk burst into jolly laughter and felt truly alive. Still jovial, he spanned his arms in peace and to his self-imposing wish, levitated out of the water and hovered over the woman. He beheld her fiercely beautiful, rounded face with jutting chin and stared into her big dark brown eyes, sharp with rage. She glared at him in noble indignation as he surveyed her naked form. Understandably, returning from such a lengthy exile, he savored the sight of such an attractive a woman so real. Her pert, tanned breasts and slender waist harkened the forgotten pleasures of the passionate brave he was. Yet, this spitfire was not for the taking, even for a man-creature as impressive as he.

To appease her anger, Lone Hawk flung his hand towards her and conjured his first creation, a twelfth-century deerskin bikini with tiny blue jay feathers lining top-and-bottom. Since it covered her private regions, she nodded to the swimwear addition with feather-fiddling satisfaction. Then with the same casual gesture but to the sky, a likeness of the woman was manifested in the heavens directly above them. And though her image was accurately produced, it took the form of a vast white cloud. In its settlement, her cumulus double spawned a bluish growth from its edges, which was reflected and absorbed by the surface of the lake.

"Sorry, good woman, but I thought you might have been my wife who'd fallen from the sky," the shoulder-shrugging Lone Hawk calmly explained to her cautioned trust. "Obviously not, however, I <u>have</u> been trying to contact you for what seemed an eternity. I can free you from this world, so now—come! I invite you to be my 'number one' on a magical quest…there, in the sky to woo you is but my <u>second</u> gift for you, with many more to come."

"Extraordinary, as you are," she acknowledged, tight lipped, in a deep, breathy voice; "you are a <u>strange</u> thing! With feathers in your arms and for your hair, with a hawk-beaked chin? <u>What</u> sort of spirit are you to have these powers of flight, 'woman adorning,' so clever…and sky-bound gifts? Yet, you speak unkeepable promises and harbor the weaknesses of an earthbound man…Ah, but it <u>does</u> make sense. You're the trickster demon I've been sensing…sent to bring me to hell! So, why did you wait so long?"

"Listen, Lady—I am <u>no</u> demon! I'm what used to be a man, but <u>now</u> I am something <u>much</u> more, as you can plainly see," Lone Hawk defended to near a growl while stroking his chin's well-fused hawk beak, which he must have missed obsessing with his feathers. "After I died, the change in me began when I was cocooned in a torturous place of nothingness, for what seemed an eternity. I have finally been released and so justly rewarded as an enhanced being with ever-growing powers. You, see? It's about prophecy—the great magical sphere of the Earth Force chose <u>me</u> as the savior of the living world.

"However, the Owlmen chose me, as well," he continued, somberly. "Yet, the power they entrusted to me only spawned my infernal <u>hatred</u> for their kind, instilling a thirst for revenge which must be quenched. They ambushed me; they killed my best friend; they invaded me—mind, body and soul. Then, seeing me a threat, the chief shaman prudently tricked me into my own demise. And as tragic as those events were, they were nothing compared to the long, dark and silent hell which I have endured until now…"

Lone Hawk plaintively stared into her distrustful countenance. She tilted her head back and rolled her eyes. Then her mirror image engraved in the sky gazed back at her. It seemed an extension of herself that wanted to believe him, yet she was still unconvinced. The woman shifted to her side and crossed her legs. However, to soften the insult to her arcane suitor, she offered an attentive look of encouragement when she returned her eyes to his.

"You <u>must</u> realize my sincerity," he pleaded, pondering the tools of persuasion it would take to convince this first recruit. "The great Earth Force depends upon my ability to awaken and unite you, the dreamers of this shadow land, and rescue our kind in the physical world from the Owlmen."

Suddenly, she cracked a smile of familiarity, as if all he had said finally hit a nerve of amusement. "Ah, yes! I know who you are," the woman scoffed with a devilish grin while she playfully paddled her feet. "The legendary Lone Hawk, the Earth Force Son…Chaser of the imaginary Owlmen, a 'fantasy' tribe of whom no one had ever seen. You caused quite a rumpus, false prophet, as Warbird folk tales had told. So, the dream still burns bright, even in death…Oh, poor diluted one, go back to sleep. Your quest is just a painful memory of a mad man."

Lone Hawk's eyes turned cold. And in one swift motion, his hovering form rolled over in the air and his feathered musclebound arm swept over the water, transforming the gentle waves into green-hued blazes. The startled woman retracted her limbs in a panicked effort to save herself from the scalding fire around her.

"You mock then patronize me when I offer you so much?!" he bellowed to her audacity while he put forth his hands in a rescuing gesture. "Sweet sleeper of ignorance, I am most benevolent. So, let's just start over and I'll forgive you. Meantime, come to my safety— it must be getting hot down there!"

The stubborn woman resented the notion that he would offer like a favor to save her from a danger of his own making. Thus, reluctantly, she reached for him and was hoisted into the air. In gradual ascent, Lone Hawk held her by the armpits and put their faces so close that barely the wind could pass between them.

"Join my quest to destroy the Owlmen," he demanded. "As these feathers and beak remind me of the hawk's avenging spirit, ours must be to quell their evil, methodical dominance—taking place right now!" Lone Hawk's voice then became gentle. "I know you're a spirit of adventure. And now that you've been sparked, you cannot possibly be satisfied with this self-absorbed dreamland."

Lone Hawk tucked the woman's slender torso under his arm and cradled her against his chest, which had broadened significantly since they first met. He soared upward, escaping the water-based inferno, and passed through her cloud's image. When she peeked over his shoulder after clearing it, the captured 'damsel in denial' was shocked to see her cumulus self, turning its head with an approving nod and smile but then dissipating to natural cloud form. Thus, beaming with intrigue, she watched as ahead of them the sky soon turned black, spattered with innumerable stars beyond a blazing, white sun. Slowing to a gentle stop, they looked back at the purplish Earth laced with pink swirls with its crisp, pale moon of peach tinge. They marveled to its magnificence.

"I've found that when I envision my wants and desires, I can make them true," Lone Hawk told with the nonchalance that one of such unbridled confidence would. "So, to you I behold this profound view of our home. And though its colors are not true, it's the same Earth. I only need to bring it back to life. Then perhaps, you will really appreciate what is at stake for the future. Hey, I'm sorry if I frightened you, but you had to believe…I <u>need</u> you! Oh! How rude of me…what's your name, 'first' recruit?"

"Well, it's about time you asked—see <u>that</u>?" she posed while pointing at the moon, like a guessing game.

"Yes, the moon. So, your name is Moon!" he answered, quite certain he had guessed the obvious.

"Well, you're half right. Now, preceded by…" she led him into the answer by bunching her long black hair into her cupped hands like a picture frame. "Color?"…she cutely coaxed while showing him the second clue.

"Hairy Moon? You've <u>got</u> to be kidding me!" he gagged, forbidding the thought.

"Black Moon, silly! Ha-ha—my hair <u>color</u>! Uh, you may have many powers, Lone Hawk, but you're as slow-witted as any man," she chided with a demeaning blanket statement that did not even seem to faze him. "Even so, I will follow you, though we <u>must</u> pretend that I had a choice."

"This is <u>not</u> about choice that's merely steered by one's own self-interest. This is about the ultimate challenge, the bestowed honor as 'the chosen' of the only viable, saving force to still exist. It's a most <u>urgent</u> situation down there, like the Earth is a person who's almost drowned, and we are the saving grace to push on their chest clear the water out of their lungs, so…" he explained to a pause, noticing that Black Moon had become suddenly distressed. "What's wrong? Your eyes, raining tears—why?"

Black Moon wrapped her arms around his neck and sobbed. "That's how they killed me. Red Bear's two henchmen came out in their canoe, during my morning swim. I thought there was news that needed my attention, for I was the Warbirds' chieftain at that time. But, as I innocently treaded in the deep water and awaited their words, one of them went overboard. Being much bigger than myself, he was able to push and hold me under until I could only breathe water…dying _so_ defenselessly, just the thought, makes me want to cry!

"Oh, my goodness—Lone Hawk! You should _see_ yourself!" she continued, alarmed yet excited. "You're _much_ bigger than before…and your beak has split your chin in two! Well, I guess as your powers grow, they make you look evermore fierce to become the world's 'ultimate' birdman hero, mm-hmm—see! Now, you're even sprouting wings!"

On his back, in fact, the wings of a fledgling had emerged and grown from his shoulders to his buttocks. Disturbed, Lone Hawk felt self-conscious and thus changed their focus.

"Look at your cloud…it's _changing_ the Earth—the transition has begun!" he remarked, twirling his much larger hands toward it as they viewed the spreading of her nimbus with natural blue, tan and green hues in its trail. "Let's return and find the others. _Then_ we can begin. For from this 'outer space' nothingness, the Owlmen have funneled through to this precious place, so it's to our good blessing from the all-giving Earth Force that we can stop them. Protecting us, it rules the wind, water, land and sky, but its powers have boundaries. That's why I was chosen. Into me has been born the _free_ and powerful, radical entity that has become its only remaining weapon! Yet, that's _still_ not enough and is why I will need many faithful ones, like you, to fuel this ever-growing strength to its _absolute_ advantage. Only then can I break through to the physical realm of destiny with _all_ of you safely under my invulnerable wings."

Pursing her lips, Black Moon observed that his ego was growing in proportion to his size. Even so, she was not particularly alarmed since they had started reeling back to the sanctuary of the changing Earth. However, she became repulsed by the 'skin-crawling' touch of a Lone Hawk who was becoming less-and-less human. She so looked forward to their landing, but Lone Hawk made it purposefully gradual. Seeing as he had her undivided attention, his inquiring mind preyed on her as they plunged into the invitingly natural-white cirrus clouds, among the first signs of the positive transition.

"So, how many years after, did your reign follow my death? And what else does legend tell of my disruption to the Warbirds' <u>ignorant</u> mentality?" he queried, steeply inquisitive, as she hoped he would not. "And what about my wife, Princess Rainbow of the Earth Force tribe? She's the one I mistook you for when I was getting a little…um, well, there <u>was</u> that dream about her up here—whatever! Was there <u>anything</u> said about what she did after I was gone?"

"There was a bloodstone totem that was chiseled in your image, hailing the sky," she admitted with reverence but avoiding the main question. "She must have loved you <u>very</u> much, this Princess Rainbow, having such an exquisite piece made for your burial marker there, at the head of the bird mound. And, how many years? A hundred between us, Lone Hawk, and it doesn't even seem to matter. I'm sure that there's been so much change since then—<u>We</u> are but relics!"

"Well, do the histories say what Rainbow did after that?" Lone Hawk dug further with a determination that was not about to let the matter rest. "She just went back to Earth Force Center after my funeral, and the <u>rest</u> is a complete mystery?"

"She left with some believers on a pilgrimage to see the great sphere, but they were never heard from again. I admit, I did <u>not</u> want to tell you anymore, but…" Black Moon begrudgingly told, feeling his grief; "it was believed that Earth Force Center was the Fire Lynx' first siege of the civilized world. It was said that after the bloody taking, the heads of every Earth Force tribesman were placed on skyward spearheads in savage celebration of their triumph. Oh, and I <u>especially</u> didn't want to tell…apparently, the women and children who remained were kept as horribly abused slaves and forcefully ravaged concubines, reduced to things that could value life no more. Suicide for many was the only escape from these human beasts…but <u>please</u>, let us close this futile conversation. The past makes me ill!" Lone Hawk was deeply saddened by the unfathomable demise of his long-lost mate, yet he would not dwell on the subject for both their sakes.

In appeasement to Black Moon's anxiety to abandon such talk and disembark, he hurried their landing back onto Lake of the Warbird's south shore so allowing her desperate separation. Once there, they noticed a dramatic change. The lake was a wonderful blue, as was the clear sky with its golden sun. The foliage retained its greenery and the towering quartzite bluffs were once again of dirty rose. Only a thin, pink haze hung in the air as a remnant of the dead world. Thus, her mood improved dramatically as they began to walk the shoreline.

"Wow, how this stirs some good memories…ah, the beauty of the valley as I remembered it," she commented ever so fondly, looking about with her hand shading her eyes. "Even so, it remains too damn still and lifeless. So, how are we to happen upon these others, Lone Hawk?"

"By my momentous presence, the layers of reality will dissolve one-by-one and so, the separate and unique realities of each destined dreamer shall be revealed for us to revive," the behemoth Lone Hawk told with an innate enlightenment that thrived in the changing world. Then showing off, he stretched his new wings forward, testing their reach. They just met at their red feather-sabered tips as she was impressed as he, continuing his words of wisdom with a maniacal grin. "Now, since I awoke near the bluffs…and you in the lake, I suspect the others linger in the areas where their <u>own</u> deaths occurred as well. With <u>that</u> in mind, let's now expand our awareness and adjust to their private layer in this 'place of death' spectrum. Perish the thought that we would unknowingly pass them over…speaking of which—look! Over there…our <u>second</u> Earth Force recruit is appearing!"

At that very moment, a tall, long-faced man in brown war garb faded into view, leaning on a big oak tree in the distance at the clearing's edge. In his right hand, a spear was cocked while a dark gray vulture shield was held in his left, as if he were in the heat of battle. Thus, while they drew closer to greet the warrior frozen in violent conflict, Black Moon expressed a note of familiarity. "I think I know him," she said, pointing a shaky finger. With eyes squinted and then enraged, she screamed, "Red Bear!" Charging at the startled man, he dropped his shield and haphazardly tossed his wobbling spear her way. The nimble Black Moon easily dodged the sharpened projectile and hurled herself against him, with a simultaneous fist and knee to his tensed face and stomach. Lone Hawk let out a ferocious bit of laughter to the incredible sight of 'so scantily clad a woman of such' attacking a fully equipped warrior much larger than she. However, when the man pushed her to the ground and pulled out a concealed knife, his amusement took an instant turn to protective urgency. In one lunging motion, he intercepted the blade-wielding warrior and pinned him against the tree.

"See this coward?!" Black Moon shouted, back on her feet with wide-angered eyes and a rumpled upper lip. "He's the <u>traitor</u> Red Bear, of whom I spoke. So, my <u>back-stabbing</u> first brave, you <u>couldn't</u> face me alone, but to send your 'no better' henchmen after me with a surprise death sentence! And now, you think you can kill me directly when I'm already dead, do you? Such gall! Lone Hawk, this one is <u>definitely</u> not worthy of your quest. In fact, if you could please torture and send him to hell, I would be forever grateful. Go ahead—show him your power!"

Lone Hawk released Red Bear and began to peacefully mediate their discord, denying Black Moon her vengeful wish. "Speak in your defense, Red Bear," he encouraged, offering him a chance of redemption; "are her suspicions true? Did you <u>really</u> arrange her murder?"

Black Moon's accused quivered in fear, yet in meek fascination looked to Lone Hawk with veneration. "Oh, Great One! Did she say Lone Hawk, the one and only Earth Force Son?" the shifty eyed Red Bear, with his big hump-ridged nose effectively praised, knowing of his legendary tale as he knelt before him. "You have become the 'Hawk God,' now arisen to battle the Owlmen, yes?"

"Look at that! He avoids the question and fawns all over you!" Black Moon protested. "He knows your story as well as I … and so, he cleverly uses it to woo you. Now, answer his question directly— you, ass-kisser!"

"Alright, it goes like this: I saw a <u>dangerously</u> lax leader negotiating with the enemy," Red Bear explained, with a self-righteous air of no regrets. "They were the savage Fire Lynx who had already taken the land of many tribes to the west. We were the last stronghold yet, during <u>her</u> seven-years reign, the Warbirds weakened as this 'fumbling' one, developed policies of trust. She invited their chief to the village and entertained him. She made a trade and river rights agreement with him while I could see his salivating gleam assessing our valley for his future conquest. I wanted to behead him, right then and there, but my attentions then turned to Black Moon as the one whose removal was essential to the Warbirds' survival. The next morning, I sent a couple of men to quietly put her out of power. However, it was seven-years too late.

"The Fire Lynx had far more warriors than we ever imagined," he continued. "They must have multiplied like locusts, as our scouts sadly underestimated their numbers. If it is <u>any</u> consolation to you, Black Moon, my reign lasted only seven days. Their army poured into the valley from every direction during the night but with no torches. I believe that every Warbird man was killed that night while I took a spear through my heart at this very spot. <u>You</u> would have been fortunate to be their breeding stock, Black Moon. That is, after they had raped you, countless times. Now, what would you have preferred?"

"I would have <u>fought</u> like a brave and died honorably, you moose's anus!" she screamed with a swift backhanded fist to his stomach. "Now, you act as though having me killed was a favor, sparing me of worse miseries. The way you distort with our good gift of speech is <u>so</u> evil. Please, Lone Hawk, you heard his confession—now send him to hell!"

Nearly twice her height, Lone Hawk looked down to Black Moon with further displeasure. "We are <u>still</u> in hell, Black Moon, and this bickering must cease!" he demanded, raising his massive arms and shaking his double-clenched fists of anger. "Red Bear, you are chosen, and so may you join us. There were <u>so</u> many times that I wanted to kill ole, heartless-clueless Chief Howling Wind…oh, how it seemed that his lame-ass being would <u>never</u> die! The man was <u>so</u> old and senile that the senior shaman, Stout Raven, ruled over him and told him every word he should say. That's how he procured my death…Ah, <u>Death</u>—but now <u>we</u> defy even that!"

Lone Hawk found Red Bear's company to be quite refreshing, as they could speak like men. Thus, Black Moon walked away, feeling betrayed, while the braves traded exaggerated versions of their masculine endeavors.

"How did you come upon the name, Red Bear?" he asked in a friendly tone which sent the newly roused recruit into an over-zealous tirade of description.

"When I was sixteen, with another young warrior on a scouting mission collecting some medicine leaves," he told, releasing a low growl; "a big and hungry black bear suddenly crossed our trail. In his foolish flight, my comrade tried to climb a tree. But, of course, the big toothy 'fur ball' was able to pull him back down to the ground with ease. So, as the bear began to maul him, I threw my spear at close range right into its neck.

"That slowed the vicious attacker down a bit and as it shook the spear out, my fellow warrior squirted away in a thankful crawl. But while he found safety, the wounded bear, almost beyond natural ability, began to chase me instead. So, I went into a full-speed 'flee from this, flee from this!'—hah! You know the feeling, Lone Hawk, or are you now so powerful you have forgotten?

"I'm not finished," he told Lone Hawk when it seemed he was about to speak; "well, naturally, I couldn't out-run a barreling bear, so, the beast was soon upon me and I was pinned down, with its gaping mouth about to devour my face. And when it seemed to be my bloody, faceless end, I rammed my sharpened knife into the soft temple of its scull where the long blade seated quite fatally. Its blood fountained upon me like rain! I was drenched with the blood of the most powerful meat eater. Therefore, I became Red Bear…but, why don't you ask Black Moon about how she got her name? Obviously, you do not know about her curse!"

With Red Bear's eagerness to muddy her name, Lone Hawk was uncomfortable yet tolerant of Red Bear's well-masked, gender bigotry. He had grown fond of Black Moon and now had her on a secret pedestal. However, so long without conversation, he wanted to hear every word, good or bad, about everyone and everything. "A curse and her name? What are you suggesting? Explain!" Lone Hawk demanded, just realizing that she had wandered off from their sight. "Oh! And now we've driven her away with this exclusive male talk. Continue and finish, Red Bear, quickly, as I <u>must</u> soon find her!"

"When her father, Chief Catching Arrow, suddenly died...the then twenty-year-old 'play girl' Rosey Fawn became Black Moon because it was the night of the shadow moon," he again described with over-theatrics, with arm-waving gestures to the sky. "Though all seemed well with the sudden change of command at that point, it was thought by many that the sky-bound event was a sign of certain doom. To the contrary, I believe that our downfall had nothing to do with this superstition. It is a woman's nature to be soft...yet it is a hard world—and <u>that</u> says it all! Well, I see that our subject matter, about whom you so worry, has taken the time for a leisurely swim."

"No, oh no!" Lone Hawk growled, with a sudden growth spurt. "She's <u>trying</u> to go back!" He quickly sped off upon his cushion of air to retrieve and restrain Black Moon. Then immediately, he scooped her up from an underwater northbound back stroke and brought her back to shore while she struggled.

"Hey, I don't like him either, but he's cunning and enthusiastic, a brave of good raw ability," Lone Hawk explained with the hopeful persuasion of his suave mediating mindset. "The last days of the Warbirds were an inevitable tragedy and best left out of history, considering the looming Fire Lynx. <u>All</u> of that was beyond your control, as well his. I do <u>not</u> expect you to forgive Red Bear. Minimal toleration is all I ask and, of course, a bit of modesty."

Placing his hand near her throat, he passed it downward before her bikini-adorned body while accessorizing it in one magical sweep. Around her neck he created a circular turquoise pendant centered by a smooth, black sphere with the same 'glitter' quality of the rocks and boulders of the earlier alter-world. On a silver chain laced with tiny roseate shells, the necklace was a beautiful compliment to the stunning, deerskin robe studded with an array of colored beads. Of perfect fit to her finely feminine form, the middle thigh-length garment was a copy of his wife's favorite; hence, it was reproduced in her memory.

Black Moon calmly admired her new outfit. "This is quite beautiful, but it doesn't change the fact I hate the man," she expressed with a disdainful frown. "Eventually, he will trip over himself when he crosses you, and I will <u>so</u> savor your response. But <u>please</u> forget my cowardice of late. I'll stay on, if only just to keep Red Bear in check. Uh, I don't want to alarm you, Lone Hawk, but…as you have given me this special apparel, you have shed 'something else'…and your feet have become something of talons!"

Black Moon brought unsavory attention to his absent genitalia that appeared to have retreated beneath the patch of feathered gray down there, and to his feet, which had transformed to five-pronged talons. He looked down at himself and, in doing so, his over-reactive eyes stretched to the upper reaches of his temples and blazed a bright red in their double expansion. At that exact moment, an old bald man in a bison mane vest with its horns wrapped around his shoulders came forward from out of the western brush. Underneath, he wore a black shaman's robe like Stout Raven, a sight which understandably spurred Lone Hawk's hatred and distrust. Pointing an extravagantly whittled, crooked cane at him, the mysterious shaman called out to Lone Hawk in gibberish with attempted intimidation.

"Speak, so we may understand you, foul Shaman!" Lone Hawk demanded, causing the stranger's immediate adaptation to the Warbird tongue.

"I, Spirit Slayer, command you, Hawk Demon, to release the woman and leave this valley! I have driven out <u>all</u> the 'tainted spirits' from before, and <u>now</u> I shall expel <u>you</u> as well!"

"Slayer of Spirits? Hah!" Lone Hawk scoffed at the gall-filled newcomer, then he spread his wings which had matured to a span of twice his current stature of three men. "See now, the future…have you <u>ever</u> driven away the likes of these?"

As Red Bear had joined them to 'case' the shaman, Lone Hawk suddenly tucked his wings to his back and turned to him, amidst a darkening sky. "Watch out behind you, Red Bear!" he warned in preparation for his most grand of impressions to which the startled brave turned his head and backed away, readying his spear. "No, they are <u>not</u> the Fire Lynx, but something far, far worse!"

Thus, by Lone Hawk's magical whim did hundreds of Owlmen appear in the clearing behind Red Bear. Strangely inhuman and willowy thin, they were reproduced just as he remembered them in their apparel of glowing silver-gray. While allowing their materialization to continue from the nowhere, even onto the shoreline, he then forced the invader's encroachment upon Black Moon from the east and Spirit Slayer from the west. Most petrifying to the three defenders, of course, were their hideous yet surreal faces. Ballooning from a pointed chin, their enormous cold, black eyes bugged out to them in paralyzing projection. And though they were but the height of an eight-year-old child, their fearless numbers, marching in an almost 'ready to float' gate, were indeed frightful as they formed a tight circle around them.

In dire respite, Red Bear tried to fend them off with his spear, but it was magically sucked out of his hands, as if he had no grip, to only disappear into the marauding assemblage. Thus, coming to a complete and abrupt 'all company' halt, one of the 'Owlmen' replicas released a luminous red, fist-sized ball that hovered above the three of them and released a deafening, high-pitched hum.

In the meantime, Lone Hawk had removed himself to view their reaction from the lake shallows while Black Moon voiced the torture that they all shared. "I <u>cannot</u> move, and that sound is stabbing my mind!" she screamed, wincing in pain as reflected by the others, gasping and groaning. "Make it stop, Lone Hawk! <u>Please</u>, make them vanish!"

The ball of persecution quickly returned to its keeper and the destructive noise ceased. However, they were still unable to move as the intruders swarmed about the helpless three, placing their bony four-digit hands all about their heads and bodies. They mercilessly roved, bringing them to their knees with countless ugly faces bombarding theirs. Then at their absolute threshold of fear, the nightmare suddenly faded into a bright light thus followed by complete darkness. A short moment later, the three of them rejoined Lone Hawk as they were before, with no sign of the inhuman presence but his own. While they were thankful to regain control of their bodies, their reactions were mixed and disturbed.

"What do you mean by this illusion of little hell beasts, and <u>why</u> did you allude to the Fire Lynx as intruders, preceding these?" Spirit Slayer asked in puzzlement, as he was about to reveal his unsavory lineage. "I was the Fire Lynx elder shaman of this Spirit Lake Valley for over thirty years before I died. You do not speak ill of the Fire Lynx—understood!"

Lone Hawk held Red Bear by the back of his neck, preventing an anticipated lunging toward the archenemy with his riled revenge. "Red Bear! Our 'war faces' are only to be worn for the Owlmen, those 'creepy' sky beasts of which I just gave you a sample. So, let the shaman explain himself…"

Black Moon erupted to his casual admittance to the torturous demonstration. "Explain himself? Explain yourself, you…sadist! Putting us through all that pain to entertain your drama! Lone Hawk, please be careful with your powers…they're making you cruel!"

"I am sorry…sorry to you all, but it was a necessary cruelty," he defended, releasing the re-tamed Red Bear who then stood cross-armed before Spirit Slayer. "For a quest of this magnitude, you must understand me and share my passion. There will be more, much more before we go. So, be prepared! Now, Spirit Slayer, these two were the last two chieftains of the Warbird tribe to rule this valley until the Fire Lynx took this land from them in a vicious siege. Had you a hand in this, or were you of the later settlement?"

Spirit Slayer scrunched his round weathered face to a maze of lines and shook his head. "The Warbirds were assimilated fifty years before I was born and, if it pleases these two, my mother's mother was Warbird," he added with no shame, rather vocalizing with soulful pride. "I lived to sixty-three as a well-respected man in the center of a strong nation. There is no more to it than that, and nothing else I care to tell. Peoples are always replaced by stronger ones, or are you so naive? Ultimately, all our people were subdued by the white plague, a pale-skinned race of people with an array of colored eyes and hair who have ruled this land in the physical present for a very long time…"

"Like Rainbow's wretched red-bearded grandfather, uh…never mind, please continue," Lone Hawk grumbled, interrupting and causing the shaman to pause and lose his train of thought.

"Ah, yes…now where was I?" Spirit Slayer said, tapping his own forehead then pointing to them, recomposed. "Oh, the physical present—is that your destination, Lone Hawk and former Warbird chieftains? If so, what is your purpose?" He cast an aura of confident sincerity that commanded respect. And so tongue-tied were Black Moon and Red Bear that their only response was to peer up to Lone Hawk in expectation.

From the lengthy pause and thoughtful stroking of his triple-peaked chin, they knew he was impressed by the shaman. "Yes, that's the plan, and we're going there for sure…however, not against the 'white plague' people but just the gray Owlmen…You are so wise, yet you do not see, my good shaman…" Lone Hawk felt it prudent to humble Spirit Slayer with reason rather than magic; "the momentum of change is in place. The final reality awaits our arrival, but there must be more participants in this sacred quest before we can proceed. Whatever your visions of this new world, I do not dispute. However, the hell beasts I call the Owlmen are very real and, if you were not aware of them before, I suspect that they have remained in a covert posture. For that, I am glad because now I know there is still time.

"You have stumbled upon destiny, Spirit Slayer," Lone Hawk went on. "I have come to believe that 'Earth Force' selection is in process and the three of you have been chosen by mystic valor. And you know of more recruits that are also worthy, I can tell…Warbirds? Yes, they are Warbirds. So, go ahead—retrieve them, shaman!"

Spirit Slayer walked back to whence he came, glaring at Lone Hawk, and was resentful because of his apparent ability to know his thoughts. "Your two cohorts will be pleased…I know of some that will suit your quest. I will bring them to you. But let it be said that, though I am intrigued, to be as physical as the living is quite impossible, even for one as great as you, Lone Hawk. However, I do not doubt that we can watch them like I have and, possibly through you, create some manipulation in the future. It'll be very interesting to see the extent to which your powers can pierce their reality…very interesting!"

Lone Hawk gleamed at Black Moon and Red Bear, but theirs was of a mutual despising towards his overbearing watchtower sights which viewed them with probing intrusion. As a result of his blatant violations, they began to think of Spirit Slayer, their common enemy of old, as more of an ally than he. And so, while the 'dominator of enormity' stood in waiting, the most unlikely pair began to converse, expressing their concerns.

"Red Bear, look at that," Black Moon whispered; "what was a man of special graces could now be a demon, using us for a very wicked deed…the <u>ultimate</u> unforgivable act of the dead tampering with the living world. We were <u>never</u> taught enough about evil. How are we to tell?" she continued whispering to Red Bear, who was even more careful as he pulled her close and spoke softly into her ear. "He can read our minds! So, if we are not 'carefully neutral,' he might punish us further. <u>Don't</u> underestimate his powers. Their growth within and without seem to know no end!"

Lone Hawk suddenly looked away from Spirit Slayer turned fetcher in the brush, and set his suspicious sights upon the teaming duo who reeked of conspiracy. "I <u>know</u> what you're thinking, you two, so I'll only tell you once: Don't you <u>dare</u> pollute the best movement for Earth and all of humanity with your paranoia. Everything's going as it should, and we are soon to be complete. When Spirit Slayer returns with the others, I will entertain you with the greatest show ever graced upon a human being, alive or dead. Afterwards, you will share my deep-rooted feelings so well that you will want this as much as I. Henceforth, there will be <u>no</u> secrets between us and <u>no</u> doubts about our cause. Yes! The sacred union of invincibility, we shall be to shatter the Owlmen' plan of earthly domination and, most fulfilling, to smother them out of existence!" He extended to them the brave-fist salute, and they obliged in fear.

After their knuckles rubbed when they dropped their hands, Black Moon and Red Bear quickly backed away from each other, put off by the coincidental contact. Though uncomfortable as it was, a far more awkward moment was yet to follow. There they stood on the beach, silently watching Lone Hawk flap his cherished wings and sporadically decorate the sky with clouds in the form of various animals. They shared a sense of not belonging with the mad behemoth, and thus, were afraid to talk to each other. They only prayed that Spirit Slayer would return as he told, yet even so short a time seemed an eternity.

Eventually, their apathetic frowns turned to unpretentious smiles when Spirit Slayer led eight big braves of conforming tanned war garb out of the woods to seal his promised delivery. The parade ended in a military formation before Lone Hawk. Then, despite the shaman's description of the sizable one for whom they were to serve, all were drop-jawed awe struck when setting their sights upon a hybrid being of such magnitude. They knelt in worship to his divine presence, extending double brave-fisted salutes to which he obliged, easily tapping them by his long-ranged arm with one knuckled sweep along the entire row. All the while, the unacknowledged Black Moon had taken the liberty of surveying the lot and though their faces launched her ancient recall into bloom, they could not share her familiarity.

"Badger, Thunderhead and Tornado Foot—I remember you! And these others…I used to know you, too," she referred to them, extending her hand in greeting, and yet they looked at her, unresponsive. "Well?" she continued, awaiting their response in flustered anticipation, but then began to understand their blank demeanor. "These are not <u>braves</u> of mind and wit! They're mere shells of the men they used to be."

"So true, Black Moon…their minds are still in a death-sleep haze, and so, they remember very little of the past," Spirit Slayer explained with a spiteful glare at the ever-changing Lone Hawk. "<u>These</u> braves are ideal for Lone Hawk's quest, as they will be <u>perfectly</u> impressionable for him to mold. All <u>they</u> know is that they have been summoned by the 'Great One' to prepare for the final battle. Defeated the last time, their warrior pride has been revived by hopeful redemption, nothing more…Besides, Lone Hawk's hands are full enough with the three of us, possessing our own minds…up until now, anyway."

"Indeed, our 'good' Spirit Slayer tells it like it is, for it is true," Lone Hawk revealed after a full evaluation with the most violating power of his mind-probe vision. "Their minds hold nearly nothing else, but that regretful, <u>embarrassing</u> 'Warbird's last stand' defeat and the <u>need</u> for a second chance. You know of them quite well, Red Bear. Please, tell us more."

"They were stationed at the north shore, a special unit called the Lynx Quellers," the pressured Red Bear explained to Lone Hawk's vocally well-deepened request while he looked to Black Moon for some 'supportive aura' effect. "From right to left, there's Tornado Foot, Bison Heart, Raging Wolf, Badger, Purple Sun, Thunderhead, Palm Fisher and Snow Blade. They were all braves who ascended the rank of warrior early in their careers. And they were the <u>best</u> in battle tactics and intelligence patrol. I would wager that these braves were the <u>last</u> of the Warbird's military to die by the Fire Lynx's deviled hand."

Smirking to the rehashing of the irreversible ancient past, Spirit Slayer rolled his eyes. Then noticing his descent, Lone Hawk took him aside, roughly, out of earshot from the others, and cautioned, "I do appreciate your contribution…but I warn you, dear shaman— do <u>not</u> spoil these ones!" he growled, face-to-close-face, forcing the humbled Spirit Slayer to peer into his repelling pupilless eye-portals, appearing as smoldering coals. Lone Hawk continued. "You have woven spells before, I'm sure. Well, I have evolved far past <u>that</u> lame trickery…for all they need to know awaits to fill the sky in 'the show of all shows' which I will now treat them. And as for you—watch! Even the rigidly proud shaman in yourself will become a believer." Then putting him back with the others like a game-board piece, Lone Hawk announced his welcome to them all: "I am <u>very</u> pleased and honored by the Earth Force to have finally summoned you, my chosen. We are now complete in number, yet sorely fragmented in spirit. Therefore, I offer my life's story for you to absorb, so that we may be truly complete. Please, recline and watch my adventure unfold for you. Inevitably, you will fully understand this most sacred of all missions."

The sky grew dark once again and the eight semi-conscious braves instantly lay where they stood, to Lone Hawk's right on the grass at the beach's edge. Black Moon and Spirit Slayer sat reluctantly on the sand, a fair distance to his left in silent protest, suspecting a painful session of mind cleansing. Of similar demeanor, Red Bear half-heartedly followed them. Yet, compromising his proximity, he lied down 'spread eagle' by himself, closer to Lone Hawk whose eyes projected two, bright white beams upon the lake. There they bounced off the water, combined and rose as one thick shaft of sparkling blue, yellow and red light that impacted the sky and painted some obscure imagery. Then to stimulate their audio sense, a loud crackle of thunder sounded off for the beginning, which was immediately followed by the desperate cries of an infant and a woman's voice, singing a lullaby. Soon, the crying subsided and was replaced by the sound of suckling while the top of a breast and an underneath view of a blurry maternal face became discernible. In the meantime, the visual range of his most impressive creation extended to the horizon of the Evermore and encapsulated their sights like a dome. Upon the effect's full development, the shaft of light dissipated and they began the journey, like that of the 'future's captive' Xavier Branion, of their ever-forceful leader's previous life, with his younger days presented in rapid-fire chronological scenes to save time.

From an elaborate spectacle of audio-video sensation no one of their era had ever witnessed, the recollections, emanating from the ancient eyes of the beholder, evolved to a 'stealing away' of the 'Evermore' braves' perceptions. Especially, when the journey to Big River City had begun, did they feel themselves a captive audience since, at that point, all of them were swept up into the view of absolute brilliance in color and depth. In effect, traveling along through the past was like the present as they were most convincingly at one with their host. His sensations of taste, touch and smell also were shared. Even erotic pleasures were felt in all their spiritual and primordial glory, which presented a clearly unique perspective for Black Moon. But it was not enough. As much as he wished to win them with so intimate an experience, Lone Hawk would soon learn upon its finale that, although the Earth Force and the Owlmen had become very real to his hopeful followers, their minds were still very much their own:

At the show's bitter end, they were spared the fall's fatal impact. However, even more disturbing was Lone Hawk's last eyeful of the smug-faced Stout Raven, tossing the Earth Force amulet with a subtle gleam of victory. Hanging in continuous replay, the dooming scene was sustained in taunting silence. Thoroughly entertained yet deeply moved to sorrow and pity, Black Moon was thankful when the hated shaman faded and the horrifying recap of his closing moments towards mortality were done. Alas, as the sky turned black, Lone Hawk bellowed with a chilling ferocity and faced them a much larger birdman, his blood-red eyes piercing and ablaze. They were completely stunned by his demonic majesty which stood before them like a feathered 'war beast' monument crowned with a dual-furnace bluff, keeper of the only light flooding the 'Evermore' earth in crimson.

The already enormous Lone Hawk had grown six-fold during his life's extraordinary sky show. And in tandem, his ego burgeoned to that of a god while he displayed the versatility of his expansive wings to excess. "It is time!" he barked in a low, rumbling military tone. "To the Warbird mound we shall now go to begin my glorious quest!" Intimidated, all of them, with the exception of Black Moon, meekly followed his huge hovering form to the mound. Untrusting toward the selfishly forceful attitude spewing from the monstrous Lone Hawk's unmoving mouth, she stood alone on the beach, her arms crossed in reticence. "Black Moon, why do you resist?" Lone Hawk grumbled from the distant mound, with the others huddled nearby. "You <u>must</u> know that I want you by my side, most of all!"

Fixed to her intentions, she remained defiant and shook her head with welling-wet eyes, sharply reflecting his red glare. "I <u>am</u> sorry, Lone Hawk, but I <u>cannot</u> go with you!" Black Moon shouted with a pained flutter in her voice. "Your life's end was truly tragic, and I feel bad for you. But I am <u>so</u> damned infuriated, huh—you fooled us!" Her shouts escalated to rasped screaming. "Why the <u>hell</u> did you bring us back from the dead, anyway? You do <u>not</u> need me…nor anyone else for 'your' self-serving quest that stinks more and more of a revenge that is none of our business. It seems the forces have twisted and torn you to madness and so, I believe you should go it alone…And if anything of righteousness remains in you, find your <u>precious</u> Earth Force sphere and make <u>it</u> serve you, without us, for 'your' sacred quest!"

Lone Hawk's response to her defection was one of primal anger with means of unknown limits at its disposal. Clenching his fists and flexing his rippling arms, abdominals and chest, the tips of his sabered wings pounded the ground with booming, tremulous vibrations while huge white sparks splattered from his eyes. "I do not need your pity and I certainly don't need your advice!" he roared, unaware that the others had started to creep away from him. "Look around you … I'm forcing the change, just as I promised. We are nearly there! So, come to me and I'll forgive your foolish stand … come!" True to his words, faint human images, growing ever more resolute, appeared on the beach, in the lake and near the mound.

At the same time, the surroundings began to change and re-arrange as boxy structures, rectangular smooth-lit clearings and replacement trees which were displaced into view. While two of the figures shone torches with straight bright beams shining around and about further down-shore, Lone Hawk was suddenly distracted as Black Moon crab-walked around to the other side of the mound. Seizing the moment of his preoccupation, she then waved the others over to the forest's edge in hopes of escape.

"Come back, you, ingrates!" the mighty master furiously demanded with the most gut-grinding yell of his vocal arsenal. "We have come much too far! You are 'in this' with me much too deep for abandonment!" Running into and through the wooded stretch, Lone Hawk's outburst only sealed their final stage as frightened rabbits spurned into a flight at the absolute height of desperation.

"Very well, you leave me no choice!" Upon his punctual fulfilling threat, Lone Hawk swept his hands and wing tips to his face and eased them back to behold his ravenous eyes. As a result, they could not continue forward and felt their feet dragging in reverse to his spontaneous, gravitational pull. Hugging the tree trunks proved a futile deterrent, as most of them were instantly ripped away into the wind tunnel of his volcanic eyes. Only Black Moon and Red Bear remained, clinging to adjacent trees with their bodies hanging in a flutter parallel to the ground.

"Black Moon!" Red Bear shouted over the imploding wind with an angst look of despair; "we cannot escape him … the others, I saw it! They were sucked into his eyes!"

Although squinting as they began to stretch into light fragments toward Lone Hawk, Black Moon was optimistic. "Don't worry, Red Bear," she reassured as they let go and were painlessly drawn to the disturbing place beyond the red walls of his cavernous, optical portals. "We are eternal and will be free of this beast soon enough!"

Then, having collected them all, Lone Hawk was pacified. He was void of their impudence and, therefore, at peace. Yet, it was more of solitude as they seemed to disappear without him. Faithfully, however, he figured that his forceful display of entrapment rendered them merely just begrudgingly silent and eventually they would forgive him. After all, it was only to prove that they were undeniably chosen and though he was too proud to admit, his actions were testament that he was deep-down painfully apprehensive. Thus, their companionship was essential.

Positioned with the bird mound to his backside, Lone Hawk fell onto it. Arms, wings and talons a spread, he was dimensionally lacking, but aligned himself as best he could. With only a sigh in satisfaction while he sunk, he allowed the earth of the mound to give him shallow cover as he submerged to re-emerge in bold fashion. The soil pressing atop his body, though cumbersome, brought about a sense of complete adulation. Unlike the Evermore, there was contact so solid and true—something of a challenge to push against and, ultimately, force aside and away.

The transition had come in its entirety, separated by only a few feet of dirt. "We have crossed over to the physical world, my friends, and we are <u>about</u> to surface in a blaze of glory as <u>never</u> seen before," he reassured with his prophecy's fulfillment, praying their forgiveness. "Please, don't be angry <u>too</u> long, because I <u>cannot</u> grant your freedom, if I forget you to stubborn silence…ah, I think a song would be in order to hail this miraculous return of the Warbirds!" As he lay beneath the grassy knoll formed roughly in his image, he allowed the pre-empting buildup to take hold with an old Warbird fight song. And though he had forgotten the exact lyrics, he recalled that they were, most appropriately, about their sacred hawk spirit's flight to battle. Thus, Lone Hawk hummed the melody imprinted in his mind, including a word or two, here and there. So inspired as he was, his mystic powers started surging and shrieking within him while his voice became louder and louder. His muscles fully flexed with explosive intent; the time had then come to officially puncture his way back yet foreword into the physical future realm. Innate to schedule, Lone Hawk knew he could hold out no longer. Henceforth, so automatically 'the unleashing' had begun.

CHAPTER X

The Devil's Code

WITH AN INDELIBLE HOLD on Xavier's fate through its projected orb lightened to a pinkish hue, the creature from the mound stooped to its talon-like foot spiked into the ground. There, with all its luminous focus still beaming, it so humanly stroked its beaked chin as if in deep thought. Meanwhile, time and action had stalled long enough for Jeff to act sensibly.

"This is Ranger Travis, ten-twenty Baraboo, extreme emergency at Devils Lake south shore!" he shouted into his smart phone with concise rapidity while the accidental spectators that fled behind the buildings, crept out with their phones recording. "Section two-five-four, back-slash-triple-zero, subject is still in full view! Maximum reinforcements and a medic airlift to Fenton U.W.H., immediately!"

With confirmation that full-scale government assistance was on the way, Xavier's fate went from bad to worse when he was lifted from the mud by the tractor-beamed cranial enclosure to where his body was dangling a couple yards off the ground. A torturous sight, the energy flowed through the convulsing body like a death-sentenced prisoner in an electric chair. Soon released from its grip, Xavier was then dropped to the muddied lawn as a shell of a man reduced to a near lifelessness.

Satisfied, the creature drew the mind-draining sphere back into its eyes, seeing its first directive through to completion. To follow, the mythical monstrosity most unexpectedly extended its half-clenched, black-clawed fist toward the unmoving Xavier and straight-arm saluted him with a gracious nod while mumbling something at a very low frequency. Then as the ritual was about to end, the honorable one raised its saluting fist to the sky and by an abrupt back-cocking motion swung open its chinned beak, partially dislocating its head from its stubby neck for a moment. And frightful as it was, behind its sliding sandstone mask, an orange-eyed hawk's face was revealed affront a lightening encased skull like a plasma ball. Thus, amidst the erupting sounds to rival the bursting Gates of Hell, the beast released a blasting roar of such intensity and so compiled a range that everyone felt as if their ears were bleeding from its 'earth shattering' announcement. After ten seconds of the vocal horror seeming an eternity, its sprawling gape closed with a forward head flip. Thus, back to relative silence, the scene had taken to a gravitating perusal by the entire, surprisingly bold audience, previously hiding nearby.

Aware of the feathered phenomenon's intent to depart, Jeff enacted his delayed show of heroism by firing three shots at the rising mass with his virgin pistol. With sneered annoyance, the so personified entity shook its head while wagging its finger at him but to no reproach. For then as Jeff had hoped, the towering birdman, thought to be anything but a 'man on a mission' behind its rough exterior, bolted off into the sky over the lake, veered off westward and out of sight. And while the entire episode consumed only a few minutes, it seemed a full-length sci-fi 'blockbuster' movie to the many witnesses clamoring to the ground's first hum.

Amidst the brutal aftermath, Jeff did what he could and performed CPR on Xavier who lay cold, unconscious and weak of pulse. "Just hang in there a <u>little</u> longer, man," he told him with hopes of acknowledgment while his heart raced to the stark reality of Xavier's life, hanging in the balance. "There'll be a chopper here <u>any</u> minute. Come on, Xavier, just stay alive—you've got this! Hey, people—back off! Goddamn it, get over to the parking lot! <u>Move!</u>" The crowd amassed around the two of them lingered with that 'sensationalism' glow a bit yet, reluctantly, dispersed to the parking lot when the sights and sounds of additional law enforcement were first detected, swinging around the bend on the lakeside road.

As witnesses to the most incredible supernatural spectacle ever bestowed upon human perception, they were quite respectful and cooperative, despite their fully adrenalized curiosity. And when the barrage of state, county and local police arrived soon flooding the area with their intimidating squad cars, the chattering crowd was rewarded with immediate detainment. Thankfully, though, during the dreaded sea of police formations, a white, red crossed medic helicopter came over the southwest ridge and shined its bright spotlight onto Xavier and Jeff, as it proceeded to land.

"All right, man, it's here!" Jeff reassured the dormant Xavier, barely clinging to life, "Got you a first-class airlift. You're gonna be just fine!" Then to the painful sight of the red, white and blue strobing lights with sirens blaring and civilians being corralled like cattle, Jeff felt very fortunate. For when the helicopter soon landed, it was to his rescue as well for mere sanity's sake, as he boarded so relieved behind the two paramedics loading the stretcher-bound Xavier.

While standard procedure would have him remain at the point of incident with the other law enforcers, he disregarded any such penalties and was glad to have escaped the mayhem. He was also aware that as a twenty-two-year-old forest ranger, they would treat him like the 'bottom of the food chain' with brutal interrogations. At least in the capital, he figured, there would be no dealings with rural, yahoo types who would push for a grass roots cover-up.

Within eight minutes, the due south flight brought them hovering down upon the roof of the University of Wisconsin's I. B. Fenton Memorial hospital in Madison. A twenty story, half city block structure of only two years since its unveiling, it was the state-of-the-art facility serving Wisconsin's burgeoning capital, rivaling Milwaukee, its most populous. Touted as one of the nation's best, Jeff was confident that Xavier's chances of survival were much better there than at the local emergency medical facility, which could very well have been the alternative if he had not specified.

"Damn! Escape one circus from hell, only to drop into another," Jeff commented with a depressed air, beholding the rivers of police cars and throngs of people below them on the streets around the building. "But then again, they probably heard that goddamn thing all the way from here! Anyway, word does get around mighty quick these days…yeah, right—cut the idle chatter…" Jeff drew not a word from the pilot, copilot or paramedics, with their blatant 'ignoring act' making him a bit paranoid as they landed on the hospital's roof.

Even though the purposeful silence was disturbing, he then tried to owe it to their professional efficiency which was quite admirable. For just after the landing, they toted Xavier, oxygen mask and all, out of the helicopter and through the large, one car garage-sized elevator door when he was barely off the craft. While he expected to accompany Xavier at least to the emergency room hallway, his start to the door beside the lift was delayed by another. There, emerging from the shadows, a tall, thin man in a dark gray suit presented his FBI badge with a halting gesture.

"Jeff Travis?" the ghostly man called while he approached with his white crewcut shining and his cold blue eyes piercing. "Agent Rutger, FBI … the Bureau sent me to discuss with you the incident at the state park. I understand that your mind must be consumed with concern for your partner. However, there is a 'big picture' aspect to which your government, my boss, has enacted a `delicate situation' sense of urgency." And while the 'intense Fed' shouted with searing facial intensity over the rhythmic cacophony of the idling helicopter nearby, Jeff began to suspect that orders to suppress the truth were soon to follow. "So, with that in mind … <u>sound</u> mind, that is," Agent Rutger continued, "what did you <u>actually</u> see up there, Jeff? What, to the <u>best</u> of your knowledge, caused such senseless destruction?"

"Well, if you really want the truth … here goes," the adrenaline-filled Jeff began in a heightened tone, presuming the agent's disbelief. "A mythical monstrosity, with feathers, claws and a red-eyed face of stone burst out of the bird mound, and took a <u>real</u> keen interest in Xavier with some kind of eye-contact, light-show thing. Then after taking care of business, it <u>screamed</u> like hell, took off into the sky and was out ta sight in <u>no</u> time! Crazy, huh?" he remarked with nervous laughter, and continued in his defense. "But, I'm not the only one … there were a <u>bunch</u> of other witnesses as you must undoubtedly know!"

"Jeff, I know that what you experienced over there has <u>your</u> mind <u>and</u> the others', swimming with some wild, supernatural explanations since the truth is <u>always</u> so mundane … who wants to be a part of that?" Rutger thwarted the ludicrous account, raising his voice into Jeff's ear, keeping the discussion outside, amidst the unbearable noise to maintain a 'confidential' environment. "Now, for continuity's sake, we will have to get your story straight…I mean, since the media will be crawling down your throat as soon as we get to ground level.

"Quite simply, there was an explosion that seriously wounded Mr. Branion and then, an incredible 'giant birdman' hologram appeared in the aftermath. Following some odd motions and outrageous sound effects, the image was simply projected into the sky, hither and beyond. Finally, to sum up the unfortunate episode, you will say that you believe it was an elaborately cruel hoax.…Oh, and don't forget to mention that you've seen similar holograms at rock concerts, so convincingly real yet certainly identifiable with the discerning eye. So, do we have an understanding?" Hand to forehead, Jeff simmered in his quandary while Agent Rutger held a glare of intimidation, awaiting the expected vote of confidence.

"That sure as hell was no hologram, Agent Rutger!" he lashed out, mildly defiant. "It was like a god…nothing this world has ever seen! But I understand the necessity for an initial cover up, national security and all. Okay, yes indeed, we do have an understanding. I will comply to your flimsy fabrication. Shit! I'll say anything you want, but I'm telling you right now that creature's far beyond our control, technology-wise or whatever we can dish out. I felt like a spitting insect when I was shootin' my gun at its majesty, just looking down and scolding me with a finger-waggin'. My God! And the way it yelled before that—goddamn scared me more than anything in my life!"

Worried about his enthusiastic insistence of a depiction dangerously contrary to what he was supposed to say, Agent Rutger tempered the madness. "Come on now, Jeff," he warned, with a firm hand around the back of his neck, guiding him through the door beside the freight lift of Xavier's transported entry; "get a grip! There'll be plenty of time for that kind of talk after your public statement. In the meantime, clear your mind and think double H, hologram and hoax, and feel it with all your sincerity." Agent Rutger released his demeaning hand from Jeff's neck, yet once his captive began to stray toward the elevators at the end of the short hallway, he reinforced his authority by lassoing him once again. "No! The stairway," he commanded in a loud whisper, redirecting his puppet to the manual door. "It'll be <u>much</u> less conspicuous while you put in a little rehearsal time."

Descending the twenty flights of stairs to the first floor, Jeff, with little choice, dashed all pride to the temporary brainwash which pleased Agent Rutger to the point of a smile. His 'proposed' lines for the charade were polished and gained the full approval of the Bureau's prescribed intimidator. And so, upon reaching the ground floor to which they stepped out of the stairway virtually unnoticed, he was psyched for the role yet anxious to be free of the travesty, if only just to rid himself of the unrelenting agent.

As they strutted abreast down the cathedral-ceiling hallway with marble walls, they passed by one of a popular chain of 'tortured life' relievers, the Kevorkian Suicide Outlet, which had recently expanded its service to the self-determined 'psychologically terminal' clients. Peering into the left side entry, there was a waiting room of a dozen clients, surprisingly of young and middle age. Looking reasonably healthy, they nonetheless glared with pained apathy from the doorway, and so the sadness was further fueled.

"Think they know something we don't?" Agent Rutger laughed somewhat ferociously while he waved to a pack of policemen by the main entryway in the lobby before them. "Oh, now wasn't <u>that</u> a counter-productive sight—hah! Well, just don't let 'em bring you down `cause you're goin' out there pretty soon, my good boy." Jeff was beginning to detest Agent Rutger to the pit of his churning stomach, but managed to ignore his cruel sentiments when he noticed the media overflow being held at bay outside the main doors. Though in relative tranquility, the spacious lobby near the mobbed entry held large ceiling-suspended TVs with dual, back-to-back panoramic screens which brought the current activities at the Devils Lake disaster site to life. There, along with several older civilians and the guarding officers, they stopped briefly for an update.

"As you can see, the bird mound at Devils Lake's south shore has been incredibly uprooted and transformed into a bird trench!"

the male reporter excitedly explained with a bird's eye view from the copter-cam's transmitted visuals. "Whatever caused such peculiar damage to this ancient Native American burial site is not yet known; however, at least one injury has resulted, apparently, by the scattering debris of the explosion. This fact, we can tell you because of a medic airlift that was observed by a reliable source, leaving the valley due south. Oh, and it seems you guys are ahead of me on this as the alleged victim has reportedly been delivered to I. B. Fenton Memorial in downtown Madison. Meantime, we'll try to go down there for some first-hand witness accounts…if, that is, those cops will allow—oh hell!" As he paused with sudden dread, the copter-cam switched to a lateral sky's view over the lake, spotting two Army helicopters. They closed in with menacing posture and search lights aglare. Then, soon to follow, an official warning was administered.

"This is a restricted area!" the loudspeaker from one of the choppers blared. "A military investigation is in progress. Leave state park airspace immediately or be grounded and detained!"

While the drama had heightened, the newsman was obviously shaken yet retained an air of levity. "I think you heard that, Collin. Our great democracy is repressing the press. So, we'd better get out ta here before they shoot us out of the sky! Reporting live over Devils Lake State Park, this is Scott James. Back to you, Collin— and not a moment too soon!" His speech sped to rapid closure, abruptly ending the transmission to be replaced by Collin Kemp, a generic, gray-haired anchorman of aged Anglo vintage in his newsroom set.

"Thanks Scott…Wow! He's sure not going to forget that assignment!" Kemp exclaimed with a wide-eyed media glow. "Now, let's go to U. of W.'s I. B. Fenton Memorial where Amanda Broderick is awaiting word on the afflicted park ranger who was just recently airlifted to the roof of the building." When the very attractive blonde newswoman, physically only a hundred feet away from them, appeared on the screen in a suffocating sea of reporters, Agent Rutger backhanded Jeff on the shoulder.

"That's your cue, kid," he coaxed, forcefully pushing him toward the automated sliding door to a second set of manual standard and revolving doors where the police granted him passage. Then as if he were going on stage for his drama debut, Agent Rutger gave him some last-minute pointers: "Go to her, downplay and diffuse … I'll be nearby." His closing words in a 'creepy' whispered rasp were more than sufficient to repel him toward a dutiful spiel, weaving into the scavenging pit of reporters.

Recognized by his earth-tone ranger's uniform, there was a 'first impression' of mistaken identity of which he was not aware until he managed to single Amanda Broderick out of the dizzying multitudes. With obvious favor toward her to do the questioning, Jeff knew his mind was near 'maximum overload' when even his libido was off its game before the lusty, blonde and blue-eyed bombshell.

Thus, thwarting the other reporters, the aggressive woman seized the interview. "Miraculously, our star witness has been released here from Fenton Memorial and looks 'perfectly' healthy after surviving what escaped witnesses, seeking anonymity, referred to as laser bombardment by a giant demon," she described, clearly and concisely, while clipping a tiny microphone to his collar. "Okay, sir, could you tell us, according to your experience, whether there is any credence to these anonymous reports? Was there a creature? Were you attacked? And, if so, what of your amazing recovery?"

Watching his puppeteer nodding impatiently from the distant hospital entrance platform, Jeff replied with confidence in his tone. "I understand the confusion, but I am not the man who was injured, Amanda," he said, steely lawman composure intact. "However, I was there to help rescue Ranger Branion … now just for the record, I'm his park enforcer co-worker, Jeff Travis, and I want to clear up any misconceptions about this heinous crime. First of all, the creature you're referring to was most certainly no more than an elaborate hologram, just like I've seen at many rock concerts. However, the only difference with the incident at the park was that this one was preceded by a very real explosion that nearly killed my associate while he was bravely investigating the situation."

Using the story as an emotional outlet, Jeff then built up his act to an eye-watering of angered sorrow and finished like he was seeking an academy award. "Whoever … and wherever you are! Techno-terrorist, hoaxing vile scum as you are … we're going to find you! And, by God—you're gonna pay! Here, and <u>then</u> in hell! I've got <u>nothing</u> more to say." Following his excessively dramatic dissertation, Jeff stormed into the refuge of the hospital, the police allowing his entrance while forbidding the press. Yet there, he was regretfully reminded of his keeper who had just slipped inside before him and stood in the lobby by the same TV-viewing area, swinging his head to beckon him over.

Meantime, the coverage continued before them, featuring Amanda Broderick's last thoughts and some surprising developments. "Well, you heard it, and you can judge for yourself," she closed, swelling with suspicion. "The park ranger, Jeff Travis, vigorously claims that a fantastic hologram with no means of support and an explosion with no apparent motivation are to explain this extraordinary 'Devils Lake' event. Is he in denial? Or was he put up to this by the powers that be? Whatever the case, our US Army has issued a hush-hush investigation at the state park and the only viably new information we have here is Mister Branion, the last name, anyway, of the wounded man. I'm sure we'll have a full ID on him shortly," Broderick looks at her phone, nodding with widening eyes to a new development from above.

"Oh, looks like we have some activity on the roof, Collin. The original helicopter has departed and there's another one, dark in color and possibly military, that has landed … and yet another? Hey, that's ours! Scott, you got the scoop! Amanda out."

With a well-timed hustle from the state park to the state capital, they intercepted the Air Force's clumsy relay where Scott James felt vindicated by their findings. "<u>Just</u> in the nick of time—yes! For everyone to see, they are transferring the stretchered Ranger Branion onto the Air Force chopper," he described the scene up top, victorious, well-defying government secrecy while broadcasting from the media's dominion where too many witnesses were already observing from the streets below. "Well, they've loaded him and there they go! They're bolting southbound like a bat out of hell and there's <u>no</u> way we can keep up with that! We <u>could</u> alert our sister station in Rockford, but the wile military will probably change course anyway. Well, I think it's <u>more</u> than obvious that they don't want this guy in a civilian hospital, Collin. Any comments?"

Jeff was beside himself in anger to the unwarranted passing of the human torch as he anticipated Xavier's doom. "What the <u>hell</u> are they doing, movin' him out of the <u>best</u> hospital in the country at a time like this? He's a <u>dead</u> man!" he shouted and stomped, attracting attention as Agent Rutger grimaced with embarrassment to the outburst. "They're <u>so</u> paranoid about this, they would just as soon sacrifice his <u>life</u> in the process. Now, they're gonna cover up the <u>whole</u> thing and say he was already dead!"

"Don't worry," Agent Rutger told the alerted police, who came to assist as he escorted Jeff out of the lobby. "He's just a little hysterical and considering…well, I think he's entitled. So, we're going for a walk and when we return, I want to see a neutral channel on that screen." The officers agreed, and ordered the news program to cease while Jeff was led into the stairway, whence they came.

"Don't blow your cover, <u>damn</u> it! Even though you were a little too emotional and unadvisedly revealed his identity out there, you did all right," he scolded while guiding him up the stairs for mere diversion. "Thankfully, my work is nearly through and <u>you're</u> going to keep a lid on it until 'my relief' arrives. Now, can you just behave in the lobby for the rest of my shift, <u>or</u> do I have to lock you up?" Jeff nodded in succumbing yet again to his threatening demands when the seasoned agent carrying on during their ascent then touted a slight scent of bourbon. "Don't be naive, Jeff. You <u>damn</u> well know that Branion is 'Citizen Number One'. His fourth level close encounter is already too widely publicized for comfort, and the government has responded to learn as much as they can to moderate the situation. And I <u>guarantee</u> that they wouldn't go through 'all' this for a corpse, or to render him so…

"Though I must say, Jeff—you were an excellent distraction as you cast some doubt, no matter how ludicrous. Even when the press is <u>too</u> good like that, it all balances out. I commend you. Here—take a little edge off and be a 'good' soldier." He handed Jeff a flask that looked like binoculars, and thus he partook in a generous sip of the high proof bourbon whiskey which brought to mind a brilliant request.

Amidst the numbing crisis, his memory drew a familiar face of past fancy worn by one also of case value, so he would take advantage of her so as not to endure the situation alone. "Thanks, I needed that. By the way, can I make a call? That is, under your <u>strict</u> supervision, of course," he asked with pleading eyes during their turn-about descent from the twelfth flight of their climb. "She's an ex-girlfriend-fiancée of Xavier's. They were really tight for like three years, but then after 'the breakup,' I unsuccessfully tried for the leftovers. So anyway, I still have her number in my phone and even though I put her off a bit, she's <u>definitely</u> the type that would be there, no question, in a time of crisis. I <u>bet</u> you'd like to talk background check with her before the press does…<u>am</u> I right?"

Stroking his chin, Agent Rutger expressed both admiration and intrigue. "Not only do you want to share the misery and take another stab at her 'charity', but you're going for extra credit ta boot," he congratulated, cracking a bedeviled grin while they turned back a couple floors up only to return to the ground floor. "I'm beginning to think that <u>you</u> could be one of <u>us</u>! And considering your acting ability—by all means! All right! But remember, if you get hold of her…get a feel for how much she knows and take it from there. Just be all the worm you can be and lure her over here." They proceeded out of the stairway and back into the lobby. The atmosphere had mellowed outside the building, but the police were still lingering about as Jeff pulled his phone out of its holster, tapped her saved number and instantly contacted her voice mail, meaning her phone was turned off.

"Damn, her <u>phone's</u> not even on! Jeanine, please pick up—what am I doing?" he pleaded in panicked desperation, then realizing he could only leave a message while her 'fine' Mediterranean face complimented the recorded greeting on display. "This is Jeff Travis calling about a serious accident concerning Xavier…Hello?" He tried three-more-times before Agent Rutger's impatient stare. Then finally, as he was about to give up, she answered 'live' after hearing his message.

"Jeff? Hey, long time no talky," she said, sounding a bit tipsy. "I just saw a <u>really</u> cool band at Spiders, but anyway, I just got in the door and turned on my phone, but your message was too distorted…so, what's up?"

"Jeanine! God, am I glad you finally answered!" he responded in joyous relief while he obliged Agent Rutger with a thumbs-up gesture. "Well, I'm downtown at Fenton Memorial because, there was an accident and Xavier was hurt really bad. I didn't know who else to call. He's been <u>such</u> a loner since your breakup—and <u>now</u> this! The guy's hit rock bottom and if you could just find it in your heart to get yourself over here…Jeanine, I'm beggin' ya, <u>please</u>!"

With a few seconds pause, she hesitated then fell for his charade. "It goes against my better judgment, but I'll <u>never</u> get to sleep tonight unless I know he's all right," she reasoned with an uncharacteristic coolness. "So, I'm leaving now. Be there in about ten minutes…" While he beamed to the good luck of reaching her, uninformed of the recent events, Jeff felt a little guilty in his vague deception.

"That was superb, Jeff—<u>Excellent</u>!" Agent Rutger commended with a forceful pat on the back. "The timing was impeccable; you led on to nothing and she's ignorant to everything. Now, assuming she gets here…you will have baited a bonus witness and <u>that</u> counts for something, I assure you. So, what's her last name? I've got to put in a little report here."

"Vercelli, Jeanine Vercelli," Jeff answered, curiously watching the agent tap away on a 2"-by-3" screen, computer-wristband with his pinky, which had been hiding under his sleeve. "Please, try to go easy on 'er. She's a <u>really</u> cool chick, and I already feel bad enough."

"This is no time to develop a conscience, Jeff. You're on a roll!" he advised with reptilian warmth while they drifted back to the lobby where the TVs were then showing a nature program about Australian wildlife. "Anyhow, you and Miss Vercelli will be talking to some agents more qualified for such interviews than myself. Until that time, which'll be <u>very</u> soon, my only responsibility is to keep you here and procure a smooth transition. But don't worry…they're <u>not</u> going to sit her in a dark room, floodlight to face and hit 'er with torturous, rapid-fire questions. So, settle down, man! When she gets here, just tell her I, the <u>mean</u> FBI guy, put ya up to it. That'll get you off the hook!"

After fifteen long minutes during which Agent Rutger made a few brief phone calls, Jeff spotted Jeanine's petite figure in a blue jean vest, white shorts and tennis shoes approaching from across the street. Since the traffic had thinned and the media had mostly dispersed, she came to the doors unobstructed by the few police who remained. Before she entered the hospital's lobby, Jeff stopped her in the exterior entry as she peered up to him with trusting eyes through the draped locks of thick, long chestnut hair. Sweeping her mane away from her face, she greeted him with a stiff hug while Agent Rutger began his intercept course from where he was phoning, towards them like a wide-eyed predator.

"The guy comin' to the door's FBI," he whispered after planting a kiss on her unexpecting lips and cheek, which made her face tense up. "They want to talk to us about Xavier. He's in <u>serious</u> trouble. I mean 'world league' stuff!"

She pushed him away with an unforgiving glare. "What the <u>hell</u> did you drag me into!" she blurted in a strong tone as Agent Rutger came to them, opening the automatic door. "I thought he was in a car crash! What's this all about, Agent?"

"Rutger is the name and <u>you</u> must be Jeanine Vercelli, the 'former' main squeeze," he joked, joining them like a gracious cold front with an inviting wave of his hand. "Well, young lady…you obviously aren't much for monitoring the news in the middle of the night, are you? Fortunately, though, <u>this</u> young patriot here has made it possible for you to not be just enlightened, but to help your country as well. Ah, and the timing <u>couldn't</u> be better. Here comes the 'relief team' who will certainly appreciate <u>any</u> information you may have on Xavier. Considering the duration of your romance, Miss Vercelli, <u>you</u> should have a warehouse full!" Jeanine was shocked to silence as she began to feel nauseous from his demeaning attitude and the intimidating arrival of a black Cadillac limousine at the curb behind her.

Emerging from the vehicle, two dark-haired white men and a black woman, all of early middle age, responded to Agent Rutger's sign language from the opened door with robotic nods of understanding. As he played host to the suited briefcase-toting newcomers, the proud agent guided them to the elevator enroute to a third-floor conference room. "This is our 'special guest' character witness, Jeanine Vercelli," he said after the elevator doors of their entry had closed. "Apparently, there's a mystery gap of time between the end of their relationship and the incident. But I'm

<u>sure</u> your speculations will get a boost in the right direction from her personal accounts. Okay, it's right around the corner here to the left, three-thirteen." The reserved room was rather intimate, consisting only of a typical oak conference table for eight and the usual video-audio, VR and communication gadgetry.

"All right, you seem well-situated," Agent Rutger happily assessed, starting toward the door while the other three agents already had set up an elaborate network of scrambled communique channeling. "Jeff, Jeanine—thank you for your cooperation and good luck." Immediately following his eager exit, one of the men also left the room to stand guard outside the door.

"Miss Vercelli, I understand that you are not aware of the recent events concerning Xavier Branion, your former fiancée and long-term companion," the woman stated to Jeanine who quietly sat across from them, shaking her head and swallowing with sounds like she was about to choke. "He <u>is</u> alive yet comatose, and is currently in transport to a 'government' medical facility for the proper care. This resulted from an explosion and an encounter at Devils Lake State Park. I believe it's only fair that Mister Travis describes for you the details, since he's 'the main' firsthand witness."

Thus, put at relative ease, Jeff was able to deliver a detailed account of the tragedy in his own words and though Jeanine shed some tears, she did not seem convinced. Afterward, detailed questioning of the past embroiled her and coaxed memories that painted Xavier as a rather odd character, prompting Jeff to realize how little he knew the man. And, though he had little to contribute beyond his surface behavior, he remained with her for the grueling duration of four hours. By session's end, they were released at the crack of dawn, subjects of 'loose' monitoring that would allow a considerable oversight.

CHAPTER XI
Xavier & the Sphere Quest

ENTERING THE MODERN WORLD as a spectacle of terror and fascination, Lone Hawk felt initially awkward and confused yet rapidly adapted to the wonderful starkness of physicality. Then freed from the ancient effigy's compression, the Earth Force's wayward son ecstatically shook the solid earth of the Warbird mound from his colossal form. Euphorically peering over the treetops, he was then caught in a delightful whirlwind of sensations. The sweet smell of summer foliage, a soft warm breeze off the lake and the moonlit, star-filled sky seemed to welcome him back from his near eternal nightmare with honor.

Soon after his brief 'appreciation for nature' spell upon arrival, Lone Hawk sharpened his awareness to an alert and focused survey of the people stirring below him. Stooping down for a closer look, all but two scurried away in mouse-sized scale to gawk from a distance. Helplessly before him, however, lay one of the two men in modern day war garb while the other shone a hand-held beam of light onto his face. The grounded man, frozen in fear, brought about to him the unpleasant realization that acceptance by the new age humans would be far more difficult than he imagined. He was indeed a huge, frightening creature in their eyes and must have appeared a global threat.

Intuitively though, Lone Hawk knew that he could not effectively proceed in this relative future, unless he learned of it through an instant form of interaction. 'The eyes,' he thought while sharing an intense stare with the immobile man; 'the master shaman's doorway to the mind and soul!'

As the notion lingered, he projected its perceived objective toward the subject, with the desire to know all. In doing so, Lone Hawk locked a round trip mind-sweep between them through a sustained bright tractor wave that managed to probe and collect its total worth, while donating his own life's experience in compensation. Unfortunately, though it was vital for the mission's success, the sight of the motionless man being violently lifted and dropped in the process filled him with thieving guilt.

Hopeful as he was that the modern one would soon recover from the ordeal, Lone Hawk feared that his chances of survival were very slim. Therefore, he saluted him with a hearty, straight-right brave fist and a solemn bow of his head. He was ever grateful for the new age warrior's sacrifice toward the sacred quest and vowed to reward him, alive or dead.

Thankfully fueled with invaluable insight, Lone Hawk released a most robust, all-encompassing yell of dedication, proclamation and warning. The great conqueror of death and future destroyer of the Owlmen had arrived, and all-too-well equipped for the task. Though his intentions would be open to a wide range of speculation, he reveled in the fact his greatness was finally known. And to further fuel his self-assessment of invincibility, the other enforcer fired projectiles at him with a small hand-held weapon and, though hot and amazingly swift, they caused him not even the slightest sting of pain. Initially perturbed by the gall of the tiny one, the futile attack was soon perceived with mild amusement. Shaking his head and wagging his finger at him, Lone Hawk giggled and launched himself effortlessly into the westward sky. When he soared over the nearby bluffs that had comfortably lost their majesty of old, Lone Hawk was reminded of his fatal attempt at flight. 'I was surely a fool in my mortal innocence,' he pondered and compared; 'and now as the all-powerful sage, my resurrection must be relished!'

By immeasurable telekinetic force, his mind propelled him through the air with seemingly no resistance, leaving him to believe that his massive saber-feathered wings were mostly ornamental.

Such was the observation, it naturally led to further curiosity about his entire appearance. Just as he wished, his ghastly image was manifested from the last perceptions of Xavier's captive mind. Initially appalled by the sight of the huge and grotesque fusion to which he had evolved, Lone Hawk soon convinced himself that his semblance was rather regal and powerful, just as a god should be.

And so, while he intentionally cruised at a low altitude over sparsely lit terrain, he spotted the Wisconsin River, formerly the Wise Crow, just moments after leaving 'ground zero' and followed its southwest course. During the momentarily uneventful leg of his journey, Lone Hawk began his analysis of the identity, thoughts and experiences of the 'future era' man to join and enhance his own. Though scattered, he found a wealth of information which was systematically generated and organized chronologically, as he relived an extraordinary twenty-two years of a very intense and recently troubled individual.

Born in Toronto, Ontario Canada a May baby, Xavier James was the second of Michael and Brigette Branon's' three children. While they were predominantly of French and English descent, Xavier's father was also of Iroquois ancestry which in southeastern Canada, was not so uncommon among the white population. Yet in the future, the young Xavier would owe it to his stubborn uniqueness.

As a couple, his parents were quite opposite in both personality and appearance. His mother was artistic and outgoing while his father, though very stable, seemed most times an introverted curmudgeon who was all too analytical. At six-foot-two, he dwarfed his mate by a foot, and had a stocky frame as opposed to her petite figure. Even their hair and eyes, his curly black with brown and hers, straight blonde with blue, solidified an obvious case of 'opposites' attraction.

Fortunately, in their wide range of differences they found flexibility and strength, supplying a stable and loving childhood for Xavier and his two siblings, Steven, three years his senior, and Michelle, five years younger than he. Even though random scuffles and mischief were commonplace in the Branion household, none was too severe due to the intimidating aura of his father. Thus, the fear of his wrath kept them in check and never needed a demonstration.

It was not until his tenth birthday that he would be challenged by a major blow to his complacency. His father, a chemical engineer in a very ungratifying position at a Toronto-based plastics research center, through his calm and calculated persistence landed a rather prestigious job as manager of his own department, specializing in aerospace plastics. And though the opportunity doubled his salary, it meant relocating to the Chicago area, a comparably dirty and dangerous metropolis of poverty and crimewaves spreading like cancer. Fortunately, the Branions would be well isolated from such elements since the move meant their graduation to a higher status. Thus, the perfect house at an affordable price was available in a fairly posh north shore suburb, so they jumped on it and moved in. For Xavier, however, a chronic propensity toward brooding had only just begun as they situated themselves in their beautiful new home.

His connections with his old 'Toronto friends' eroded in only two years. And through only a mediocre showing in the elite public middle-school of his uppity community, Xavier adapted to the environment with hidden reservations. He was cynical yet polite and consciously bold, yet shy. His roundabout demeanor could evoke admiration, confrontation or even pity, given his mood. Hence, he was labeled a 'misfit' underachiever by 'the overlords,' his reference to authority figures. Given the situation, enrollment into a strict disciplinarian high school was highly recommended and implemented.

Caught off guard and arranged against his will, Xavier's second year of teen-hood traveled a path to a Catholic college preparatory school which resulted in a most contemptuous phase, due to his parents' forceful decision. His thoughts grew hostile toward them and the whole of Catholicism, the very faith to which he was indoctrinated by a baptismal ritual of water and words. As a result, he suppressed rebellious temptation and accommodated his parents' wishes, even though his attitude of 'I'll go, but I won't like it!' prevailed at the time.

To his surprise while it seemed to him that his contempt would never cease, he found sanctuary and forgiveness when he discovered the sports curriculum in which he flourished. While inspiring physical fitness and teamwork, the program also aided the demands of college and professional sports. Thus, the controversial additive to academic credit was upheld, because the pool of quality athletes was dwindling as were the fans in direct proportion. Knowing his classroom work likely could not rate better than his nominal interests, Xavier relied very heavily on the sports program to compensate for what he thought he lacked.

His advantage of early physical maturity, six feet tall and stoutly built at only fourteen years of age, drew some attention. So, with the encouragement of his physical education instructor, Xavier joined the football team as a running back. As the youngest member, he was treated quite poorly at first. But when he began to break tackles through the defensive line on the field of play, respect soon followed.

Xavier saw limited action during his first season, only playing in six games, four of which they lost. Hence, he attributed his lackluster performance to his clumsiness and untimely spontaneity. To quell the shortcomings of the raw nature that he was, karate and martial arts filled the void. Discipline and grace were then added to the mix of his improving overall being, spurring his life toward a positive light.

While the ancient East Asian techniques improved his mind and body control, his studies excelled proportionately from an unimpressive 'three' to a very good 'four-point-five' of a possible 'five' grade-point-average in his third year. Most importantly, as was his main goal, his confidence and agility were especially enhanced on the football field. By his senior and final year of high school, all was glory with the discovery of his accurate and exceptionally powerful throwing arm. Combined with his six-foot-three-inch muscular stature and running back experience, Xavier's talents provided a double threat against woeful defenses that usually struggled, chasing or trying to block the ball in vain. He developed into a true leader as the 'highlight quarterback' of multiple ability and so, brought the team to the state finals. And while they were crushed by a talent-packed East St. Louis club, thirty-eight to seventeen, he was still aggressively pursued for college play.

After high school and a summer working as a martial arts instructor, Xavier started his college education and recreation at the University of Wisconsin in Madison on a sports scholarship. He was hired to back up the well-established star quarterback for the Badgers, among the top ten teams in the college league. Even though his studies had slumped with the demands of football during the first semester of his senior year, his high $KRCQ$, Knowledge, Relations and Communications Quotient of nine-hundred-thirty of a thousand made him a worthy draft choice.

Focusing on his NFL dream, Xavier then had no serious plans for an alternative career. In turn, Xavier, a natural jock on the apparent rise, settled for the curriculum commonly chosen by those unsure of their 'real job' future—political science. At the time living in the crowded dormitory, he found his classes to be of minimal challenge and sat on hold merely a bench warmer for the team. Seeing no action on the football field, he languished until that fateful Saturday afternoon in late October, when the starting quarterback was brutally sandwiched by three defenders, suffering a major concussion and dislocated shoulder. Midway through the game, Xavier was then given the nod and made his debut a 'come from behind' victory with two touchdown passes and one he ran in himself from sixteen yards.

His stellar performance which was broadcast on the Sports Vision Network, made him a minor celebrity. And when he won five more of seven games, he earned hero status. Enjoying the spoils, women flocked to him and his reputation as a stud became renowned. At that point, the 'so full of himself' Xavier was sure that he would be the hottest contender in the National Football League's Spring Draft, and thus he began to consider his academics a pure waste of time.

Brimming with confidence, his plans were not far from reality until a linebacker from Nebraska State University barreled into his knee over his planted left foot. Tearing the inside ligaments and severely damaging the surrounding cartilage, Xavier never fully recovered from the extensive surgery; hence, attaining his ultimate goal was shattered. No longer could he dream with any seriousness of being a Super Bowl quarterback in the NFL.

His claim to fame had ended 'that' Thanksgiving weekend and meant a promising career in the pros was an impossibility to say nothing of the sudden anonymity. He gambled on a 'story book' occupation and lost it all. Apathetic, discouraged and basically depressed by his physical downfall and lack of a bright future, Xavier began to drink whiskey, wine and beer quite heavily. On his crutches, he often went to his classes drunk and started cynical arguments with the teachers and other students whenever the opportunity arose. He was bitter and unapproachable during his two-month alcohol binge. However, in early February after the Super Bowl, he vowed to change.

Though he did not quit completely, Xavier curtailed his consumption of the spirits considerably. With a sober mind and the distractions of glory far behind, he re-established core relationships, family and friends he so selfishly alienated atop his fragile pedestal. In his humble attempt to mend broken ties, only one responded with any impact; his former good friend, Greg Shannon who used to play on the offensive line for his tremendous high school, senior year season. Carefree and forgiving, Greg picked up on his call in a very big, impulsive way. Besides a sense of loyalty to his old captain, he was itching for a change of scenery and promptly quit a lucrative yet dull manager's job at his father's warehouse in Chicago to be enrolled at U of W on a delay-modified curriculum.

Sporting the latest Mercedes Benz roadster, Greg pulled into the driveway of his American colonial, two-story house right behind the moving truck. Via his rich father, everything was paid for. And so, with more than adequate space, Xavier was offered residency in the stately abode, rent-free. Right outside Madison's south belt, the location was perfect for being near, though not in, the trendy loop. However, there was one problem with the deal and that was Greg's obsession with being popular. He had to provide the most party-friendly house in the city or he would feel like a failure. Therefore, he would in no way be an underachiever in that category, thus, 'parties ruled!'.

The festivities seemed to never cease. Drunken, drugged and passed out strangers were ever-present like old furniture, but Xavier did not complain. With nothing asked of him in place of rent, he volunteered his services, cleaning up and tossing undesirables out the door. He was the key to 'functional' in a mayhem environment. The parties rolled on, but never too overboard when he was around. And while he met and slept with many of the women who came to the house, only one merited long-term interest:

The lovely Jeanine Vercelli, a 'Boston girl' of Florentine Italian heritage, stirred his fancy like none before. With her beautiful classic features, big golden-brown eyes and contagious optimism, Xavier was hooked. Her strange mix of accommodating ways and a headstrong, independent attitude was initially confusing and uncomfortable. However, he soon adjusted to her with surprising ease, thus allowing them to fall in love. Interchangeably, they spent the major holidays with her family in Boston and his near Chicago. Their parents whole-heartedly approved of their mates and hoped that they would eventually marry. After three years of dating bliss, they met their expectations and were engaged. Yet, with mutually arranged curriculums in their favorite subject, psychology, a regrettable 'test case' field trial would be played out in a 'meltdown scenario' that ended a wonderful relationship.

One tragically unforgettable, late spring evening just before their passing as undergraduates, Xavier and Jeanine came back to the house from a concert at the university. Upon their return, an ambulance and two-police cars awaited the stretcher holding a zip-bag-covered overdose victim of fentanyl-laced heroin. There before his welling eyes, Xavier's good, most generous and suddenly dead friend, Greg, was then loaded into the ambulance.

After Xavier went over and learned the nature of his death from the police, he came back and told Jeanine about it. Expecting sympathy, her crass response sent him over the edge in a psychological upheaval that unleashed itself with a fury. "God, I knew he was a total alcoholic, but didn't know he was such a…junkie!" the uncharacteristic Jeanine blurted, a little drunk herself, of his pal who she never really liked or respected. "I <u>am</u> sorry, but did you <u>know</u> about this?"

His reaction was violent and swift as he hoisted her above his head by the upper arms and shook her with a hateful stare she had never seen before. "The guy's fuckin' <u>dead</u> and that's <u>all</u> you can say? You, goddamn bitch!" he yelled with frightening conviction, then whimpered. "He was my best friend, the only one who I could count on when I became a nobody!"

After the police on the scene witnessed the incident and saw the furious Jeanine throwing her engagement ring down the street, they sought her accusations to convict Xavier for assault. While she did not press charges, Jeanine had a court order placed on him, preventing all contact. Once exposed to his violent side which left deep hand-marked bruises on her arms as a brutal reminder, she feared for her safety and possibly her life, considering his great strength and proven lack of control. Her decision to break it off was a prudent one since, as a part time social worker, she counseled many a battered woman and by no means wanted to share their hell.

A very quiet Xavier went to Greg's funeral, alone. Afterwards, he visited his own family, pretending that everything was fine. His acting rated with the best in Hollywood as he convinced them, with a forced smile, that he was only looking forward to graduation and hoped to see them there. All the time, though, he felt embittered and hollow, inviting his dark side to seep in and entertain his needs. Hence, a fantasy world of warfare developed upon his return to Madison.

As he dared, with all forbidden aspirations available to him by the mind meld so thorough, Lone Hawk delved deeper into Xavier's post break-up psyche and found a man more cynical of the world than ever before. In his devolving mind-set, society's entire setup was a travesty, enshrouding a natural hellhole that he wished to someday expose as his killing field. A trailblazer of justice, he would be the real-life 'X' Man, destroyer of the ever-abundant misery makers of whom there was a virtually endless supply. While fantastical, his goals were even more unrealistic, if only by the fact that he had merely a criminal psychology degree and a summer as a state park forest ranger to his credit. However, from a practical standpoint, he did intend to follow the proper channels and try out for a career in undercover law enforcement, perhaps with the CIA, DEA or FBI. And if by slim chance he was accepted, his advantageous position as an agent with entrusted power would have provided the perfect element for promoting his fantasy, one he could so easily abuse.

To add to the frightening level of Xavier's obsession, Lone Hawk found his constant review of a decades-old, 'high drama' movie classic to be rather alarming. The story, revolving around a lowly cabbie who, in his quest for justice and fame, courageously terminates a drug-dealing pimp and saves the 'baby girl' hooker from under the guy's 'degenerate' wing in the process. The pop culture flick never grew old to him. In turn, Xavier's admiration for the main character was so strong, he began to secretly imitate and role-play before the mirror with guns and knives while continuing his warped dream of an obscure and violent rescue of society.

Realizing the outrageous intensity of Xavier's plans, Lone Hawk figured that he may have done the modern world a small favor. A fanatical, over-zealous avenger could potentially kill the innocent in pursuit of his self-righteous agenda. As Xavier was heading toward such a scenario, Lone Hawk became well-cautioned in his own mission to use impeccable judgment. He would be careful not to harm any humans while seeking out the enemy.

Then switching up when his thoughts turned to the Owlmen, there was a cross section with Xavier's knowledge of these entities to be of pseudo-realism. The Grays—stereotypical, extra-terrestrial beings blamed for countless human abductions fit the image and the behavior traits too well to be a coincidence. They were in full operation and even without adequate proof of their existence, many believed the government was in active cooperation with the aliens. General speculation had it that an exchange program of experimental human subjects for advanced technology was long in progress and guarded to an impenetrable degree.

Lone Hawk did not lend much value or thought to the 'government involvement' theory, since there was so little trust in the rulers of the time, anyway. However, the wide-spread awareness of the actual abductions made him tingle with the vibrant anticipation of finally exposing them not just for his own nine-centuries-old experience, but for the many others who had been violated as well. How very fortunate, he felt with reconfirming relief, that the Owlmen chose such a gradual course in their world domination scheme. But then more careful to reason, he began to wonder if they were, perhaps, the very ones awaiting his return...

As his chest brushed along the treetops, Lone Hawk realized he must re-focus his thoughts toward locating the Earth Force sphere. Yet with the approach of the Big River, Mississippi in the contemporary, backtracking became necessary since he knew his destination to be northeast of there, not far on the Wisconsin River's north side. Still not quite sure exactly where, he passed over the sacred cave on the way back without recognizing it and questioned his power of observation until he tapped into Xavier's visit to the very same location. Concealed by a commercial structure, it had become a tourist attraction named Kickapoo. And though the sphere was not known to the modern age inhabitants, its aura emanated most prevalently in the distance from below.

To avoid discovery and destruction by irreverent newcomers, the mystic sphere cleverly burrowed underneath its home in waiting. Lone Hawk sensed submissiveness in the great orb's psychic vibes of increasing intensity, and so desired to be the master of that which he once feared. In his plunder, as he thought, he would absorb all of its magic and score his first triumph in the new world. Then, over-designed and ever invincible, the second and ultimate victory against the 'Evil One' of the Owlmen would be naturally insured. Lone Hawk's burgeoning confidence began to simplify and predict, little knowing that the complexities of the planet's situation were far beyond his or Xavier's immediate comprehension.

After coming about again but then getting warm, he scanned the specified grounds with infrared clarity and, just as the notion of great military aircraft spoiling his mission arose, so did a near collision. Although it was only a private jet descending from the southeast for landing, the preoccupied Lone Hawk was caught off guard. The encounter evoked a sudden rush of anxiety and demanded an immediate arrival at his destination. In response, he swooped down to a lower altitude, once again occasionally brushing the treetops of the rolling wooded hills. Thankfully, the first clearing he came upon held the big log cabin of Kickapoo, latest desecrators of the Earth Force's sacred hollow. There, landing beside the building, Lone Hawk began to dig into the earth. Though his well-clawed hands and taloned feet created a deep ditch in but an instant, he suddenly stopped to the ridiculous approach.

`This is <u>not</u> the way!' he thought in disgust of his unimaginative, menial approach. 'The Earth Force would merely flow and be its own path, the way I must go.'

As he sought a prompt solution, Lone Hawk calmly reflected to the moment before his grand entrance, when he seeped into the Warbird mound. By simply expanding on that feeling of submergence, he imagined the solid earth as a great pool of water. Upon his element-reversing vision, the most pleasing effect became so and thus sent him plunging into the ground with a muddy splash.

Lone Hawk swam through the rocky soil in complete exhilaration. Then before proceeding to any great depth, he peeked curiously into the cave's temple room and was amused by its tininess, considering how it so impressed him long ago. His confidence boosted even further by his own grand scale, he continued to descend below the cavern into the deep underworld's murky sea with nothing more than the presence of its expectation. Thus, his blind search came to an end when the sphere, preceded by a guiding wave of warmth, glowed like a beacon in the distance.

There, seemingly awaiting their reunion, the orb was fixed, inviting the already bolting Lone Hawk to apprehend it. So, in seizing upon his immediate conquest, Lone Hawk grasped the docile sphere, barely fitting into his out-stretched hand, and held it out with a beholding straight arm.

"It's been a long time, old friend," he said, flaunting the role reversal of their lengthy separation. "You were the master then, yet now, you are <u>mine</u> with <u>all</u> your power. You <u>cannot</u> abandon me this time, as you did before when…you portrayed me as a fool! Even if they did have faith, it doesn't matter. I never returned to them. Well, the score will now be settled because you, my precious jewel, shall accompany me on this sacred quest as a part of me, so I will <u>never</u> have to concern myself with your abandonment <u>ever</u> again."

Following his bold words of intent, Lone Hawk smashed the sphere violently into his chest with a tranquil groan. Then glowing a searing red, it was imbedded like an eye just below his breastplate.

"Beware, Evil One and your silly little Owlmen! I am now <u>fully</u> empowered by the Earth Force! I only need to find you, and soon … as you cower before me—oh! How I will ever savor the moment before your execution! Then after clearing you out of existence, your infection here in this world will vanish and fester no more!"

While bathing in the momentary glory of presumably achieving omnipotence, Lone Hawk was suddenly jostled from his complacency. He began to experience a most heinous sensation of falling. Fearing his return to the Evermore, he struggled like a drowning man which only accelerated the process.

"So, you would have me drop as before? Yet, in addition, you'd even sacrifice <u>yourself</u> and the entire Earth?" he scolded, blaming and pounding the pirated sphere in sinking desperation. "I suppose while the 'mighty orb' cries in defeat, I must stop this alone!"

With the obvious futility of frantic resistance, Lone Hawk implemented the opposite by way of doing nothing. Relaxed and clear of mind, the falling slowed to a stop. After a brief period of meditation in the non-sensory darkness, a vision appeared of passing the clouds above with an ever-shrinking view of the landscape left behind, turning into the curvature of the globe beside the black of outer space. Hence, his amazing power of suggestion ignited an upward surge.

Once he passed through the cavern, he was indescribably relieved to be freed from the mysterious clutches below the crust. Relief then graduated to adulation when the catapulting effect hit open air. Imitating his vision of liberation, Lone Hawk broke ground and before long, he watched the land and river diminish in the early sky of morn, indicating that his duration below was much longer than it seemed. The opportunity to test the extent of his flight-ability became the next obsession as he regained control and continued full force to the outer limits of the atmosphere.

"Now, behave yourself, my little globed wonder," he advised with an air of condescension, petting the chest-laden sphere; "my powers have grown far beyond your control. So, here forth, you would be <u>most</u> wise to cooperate."

Into the stratosphere he soared with minimal resistance until when nearing its midpoint, Lone Hawk suddenly hit an invisible barrier that almost shocked him into unconsciousness. And though he did manage to smash through its powerful membrane, the phenomenal impact rendered his perceptions a dizzied haze. But then amidst some re-calibrating above the dangerous crossing, his cleared mind sensed a definite abnormality surrounding the entire planet.

As his inertia carried him further away from the point of aerospace puncture, his suspicions were reconfirmed. In a thorough analysis of the sky's middle layer, an all-encompassing weave flashed sporadically throughout the curved plane within the stratosphere. Lone Hawk felt he was on the verge of solving the puzzle. There had to be a connection between this strange phenomenon and the Mars expedition's tragic end as Xavier's suspicions also would suggest, but from different 'bad actors.'

`The space craft hit this unnatural matrix and was vaporized, on purpose … is this a concoction of the Owlmen? Or manmade, like Xavier thought? Or can it be that these are natural energy surges as the government claims? Hmm, how curious,' he asked himself, trying to rationalize; but then in his haste, he started dismissing it. 'These new eyes are just <u>too</u> good, over-discerning … maybe? I <u>must</u> learn to adjust them—oh! Questions, questions … this web's origin, its brightness—they're only clouding my judgment!'

Addressing his immediate concern, Lone Hawk toned down the distractions and scanned the abundant space clutter of countless satellites and various ships and stations, which were seemingly powerless and adrift. Then from one of the vessels far off in the distance, he detected befogged cries for help. With good intentions, he started toward the anguished source; yet, after careful consideration, he came to a halt, seething with reluctance. "A trick!" Lone Hawk surmised suspiciously, with a growling shout. "Below the ground, the Evil One. Above the sky, the Evil One … I <u>must</u> investigate, but cleverly."

In seeking a disguise, he found use for his previously thought obsolete wings. Stretching and swinging them foreword to a close, he totally shrouded himself, body and face, appearing as a dingey red, white and tannish-gray chunk of orbiting rock. Thus, on a swift yet indirect course, he intercepted the cryptic craft and realized that the recently departed lay within it, all too aware.

———

Upon further investigation, Lone Hawk, feeling no threat, rested atop the triangular white space plane, marked 'SPACE X SP-LL 777'. Sizably fit, he cloaked himself around the wings and fuselage of the aerospace liner which was a recent commercial advancement of runway take-off capability, needing no disposable rockets. Relieved they were legitimate, he marveled seeing through to the throngs of 'crew and passenger' ghostly apparitions cringing in the light of his envelopment. Fearful that their not-so-perfect lives of wealthy indulgence had called the great Satan to deliver them, the sixty-four captive spirits began to pray ever feverishly, a natural last-chance effort to save their souls from eternal damnation.

"Fear not, worried spirits," Lone Hawk's penetrating baritone firmly conveyed, attempting to instill some order among the anxiously squirming spirits; "I am no <u>hell</u> beast! I only want to know what happened. <u>Why</u> is this ship not damaged on the outside while all of you have been rendered dead, inside?"

After a moment's hesitation, the plane's chief pilot mustered the courage to answer him while restlessly stirring amidst the swirling menage of ghosts. "Great Spirit, the upper atmosphere is possessed by <u>something</u> very cruel and unnatural. My first impression of this phenomenon, a super bright pale-green spot floating in the flashing grid, was only that of a curiosity—a rare opportunity to get a good look at a UFO. However, I put <u>everyone's</u> life on the line when I unwittingly put the plane into a gentle rotation so all of 'em could witness the anomaly…you know, really getting their money's worth.

"As the passengers were marveling at the spectacle, our sensors picked up unbelievably high levels of electro-magnetic energy concentrated in the observed area. However, once the danger was known, we <u>tried</u> to pull out, but…it was too late. A powerful bolt from the point of interest shot out, encompassing the plane with a deadly, blinding light of coursing red and purple streams. And now, you see here—the <u>tragic</u> result.

"So, if not be the devil, who or <u>what</u> are you?" the pilot asked. "A messenger from God or, perhaps, an alien god that just <u>happened</u> upon our planet. <u>What</u> is our fate? Are we condemned to an afterlife as space clutter?"

While the other spirits diligently prayed with Christian 'Hail Marys' and 'Our Fathers,' Lone Hawk became theologically intrigued. 'This Christ, Satan and One God Almighty,' he thought so boldly in the parallel, 'Myself, the Evil Chief of the Owlmen and the Earth Force—of course! Have two layers of reality intersected, coincidently, as one's destiny become the rescue of the other? Hmm...'

Reasoning time would unveil the truth about that soon enough, Lone Hawk acknowledged his first suspicions to be of fact. The Owlmen had already imprisoned the planet. Thus, as the sense of urgency had been escalated by his confirmed realization, the spirits praying so chaotically within the craft began to prey on his benevolent nature. As well, he offered an ultimatum: "If your annoying, self-pitying chants cease immediately, I <u>will</u> take you back to the surface where, perhaps, you can find your god. Otherwise, I will leave you as <u>nothing</u> more than a sorry mass of crying space clutter. Though adrift in a seeming eternal orbit, eventually, in several years, you'll merely <u>burn</u> up like a meteor upon re-entry. Shall I tell you more?"

His stern proposal was received with prompt affirmations of silence, a communal latching onto him as their only chance for a viable afterlife which, in fact, was only a plea to be close to home. Thus, appreciating their subservient hush, Lone Hawk prepared to direct the plane back to Earth. His sympathies, of course, were with them as he felt such pain before in the Evermore. Yet, the favor to shuttle them back to the surface seemed just the action to turn his covert operation rather overt. However, he was committed and would treat the minor mission as an immediate priority.

At full speed, he plunged into the ionosphere as a space plane sandwich, exerting all his remaining energies to create a protective force field. In direct response to his actions, the phenomenon of which the dead pilot described began to flare in its glowing matrix, readying to snag them. Though when it released the same deadly streaming bolt, Lone Hawk with tremendous velocity already dove into its epicenter. Prepared for the shock barrier, he shot through, his path piercing and dispersing the attacking field. Surprisingly, he felt no impact as before. He was sure that he defied the Owlmens' most advanced tool of weaponry and so passed a vital test. Hence, self-assurance in ever-bold form resulted in stride, with the satisfaction of calming the desperate souls in tow.

"We're through the danger zone," Lone Hawk announced while exiting the stratosphere and descending into the cirrus troposphere over the eastern edge of the southwest Canadian Rockies. "I will shortly have you on the ground, where you can roam freely and find peace."

Cruising high in altitude and attitude, Lone Hawk dipped below the thin cloud cover and witnessed the majesty of the towering mountains reflecting the reddish sun at post-dawn. While he considered the tall, rugged terrain as the perfect place to commence a brief solitary hiatus, five military aircraft of camouflage green with rainbow trim suddenly converged upon him. Thus, with what became a pressured delivery, he began a steep descent in avoidance of the abrupt pursuit. However, one of them fired a laser-guided missile that unshakably followed his course. And so, straight down, he held his high velocity dive into a deep valley, which was followed by a lateral swoop. From there, he then released the space plane to a gentle slide along the grassy bottom ground.

"Scatter, good spirits!" he advised in their throttled send-off; "let no walls hold you … Prepare yourselves—here comes the explosion!"

Lone Hawk left the violent detonation of the vessel behind and by its blasting force, he entered the base of an opposing mountain in spirit form, re-submerging into the sea of the underworld. Shortly after his subterranean diversion, the anxious 'falling syndrome' crept back into his psyche and forced him to immediately resurface. So, at the bottom of a nearby rocky ravine of pine tree lace, he popped aggressively out into the majestic scenery, solid and free of the dismal nether land below which harbored a weakness in him that he was later to overcome.

Much to his relief, the fighter jets were nowhere within his sensor range as he emerged to daylight. Even so, he would not underestimate their tracking ability and so began searching for a suitable area to discreetly absorb the environment and the much-needed psychic waves, which would guide his quest. Then, however untimely, Lone Hawk's mind went adrift amidst his low flying exploration through the winding mountain range when he found through Xavier's travels a familiar serenity in the rustic beauty.

During their second summer together, Xavier and Jeanine went on a road trip to Alaska. It was an incredible journey full of many fond memories in the natural wonderland of Northwest America. Venturing all the way from Seattle to Mt. McKinley National Park, they were graced with a view of the hemisphere's highest mountain, the midnight sun and the aurora borealis, all in the same day.

While Lone Hawk from his ancient knowledge was aware of the far-off magnificent mountains to the west and the different angles of the sun in the sky, north and south, the northern lights 'so intense' were new to him. And though they were not so geometric like the aliens' unnatural grid in the stratosphere to be of pertinent effect, there was an uncanny similarity to the colorful threads of light held by the Earth Force sphere in their first encounter. Every new memory and experience, it seemed, formed further connections in solving this great puzzle to complete understanding. To know it all as he must, the pledge rang in his thoughts that nothing would be whisked away as trivial.

Confident in his growing brilliance and ability to lose the disadvantaged aircraft, a cocky Lone Hawk began to playfully career northwest through multi-forked ravines. Eventually, he dared to widen his path, elevating near the sky-jutting peaks atop the rugged range. In his carelessness, he was once again detected by three of the same military jets that had cleverly swooped down upon him from behind the tallest, most massive mountain in the vicinity.

Lone Hawk easily stayed ahead of them and with his flight capability calibrated to its optimum, he tested his superior maneuverability. Scheme in place, he looked back at the jets in hot pursuit, and launched a surprising move by flipping over, face up, and instantly darting beneath them in the opposite direction. As he tauntingly waved his hand in passing, the feathered flight pro laughed to himself, enjoying a long-buried sense of humor.

Bathing in his well-sustained mirth, he bolted back through the veined maze etched in the mountainside rock, at speeds they could not possibly retrace. Fortunately, his random path stumbled upon a deep and narrow gorge which he ducked into, a custom fit. There, while he wedged himself between the sheer cliffs of its interior, Lone Hawk felt a breath of life from afar. Well familiar with the 'mind signature' at even but a fragment, he knew the thriving source in broadcast could only be that of Xavier Branion.

"Ah, Xavier, so you survived," he congratulated, with a call to duty; "well, just be sure to redivert your 'vigilante' herodom energy towards the west, where in the mountains you must go…for you have been chosen for a sacred quest. Your mind has been and will be ever precious to me, but with your body now free to roam, you must join 'us' for battle." He transmitted the balance of personal intellect, Xavier needed for his memory's regeneration. Though uncertain of its process duration, Lone Hawk added, "Remember yourself…now, and as I vowed before, my modern warrior, you <u>shall</u> be rewarded."

The conscience-cleansing news created a short moment's solace until a very different signal emanated nearby that was identified in a painful instant. The vibe stirred a flashback of his alien abduction, a time long gone when he was powerless against the Owlmen. For the first time since emerging to the physical realm, he relived the brutal experience in its entirety, which led to explosive anger.

Hatred then arose ever fresh and was savored. There would be no rest. For as his instincts told, they were not far off. Therefore, the hunt would begin in earnest for the newly vulnerable Owlmen, the self-proclaimed future race that was about to face a most frightening nemesis from the past.

CHAPTER XII
Metamorph 'X'

A FTER HIS JET TRANSPORT from a clever chopper transfer via the New Savanna Army Depot in northeastern Illinois, Xavier arrived at a U.S. Naval Medical Research Facility outside of Baltimore, Maryland near Chesapeake Bay at 4:30 a.m., eastern standard time. There, he was immediately brought to the high security section of the building, Third Floor Center. As priority patient number one, he was examined by a host of top specialists with the most advanced medical equipment the government could offer and was initially declared comatose yet stable. However, just after a couple hours under full life supports, Xavier's body temperature suddenly plunged and his heart rate flat-lined. Shock revival techniques were administered but failed due to instant rigor mortis setting into his flesh which, in turn, became stone cold. While the patient died by inexplicable means, the five-member team was baffled, exchanging glances of disbelief and shoulder shrugs in their white encapsulations of protective attire. Thus, as they readied for a fresh autopsy, the chief physician noticed that the once cold forehead of the supposed deceased was starting to warm to the touch. Yet, the monitor showed no such gain.

"We'd better get another CAT on this," he calmly advised, concealing his excitement, while two of the others reset and positioned the arched scanning apparatus with a rolling stand over Xavier's head. "There should be <u>no</u> brain function, but he's feverish. Very odd..."

The CAT Scan was activated, and the medical staff was astounded by the peculiar imagery appearing on the monitor's screen. There was definite activity. But instead of the usual stagnation to slowly fluctuating hemispherical patterns of a live human brain, only a single winding swirl of bright red, purple and green was transmitted. Like a satellite's view of a hurricane building momentum, the cranial anomaly spun from a black eye and steadily increased to a dizzying rate. The surging and flashing phenomenon became a psychedelic strobing ellipse, which began to make them nervous and nauseous as well. The situation was becoming that of a bomb squad, attempting to diffuse a live scull by the administration of heavy tranquilizers to prevent its violent eruption. Into the top of the jugular vein, the anesthesiologist started to inject the first dose.

"The needle punctures okay, <u>but</u> there's some kind of back pressure!" she warned, wincing, as she pulled out the syringe with shaky hands that were nearly burned by the heat. "<u>Nothing</u> will inject! And what about that <u>head</u>? It's like a campfire! I suggest we open it up, relieve the pressure and ice it down or … 'abandon building'?"

"Agreed! A standard frontal flap with the auto-scalp and a Freon flush—immediately!" the chief surgeon proposed, fearfully watching Xavier's red, steaming face he prayed to neutralize. "Also, alert security … even though they should be monitoring all this anyway."

Before they could even prepare for the incision-cooling process, 'dead man' Xavier suddenly ripped away the tubes and sensors, and hurled himself off the examination table. Then by a coincidental swiping forearm, he knocked the chief surgeon to the floor, rendering him unconscious. In immediate response, the medic standing closest to the exit bolted into the hallway to alert security while the wild-eyed Xavier, fresh from his resurrection in a white-green-patterned hospital gown, had backed himself into a corner.

"Don't touch me! Get away from me!" he hissed then raved. "I've <u>got</u> to get outta here—go west, it said!" And though in an acute state of paranoia, Xavier did not obstruct the remaining medical staff from assisting the downed chief surgeon nearby. With cautious eyes on the looming madman, they helped the team leader to his feet and were very relieved to see that he was fully conscious and able to walk. However, when they tried to lead him out of the room away from his assailant, the brave doctor insisted on staying to diffuse the crisis.

"Mister Branion…Xavier, you were in an accident and now you're in the hospital to recover. Nobody wants to harm you," he said, causing a taming effect that left Xavier with only a needful look while he whispered his own name as though so unfamiliar. "That's it…easy. Don't worry—we'll help you remember everything, and then you can go home." Xavier began to emerge from the corner with a trusting demeanor, but then he stopped in his tracks, scowling at some commotion outside the room. When suddenly, three youthful 'southern fried' Naval guards, led by a 'Cool Hand Luke' type character, burst into the room.

In militaristic haste, the brash 'guard in charge' stepped forward and drew his pistol, forcing the compassionate physician aside. "With all due respect, doctor, this is a security matter and you'd better step back for your own safety," he warned in a thick southern accent while Xavier reverted to a defensive stance, crouched with his fists clenched and his teeth grinding like a chain saw. "Now, he sure don't look to me like he understands a goddamn word I'm sayin'. So, we're just gonna have ta wait for the back-ups with the tasers. And they'd better hurry, cuz I don't wanna have to blow his head off!"

As though the macho guard had spoken the magic 'escape launch' words, Xavier charged him from fifteen-feet-away and bowled over all three of them. While not one could pull off a shot, someone did manage to set-off the alarm. Thus, seizing the moment, he barreled out of the examination room, smashing through a pair of double doors into the main hallway, and collided with seven security-back-ups, picking up the 'bowling' spare. Continuing his high velocity sprint down the well-cleared throughway, he was rapidly coming to its crowded end where two-elevator-platforms awaited on either side. Finally, then with nowhere else to go, he careened left toward its short hallway. There, with throngs of hospital personnel just standing and holding their ears due to the blaring alarm noise, Xavier spoke out while ducking into the lifts' waiting area. Yelling like a mad man, he headed towards the tall-windowed dead-end. "Get out of the way and, what the hell—get outta town!" he warned while pointing outside the fast-approaching window barrier. "Something big, <u>really</u> big is about to happen—and it ain't good!" Then in a blurring, supernatural three-step lunge past the platform, he right-shoulder crashed through the window with a thunderous, glass-shattering bang. Airborne, Xavier launched himself fifty-feet and two-stories down to a sparsely filled parking lot. There, he landed in a double-roll, got right back on his feet and easily hurdled a six-foot, concrete perimeter-barrier.

A little further, he was confronted by a ten-foot, barbed wire fence with a sign reading, 'WARNING: ELECTRIFIED FOR YOUR PROTECTION'. Without hesitation, he carried his momentum forward, leaped and grabbed the fence's top frame bar then flipped over the barbed cables, with sparks flying onto the graveled stretch before a rural highway. Finally free from the hospital grounds and desperately determined, Xavier tested his open-air sprint ability when he reached the well-travelled road and executed an incredible, long-jumping-double-step move on the roofs of a tan SUV and a silver cargo van. Such a move could not be better orchestrated as they passed from opposite directions, giving him the footing that landed him with a self-congratulatory smile breaking into a full gallop over an open field of rolling farmland.

Looking behind and over his shoulder at the early-rising sun, Xavier reaffirmed to himself, the mysterious message he heard just upon his resurrection. "Ah, <u>just</u> according to plan—go west, young man!" he shouted in joyous release and while running at 'express way' speeds, he ever-miraculously saw a well-timed opportunity. "And there's my ride!" About a quarter mile in the distance, he spotted a long, multi-car freight train traveling at a good clip on an elevated track, bending northwest with an open-car he caught up to and jumped inside, quite proud of himself. "My God— powers bestowed is right! Must've been doin' seventy—I am <u>fuckin'</u> invincible! And I've got the <u>whole</u> car to my…oh, excuse me, I didn't see you there and—hey! Careful with that thing!"

After Xavier perused the car's empty front-half, he then swung his head toward the back and realized he had spoken too soon. There, sitting in the corner, he discovered to his shock a mangy, gray-bearded bum in a dirty-tan trench coat facing him, with a bottle of booze in one hand and an old-fashioned, snub-nosed revolver aimed at him in the other. While the 'unwelcomed' raised his hands and crab-walked toward the open door on the other side, the sorry old man flared his glassy-blue, blood-shot eyes in distrust and pulled the trigger. With a bang muffled by the train's rolling racket, the vagrant scored a shot into Xavier's left temple which forced him out of the car, holding the side of his head. He rolled down the graveled mound beneath the tracks into a drainage ditch and crawled out of it, rather dazed. Certain that he had taken on a massive head wound, Xavier inspected his hand and, despite being a little muddy, discovered there was not a drop of blood. Surprised, he panned his hospital gown, tattered to immodesty, and noticed his arms, legs and the rest of his body had not even a scratch. Triumphant over what certainly should have been lethal, he sprung back to his feet, took a deep breath and continued his westward run toward a suburban residential area, with the back of a fenced baseball diamond in the forefront.

Thinking about the 'good old days' playing ball as a kid, Xavier paused for a moment behind the fence near third-base when he observed some 'actual' kids in baseball caps, carrying their bats and mitts in approach from the far-right-corner of the field. In response, he blurred into his signature high-velocity sprint to a row of pine trees behind left field and slinked between their ample cover by the fenced yards of the perimeter houses. Confident he did not attract any notice, Xavier crouched out of sight, whispering to himself. "Shit—that was close! Okay, first thing: Get some clothes; Secondly, some money would help, but don't want to stoop to stealing; and third, a ride…some wheels, a car—damn! The criminal mind at work—oh!" Suddenly, his love-lost interest came to mind full-force, becoming an obsession. "And then there's her…Jeanine? Yeah, great—now I'll never get her out of my head! How did something <u>so</u> good, go <u>so</u> wrong? Whatever, maybe <u>someone</u> around here can help—wait! How about <u>this</u> guy?"

From his hiding place, peeking into the neighborhood next to the field, Xavier spied a young, black high-school-aged kid, strutting down the street in a purple tank top and baggy blue jeans, which prompted him to sneak around and hop the fence into the next yard. Then waiting behind some tall, thick bushes in the front yard ready to pounce, he watched the fast-walking teen turning and heading toward a modest two-story-yellow-bricked bungalow, a couple houses down across the street. Just after the tall and thin adolescent stepped onto the front porch, Xavier rushed over to him in a phantom-like blur and took him down while twisting his arm behind his back and covering his mouth with an iron grip. Thus, once the tough kid, then pursing his lips and trying to fight, was finely subdued, Xavier demanded his cooperation in a low, raspy whisper. "Don't make a sound! I just need some clothes and a place to get my head together. So, just go inside as you were, act natural and, of course in your own words, introduce me as your unfortunate guest that just needs a little charity right now…And don't try anything foolish—or I'll rip your arm off!"

The rattled young man unlocked and opened the door with his trembling hand. Xavier pushed him by his twisted arm and scooted his way inside, quickly closing the door behind them. The smell of coffee and the sound of a barely audible television emanated from a nearby source. "Derek! Your father and I would like to talk to you!" a woman's voice hollered from the kitchen off to the right, behind the living room where they stood below a second-floor stairway. "We've been up since 'four' this morning, worried sick! Now, get your ass in here and explain yourself!"

"Tell them to come out here," Xavier whispered, planning to lure them into a common area for a more controlled situation, even though he did not consider another, lurking upstairs. "Say you have a guest who will explain your delay."

"Mom, Dad, sorry…left my phone in someone's car and it was a long night getting it back…anyway, there's someone right here in the living room, a real 'charity case' you can help out on this fine 'church' Sunday," Derek tempted to the narrative, in preservation of his arm. "This guy, you're not gonna believe it—he must've been in some kind of accident!" His mother, a thin medium-complexioned woman in a sky-blue robe, complied and ventured out there with more curiosity than her husband. After she walked through the doorless frame into the front room, however, she was horrified to find that her younger son had decided to play the hero.

"Scotty! No!" she cried out, pointing at the daring twelve-year-old boy in his tiger-striped pajamas who had just leaped from the stairway onto Xavier's back, stabbing and slicing his neck with a pocketknife. "Good Lord! <u>Get</u> off of him, Scotty! What? Now, <u>put</u> him down, you maniac!" she demanded of Xavier who had torn the junior assailant from his back, and pressed him with one hand to the ceiling like the liberty torch.

At the same time, he stripped him of his pocketknife and admired it. "Well, well—a Swiss Army knife...I used to have one of these! When I was a little kid in Toronto. <u>Why</u> do I remember <u>that</u>, but nothing important?" Xavier complained in frustration as the boy's father, a man of his size wearing gray boxer shorts and a white T shirt, rushed into the room and started cautiously to close in on him. "Can I <u>now</u> assume we have the 'whole' family here?"

"<u>Put</u> the boy down, mister!" his paternal-half demanded with a roar while reaching for his son with one hand and guarding against the knife with the other. "Only then can we talk, so put him down—now!" Xavier lowered the brave Scotty into his father's arms and gave him the knife as well.

"Dad, he should be bleeding all over the place! He should be dead!" the mystified Scotty exclaimed to his head-shaking father, carefully weighing the bizarre situation. "I got him really good! Didn't I, Derek?"

"That wasn't very nice, little man...and it's <u>nothing</u> to be proud of," Xavier scolded and started looking even more crazed, as he began to shake into traces of blurred anger. "Now <u>please</u>, just <u>get</u> me some clothes! Isn't it <u>obvious</u> that I need some clothes!" At that instant, the father of the house came to realize that Xavier was no ordinary, half-naked white amnesiac. He was rather sure, from the top news story, of his true identity. Thus, he chose to be accommodating and not confrontational, for his family's safety's sake.

"Derek, go up to the attic and get the box in the right rear corner, labeled 'Wild Days'," he instructed his all-too-eager son who had a plan of his own, which was squashed. "And <u>don't</u> get any ideas about calling the police when you're up there!" Most effectively, he gained Xavier's trust as Derek bolted up the stairs, shaking his head in disappointment. Thereafter, sirens were blaring in the distance but coming closer.

"Thank you, sir," Xavier said in a most gracious tone, bending to one knee and covering his crotch with his bunched-up gown. "Here I am, this <u>vile</u> intruder…and you're going out on a limb for me. But I'm gettin' the feeling that you know <u>more</u> than you let on…what gives?" He looked toward the father with delving eyes of intimidation while his wife came forward to intervene.

"I <u>knew</u> you looked familiar! But with all of the commotion, I didn't make the connection right away," she explained, with a closer examination of Xavier's face. "You're the guy from that 'weird' Wisconsin thing with the hologram explosion. We started watching over coffee about an hour ago. It's the only story going. <u>So</u>, let the big screen tell ya what's what!" On the wall opposite the picture window with silver-blue drapes drawn, a three-by-five-foot oak framed picture of the famous 'Christ's Last Supper,' modified to an 'all black' messiah-disciple cast, hung above a spinet piano. When she picked up the small rectangular remote control from atop their mahogany coffee table, the mother of the house sat casually on their gray leather sofa and transformed the 'holy' reproduction into a functional television screen. Turning on to a cartoon, she flipped through the channels for a related news program while Derek came down the stairs with the prescribed box of clothes. Xavier quickly fished out a pair of black jeans with blue zippered, bell or straight bottoms and put them on. Though a tad too long and out of style, they fit rather well.

"No underwear?" Scotty blurted with an ewe, lip-rumpling expression, causing everyone to laugh; "that's <u>disgusting</u>!"

"I'm in <u>no</u> position to be demanding undergarments, kid," Xavier defended as he slipped on some well-worn black work-boots that were about a size too big, then recognized himself on the located news channel. "My God, <u>that's</u> my picture! And <u>whoa</u>—a breaking story…<u>Please</u>, turn up the volume!" Illuminating the screen was a recent photograph in his rangers' uniform transposed to the corner of the Devils Lake `sky-cam' scene from the early AM, before the federal government forced the media out of the area. Dread and intrigue irrepressibly cascaded into Xavier's baffled mind as he watched the most current report:

"Driven by an obscure power of insanity, or the result of his 'alleged' paranormal contact, Xavier Branion, the well-publicized victim of the Devils Lake tragedy, escaped from a high security Naval Medical Research Facility outside Baltimore, just moments ago," the perfect newswoman's voice reported in background commentary. "While government officials declined to comment, insiders and civilian witnesses claim that a man of his now well-known description survived a three-story plunge to the parking lot, a climb over an electrified barbed-wire fence, and was seen jumping over traffic at an incredible speed then running westward into the rolling countryside. <u>Anyone</u> who has information as to his whereabouts should <u>contact</u> authorities and be aware that he is <u>extremely</u> dangerous and unpredictable.

"Like a cheap, sci-fi tabloid story come to life," the reporter continued; "this 'very real' situation has yet to come to full bloom, now, with national and international attention <u>swelling</u> to alarming proportions. And <u>all</u> we can do for now is ask, 'what really happened at Wisconsin's Devils Lake State Park?' Is this a case of government experimentation gone amuck, or is there a <u>manipulative</u> unknown entity at work here? Two things are for certain: First, the federal government has closed off an entire state park in response to a flimsy explosion/hologram explanation, which nobody is buying. Secondly, during the incredible mass sighting, a simple park ranger was severely injured then airlifted from the area and <u>now</u>, it seems, he's no less a 'super-human' maniac on the loose—oh! We will now switch from the pre-recorded Devils Lake scene to some live coverage from the Naval Medical Research Facility with Jack Damon…Jack?"

Immediately, in a crowded view on the road outside the facility, the suave, graying newsman looked back-and-forth, pointing at the taped-off broken window of Xavier's escape. When it was zoomed upon, Xavier commandeered the remote control and turned it off.

"Xavier Branion…'simple' park ranger turned super-human maniac, and you're not even scared?" he asked, astonished, without a response as he was buttoning a colorful, random-patterned shirt which he selected from the 'goodwill' box. "Well, all I know is…I escaped from getting my goddamn scull cut open by those 'brain-munchin' Navy doctors. But, the Devils Lake stuff and the hologram, I'm not sure. Though, there is something of an entity. A big nightmarish set of satanic eyes! If this is a 'government' thing, I guarantee that this simple park ranger is gonna cash in on the biggest lawsuit in history!" There was a lull of silence as Xavier held his forehead and looked down in painful contemplation at the black and white peach-mesh carpet, exhaling loudly.

"I think you were abducted by aliens, and they gave you an implant for super strength and skin that heals instantly," Scotty surmised, sharing his comic book opinion with everyone while not being taken so un-seriously. "That's why you don't bleed! Now, the question is, 'what do they want you to do with this ability?'. My guess is that you're like, their spy and they plan to use you to infiltrate the government. But, if they try to remove the implant, you'll probably explode! Then—Kaboom!"

His mother cut his monologue short, "And, you have said enough, Scotty! Excuse him, Xavier. He's got quite an imagination, yet, then again, you can't blame anyone for wondering or being concerned, considering your condition. So, you have your clothes. What else can we do? You must understand that we don't want to be accomplices, but don't want to turn you in, either…well? You hear the sirens! They'll be searching every house in the area pretty soon…"

Xavier scratched his head in dazed apprehension, then sheepishly responded, "A phone call, maybe? I've got a number in my head and a woman's face—Jeanine, something…it could be of help, remembering stuff." She looked to her husband as he nodded reluctantly in approval. Thus, to appease his request, she demanded with a stern face that Derek lend his phone for the call, rather than theirs, hoping a teenager's number would be less risky.

"Derek, let Mister Branion use your phone for the call," she ordered him, beholding Xavier's begging demeanor, while he handed it over with a smirk. "If they track it, just ditch it somewhere and say you lost it last night—who's to know? Proceeding, Xavier tapped in the 'top of mind' number to its ID that checked correctly as her video voicemail greeting played, sparking his memory with brightened eyes. "Jeanine Vercelli—that's her! And look at that beautiful face!" he showed them, wearing polite smiles, while Derek offered a compliment. "Yeah, hot—totally!" Xavier nodded in 'all that' concurrence. Yet, when he started to leave a message, a high-pitched, number-crunching sound emanated from the phone with a jumbled screen that looked to be purposely scrambled. Amidst the panic, Derek's mother snatched the phone, visibly shaken, and pushed him out of the way then trotted into the kitchen from where she threw it to a well-distanced slide down the alleyway.

"She's very pretty, Xavier, but I think that was a call-trace and I hope I turned it off in time, ha-ha…probably not!" she expressed upon her return, making light of it but with mounting intolerance. "So, you had your call and now, it's time to go!" While she was adamant about his immediate departure, Xavier delayed her wishes when he became entranced with the white pine-framed, full-length mirror. With an intricately whittled crucifix on its crest hanging next to the front door, he strolled to it with intense curiosity, talking to someone inside.

"Who are you? What do you want from me? Go west, still?" he demanded of the banding red eyes in the mirror that only he could see. Yet, the experience was soon shared by an obscure contact that caused him to levitate and smash his head against the ceiling, as the floor shook. And while the eyes only intensified and became his own in the reflection, his face and body contorted in kind. Then suddenly, with no answers to his desperate query, the intruding orbitals shot out of the mirror into his own. As if hellishly anointed, Xavier fell back to the floor, covering his eyes. Then to top it off, the looking glass shattered all over the floor. While everyone else stood aghast, he only worried about the state of his burning eyes.

"I'm sorry—so sorry! But do my eyes look okay?" he asked in a frantic state as he turned to them, playing a frightening game of peek-a-boo. "They're not all weirded out, are they? I've got to know!"

"Never mind your damn eyes! They're fine!" the enraged father shouted with fragile temperament. "You just destroyed a very expensive mirror, a family heirloom, and you probably have the authorities on our ass and, quite frankly, you're scaring us like the devil himself! Find another refuge, Xavier. You've more than worn out your welcome here!"

In quick response, his dutiful wife guided Xavier by the arm and hustled him toward the kitchen while the less-than-shy Scotty called out his parting words: "Good Luck, Superman!" he beamed with admiration, as Derek and his father restrained his tagging along. "Show those dirty cops who's boss!"

Entering the kitchen, his exasperated mother then shook her head and rustled up a fifty-dollar bill out of her tan leather purse, sitting on their butcher-block counter. "It's not much, but it might buy you a little more time to remember things…and as you mentioned going west, may I suggest heading to the main strip just four-blocks over," she advised with a maternal smile while she gave him the money via-la-handshake and opened the back door. "And I hope you see that girl again…I think you both need each other, now more than ever…" Xavier thanked her with a gracious kiss on her hand, but then he managed to freak her out yet again. "Yeah, me too—gotta make that happen, but tell me…are you <u>still</u> going to church today?" he asked, reaping an uncomfortable nod and a 'mm, hmm' while he looked about cautiously crouching around on their rear deck. "Well then," he rasped in an ominous voice; "pray like you've <u>never</u> prayed before…and not just for me, but for <u>everyone</u> you know and love! Oh, and thanks for everything." He scampered off into the alley, a hunted fugitive, and left her, a religious woman, in an apocalyptic chill, prompting tears and the crossing gesture.

After weaving through some side-streets and alleyways westward, Xavier found a Seven Eleven convenience store across the main street where Derek's mother suggested to go. There, he purchased a few common-sense items, including a pair of wide-banding, chrome-framed sunglasses which he put on right away. Then, in the back of the building, he discarded the colorfully loud shirt and slipped on a Baltimore Ravens T-Shirt and an Orioles baseball cap he wore backwards in the 'cool guy' style. Lastly, out of the big plastic bag, he pulled a Motor Trend magazine out with a quick page-thumbing and tucked it under his arm. His 'innocent tourist' look completed from the waist up, Xavier then peered down at his funky-weird, black an' blue jeans with a sigh of incompatibility and nonetheless continued to the main strip, heading north. Along the moderately busy street, the scattered racially diverse pedestrians paid little notice and so he strutted casually looking about and spotted some Harley Davidson motorcycles parked on the south side of a ranch-style bar. Seeing also a few cars parked there and thus assuming they were open for business, he hurried his pace toward the drinking establishment with its big neon sign, 'Ace in the Hole Bar & Grill.'

Upon treading its graveled parking lot and unable to resist, Xavier swung his boot awkwardly over the flamed-blue tank of one of the six-classic motorcycles, grabbed the handlebar grips and took a seat. Saddled in reminiscence, he gained access to a sweet memory and spoke softly, half-whispering about it to himself. "Ah, the timeless 'Hog'…that was so excellent when Greg let me borrow his Harley, with the flaming roadrunner on the tank—so cool! And looking so cool, impressing the hell out of Jeanine, cruising her to Devils Lake and…wow! What a perfect day—oh, shit!" Xavier rasped as he suddenly jumped off the mint-conditioned, black an' blue beauty and backed away from it, remembering Harley etiquette. "Never sit on a Harley-dude's 'pride an' joy,' that is, unless you want your ass kicked!" Then eyeing the 'low life' bar and shaking his head, he convinced himself to 'dive the dive.' "Ha-ha, yeah—why not? Bikers, beers and the 'bar from hell' on a Sunday morn…what's the worst that could happen?" the brave one jested, though, just as he walked to the double-doors of the T-shaped, gray aluminum-sided structure and reached for the door handle, Xavier was startled by the loud revving rumble of a rather gaudy, orange-and-chrome Harley with a prominent Mexican flag on its sissy bar.

Hot off the street and generating a generous dust cloud, the rider pulled onto the white gravel-stoned lot to a sideways, skidding stop. There, a short, stocky Hispanic man in black leather dismounted, brandishing a huge, Aztec feather-snake tattoo on his right upper arm and shoulder. Instantly triggered by the mere sight of the man had Xavier wondering and somewhat aware that he resembled one of the Toltec warriors that executed Lone Hawk's uncle in the ancient past. The mind-meld flashback with their serpent-bladed swords as well had him whispering in utter distain, "Toltec Demon—what? I never even saw that guy before!" But then hopping off the brawny street-bike's 'bitch seat' stood a pretty, hips-barely-coming-in Latina girl of about fourteen who three-stepped to the at least twenty-year-older man and initiated a make-out session in their mirrored shades. Shaking his head in disgust, Xavier entered the bar and nodded to the plain-faced, bleached-blonde bartender and a few elderly white guys in fishing hats seated in front, sipping their hard mixed-drinks and watching baseball highlights on one of the eight-ceiling-mounted TVs. Proceeding to his right, he swaggered alongside the impressive maple-topped, U-shaped bar loudly on its vinyl-wood-planked floor in his loose-fitting, steel-toed boots—making an eyebrow-raising impression. He took a seat in an armed stool at the end of the bar and perused the quaint setting of two, new-looking pool tables behind him, a dart board in the back next to the restrooms and sports paraphernalia accompanied by various American flags all about.

Amid the only action being at the dart board with two of the six people there playing, Xavier placed the magazine and the fourteen-dollars change from the Seven Eleven on the bar. He read the Motor Trend headline in an amused whisper, "Flash: If You've Got a Million Bucks to Burn, Introducing the 'Long-Awaited' Flying Cars—Three Models Available to the Public for Purchase This Fall!" he giggled under his breath, skeptical, then burst to intrigue when another memory was sparked. "Wow! That's right! Jeanine and I saw 'em at the Air Show, and lookin' like <u>actual</u> muscle cars—totally awesome! Oh, hi…" The bartender stole his attention and introduced herself, speaking in a warm southern accent. "Hi, sorry to tear you away from your magazine, sir, but I'm Betsy, your bartender here on this fine Sunday morning," she cheerfully greeted then pointed to the swinging double-doors behind her at the other end of the bar. "The kitchen doesn't open up till eleven, so chips-and-salsa will have to do for now, if you're hungry…Anyway, what can I get ya ta drink? We've got three-dollar Buds in the bottle on special, if ya want?" She awaited his order with an expecting smile as Xavier charmed her right off the bat. "Sure, that sounds great, Betsy…in fact, your sales-pitch is so persuasive, I'll take two-ta-start and how about with one of those 'big ole' steins ta boot!" She replied with a joking military salute. "You've got it, Sir!"

While Betsy bended over a big old cooler before him in her 'Daisey Duke' blue jean cut-offs to fish out a couple beers, the

Mexican biker and his 'underaged-minor' girlfriend strolled inside, with her skipping girlishly ahead then coming to an abrupt halt next to him. There, she took off her sunglasses and thus revealed a set of vacant dilated eyes accompanied with a ditsy smile, obviously smitten with him. Xavier smiled back, flashed the peace sign and rolled his eyes as her vulgar keeper caught up, pinched her butt and pushed her along to which she shrugged her shoulders, blushing and giggling. While Xavier delivered a disapproving glare, the raunchy guy sneered and winked at him as he hump-walked behind her around the bar toward the dart board area. There waving, one of the bar's stand-out patrons, a 'Thor-like' body-builder type in a tan leather vest, cowboy boots and black denim jeans called out to them. With a comfortably sauced, southern-accented demeanor, he berated his mal-tempered acquaintance who was also sporting a three-inch, gloriously embellished pentagram tattoo on the left side of his neck. "OMG, if it ain't Cartel Carmen, whoring minors and probably still selling those fen-laced drugs—and <u>candy</u> now?!"

Not so jokingly, the head-shaking, finger-wagging Randy tried guilting the notorious Carmen, but in vain as he caressed the drugged-up girl's shoulders from behind. "Hey, Randy—it's been a while...so I thought I'd check in. And, come on, <u>don't</u> hurt her feelings. Even though she's 'no speak the English' fresh...she's just a late-bloomer like all my girls, totally eighteen-plus—tee-hee!" he spewed sarcastically, with curiously naught an accent to then continue chuckling through his toothy smile laced with predictable lies and no sign of a conscience. "And enough with these 'tainted drugs' accusations! All I do is provide services to help asylum-seekers become productive U.S. citizens-of-color...who are definitely <u>not</u> pressured to vote in any particular way, nudge-nudge—hah!" The suddenly agitated Carmen then redirected his attention to Xavier, voicing concern as he continued. "So, what's the story with that freak, sitting <u>alone</u>? At the end of the bar over there? He looks undercover..."

Carmen's paranoid accusation did not sit well with Randy, thus casting his firm doubt. "No way—look at him guzzle that king-sized beer!" he raved, pointing at Xavier gulping down the rest of his foamy double-beer-filled stein then loudly slamming it down on the bar in thankful relief. "He's probably just some hung-over college kid, gettin' some hair-of-the-dog and tryin' ta figure out how in the hell he wound up 'round here…" Scheming, Carmen sounded agreeable enough with a seemingly harmless suggestion. "Well, whatever…how about some call-ball at the table behind him, best-outta-three, fifty-bucks?" he said, imitating the pool-shooting motion, then added, "plus there, I can keep an eye out…" Somewhat distrustful, Randy agreed but with one condition. "Okay, but don't start anything…he looks like the 'big jock' type and even I, 'the Mighty Randolph' don't want ta tangle with 'im!" Then nodding to each other, they started toward the other end of the bar with the girl, tagging along while the other bikers, a couple of tough-looking, tattooed white women and four-mixed-race male ruffians stuck around, drinking and playing darts.

Meanwhile, Betsy brought Xavier a third beer and warned him in whispered rasp about the criminal element in the room, coming his way. "Hey, though I'm sure you're well aware, this guy Carmen—he's <u>bad</u> news and with <u>lots</u> of back-up, if you know what I mean? So, just <u>play</u> it cool—I don't want <u>anyone</u> gettin' hurt!" she emphasized, eyes flaring while discreetly finger-pointing behind her view-blocking hand at the meekly female minor; and with an eyebrow raising, Betsy assured, "and don't worry, I <u>won't</u> serve that girl…wait—I've got an idea!" Her face brightened up as she continued, from a whisper to normal volume. "Maybe if I just stand here, talkin' yer ear off, he won't give ya any shit…so here goes: Anyways, what's your name, stranger? What brings ya ta these parts? And, as long as we're at it, how's about tellin' me yer 'whole life story'? Ha-ha—oh!" she suddenly got serious, with 'the story,' hitting him close-to-home. "Did ja hear about the <u>giant</u> gargoyle that <u>exploded</u> out of the ground in Wisconsin? They say it <u>killed</u> a park ranger, and then flew off somewhere…Brandon Xavier, I think was his name?"

Xavier paused his response while engaging a stare-down with the passing menace, to then answer her 'busy talk' questions with a devil-may-care attitude. "Wow, Betsy, that's quite a list! Hmm…" Xavier scoffed with a stroke of his chin then delivered, playing the game with the utmost efficiency. "Well, here ya go, rapid-fire style:

The name's Greg; I'm in town, visiting a college bud; picked up a chick last night and we both got totally wasted; came to, about an hour ago in her apartment; ditched her, hardly remembering any of it; then wandered around out there, kind a lost, and ended up in here—the end! And my life story? Hah, forget it—you <u>don't</u> want to know! And finally, the 'Wisconsin gargoyle' thing…sounds like some psycho-geek, domestic terrorist's 'the earth-god's angry' hologram-attack gone <u>way</u> too far!" Xavier, looking smug in his perceived brilliance, then wrapped it up like the hard guy he was. "And 'for real' finally, as far as anyone gettin' hurt around here, you best be worryin' bout <u>his</u> safety…as I am defensively, of course, <u>very</u> well-trained, if you know what I mean? Now, let me just chill and check out these flying cars—I think I might get one!"

Betsy giggled most endearingly to his unusual speaking style, causing her generous breasts to jiggle in her skimpy yellow tank top while she leaned over the bar and patted him on the shoulder, offering a better cleavage view. "Gotcha, loud an' clear, Greg, but I'll stay standing here, just in case…ha-ha, flying cars—<u>it's</u> about time!" They shared a little laugh when meantime, going on behind Xavier's back, Randy made the break on the racked-up triangle of billiard balls and sank no pockets, leaving the table to Carmen who from the far corner jumped the cue ball in Xavier's direction. Nearly hitting him in the head, he positioned his hand to block and miraculously caught it without even looking. He then nonchalantly tossed the ivory orb back on the table and flipped him 'the bird' while gazing back at him with an impish grin. After some dirty looks between them, Xavier got back to his magazine with Betsy covering her mouth and smirking at the then infuriated Carmen, pounding the pool cue handle on the table like an angry child having a temper-tantrum. Amid his annoying thumping racket combined with the blaring TVs, Xavier poured his beer, took a gulp and slammed the bottle down only to project an intense stare upon it. Not so consequently though when he turned his head to address the obnoxious behavior, the bottle followed his sights and flew directly into Carmen's forehead, instantly falling him to the floor.

While his 'teeny bopper' girlfriend knelt and tended to him babbling in high-pitched Spanish, Randy slid his pool cue into the nearby wall rack and watched the old guys near the front entry file on out the door. Meantime, as he readied to follow them, Xavier just shrugged his shoulders at Betsy, standing there shocked and tongue-tied like the rest. Yet upon her suspicion, she soon rustled up enough gumption to say something. Though not till after she carefully removed his sunglasses, did she get a better, confirming look at his face to dare say. "Greg? Not even! You're the <u>ranger</u> guy from the Wisconsin thing, but—nice disguise!" she complimented, with her then signature smirk and a whisk of her shaky beholding hand. "Of course, you would've known that your pic's gone totally viral by now, unlike these anti-news, ignorant country folk—but not <u>this</u> girl!" she tapped her collarbone, proudly touting herself above the rest, and continued. "So obviously, you managed to escape from some high-security government facility. And now, you have <u>mind-over-matter</u> capabilities? <u>Whoa</u>—this is too much! What other abilities did that giant gargoyle give you, uh, like 'levitating' maybe?"

Loudly exhaling with his hands up in 'clear the air' surrender, Xavier admitted some of his paranormal enhancements but vaguely so. "Yeah, well—I <u>knew</u> I couldn't hide it for long! But yeah, some <u>really</u> weird things actually already <u>have</u> happened between my unbelievable Naval facility escape and hiding out at some black kid's house near here where his parents, very nice, gave me some clothes and money. Anyway, things like levitating? Uh, for sure…<u>right</u> in front of a haunted mirror—hit my head on the ceiling! And, running maybe as fast as a <u>cheetah</u> to catch a freight train way off in the distance is another…I suppose other new superhuman abilities will just keep cropping up—<u>so</u> freaky!" After Xavier's confession of his transformational secrets frankly delivered with an air of unfazed acceptance, Randy, then intrigued, stood up for himself with a theory of his own. "Well, little do you know, <u>Betsy</u>, <u>I</u> keep up with the news and admit that, at first, I just thought it was a sick but 'damn impressive' hoax that would eventually have a reasonable explanation—how <u>wrong</u> I was!" Randy fervently declared. But then while shaking his head and looking Xavier square in the eyes, he broke the bad news to him in a sympathetic, syrupy tone. "I'm now convinced that, that 'gargoyle' <u>thing</u> you encountered is a denizen from hell. And I'm sorry to say, Ranger Brandon, but with this telekinetic ability you've got goin' and the other stuff you mentioned…you are <u>undoubtedly</u> demonically possessed! I'd help ya, if I could…" Then he prudently changed his tune; "but, I sure ain't waitin' till ya go full-blown 'Carrie' on this place! Come on, people, let's get out of here quick, before things get <u>really</u> fucked up in this about-to-be 'Hell on Earth' bar-burnin' disaster!"

Xavier paused in response to the riled Randy as he paced back-and-forth while waving the others over. Hence, while they were slow to move and whispering among themselves, Ranger 'Brandon' commenced a downward air-patting gesture, trying to preserve what little peace might remain in the rattled place, and thus promised his timely departure. "Settle down, everyone…don't worry, I'll be moseying on outta here pretty soon, but <u>not</u> till after I finish my 'flying cars' article—<u>interesting</u> stuff, I tell ya! And see…maybe a little cross-eyed, but I think ole Carmen's gonna be ay okay!" Then as a precaution to keep an eye on him, Xavier turned his bar stool around and sat, facing the pool table. Alas, just peering back at Betsy and reaching for his magazine, her bright blue eyes widened in terror when Carmen elbowed the girl in the face, pleading to him in Spanish and trying to restrain him. But he pushed her down and whipped a good-sized knife sent spinning toward Xavier's unguarded neck. Scoring a perfect strike into his throat, Carmen celebrated with a double-pointing, finger-shots gesture at him, then dragged his bloody nosed girl-toy by the wrist off the floor and around to the far side of the table.

With Xavier lying slumped back in his seat, Betsy leaned over and cradled his head, hanging over the bar, then reached for the knife deeply lodged in his throat. A little shaky, she got a hold of its fancy, silver-laden redwood handle and started pulling out its bloodless, five-inch stainless steel blade in curious examination of the rapidly resealing wound left behind. Then to her thankful surprise, Xavier smiled at her with a wink and yanked the knife completely from his throat, as the shrinking gash sealed back up in an instant. Astonished and relieved by his death-defying comeback, Betsy planted a quick kiss on his forehead dampened by her dripping tears yet backed away when he suddenly jerked forward and looked around, undaunted. At the same time, the six-other bikers from the back-bar had meandered to the scene but then stopped in their tracks, not daring to pass since Xavier sprung abruptly to his feet and blocked their way. Gloating with a smug glare, he waved the failed knife in the air like the victor's prize for all to praise while a somewhat heroic Randy wrestled the girl smoothly away from Carmen and effectively kept him at bay. Acknowledging his good deed, Xavier gave him the thumbs-up and a stern 'not bad!' smile as he approached with heavy boot-pounding steps to neutralize the relentless degenerate, refusing to leave without her.

Thus, with a crushing backhand to Carmen's chest which knocked the wind out of him, Xavier started first by examining his attempted-murder weapon, twirling the knife and running his finger along its blade. "God, you sure know how to pick 'em, Carmen…this thing's weighted <u>perfectly</u>—an <u>excellent</u> throwing knife indeed!" Xavier whimsically assessed while leading to a proposal, an ultimatum that would not end well for the 'all too proud' cartel coyote. "Now, to the point…you have two choices: One, leave this place <u>alone</u>, nice an' peaceful like, then I give you your knife back on your bike outside, so I can <u>personally</u> see you on your way. But, if you choose the alternative and so <u>stupidly</u> insist on sticking around…uh, really?" Still thinking he had the upper hand, Carmen foolishly whipped out his phone and before he could even tap the screen, Xavier instantly foiled his plan by ripping it from his guarding clutches and crushing it into a mangled, shattered plastic mass.

Spattering sparks and smoke in his presenting hand, Xavier smirked at the enraged Carmen and tossed it over his shoulder. Then crazed beyond his own safety's sake, the prideful adversary lunged and tried to strangle the eye-rolling Xavier who swiftly grabbed his wrist and ankle, and thus dwarf-tossed him onto the cleared pool table on the other side of the bar. In a flash, he then rushed over and, with just one hand, dragged his battered carcass off the table by the back of the neck and brought him before the shaky and confused girl, wiping her own bloody tears, to apologize. "Well, I suppose <u>this</u> <u>was</u> the better option, Carmen…like, seeking redemption?" Xavier proposed with a crimping neck-lock, the novel concept that otherwise would surely never have crossed such an uncaring mind. "So, go ahead and tell her! Tell her you're sorry for every vile thing you've ever done to her, and that you promise to <u>never</u> bother her again, meaning no contact what-so-ever—understood! No?" Still resisting in futile struggle, Carmen started to reconsider when Xavier followed with a plausible threat at hand. "Well, let me clarify...<u>don't</u> comply then, don't recommend it...I'll do to your neck bone what I did to your phone!"

Defeated, Carmen cleared his throat with his shifty eyes darting nervously all about and, though not fooling Xavier, half-heartedly gave in only to preserve his own neck. "Alright—<u>alright</u>!" he shouted in frustration only to then shift to 'sweet talk' mode when fake apologizing to the girl. "Cindy, *mi amiga especial*, I'm <u>so</u> sorry for how I've been such a total asshole to you, disrespecting and mistreating you all this time. So, don't worry, you're a 'free girl' in a 'free land,' but on your own? ...Hmm. Well anyway, what I'm <u>trying</u> to say is I'm no good for you, so for your <u>own</u> good...I'll <u>never</u> try to see you again—I <u>promise</u>!" he vowed, thrice-gesturing the 'sign of the cross' and delivering a 'satisfied?' snare to Xavier left sighing and releasing the 'lost cause' in return, to then just get the whole thing over with. "Uh, <u>not</u> good enough, Carmen, but it'll have to do because time's up..." he warned with a nod to Betsy for assistance.

"Betsy, call the police and tell them you have the fugitive Xavier <u>Branion</u> detained by his own free will, unarmed and ready to cooperate—oh!" he added, merrily, with a slap to his own forehead, "and be sure to mention Carmen here, seeking a clear conscience, who's in custody voluntarily as well." Naturally as expected, Carmen protested, reminding him about the deal. "Hey, I thought since I apologized to her and stuff, even though in English, you were going to let me go and <u>give</u> <u>me</u> my <u>knife</u> back!" In all fairness to him, Xavier picked the knife up off the floor where he dropped it and, as a safety precaution, bended the blade amazingly to the handle without snapping it. Then pressing them together between his magical forming hands, he produced a harmless bar of metaled wood which he tossed to Carmen's fumbling catch. Dumbfounded and since freed from Xavier's grip, he then sat on the floor against the wall and shook his head, holding his mutilated knife in disbelief.

With the drama subsiding, Randy left Cindy's side with a nod and a pat on her back, trusting her to Xavier's care and parading out of the bar with the others. Then to the rumble of Harleys starting up outside, Betsy returned from the kitchen where she made the call. And while offering a maternal smile to Cindy who looked to her with hopeful eyes, she confirmed the 'quick response' and reassured the needy young teen, holding and leaning on Xavier's arm. "They said five-minutes, and I can already hear the sirens—lots of 'em! So, don't worry, honey…Cindy, is it? I'll do <u>everything</u> I can to help you get your life back on track…" Xavier nodded with an approving *'numero uno'* index finger gesture and started his exit with farewell words and a pouting Cindy reluctantly letting him go. "Thanks, Betsy and take care, Cindy—you're in <u>good</u> hands…" He paused with a forward-motioning wave and pointed to the door for the sorely slow-moving Carmen to join him. "Come on, Carmen, <u>time</u> to turn ourselves in—bye, y'all!"

Still to traumatized to speak outright, Cindy peered up to Xavier just starting away and merely said in a most sincere yet strained whisper, "Thank you, Xavier." Accompanied by a fragile smile and a girlish, finger-trilling wave goodbye, such heartfelt appreciation, he had never quite experienced before. Begrudgingly then, Carmen finally got up off the floor, raised his hands and started towards the door, with Xavier following him and Betsy racing behind the bar on an intercept course. In turn, she opened the gate in front and stalled them near the door as the sirens grew louder, and the police cars became visible down the street through the window.

"Wait <u>just</u> a minute there, Xavier…uh, besides all the weird shit that's gone down here, what the <u>hell</u> are we to expect from your encounter in Wisconsin, with that whatever-it-is on the loose? What's gonna happen? What should we do?" she so anxiously stressed with pleading eyes, prompting Xavier to pat her on the shoulder and reveal his discomforting forecast. "Okay, I'll level with you…this is big—'height of humanity' big! It's <u>all</u> coming down to <u>something</u>…catastrophic! And I, whether I like it or not, am like…<u>totally</u> roped in at a very high level. Now, my only advice to the two-of-you, and <u>anyone</u> else is go west, away from the coast to the higher elevations—hell, the mountains aren't that far at all from here!" he beamed with hope and added for Cindy's sake; "at least, it would give the kid a chance…" By the mere suggestion of a 'safe mountains' haven, Betsy then sported a big ole country smile and waved the 'still a little spacey' bar-stool-sitting Cindy over to join her. "West Virginia, here we come!" she joyfully declared with Cindy then by her side, nodding and clapping to Betsy's exuding positivity. "Got a <u>lot</u> of family and my parent's big ole house is up there! So, good luck Xavier and thanks for…well, as for you, Cindy, not to sound too cliché, but '*mi casa es su casa*'!" As Cindy smiled and made the '*numero uno*' sign, like Xavier did earlier, to her corny invitation, Betsy got on her tiptoes and gave Xavier a kiss on the cheek. She then escorted both him and the frowny-faced Carmen to the double-doors which she opened to multiple police cars swarming the parking lot, flashing their red-and-blue lights.

First to step out, Carmen got the 'last word' as he stopped just outside the doorway and shouted their doom, looking back-and-forth at them and the police with an ominous laugh and a maniacal grin. "Hah, ha-ha—you <u>do</u> know, none of this, matters now! <u>This</u> is fuckin' <u>biblical</u> 'end of the world' shit! The joke's on <u>all</u> of us because there's <u>nowhere</u> to go, no escape—<u>true</u> equality, baby! We're <u>all</u> screwed this time!" Xavier shook his head and followed him to the awaiting authorities, well knowing he could not quite argue his point. But then to look back at Betsy and Cindy, he prayed to disprove him.

CHAPTER XIII
Prisoners Ally

"I T IS CALLING US!" the alert Black Moon announced to the others whose lack of direction she resolved, alone, by detecting a hopeful sign. "No longer will we be slaves of darkness to Lone Hawk, 'the beast' and his selfish quest…hurry! To the blue light, our gateway to freedom!"

In trust of her intuition, they followed and soon shared her superior awareness. Like spermatozoid swimmers to the ovum, the school of tortured spirits swam through the swirling sea of struggling energies to an unknown refuge. After passing the violent storm of Lone Hawk's vast interior, they came upon a space of absolute tranquility. The eleven then bathed in the blue light, a sudden contrast to the black and red of which they escaped. The horror was gone and, with their most welcomed passage, fear, pain and frustration disappeared.

Immersed in harmonious joy, they were drawn effortlessly to a warm, aquamarine sphere which protruded from a dark, misty barrier. As they aligned its soothing curved surface in semi-circle formation, they began miraculously to change back to their former selves. From mere shadows, some of them transformed completely while most stagnated in an intermediate, apparitional stage. Whether purposely or coincidental, the majority was stifled in their overall development, including the ability to communicate.

"The Earth Force Sphere!" Black Moon delighted as eleven emerald, body-conforming thrones symmetrically emerged from the floor, comforting them even further in the surreal room of questionable boundaries. "Though we hated Lone Hawk for his treachery, we can be thankful that he did heed to my advice."

No one expressed notice of Black Moon's revelation, including Red Bear and Spirit Slayer who were fully formed and seated on either side of her, back and center of the orb. She looked about in frustration, wondering why most of them remained translucent self-images. And most infuriating, she wondered why those of complete reformation sat passively in silence.

As Spirit Slayer locked in a sphere-staring trance seemed the most cognitive of the lot, the challenging Black Moon directed her attention to him with desperate eyes. "Are you so overwhelmed that you must sit like a zombie?" she asked the motionless Spirit Slayer in disappointment. "Please, awaken, good shaman. Oh! This conversation with myself is growing most tiresome…"

To her lonely plea, he tore his sights away from the orb, only to offer Black Moon a glance as he stood and put his hands near its surface. "Excuse my preoccupation, Black Moon," Spirit Slayer whispered then raised his voice to a nominal volume while making circular, tactile motions before the hypnotizing sphere of a half-more his arm-span's diameter. "But it is not every day that one is in the very presence of a god! So, I was thinking about an address to begin formal contact. If you do not object, I would be honored to establish good rapport with this power that may be our only hope for freedom." Black Moon agreeably extended her hand toward the sphere in a gesture to proceed.

"Earth Force, your Greatness…please, in your kindness, grant us passage away from this body of Lone Hawk as he has taken us against our will. We only wish to join the new world 'independently' as braves who seek peace and do your bidding on our own; however, if there is a purpose for our forceful captivity, please offer us a sign, oh merciful one…and we shall abide."

With the conclusion of Spirit Slayer's heartfelt plea, the sphere cleared to a view of some rugged mountainous terrain passing underneath, much like an eagle's perception in rapid flight.

"It's a window to the real world!" Red Bear hollered, suddenly jumping out of his seat into a celebratory dance. "Lone Hawk has delivered us as promised—wow! But just in case, let's now test and make sure it's not but a tease." When Red Bear tried hastily to put his hand through the window to feel the wind outside, he was instantly rejected and thrown back to his seat in a trail of red sparks. Then quick to follow, the overly eager brave's contact triggered a thunderous rumble! Like the clearing of a volcanic throat, fair warning preceded the linguistic eruption that would cascade and resonate throughout the newly reborn.

"*Patience, my chosen ones,*" the penetrating baritone whisper of the Earth Force echoed in their consciousness, demanding absolute attention; "*your time will come very soon, as Lone Hawk 'unknowingly' delivers you, his disciples, back to the living world. Please, forgive his forcefulness, for he was only desperate to have your familiar companionship as security into the unknown.*

"*However, as he is unaware that you have successfully crossed over with him, he did not remain alone for very long,*" the Earth Force continued. "*Upon his emergence in the form of a most massive and powerful entity, he readily absorbed the mind of a man from the present era. Let this Xavier Branion's knowledge and experiences rain down into your minds while your commune with Lone Hawk's subconscious will prove invaluable as events unfold.*

"*The ultimate cure for the wicked disease which has invaded and now envelops the Earth relies on your combined wisdom and Lone Hawk's vengeful tenacity. Together, you will reach the source of the evil, and all will become clear. At that time, passage shall be granted to accommodate your vital roles. The balance of the world is entrusted to you, honorable braves, so…*" the Earth Force concluded, "*show yourselves worthy for all its natural life which is at stake!*"

Their reaction was of pure appreciation, being selected for a task so grand. And, upon further reflection of the omniscient address, they gazed, pleasantly stunned, into the Earth Force window with renewed hope and purpose. Eventually, while dreamily watching the interesting topography passing below Lone Hawk's careening flight pattern, a lifetime of perceptions seeped into their minds. Good, bad and indifferent, all of Xavier's experiences were shared, even the deepest secrets in his darkest zones of thought.

Although accessed, those filed too personal or shameful were generally ignored as they focused their attentions on the world's present technology and sociology. Thus, with the intermediary mind meld completed in a fraction of the time that it seemed, they were all quite dazed by its encompassing surge. However, when the view through the window suddenly made a one-hundred-eighty-degree reversal from the ground to the sky, even the ghost-phased disciples bulged their thrilled eyes to alertness, but only for an instant.

"Look!" Black Moon shouted, pointing excitedly. "Military aircraft passing right above us and his hand…I believe he just waved at them, ha-ha—<u>Lone Hawk</u> is <u>really</u> enjoying this!"

After the sudden turnover and their first real glimpse at the impressive flying machines of the modern era, the scenery returned from a sideways angle to the winding ravine, which sped by in a blur. Eventually, they came to a dead end that lay within a towering crevice, leaving only a stagnant view of tan and gray rock-face beneath the shadows. During the repose, with little to see outside the magic window, intense discussion and comments were to naturally follow.

"This is <u>so</u> amazing!" Black Moon reveled in the knowledge so recently bestowed. "All of these <u>wondrous</u> inventions and their <u>sheer</u> awareness of the 'surrounding world's realities' are so impressive. Just to imagine the variety of people, places and animals that exist nowadays is <u>such</u> an unbelievable gift, but there it is so true. How <u>little</u> we realized the vastness of it all…our world was <u>so</u> small."

In retort to what he considered wasteful words and unfocused to the task, one of the formerly sheepish let his wolfish demeanor surface. "Warriors! Let us not merely <u>gaze</u> into this window with dreamy-eyed awe," the lean, fierce-faced Tornado Foot demanded. "This is <u>all</u> very interesting, but the Earth Force has chosen us for battle with the Owlmen. Am <u>I</u> the only one who is aware that we <u>have</u> no weapons? Though my feet were fast and even deadly in the world of old, I always needed my arrow and bow.

"To rely on this esoteric notion of 'combined wisdom' forming the balance is <u>pure</u> rubbish. We are merely ancient warriors whose descendants were nearly wiped out by superior brute force. Let us learn from their mistakes and be prepared. We could have all the knowledge and wisdom in the world, yet without superior firepower, we are but 'helpless voyagers' on a cruise to doom. We need <u>real</u>, tangible weapons. Earth Force, please, if you're listening, grant us these…I only make perfect sense!"

Answering his long-winded plea, the Earth Force responded with gifts of appeasement. Into the right hand of each, a shimmering gold-pointed spear with a deep red, glowing shaft appeared. And with slight delay, another materialized into the 'doubly surprised' Black Moon's left-handed origin. While most still remained in the mute ghost phase, the Earth Force's bestowal of the mystic spears was thoroughly cherished. Only, a couple of the less faithful expressed disappointment.

"A fanciful spear?" Red Bear protested. "I do <u>not</u> think this is what Tornado Foot had in mind. We saw Lone Hawk's 'elaborate demonstration' in the Evermore of what the Owlmen can do—hah! They would make <u>fools</u> of us with these toys…and anyway, <u>why</u> did you get <u>two</u>, Black Moon?"

"Jealous of a toy, Red Bear?" she laughed. "My, what an 'aged child' you are, and it seems that your friend here is <u>even</u> worse!"

Throwing his spear to the floor next to the divine orb, the ingrate Tornado Foot stood with irreverence. "It's <u>just</u> a placebo to nurse our so-called combined wisdom," he angrily declared; "Earth Force, you <u>must</u> do better, or we stand not a chance!"

And there he stood, tapping his foot while awaiting improvement of arms. Though backing away from him, the others, even turncoat Red Bear, looked at him in silence with shaming eyes saying, 'oh no, you didn't!'. Growing impatient, Tornado Foot then stooped over to reclaim his discarded spear yet was put off when it coiled up, seemingly taking a life of its own. Like a riled cobra's hooded head, the golden spear tip began to curve and fan out as it rose from the coiled shaft. Rhythmically swaying to-and-fro, the strange snake-spear emitted a fist-sized bubble of bright, bloody red from its eyeless face. The object then floated toward the regretful brave.

With an obnoxious high-pitched hum, the ball, much like the Owlmens', spiraled Tornado Foot's unflinching body head-to-toe and promptly returned to its source. At that point, the inflamed serpentine spearhead stopped in the cocked position and instantly struck him with a fury. Afterwards, a blinding white light filled the chamber while the spear returned to its original form. And to no one's surprise, the luminous burst faded off without a trace of Tornado Foot.

"<u>Please</u> forgive my impudence, oh superior one!" he woefully pleaded while cast back into the dreaded energy storm that then was hosted by Lone Hawk's opposing 'blue versus red-eyed hurricanes' in the heat of battle from which they had earlier fled. "I had a lust for power that I could <u>not</u> control, and I'm <u>so</u> very sorry…<u>please</u> take me back—I <u>promise</u> to humbly serve with no doubts! <u>No one</u> has learned their lesson as well as <u>I</u> who shall redeem himself to your <u>absolute</u> satisfaction."

Most mercifully, Tornado Foot was granted a second chance and thus ascended through the benevolent blue eye and returned to the warm aquamarine light. Eventually, he found himself in his throne rejoined with the others. Thus, as he felt as though he had awakened from a dream within another, he asked so ever meekly, "Am I <u>really</u> back among the fold, again?"

"Yes, you are back!" Black Moon scolded to cleanse and unify the lot; "yet, we are <u>still</u> not whole…you, two!" she then raved, accusingly pointing at Tornado Foot and Red Bear; "you could end up <u>sabotaging</u> this quest with your <u>blind</u> pettiness! Have you <u>no</u> respect? Let me just say that you, Tornado Foot, seem to be cured of your skepticism, and I <u>hope</u> this is true. But as for you, Red Bear…have some honor and choose a side for once in your <u>despicable</u> existence. Now, since you both to my absolute surprise remain with us, at least be appreciative and reinforce our focused efforts ahead…

"Our power is <u>much</u> more than tactical weapons of convention—it goes <u>far</u> beyond that! We are nearly gods, and with our unified…" Suddenly, only Black Moon's throne began to rock back-and-forth, up-and-down and around to the point of hilarity, as she was caught off-guard, bouncing every which way. "I'm sorry, Great Earth Force!" she pleaded, voice and breasts a jiggle, well-knowing what she had said to anger the sphere. "I take back what I said…my bloating ego got in the way and has retreated—I <u>positively</u> regret my godly presumption! And, of course, I will <u>only</u> use my powers bestowed for the Earth's greater good?" Immediately, her throne calmed to stillness while Red Bear chimed in at her expense.

"<u>Nearly</u> gods—ha-ha!" he chuckled, enjoying being the 'thorn in her side.'" "Even <u>I</u> know better!" Black Moon pursed her lips and flared her eyes at him in retort. "Well, nobody's perfect…and <u>I</u> for the renewed life of me <u>cannot</u> understand why <u>you</u> get a pass…so anyway, umm, forget the 'godly status' thing I was about to say. Rather, in light of the incentive that our freedom will be granted to procure victory in this quest-of-all-quests, let us delve into Lone Hawk's stubborn mind and inject a healthy dosage of 'combined wisdom,' and—what's this?! He is taking us <u>right</u> into the rock!"

In response to definite contact with the enemy, Lone Hawk, to the complete astonishment of 'the Earth Force eleven,' ventured into the sheer cliff before them. Void of desecration, he flew like a spirit in untethered defiance of the rocky underworld's night. Then while blazing a trail deep into the great mountain, Red Bear accurately voiced all their impressions, scouring away any residual doubt: "Whatever disbelief and uncertainty I may have had, I now relinquish," he said with a sweeping hand of the window's grainy view, hinting at a boundless range. "Lone Hawk can go <u>anywhere</u>…and with him, our fusion is <u>invincible!</u>

"Oh, and what direction! Now, here…what sort of strange cave etched so deeply into the rock is this?" Red Bear asked suspiciously but in wonderment of the Spartan, yet finely appointed hexagonal hollow upon which they had arrived. "Those signs, panels and controls, they are <u>so</u>—you know! Of course, I'm talking Owlmen, Gray Alien base and there they go. Ha-ha, he sees them fleeing for their ship in the tunnel without a chance. Hah, look at them <u>pathetically</u> scamper…get those freaks, Lone Hawk!"

In the excitement of the chase, Red Bear then unwittingly lunged like a cat after a bird outside a window, only to be deflected once again.

"Have you no restraint, Red Bear, oh <u>delirious</u> wild man that you are?" the deep-voiced gentle giant, Thunderhead, heartily laughed upon his full development as Red Bear tried to regather his composure. "We share your enthusiasm, I am sure, but please do not narrate everything and disrupt our view. Ah, and see…you could not have caught them even if you were set free. Their ship has sucked them inside!"

True to Thunderhead's observation, three Gray Aliens blurred into the bottom of their levitated silver craft of a bubbled-center, flying saucer design. Then almost instantly, the vessel disappeared into the oval tunnel where they would follow. In a flash, they only caught one last glimpse of the near colorless alien station of geometric perfection, and thus were taken on a wild ride inside the eerily cumbersome passageway into which the saucer retreated. As they plunged into occasional curves dotted by dim red and white lights, initial pursuit saw nothing more until the splashing impact of water.

Though the chase had slowed until the white bubbles cleared, the alien vessel was faintly in sight. With an incomparable advantage in the aqua tunnel, Lone Hawk quickly gained on the target. And in fulfillment of their expectations, he came into rapid contact and latched onto the surging craft.

"We _have_ them!" Black Moon announced, triumphant; "now, he can find the source from where they hail, down there…"

When the opposite end of the winding corridor soon opened up hundreds of miles off the British Columbian mainland into the deep dark sea, Lone Hawk brought his prize to a halt, remaining fully adjoined to it. Then like the plane he retrieved from outer space, he attempted to communicate with those within its chamber. Only in this case, forceful mind absorption would be the order of the day and so, implementation had commenced. However, the alien crew was of the ultimate resistance and, as such, proved themselves 'mind-probe-proof' by resorting to the only for certain deterrent: 'Abort Existence!'. Hence, their self-destruct mechanism was activated.

The impact of the deep-sea explosion caused no harm to Lone Hawk and his ghostly detainees, yet they had been violently thrown aback without the guaranteed link. Invariably, the loss left him in an obvious state of perplexity as he spun above the steps of the North Pacific Ocean, pondering his next move. In turn, nearing the surface in such a dizzying manner only made Black Moon and everyone inside him even more anxious. Even when they cracked the ocean's surface with no land in sight, the rotation continued at such a rate so pressing the limit of their bear-ability.

"The explosion has stifled his drive. He is <u>totally</u> confused!" Black Moon voiced with great concern. "We <u>must</u> break this cycle. Lone Hawk! You've <u>got</u> to rest and <u>clear</u> your thoughts. The sign will soon come!"

Calming to her request even but for the moment, Lone Hawk's spin slackened to a comfortable rate between the sea and sky. He was still in a quandary, yet reprieve was granted as the window's view of the splashing deep blue waves below a cumulus sky cleared to a halt, facing west with sighs of relief.

In the meantime, Black Moon attempted to solve the puzzle. "He is most <u>certainly</u> torn between the great ocean and the sky. But where do their ships come and go? Well, the sky's too obvious and he's been fooled before, and so has vowed, 'Never again'!"

In agreement, Thunderhead elaborated on her raw assessment. "You're on to something, Black Moon, and <u>I</u> think they are most <u>definitely</u> in the depths of this vast ocean," he surmised to then present his theory with ancient flair. "The sky holds nothing to fortress. Their travels would be <u>so</u> exposed to these modern humans with their fighter jets, space ships and such. I contest that like clever worms in an apple, they lurk in the very core of our Earth. Theirs is a place from which to surface, do their dirty deeds and retreat, unreachable by any man…yes! In the <u>deepest</u> of the deep, they do nest…I am <u>most</u> certain."

While mutual nods of concord spread among them all, Spirit Slayer posed a vital question: "That was very well put, Thunderhead," he complimented, leading to the point; "though under the ocean they could very well be, it is so huge that we may spend years combing its floor in a search destined to lose momentum. This sign or guide soon to come is a most abstract concept. How are we <u>or</u> Lone Hawk to recognize this 'profound thing' of which you speak, Black Moon?"

Righteously responding just as he spoke her name, the exasperated Black Moon once again felt like the bonding force of 'the sphere's chosen.' "Because <u>I</u> have enough faith and intuition for <u>all</u> of us," she proudly touted; "and do <u>not</u> underestimate Lone Hawk. The way he found their station by internally superseding a mountain only proves his sensory abilities are absolutely phenomenal…ah, we <u>are</u> submerging—<u>see</u>? He has recovered and taken our advice.

"Oh, and what is this?" she remarked of a big white 'battering ram' creature fleeing in the distance. "A great white fish, it seems…and in an 'awful' hurry!"

In correction of her hasty observation, another disciple emerged whole and broke his silence. "That is <u>no</u> fish," explained Badger, a lanky brave with a boyish face and amiable disposition; "that's a whale, a 'sperm whale' to be precise!" he plainly added, with his obvious interest 'selectively' tapping into Xavier's ample zoological knowledge. "And look at how <u>badly</u> wounded it is. That trail of blood has made him prey for those killer whales, swimming after him …" his voice became frantic; "Lone Hawk, you <u>must</u> save this <u>poor</u> animal!"

Sharing his sentiments, Lone Hawk promptly chased down the rare ivory whale and vigorously whisked the violent pack of male yin-yang marauders away with his huge and powerful hands. Even in the blood-drenched waters, their near-feeding-frenzy was wisely abandoned due to his mighty presence. And thus, they chose instead to chase a great white shark drawn to the bloody scene.

"Thank you, Lone Hawk," Badger continued with immeasurable relief; "you have done well to save this one from a very torturous death, being eaten alive, chunk by torn chunk…oh! I'm <u>so</u> glad he rescued the creature," he gushed with compassion then shared more with the others. "They are among the most <u>fascinating</u> and <u>intelligent</u> aquamarine mammals on the planet. Look at his frightened, yet knowing eye…I <u>believe</u> we have found our guide!"

After pulling a broken harpoon out of the petrified whale's side, Lone Hawk passed his hand over the huge puncture wound. Once gushing with blood, it was then miraculously sealed, unscathed, as though it had never been inflicted. Then proceeding to calm the cetacean adolescent, he stroked its brow with little resistance. Eventually, he would gain its trust and learn about the oceanic world from its largest predator's point of view.

CHAPTER XIV
Branion's Way

AFTER ABOUT AN HOUR'S limousine drive south from the 'Ace in the Hole' bar to a top-secret CIA location nestled in the bowels of an office building just north of the Washington D.C.'s Capital Beltway, Xavier constructed every possible scenario he could conceive while waiting for the black bag of his gracious submission to be removed. Through wide, deep green double-doors into a finely appointed, theater-like conference room, the black-bagged Xavier was escorted inside by four-male federal agents, two-white, one black, and an Asian man who would later accompany him for his initial transport. As the doors closed behind them, they removed the bag and the handcuffs, allowing him a moment to look around and rub his hands together for reassociation. First to impress him was a twenty-five-by-fifteen-foot IMAX screen, in front and to his left of the side-entrance whence they came. On screen, the 'larger than life' Secretary of State Dan Dwight's 'live' elfin-faced image was on display, sitting at a desk in Geneva, Switzerland with his hands folded. Then next to catch his eyes were four, ten-foot-square faux skylights with passing 'cumulus skies' imagery, evenly set in an ornate cathedral ceiling.

Among the dozen or so dignitaries present near the front of the voluminous room, CIA Director Charles Wilkins, a tall black man of about sixty, was the only one to break away and approach Xavier since he filled the primary role as host of the ten o'clock top-secret meeting. Emanating a comfortable air of authority, he instantly gained Xavier's trust and then more so by a welcoming proposal he was soon to deliver from a large jade podium amid the mostly grayish-green setting with subtle red, white and blue accenting. Before the centered podium stamped with a two-foot CIA emblem, a soft-U-shaped marble table curved around it where the primary bureaucrat participants, including the 'Eisenhower' resembling Joint Chief of Staff, General Sean Fletcher, began to seat themselves.

Thus, taking his cue from the building tension, Director Wilkins shook Xavier's hand and in a deep bellowing voice, cracked a little joke to break the ice for an amicable start. "Pleased to meet you, Xavier…Chuck Wilkins, CIA Director. Ha-ha! I'm sure glad you didn't squeeze _my_ hand as hard as you did that Cartel dirt-bag's phone—_wish_ I could've seen the _look_ on his face!" Wilkins mused so jolly, but then got dead serious. "However, that was just the tip-of-the-iceberg as to your supernatural abilities, I'm told, that you put on display back there…" Brimmingly unfazed by his budding supernatural confidence, Xavier spoke as if he had all the leverage and thus intended to get his way through some kind of deal. "Yeah, and much more to come, I'm sure. Now let's just cut to the chase—you _need_ me as a tracker, don't you! Well, tell me what you've got planned so far, Director Wilkins, and…if I like what I hear, I'll see what I can do for you…" he spouted in a brash tone, smirking, to then continue with suspicion. "And by the way, there was a 'weird' alarm that went off when I was scanned in the elevator…_which_ I could _tell_ took serious notice from one of your agents here…uh, anyone?"

In ill-eased response, the Asian agent, a good-looking guy with a long-thin 'Japanese' nose, pointed to himself and looked to Wilkins for permission to comment, prompting the Director to give him the go-ahead nod. "Mister Branion's bio-scan, as he so aptly sensed, was most unusual to say the least," he said in a stiff manner then elaborated, somewhat distressed, with intense glances and a twirling hand directed at the squinting Xavier. "He entered as a detectable yet unknown quantity…so according to that, the contact at ground-zero has rendered Mister Branion here to have a not-yet-identified, nor classified life signature. Also, right after his anomalous scan was read, I was thinking it could be a malfunction, so I checked my own which came up normal. Uh, conclusion being—he's been <u>transformed</u> beyond human." Director Wilkins pursed his lips, obviously disturbed by the evidence, and thus wanted confirmation. "Well, just to make sure, have it fully re-calibrated and check him again on the way out…" Meantime, Xavier added another angle to the mix that had most, within earshot, rolling their eyes. "Not to scare you, guys, but people have suggested that I'm <u>probably</u> demonically possessed…yet I don't think that's the case. From what I can gather so far, it's like 'not quite evil' nor 'all that good' but a strongly determined, persuasive presence in my head, goading me to go west…uh, to the mountains? Maybe describing from where it was messaging…and I'm envisioning the northwest Rockies, so—<u>that's</u> where it's coming from, I bet!"

In elated response, Wilkins hailed Xavier's mystic message to its confirming alignment with the investigation. "Wow, does that ever fall into line with what's been going on up there in the Canadian Rockies…Dan, Sean—could this be 'more perfect'? There's a definite connection between Mister Branion and the entity! Come with me, Xavier, I'd like to show you a rough depiction of your multiple-witnessed abduction that we <u>had</u> to put together due to some kind of interference, rendering the confiscated phone videos too scrambled for viewing…oh, Dan?" he paused for a moment, turning the conversation to Secretary Dwight, and continued with his introduction. "You raised your finger…want to say something before we start the video which will <u>temporarily</u>, ha-ha, displace you to the corner-screen? Uh, Xavier, our Secretary of State, Dan Dwight…"

The Secretary then took the virtual stage, with a slight Southern drawl that made him sound a bit less stodgy than Wilkins whose accent was business non-descript. "Welcome aboard, Xavier…well, after Director Wilkins' presentation of the 'Devils Lake' incident, featuring our 'hurry-up' CGI-depicted account of your <u>possibly</u> 'other-worldly' encounter, we will further discuss the initial itinerary as Wilkins hinted at, the what-ifs and other plans, depending on how it goes…" Dan described with open-minded flexibility, and went on; "I'm glad we seem to be on the same wavelength here from the get-go, and if you have any questions or concerns, please feel free to speak up. So, once you get your bearings on the flight out, trust your instincts, psychic impressions and such for your team members accompanying you as their primary mission's guide." In all politeness, Xavier responded then, with a raised eyebrow to Wilkins and the Secretary, hinted at something that would meet regretful resistance later on. "Thank you, Mister Secretary, I appreciate your confidence in my 'potential' value here, but I <u>do</u> have a special request that can wait till after the Director's presentation…which he looks all-to-eager to get rolling with—so on with the show, if you please…"

Wilkins nodded with an unsure-figuring grin then escorted Xavier to the podium area and rolled a deluxe, tan-leather office chair from the side to front-and-center where he took a seat facing the director. As he calmly looked about and back at the row of bureaucratic stiffs behind him, Dan's image shrunk to the lower-left-corner of the big screen while the CIA emblem cut-out of the scene to a luminous, night-time lakeside setting's fade-in view. In 'Anime' style, the video began with a wide-angled perspective of Xavier's march from the beach to the bird mound while Director Wilkins narrated the action play-by-play with great enthusiasm. "Okay, that's you, Xavier—you've broken away from Ranger Travis and the others at the beach, then…you're crouching around on the upper part of bird mound, trying to identify the strange humming vibrations coming from it," he started with the set-up then moved on to the nitty-gritty horror of the situation.

"And here, is when it gets ugly…the weird effect stops for a bit and you call over to Travis, but then it starts up again and—boom! The ground <u>bursts</u> beneath your feet and launches you approximately a hundred feet southwest of the mound. Oh, and did the animators ever do an <u>excellent</u> job, as you can see with this at least seventy-foot-tall, gargoyle-birdman creature emerging from there that reportedly had a tan, triple-crested 'Gray Alien' face and a giant feathered headdress. Now, watch this—first thing! It casts these wild laser beams out of its huge banding-red eyes, lifts you up with a projected pink sphere for about ten-seconds and drops you back to the ground. Then, strangely enough, it salutes you with some rumbling, low-frequency whispers and then curses the sky, temporarily hawk-faced, with the loudest 'rebel yell' <u>ever</u> heard! So here in this part, the best <u>actual</u> audio recording that was confiscated plays out—now listen!" During the frightening replay of Lone Hawk's painfully real 'shout out to the world' recording, Xavier grimaced, curled forward and covered his ears while everyone else, besides the video-focused Wilkins, took concerned notice.

Meanwhile, continuing his ground-zero narration, the Director glanced over at Xavier and realized the traumatizing effect that the vocal anomaly had had on him. Yet, he decided to go ahead and wrap up the video presentation before addressing his unique reaction. "Yes, like the gates of hell unlatching and unleashing, roaring and screeching—oh! I know, Xavier, just let me … so, nearing the end here, Ranger Travis fires a few shots at the creature with no apparent effect, but look at this—only to have it wag its finger and shake its head at him like saying, 'naughty-naughty—<u>behave</u>, you!'… hey, <u>that's</u> just what they reported!" Really into it, Wilkins gestured wildly while being uncharacteristically silly in his amusement, then promptly retained a cool composure and concluded his video narrative. "Finally, then, the 'Gargoyle Chief' birdman creature flies off <u>without</u> even flapping its wings and disappears over the western ridge. How it propels itself is thought by our experts to be with some kind of telekinetic anti-gravity technique … uh, Xavier, do you want to talk about the actual recording of that hellish yell—did it speak to you in any way? Judging by your reaction, it must have hit you like a ton of bricks!"

Still a little shaken, Xavier sighed for a moment then found himself, curiously, brave fist saluting the ceiling just as Lone Hawk did the sky. And though he quickly retracted his hand to his chin, everyone nodded to him, making the connection and eagerly awaiting his response which he delivered in atypical form. "So, you want an interpretation? Well, get this: 'Evil One—I'm back! Your worst nightmare has only just begun!'… or something like that. But whatever of this, I am sure—<u>He</u> … <u>is</u> … <u>pissed</u>!" Intrigued, Wilkins cued in on Xavier's pronoun usage as he grew fascinated with a potential nemesis coming into focus. "So now, <u>it</u> is a … <u>he</u>? Hmm, so who does <u>he</u> consider to be this 'Evil One' with whom he obviously has a score to settle, do you suppose?" Calm and cool once again, Xavier elaborated in response. "All I know is it's definitely not about us, but rather an invader that maybe banished him to a very-very long exile and now, free at last, he's totally gung-ho on getting his revenge." Xavier flung his beholding hands widely and, while sporting his 'signature' annoying smirk, looked around to close his point. "And that's my 'crack' analysis…"

In a gruff voice, General Fletcher interjected and expressed his military concerns to properly re-identify who the 'true' enemy really was. "Well, folks—it's pretty damn obvious to me! Our target has become our ally against a common enemy as I will explain in reference to a very recent happening, a bizarre incident in southwest Alberta," he passionately surmised while connecting the dots with logical precision. "This all ties in with the 'Santa Marsia' Mars mission disaster as well, which has triggered ever-increasing, communication satellite interference and hailing-to-zero-response manned orbiters, including the space plane involved. Brought down from low-orbit to a controlled landing there, a huge grayish-tan form was observed piggybacking on the disabled vessel by a Royal Canadian Air Force squadron, performing exercises in the area."

The General then raised his voice to emphasize the climactic point of the encounter. "Unfortunately, though, a young trigger-happy pilot fired a direct-hit missile at the creature-cloaked plane while they slid intact toward the mountains. And though the space plane was completely destroyed, your 'bird chief' friend resurfaced and, for a second time, gave them the slip but with this occurring quite a distance to the west in British Columbia." The General concluded his long-winded spiel with an 'other worldly' twist that surprised no one. "Now, before I lose my point, I am convinced that the common enemy is extraterrestrial, taking us out first—in space, second—in the upper atmosphere and now, down here where its 'I'm now certain' terrestrial nemesis forges a westward pattern for us to follow. That's why our as well…your mission, Xavier, will begin at the Cache Crown Airport, about a hundred-thirty-miles from Vancouver, to hook up with the Canadians for an investigation of the last-sighted location."

Upon hearing the 'whole story' of the mission trajectory aligning with his own, Xavier suddenly sprung to his feet and backed away to his right near the edge of the podium next to Wilkins, gaining a more dominant presence. Then in a firm voice and a bit of a sneer, he turned his request, hinted at earlier, into a demand while gesturing in an intimidating manner. "With all due respect, General, Mister Secretary, uh, Ladies and Gentlemen—here it comes!" Xavier blurted in warning to their cringing faces, not to be soon relieved. "The request I alluded to earlier…which is that I will require a minor adjustment to our itinerary—a stop-over at Madison-Dain County Airport." To the further-soured faces abounding, Xavier, unfazed, then looked around with a stout grin and continued with some heartfelt persuasion. "There, I'll need you to arrange a rendezvous with Jeanine Vercelli…who I'm sure you already contacted and have under surveillance as we speak. Dealing with this situation, clearing the air and just maybe having a second chance will be essential to my on-going 'positive' morale which can only benefit the mission. So, do we have a deal? Or, do I pursue this on my own? You know you can't hold me…"

Alarmed, Secretary Dwight tried to dissuade Xavier from his unanimously perceived, selfish condition placed on the mission's plan. "Let's be reasonable, Xavier…to stifle the mission with this 'wild goose chase' for an old girlfriend is just plain impractical! Especially when the security and quite possibly the core-stability of the entire 'good world as we know it' is at stake." Even though Xavier started pursing his lips, shaking his head and squeezing his hands together with a crimson glow, Director Wilkins chimed in, clumsily, offering only a flimsy alternative. "Really, Xavier, this is much more important than trying to patch up a relationship that went sour," he reasoned away while tilting his head and beholding him for a solution. "I'm sure we can arrange a 'compromise' as in setting-up a zoom call with her while you're on the plane, you know, so we don't waste any time on the ground…"

Then trying to appeal to Xavier's burgeoning ego, General Fletcher inadvertently made things worse. "Yeah, we could do that and…just look at it this way, Xavier: Have faith in our champion out there who, out of everyone else in the world, chose you to follow his lead," he charmed as best he could, smiling wide-eyed and nodding to him, over-doing it a bit but only in hopes of putting the notion to rest. "And with that, we're gonna win this thing! Then, when you go back to her 'a hero,' she'll be worshipping the ground you walk on, along with lots of other pretty gals, I bet!" Thus, sudden 'inhaling thrusts' of shock spread and echoed around the room as Xavier looked back-an-forth, red-scrunch-faced enraged. And thus, he started shaking into blurring traces while making the floor vibrate and rumble like he did at the 'shattered mirror' incident a couple-hour earlier, only ten-times worse.

Out of control in what had turned into a simulated earthquake zone, Xavier pointed his finger like a shootist at Dan Dwight's screen image while glancing back at the General who he telekinetically forced to draw his concealed pistol. Then in sadistic synchronicity, Xavier, with a gleaming smile pretended to shoot the Secretary's image as the frowning Fletcher fired three-live-rounds at it, shattering the IMAX monstrosity to a striated rectangular plane of downward flowing sparks and smoke. Instantly, while feeling his demonstration a success, Xavier quelled the tremors and cleared the smoke with downward-pressing hands and resumed his alpha-male composure, wearing a 'need I say more?' smirk.

In turn, Director Wilkins conceded to his demand, with the stunned General Fletcher shakily re-holstering his sleek-compact pistol and nodding meekly in concurrence to the change of plans. "Well, alright, Xavier—you've made your point!" Wilkins folded reluctantly to the stop-over demand but with a loud exhale, none-the-less, of unwavering relief. "Agent Lee, you heard the man—arrange for the Madison stop-over with our FBI counterparts handling ground transport, etcetera…Xavier, you've got us over a barrel, for sure, but could you 'at least' just make it as brief as possible?"

Xavier responded with his continued psychopathic demeanor as with the reckless demonstration of terror he just wielded at them, deeming it merely 'par de course.' "No problem. She lives pretty close to the airport, so all I ask is about a half-hour on the ground—cool?" Wilkins, just itching to get the meeting over with, allowed a more reasonable extension. "Let's just say forty-five-minutes, with church traffic and all…" He paused and took a deep breath, with a nodding look around and a pitying headshake at the tattered IMAX-screen mess. "Well, I think we're through here…meeting closed and adjourned—whew!" Xavier clapped for a couple-seconds then shrugged his shoulders, unconvincingly wide-eyed and innocent. And while he followed Agent Lee with the other three-agents out of the conference room, the rest of the attendees were left chit-chatting and breathing sighs of relief.

After Xavier's bio-scan results from the re-calibrated system registered same as before, the Agent Lee-led team-of-four exited the elevator and made an immediate left back into the multi-tiered garage of his black-bagged arrival, and onto its narrow walkway with that familiar sound. Clicking and clacking in echoed disunity, their hard-soled shoes struck the concrete floor with a 'G,-3' painted pillar where they took another left across the bottom of an up-ramp. On the other side, they approached a fleet of six, dark-green sports sedans parked grill-out in a row of 'special' reserved spaces. Like the latest Dodge Charger EC model but huskier with high-mounted doors and an unusually tight passenger compartment, Xavier jumped for joy when he realized that the type of automobile they were about to board was of the flight-capable variety.

While the other agents got into the first 'fly-car' parked in the row, started it up to a smooth roar and pulled out, Agent Lee tapped away on his phone and paused in front of the second one in line, with a motioning nod and smile for him to check it out. Relishing the invitation, Xavier beheld the ultra-high-tech vehicle and gave it a thorough looking over as he gushed about it and impressed to 'the connection' he left back at the bar. "My God, I was just reading about these babies—this is the tits!" he raved, googly-eyed and most honored while bowing to its majesty. "Wait a minute, you could have just had me air-lifted in a fuckin' helicopter to the airport…a 'special favor,' perhaps? Come on, you must have known about the magazine at the bar…" Thus, Agent Lee readily admitted to Xavier's innocent suspicion. "Motor Trend? Yeah— excellent article! But they'll run ya plenty more than a million- bucks…properly equipped, that is." Agent Lee confirmed, most graciously, and with a tap on the magnificent machine's hood, he tempted to Xavier's delight. "So, what you say we take 'this baby' up there, and catch a mega-cool view of the Capitol?"

Xavier could barely contain himself while he got as hopping-giddy as he could ever be. "I'm with you, Lee, ha-ha…let's get high, Mon!" Agent Lee shared the laugh then wrapped up his phone work and slipped into the driver's seat, tapping on the inside window to prompt the pre-occupied Xavier, rocking the car from the roof's edge, to get inside and ride shot gun. Once inside, the agents in the other identical vehicle proceeded and took a right on the up-ramp, with Lee and Xavier following in the three-floor-ascent to the ground-level exit gate. Both flight-capable cars checked out and passed into an outdoor parking lot that was packed close to the six-story office building, but clear in the back near the outer gate. There, they pulled up and stopped a few car-lengths apart, with the lead vehicle revving its multi-thrust engines which sounded like a symphony of low-to-high-frequency vacuum motors.

Within seconds, the flying car smoothly levitated twenty-feet and surged forward in a steep southward climb over the north Capital Beltway/interstate junction toward the Capitol, with the Washington Monument barely visible in the distance. After Agent Lee took off the same and began to gain on the others at about five-hundred-feet and climbing, Xavier cleared his throat about to break his ecstatic silence. Yet holding his blurting tongue for the moment, he only observed with bugging eyes, Agent Lee's maneuvering expertise in handling both the steering wheel and the joystick on the console beneath the multi-gauged dashboard. He eyed the digital-dial speedometer cruising a steady two-hundred-fifty-MPH and hinted toward a thrilling request. "Now, tell me, Lee, what does it top-out at?" More than happy to brag, Agent Lee rocked and thrusted his beholding hand forward to the clear blue sky, sounding like a glorified test pilot. "I actually had one of these 'Charger Rockets' over three-fifty, cruising at five-thousand-feet, but these particular models are the super expensive, 'souped-up' versions with the deluxe anti-gravity-assist package and all…" Lee paused to boast about the classic scene before and below them. "Now, that's a beautiful view of the Capitol, since the haze has lifted."

Though impressed, the always competitive Xavier continued to pressure with his suggestion by means of a 'lively' sky diversion.

"Yeah, beautiful…but back to your magic chariot here—how about <u>blowing</u> past your comrades in front of us and <u>taking</u> the lead? I'm <u>sure</u> you know the way, without them!" Lee was a bit reluctant, at first, then warmed up to the idea. "Umm, okay…just let me alert them, so they don't get <u>freaked</u> out…" he cautioned to Xavier's near mocking the notion. "Oh, <u>dare</u> no—we sure wouldn't want to do that! So, fine…fair warning <u>then</u>—go for it!" Xavier waited in suspense while staring at the speedometer, once again, on the elaborate dashboard that was then maintaining a slower two-hundred-thirty-MPH and falling behind, perhaps for a more thrilling effect.

Meantime, Agent Lee made some lever adjustments on the steering-column and gave the driver-pilot in the lead a heads-up before implementing the maneuver. "Yeah, Larsen, I'm about to aggressively take the lead, per the passenger's request, and take it down to the tarmac ahead of you—copy?" Thus, right after Agent Larsen's generic "Roger that!" reply, Lee gunned it and raced ahead with such tremendous acceleration, Xavier sat pinned in his seat, hooting and hollering, as they passed rapidly over and high above the other flying Charger beginning to descend. Then taking it from two-to-three-thousand-feet, Lee only nearly topped it out at three-hundred-thirty-MPH, but soon cut to half-the-speed as they neared the Potomac River above Capitol center.

As Agent Lee began to descend sharply and cross the river into Washington National airspace, Xavier voiced his concern about the two 'unlikely' fans he left back at the Baltimore bar, so as to subtly reveal whatever of their fate in the 'supernatural bar fight' aftermath. "By the way, Lee, do you have <u>any</u> idea what happened to the 'Ace in the Hole' bartender, Betsy? She should be commended for how well she handled such a tense, down-right bizarre situation." Lee glanced at him, held his own chin in recall and delivered the best-case-scenario report he could have ever expected. "Uh, Betsy? Oh yes, Miss Schroeder…she gave a satisfactory statement to one of the officers. And then, it is my understanding that she left with her daughter. So, would you like us to send her a message for you?" Not to stir-the-pot, Xavier declined for their own good. "Nah, leave her be…she's been through enough. Just wanted to put in a good word for her."

Xavier smiled broadly to the good news that they would escape the coastal city and, as he envisioned, find refuge at her family 'mountain haven' homestead. But his premonitions of global disaster soon over shadowed such sweet thoughts and thus grew ever stronger. So, before he could brood about the everyone else's fate too much, Xavier refocused and watched excitedly as Lee took the fly-car into a well-controlled descent then to hover for a moment above the airport's northeast tarmac. Parked down there as he correctly assumed it to be, his private military jet awaited with the other passengers standing before it. "Alright!" he blurted, rubbing his hands together in anticipation. "<u>This</u> must be my Madison Express in waiting—wow! Now, <u>that</u> is one sweet-lookin' plane! And with the Marines, seeing me off? Uh, or…more like coming along, for my <u>own</u> security's sake? Yeah, right! But gee, I am so <u>VIP</u> flattered…"

Agent Lee then rode his wave of sarcasm quite well in retort. "Nothing but the best for you, Citizen '*Numero-Uno*', ha-ha…so here, I'll just quick-introduce your new teammates, special agents and, yeah-yeah…like in the old series, 'X-Files', paranormal investigators who I know very well," he assured, sounding a bit hurried, and continued. "So don't worry, you'll be in 'good company.' And after that, who knows? Maybe <u>I</u> should get the <u>hell</u> out of this city, and 'go west' as well!" They chuckled half-heartily, well knowing it to be a sensible move while he carefully landed with the two 'special' agents meeting them outside the car, fifty feet from the plane. Immediately, Agent Lee got out to brief them while Xavier took his time exiting the 'thrill riding' vehicle to take one last look and allow the three agents ahead start towards the plane. Soon, he caught up and rushed to Lee's side for introductions. Then facing each other, they felt a little awkward until Agent Lee, most aptly, smoothed things over with a beholding hand towards the tall-lean, facially 'Spaniard' Latina and the hulking Slavic man, both in quasi-military attire and about forty-years-of-age. "Xavier Branion, meet our CIA premier paranormal specialists, Special Agents Sandos and Andrewska. They will be at your disposal throughout this expedition to interpret, advise and annoy you with scans and questions. And, of course, we've supplied a small security force to accompany you. So, good luck, Xavier, and let it be known that you are in <u>very</u> good hands with these two. It will be a very productive, revealing and…'adventurous' investigation, I'm sure, so good luck to you all!" Between handshakes with the two individuals, Xavier offered a punching thumbs-up gesture and nod to Lee who looked off and left them as if he could not vacate the scene soon enough.

Then with Lee's departure, the proud 'security force' Marines exploded into a planned 'welcome chant' in Xavier's honor: "Let's go, Branion!" they shouted out a few times, all smiles, rhythmically clapping and pumping their fists to which he brave-fist saluted them, half-clenching his hand like a lion's paw with them copying the same.

While the disapproving special agents shook their heads so quelling the soldiers' inappropriate mirth, the CIA flying Chargers' turbine engines roared to transcend any conversation level. And thus, they wasted no time boarding the ninety-foot, white with red and bluish-silver-trimmed aircraft. Sporting sleek, futuristic lines and Mach 2-plus capability, the plane was more than aptly equipped and designed to task. And with an interior plush as any first-class airliner, Xavier was impressed at first sight when he saluted the pilot and copilot then perused down the aisle through the well-spaced rows of a mere two seats per side. Waving toward the rear in a hurried demeanor, Andrewska guided him further aft through a pair of automatic sliding doors to a spacious conference cabin. Like the rest of the plane, the red and bluish-silver on white color scheme pervaded throughout. Once inside, Xavier seated himself at the far end of the table, facing forward in one of the ten swivel, high-backed armchairs anchored to the deck. Set around a twelve-foot, oak-veneer conference table, there was also a curious, chromium platter-like centerpiece that caught his attention until the doors suddenly slid closed. Taking their cue, the agents seated themselves as well, allowing an empty one on either side, so as not to crowd him.

The plane began to taxi toward the runway and Sandos cleared her throat to begin the phase-two briefing. "Well, Mister Branion, let me open this briefing by assuring you that your request to stop over in Madison will be honored and we should arrive there in approximately an hour," she opened with a very businesslike monotone voice as she forced a robotic smile, sporadically glancing at him with big dark eyes while she referenced from her phone. "There will be a limousine with a couple of agents from the Bureau and, of course, they're fully instructed as to the location of this Vercelli woman's residence and, with minimal surveillance, we're sure that she is home. The question now is…would you like to call her first for some preparation, or is your intent one of surprise?"

They were accelerating down the runway and his mind did not even consider the former suggestion. "Surprise, <u>definitely</u> surprise!" he shouted with an impish grin, just as they became airborne. While Sandos acknowledged his choice with a raised eyebrow and pursed lips, the broad-faced, big-shouldered Andrewska seemed to make fun of her reaction with a smirk, rolling his slit, gray eyes.

"When we get to cruising altitude, you can get out of that crap and help yourself to some top-quality Air Force duds which they've supplied in the back," Andrewska suggested, lumbering over to an aft storage compartment from which he started to extract some clothing basics. "Socks, boots, underwear and jump suits, or pants with separate shirts. If you wanna change, take your pick and we'll forestall our discussion till you're ready. We're pretty much leveled off now, so how 'bout it? The restroom's right over there…"

If only to get a better fitting pair of boots, Xavier obliged Andrewska's invitation and fished out his selections, first making sure the footwear was the right size before going in to change. "All right, I'll be just a moment!" He stepped inside the spacious lavatory, stripped himself naked and relieved his bladder, but then steered his eyes toward the mirror to his side above the sink. Hypnotically possessed, his transcending-self faced his fading reflection and delved into an alternative consciousness that transported him to an aquatic encounter. While seemingly immersed in an oceanic environment, his surreal, gigantic hand stroked the brow of a frightened whale of milky hue. "Are you okay, little guy?" he asked, entrenched in the realism. "Don't worry…I'm <u>not</u> gonna hurt you! What the <u>hell</u> am I doing here?" Suddenly, due to the vision's swimming sensation, Xavier lost his balance and fell to the deck with a roaring 'whoa!' and a loud thump. Mentally realigned by the collision, he immediately bounced back to his feet and managed to slip on his selected pair of Navy blue boxershorts by the time Andrewska checked in on him.

"Excuse the intrusion, Xavier, but is everything all right?" he asked politely yet with a knock and an intrusive crack of the door to see him innocently pulling on his baggy camouflage pants. "It sounded like you yelled and took a tumble, but there's <u>been</u> no turbulence. Is there anything we should know about?" After he buttoned his spiffy, olive short-sleeved shirt, Xavier bundled the old clothes and brought them back into the conference cabin along with the new socks and boots. He sat then adorned his feet, not saying a word. When he was through tying his laces, he held the former outfit toward them in a wadded state. "Would you like to keep these as evidence?" His tone was sarcastic and evasive as Andrewska took the pile and looked to Sandos for support. "Do you <u>really</u> want to know what happened? I sure wouldn't want you thinking I'm just a klutz!"

"Mister Branion, nothing is too trivial to report," Sandos assured him in a soothing, almost mothering tone; "please, tell us what caused you to fall."

Xavier started to laugh hysterically in disbelief at what he was about to tell them, yet decided it best to share the bizarre experience, if only to preserve his fading sanity. "You're not gonna believe this one, so get ready!" he prepared them with a tinge of embarrassment while he tried to cover his fear with a humorous disposition. "I mean, don't laugh, because it makes no sense. Okay, here goes…I saw something in the mirror, and it grew till the whole scene enveloped me like the most resolute VR you could <u>ever</u> imagine. Now, get this! I was in the ocean petting a whale that looked like a miniature 'Moby Dick' type, you know—whitish, big blunt nose and everything? Then anyway, I could tell he was sad and frightened, but I didn't know what to do. Oh! And my hand was black clawed, like as if it were the devil's hand. Oh, I don't know…it was kind of nice, helping the little whale. But so, disturbing too, like an out-of-body experience—I was <u>totally</u> displaced!"

Sandos hung on his every word and so, moved over a seat to sit beside him while she offered her own theory: "First of all, considering what we already know, I would start with the premise that this was no hallucination, but rather an episode of psychic contact with the entity," she began her analysis, hand-to-chin and her legs crossed in her loose-fitting trousers. "You are sharing a telepathic wavelength, it would seem, and the vision would suggest that in its westward movement, it has taken to the Pacific Ocean. There, like it did you, the being has located this intelligent aquatic creature for, perhaps, informational purposes. Although pure conjecture, this makes perfect sense and if distance has anything to do with the level of intensity, you should be a data magnet on freshly trodden grounds. Don't be shy about these visions, Xavier. Already, you've made great strides. I'm absolutely thrilled in anticipation of what you'll turn up at the Canadian site!"

"And depending on its depth capability, such an oceanic maneuver would put our military at a serious disadvantage," Andrewska added to the theory, rubbing his hands together with an intrigued grin. "Rather crafty, this one, as a naval pursuit could very well prove quite pitiful. But, then again, it could be down there for another purpose other than to hide. Perhaps..."

"Goddamn it! Didn't they relay my feedback from the initial conference?" Xavier blurted in frustration, glaring back and forth then with a sweep of his hand, he dispersed their all-too-patronizing discussion. "He's searching for his enemy and he's going to turn this world inside out in the process, if need be. We are something more than mere consequence, but we're not a threat to him. Don't get me wrong—the ocean/whale explanation, Sandos, was good. His incredible resourcefulness, now that I think about it, is his ultimate strength. He uses everything in his path like insurance or something. Anyway, before I burn out on all that, let me just focus now on my business in Madison. There lies a delicate situation, and I don't want to screw it up!" Sandos left her seat and opened a black briefcase she pulled from a compartment across from the clothing locker.

While she began to calibrate the portable scanning device inside of it, Andrewska took the unit's wireless gun that looked like a Walmart price scanner and pointed it to his own forehead for a control-subject reading for a base comparison. "As long as we've put our discussion on hold, I hope you don't mind if we run a few harmless scans," he suggested, rather presumptuous; yet even with a very cooperative Xavier, their equipment would prove obsolete. After their failed attempts to get a fix on Xavier's physical make-up, Andrewska formed a conclusion that would at least, in the meantime, put the matter to rest. "As I register within the expected parameters, malfunction of the test equipment is highly unlikely," he spoke into his phone recorder to document the findings with Sandos' nodding in support. "Since Xavier Branion remains an unknown life-form with our maximum scan range, fundamentally identical to the lift-bound device used during his induction, we can only reconfirm the base results. However, with all scientific data aside, the metamorphosis which has taken place could be described as a 'matter to sustained antimatter' transformation. Thus, in layman terms, he seems to have changed from a living man to a spirit of substance, his former self synthesized to a mass beyond all but obvious detection by the physical senses. Physical analysis concluded."

"A 'solid' ghost? Well, I'll be damned!" Xavier chuckled, despite their mutual lack of denial. "So, the Grim Reaper only met me halfway, sort of trapped in immortality…<u>pure</u> speculation, people, as you damn well know!" The concept frightened, yet intrigued him to consider the possibilities as vocal silence would ensue amidst their incessant phone-screen tapping until a smooth landing at the Dain-Madison Airport.

There, engulfed in a steady, fine mist, the familiar locale would then stir in him a flood of romantic anticipation.

CHAPTER XV
Giving Windows

"**W**ELL, WISH ME LUCK," Xavier announced for some moral support as he peered out the airplane's porthole and could see the dark gray Cadillac limousine, awaiting his arrival between the runway and the gate of the restricted area. "It's soap opera time!" The plane taxied and stopped abreast of his ride which had him eagerly jumping to his feet, ready for his rekindling quest.

"Please remember that in those forty minutes, you only have about twenty or so to actually visit with her," Sandos warned him, respectably yet with her slightly restrictive hand holding his forearm. "So, <u>try</u> if you can <u>not</u> to get embroiled in some lengthy interaction, or should I say … keep your expectations realistic? And, of course, good luck."

"Yes indeed, good luck, Xavier and here …" Andrewska expressed as well while giving him his black and gold sports watch with a stylish, archaic standard face. "It's not digital, but it looks cool. And at least you'll have a little 'time reference,' so you know when these Bureau guys will be storming the building."

"Thanks, man," Xavier said as he buckled it to his wrist, but then he began laughing as he started into the main cabin. Looking back at them, he added, "Agency versus Bureau, I can tell—'you people' mix <u>really</u> well!"

"Sure, that's why I'm not going with you," Andrewska agreed in their male bonding ritual that seemed to bother Sandos, who only pursed her lips. "But, since the last decade or so, we've been virtually interchangeable. And so, as a good sport, I sure wouldn't want to impress upon them that their operations are inadequate to handle you."

After Andrewska saw him past the jubilant Marines with their thumbs up gestures seeing him off the plane, a short, stocky African American man with a black umbrella was impatiently tapping his foot by the opened door of the limousine. "Greetings, Mister Branion…Agent Harper, FBI," he said in a gruff voice, presenting his badge and wearing a dirty-beige trench coat over a dark tweed suit, despite the steam-bath weather. "Your destination has been monitored to confirm that Miss Vercelli is presently at her residence. If she happens to leave for any reason, we will be contacted and advised. We are scheduled to return here at noon. There will be no interference, assuming that our time restraints are honored. Do we have an understanding?"

Xavier nodded the affirmative as he sat down and was boldly motioned by the pushy one to scoot over for an uncomfortable side-by-side seating arrangement. While equating his undaunted behavior with a general compensation for his lack of stature, Xavier exercised self-restraint and shared some small talk with the male driver, an amiable, sandy haired Anglo type. "So, do you guys have any anti-gravity turbine flyers in your auto fleet?" he agitated, leaning forward to direct his query towards the man up front while ignoring the sneering one beside him. "One of the agents with the Agency took me for a wild ride over the Capitol in one of those things earlier this morning. And <u>wow</u>—I'm talkin' <u>way</u> cool!"

"Yeah, yeah…they get <u>all</u> the cool toys in the 'big name' cities…and we don't get <u>shit</u>!" he complained with the relaxed manner of a friendly cab driver. "Although, I do think they've taken notice that as Madison has become one of the country's premier 'boomtown' cities, an explosion of illegal activity has come with it. They'll have <u>no</u> choice, but to give us the funding to keep up with this growing cesspool here—<u>believe</u> me!"

"<u>Enough</u> of this <u>idle</u> chatter! Just drive, Jensen!" Harper snipped as he became thoroughly fed up with the non-professionalism, prompting the subordinate, Jensen, to obediently revert to silence. "Mister

Branion, please do <u>not</u> encourage any conversation. Jensen here's a little green, but he should know better our way of depersonalization. It's got <u>very</u> little to do with intentional rudeness. However, it's got <u>everything</u> to do with survival in this line of work. Certainly, with your reported interest in this profession, you can understand that."

Xavier rolled his eyes at him and looked through the fogged glass to realize that they had reached the Madison Beltline westbound and were already halfway there. "Sure, but make that my former interest, <u>wisely</u> abandoned," he quipped, displaying an expressive dislike for the man. "Though I must admit, it seems there's hope for the Agency as I have them almost completely trained. Uh, right here…I believe 'this' is the exit you want to take, Jensen. Oh! That wasn't too personal, now was it, Lord Harper?"

He did not respond to the flaunted sarcasm, since he was well informed of the potential dangers involved. Thus, the remainder of the ride to the integrated, middle income southeast side held no more than occasional throat clearing. There, they pulled up to the curb in front of the three-story taupe colored brick building which was about thirty years old. While they parked and paused for a last-minute's briefing, the blue Chevrolet sedan of the monitoring squad drove up the street from the same spot a half-block to park before a similar unit. As there were many parking spaces available due to churchgoer vacancies, the time was ripe for such an operation.

"We made very good time, so you have twenty-three minutes," Harper told Xavier who then jumped out of the vehicle as if spring loaded and tapped his new watch to signal concurrence. "And be <u>sure</u> to exit from the <u>rear</u> of the building to the alley. We will run a circle route and pick you up there…"

Xavier nodded and waved from over his shoulder as he strutted across the lawn to the door. He pressed button number-four, as he recalled, on the intercom/mailbox panel and impatiently stood at the street entry, with no reply. Repeating the summons three more times, he looked at his watch and anxiously realized that two minutes of precious time had already been used. Then when he began to contemplate forceful entry, she was finally summoned with her answering simply, "Yeah?" to his, "Jeanine!" while laughing nervously.

"Xavier?!" Jeanine surprised in a raspy squeak. And though he could not see her, she was jaw-dropped in shock while pulling her messed hair away from her sweaty cheeks and brow. "How could you <u>possibly</u> be here? We thought you were <u>dead</u>!" She seemed very nervous and 'not at all' glad to hear his voice. Yet, he ignored the subtle signs and put forth his best demeanor.

"Well, I'm not…if that's okay with you," he replied with a charming smile and a chuckle. "Anyway, through all this strangeness, one thought allowed me to survive and <u>that</u> was <u>you</u>, Jeanine. I've missed you <u>so</u> much! But unfortunately, I have <u>very</u> little time. So, come on—would you <u>please</u> let me in? I've <u>got</u> to talk to you before I go!" Speechless, she breathed heavily with a mortified expression while a man's voice could be heard, yelling in the background.

"Hey Jeanine!" the familiar voice bellowed. "Got anymore beer?" Amidst the treacherously awkward situation, she gasped to silence as her hidden eyes began to well and drip with tears.

And as all became clear, Xavier snapped with a fury. "Jeff?" he steamed, pounding his sledgehammer fist against the brick wall. "That little prick! How long has <u>this</u> been going on? Well, I guess when X-Man go-eth, J-Boy cometh! Is <u>that</u> how it goes? Goddamn it, Jeanine, let me in!"

She was then heard sobbing in remorseful fear and thus, cut-off the intercom as Xavier's inflamed presence grew to a most frightening intensity. "Jeanine!" he wailed, becoming absolutely enraged when she ended their brief exchange most prudently, just as she did their breakup a few months before. However, this time, his superhuman ability gave him free reign to overreact accordingly. So, within seconds, he leaped to her second-floor balcony sliding doors; he crashed through them with a lunging head butt and swinging elbows; then he busted their frames and tumbled onto her living room floor in a pool of broken glass. From there, on an Oriental rug surrounded by a similar motif, he quickly rose to his feet and became the hunter. Soon, after detecting some frantic breathing emanating from the kitchen broom closet, he opened the door and discovered Jeff, drunk and wearing nothing but 'Jungle Book' boxer shorts and guilt-ridden fear.

"So, how long have you been doin' her, Jeff, oh loyal comrade?" Xavier asked with a sadistic smile as he allowed him to creep out of the closet, under his barricading arm. "Is <u>she</u> the mystery girl you've been seeing? Tell me!"

Jeff scurried toward the refrigerator and tried to think of a way to neutralize his unexpected rival's rabid poignancy. "It's not like that, Xavier," he defended nervously in a sporadic, slurred and trembling tone. "Those <u>goddamn</u> FBI guys were questioning us till <u>fuckin'</u> dawn…and sorry, man…we were just 'thrown' together! It was a one-time, weak moment-type thing. It didn't even go <u>that</u> far—just went 'downtown' a little…" he apologized thinly with a whimper while strangely signaling the 'peace sign' in a vulgar tonguing way, then continued. "But hey! The important thing is that you're back, super-charged," he laughed to create some levity. "I mean—wow! You really got something 'kick ass' out of that god-awful encounter, it would seem. Why don't you tell me <u>all</u> about it while these brews I just put in the freezer cool-off. We can make it a 'celebration' for your <u>triumphant</u> return!" His smoothing of the situation was not reaping the desired results as Xavier scowled and closed in with cold-blooded vengeance. To this, Jeff began to squirm in the counter-cluttered trap.

"So, the opportunity <u>just</u> presented itself, and so you <u>had</u> to take the plunge…you, scavenging bastard!" Xavier roared, so unforgiving that his frantic target climbed onto the kitchen counter, crouching, with nowhere else to go. "I think it's time for you to pay for your indiscretions, you, <u>sorry</u> little prick!"

"Come on, Xavier…let's be reasonable about this," he pleaded with bloodshot eyes, standing above him on the regrettable pedestal. "Do you <u>actually</u> think a brutal display like this will have her running into your arms? Face it! You two are <u>history</u>…and <u>she</u> can see anyone she wants!" As the proverbial 'straw that broke the camel's back,' Jeff's blunt words triggered a brief tirade. With a swift backhand to his stomach, Xavier knocked the wind out of him and forced him to buckle over. Rendering him helpless, he then clutched and jammed his throated jawbone shut, resulting in a badly bitten tongue.

"That's right!" the seething Xavier celebrated as he hoisted and pressed him one-handed up from the counter, smashing his head through the low integrity gypsum board ceiling. "Taste the pain, asshole!" Gradually, he reconsidered his actions vile and lowered his victim's struggling body to the floor. Hostility vented, he began to shed tears of shame as he released Jeff, who promptly rinsed the blood from his mouth and face at the kitchen sink.

"What the fuck's happening to me?" he cried, standing under the hole in the ceiling, with gypsum-powdered hair and his former guard diminished. "Mercilessly torturing this guy and scaring the hell out of the woman I love…that thing's turned me into some kind of monster too!" Suddenly, both the front and the fire escape doors were broken open by two black agents of the monitoring squad, and Agent Harper as well who came up from the alley.

At that moment, Jeanine finally emerged from her bedroom-hiding place, expecting the police. "Thank God! You must have been in the neighborhood when I called," she greeted them in relief, wearing only a big gray T-shirt with the U. of W. mascot, Bucky Badger on display. "He's in the kitchen! Wait—you're not cops! You're the Federales, right?"

As they could see, Xavier and Jeff were drinking warm beer and talking most amicably, pretending the ruckus had never occurred. "Oh, hi! I still have a lot of time, guys, so take it easy," Xavier said to the lot of them clustered and sneering at the doorway while he continued nonchalantly to explain his experience to a most impressed Jeff, holding a bloodied paper towel over his mouth. "Anyway, it's like I have this mystical psychic connection to the creature, man. And I think I started realizing this after I escaped and took a fuckin' bullet to the head. Besides the fact that I could run as fast as a cheetah right before that, it kind of tipped me off to 'the change' because, even with the amnesia, I knew I should've been dead. And then the visions came…"

"Big mistake, Branion," Harper interrupted; "you've made this simple task anything but covert, and have forfeited your remaining time."

While bloodied and clownishly wearing gypsum powder in his orangish hair, Jeff sprinkled some humor on the situation that only further angered the frustrated agent. "Everything's cool, sir," he said with a smirk, giggling. "He's just a <u>violent</u> alcoholic who was comin' down, like really bad! See? He's got his beer, and all is well."

"Very cute, Red Nuts!" Harper assailed Jeff, then yelled at his back-up team: "How <u>incompetent</u> could you guys be to miss 'his' being here? Well, you can sure as <u>hell</u> expect this pathetic oversight to be well noted in my report!" he shouted, disgraced by his own outfits' ineffectiveness while the two surveillance agents responsible looked to the floor in embarrassment. "You two, <u>grab</u> some clothes—Now!" the livid Harper roared as Jeff and Jeanine went obediently to the bedroom, got dressed and gathered their things. "As for <u>you</u> guys, stay here and take care of the cops. And as for them, they're <u>all</u> coming with <u>me</u>…" Amidst the faintly audible police sirens, Agent Harper went forward with the exit strategy, leaving his bewildered subordinates to deal with the mess, as he ushered the three of them down the fire escape stairs with Xavier leading the way. Even in the alley, onlookers were peeking around the corner as they piled into the awaiting limousine and bolted onto the street, almost hitting some bypassing pedestrians. Within a block, a couple of police cars could be seen, racing across the street behind them, most assuredly answering Jeanine's emergency alert.

"Whew, doggies—out of there by the <u>skin</u> of our teeth!" Xavier savored with an adulated gleam in his eyes, frightening Jeanine as she looked to him, a stranger. "Don't worry, Jeanine. Now, everything's gonna be <u>just</u> fine!" Then, establishing eye contact from which she could not break, he found yet another of his new abilities. For when in an instant, he managed to hypnotically transform her sights from fearful to inviting. And so, he ventured past the warmed windows into her mind, planting a powerful bit of persuasion to hopefully redeem himself: 'Forget the tragedy that forced us apart; remember us as we were, totally in love, with sweet anticipations of our future together; and, most of all, feel with all your heart that we are the sweetest of lovers, soul mates forever and nothing less.' Hypnotic suggestion in place, he released her to regain semi-consciousness and saw in her eyes the passionate glow he so deeply missed. Followed by a sensuous kiss of tongue-bathing serenity, theirs was a blissful encounter far removed from Agent

Harper and Jeff, who turned away after some uncomfortable 'get a room' glances.

Ten-minutes ahead of schedule, they arrived at the airport and pulled onto the tarmac, intending to park alongside the refueled aircraft to drop Xavier off as Andrewska waved in the distance from the opened hatch. "Well, I can't say it's been a pleasure, Branion…" Harper said with his continued tone of disappointment; yet, before he could finish, Xavier kicked the door open and whisked Jeanine out of the vehicle while it was still moving. "No! Branion, you can't do this!" Harper shouted, with Jeff's obnoxious cheering to follow as Xavier cleverly made off with the 'so in the mood' fair maiden, then trotting up the plane's stepped ramp. "Shut up, Red Nuts! You won't be so glad, when you're being held indefinitely for knowing too damn much," he told Jeff, who was quickly muted by the threat while Andrewska came to the limousine door to reassure the frustrated agent.

"It's all right—you did great, considering…you really can't stop the guy from having his way," he said, dismayed, through the half-cracked window; but then with an amused look at the captive Jeff, Andrewska added, "but tell me, how could you let this guy here sneak in under your nose like that?"

"I don't want to hear about it!" Agent Harper lashed, not amused, but then offered his own retort: "And, hey, look at it this way…I'm through with that asshole! And you've got to kiss his ass to the very end. I wouldn't trade places with you for all the coke in Columbia…good luck!" He closed his window with a smirk and thus they sped away, leaving Andrewska shaking his head in dread of an even more unpredictable flight ahead. After a short trot back into the plane, he saw a very angry Sandos, sitting alone in the back of the main cabin. There, in the front, the 'Merry Marines Dozen,' this time, quietly chanted, "Way to go, Branion, way-to-go!" even though Xavier and Jeanine had already passed by moments ago, and gone into the conference cabin with a closed-door policy in effect.

"Lover boy said that they want some privacy. Something of a 'conjugal visit,' I'd gather. Can you believe it?" she complained most prudishly, with venom in her eyes. "And did you see that girl? She looked totally wasted and was writhing against him like a cat in heat—I think he put some kind of a 'horny' spell on her! But, I know, we can't do anything about it…<u>just</u> observe—you got the link?" Sitting across the aisle from her next to the cabin door, Andrewska started tapping on his phone as did she. "Yep, and <u>look</u> at that tattoo…and on the front—she just doesn't <u>seem</u> the type!" he surprised to Jeanine's crotch-laden body art, about which Sandos commented further as the soldiers ceased with their obnoxious chant and began to quietly chatter among themselves amidst the plane's revving engines.

"Hmm, a peace symbol over the Earth, 'Peace on Earth'—how darling!" she demeaned, sounding a bit catty, then noticing with concern. "But would you look at that <u>face</u>—'weird' expression! God, I <u>hate</u> the voyeuristic side of this job…this should be private and beautiful." Acknowledging her sentiments, the nodding Andrewska reminded her about the 'top of schedule' VIP engagement looming. "Yeah, know what you mean. But anyway, they <u>better</u> hurry…with the Prez, paying us a visit pretty soon…" Sandos rolled her eyes and watched the raunchy action with a soured face as the plus-one aircraft accelerated down the runway to a swift westward takeoff.

Meantime, next door on the table in the conference cabin, Xavier and Jeanine were well past their frantic disrobing stage with her riding him like a bucking bronco, wavering and jerking unrhythmically at every plunge. She seemed detached in her disingenuous enthusiasm whose dead stare reminded him of a Luciferian succubus, knee-squatting around his groined base until her slapping plops soon led to a sloppy trilling of climaxes. Satisfied in only a raunchy primordial way yet just mostly relieved, Xavier became repelled by the unnatural plumping of her breasts so vascular and hardened to the touch that the strangely morphing nymph she had become terrified him to the limit, and thus he thought to himself in 'rejection mode' for both their sakes: 'My God! Who…<u>what</u> is she? That's <u>not</u> her style, not even as a joke…that is <u>not</u> my Jeanine—<u>must</u> end this!' He stared back into her dark lustful eyes, ventured back into her mind and managed to remove the nymphomaniacal spell he so recklessly instilled. In turn, the stunned Jeanine instantly dismounted and slid her pert little rump off the slippery table looking around, confused, then she followed Xavier's lead in getting dressed. While emerging from her haze and zipping up her Capri blue jeans, Jeanine peeked down under her mint green panties at her shaven tattooed crotch and looked outside the airplane's window at the herds of pillowed clouds, passing far beneath them. Shaking her head, she darted her eyes at the fully clothed Xavier and scowled with suspicion in her raspiest tone.

"I did _not_ get that drunk last night, Xavier," she declared, thinking it was the day after their tragic break-up which, along with the past few months, had been totally erased. "Did someone slip something in my drink? And _how_ did I get on this plane, get this tattoo and…'I'm dripping'—was it good for you? _Damn_ it! Don't just _stand_ there with that 'fake' innocent look on your face…It's like I was just at the concert for your 'birthday' date night, then all-of-the-sudden…_here_ I am—well?" Incredibly calm considering the situation, Jeanine zipped and buttoned her jeans then, hands-to-hips, glared at him while he opened with an unconvincing compliment that led to a serious explanation.

"Jeanine, uh, Honey-kins…where do I begin?" Xavier sweet-talked then paused to best present his wording. "Well no…it wasn't good for me because _you_ weren't even there, but I _do_ love your 'Peace on Earth' tattoo—so 'hippie' cheche! And now, _that_ is a good place to start since you must have gotten it at least a week ago. And hate to tell you, but my birthday was three-months-ago. You see, something _really_ freaky-weird happened at the park last night, during our patrol, that has received worldwide attention. I had some kind of 'supernatural encounter,' there, that gave me _exceptional_ abilities and a psychic connection that's proven 'extremely valuable' for this CIA mission now in progress. So, here we are…I arranged to have you come along and, about your…" Suddenly, Xavier was interrupted by Agent Sandos' voice on the intercom.

"Sorry to disturb you, Xavier, but we have an urgent communique for you from Madam President Julia Galgano, currently streaming from Brasilia, which requires the use of the holographic projection port, at center, on the conference table. Also, Agent Andrewska and I would like to welcome Miss Vercelli whose 'surprise' addition will not be a problem. May we enter to set up and begin transmission?"

Jeanine's dark demeanor then took a sudden turn to that of ecstatic anticipation as she cracked a bright toothy smile and gushed about her heroine, the first woman president of the United States. "No way!" she shouted, then covered her mouth to continue in a loud whisper. "President Julia Galgano wants to talk to you? My God! I campaigned for her, a 'fellow Bostonian' and all, and—oh, wow! Well, tell 'em just a couple minutes...I've got to go to the ladies' room! While meantime, you can clean up..." Xavier complied, feeling he dodged a bullet, and re-affirmed their readiness to the 'listening in waiting' agent.

"You heard her, Sandos—just a couple minutes!" While Jeanine darted aft into the lavatory, Xavier found some cleaning products in the locker area and took care of the conference table's aromatic spot of 'possession steeped' passion. When Jeanine soon emerged from the restroom, fresh-faced and bright-eyed, he promptly opened the sliding doors to the visibly anxious, special-agent duo.

CHAPTER XVI
Communion Chasm

I N PREPARATION FOR THE world's most honored communiqué left awaiting transmission with his 'testing' whiff of approval, Agent Andrewska wasted no time setting up the holographic projector. Once a go, it produced a slightly downsized, 'live' three-dimensional image of the president, between the overhead and conference table reception plates. Smartly dressed in a charcoal gray suit jacket, a white-blue pin striped blouse and a black knee-length skirt, Commander in Chief, President Julia Galgano stood regally before them, appearing real enough to touch. A tall, thin and femininely handsome matriarch of fifty-two, she was the Republican 'can do' senator out of Massachusetts who was struggling through the third year of her term. With only a mediocre approval rating so far, her sincere efforts did little to spark a generally apathetic nation, whose presidency she won by a very slim margin in one of the lowest voter turnouts in modern US history. Nonetheless, with warm hazel eyes and a genuine smile, she gestured fluidly and emanated a unique brand of charisma.

"Xavier Branion, the super-human wonder of the world! It is such an honor to finally meet you, though it be via VR conference," the president began in a medium pitched yet gutsy tone of voice, with her trilling pink-polished fingers beholding him in tribute. "Your personal triumph over the mortifying effects of the alien, or otherwise determined, contact is most commendable and the resulting physical and psychic enhancements are truly amazing.

While we do wish to harness your special bond with the anomaly, you may feel the weight of the world is on your shoulders, and to that…<u>believe</u> me—I can relate! So, helping to carry the load, I trust that our supporting staff has been accommodating your needs and, considering the esoteric nature of this foreseen bond, they shall remain flexible in response to your instincts, however and wherever they may guide.

"Now, I'm not here to give you a State of the Union Address, but I do want to be reassuring and remind you of what we have overcome in the past: Terrorism, foreign and domestic—'9-11', <u>still</u> the worst; the Covid pandemics and natural disasters—'Hurricane Katrina', most notably; economics, with crippling recession, inflation, unemployment and thus…the 'Corporate Bailout', embarrassing yet necessary and so on. Also, let us not forget the <u>insidious</u> social engineering movement orchestrated by foreign governments and 'Big Business' oligarchs with their <u>Marxist</u> infestations, <u>fueling</u> racial divisions while trying to bring down our Republic. To these crisis situations and so many others, Xavier, we responded time and again, allowing our <u>most</u> resilient, freedom-loving civilization to prevail and thrive once again.

"The point I'm illustrating here is that no matter <u>how</u> bleak things may look, the 'human spirit' bounces back, regains control and hopefully learns something in the process. As this pertains to the present situation, Xavier, it is through you that we would <u>ultimately</u> wish to establish peaceful coexistence with the newly discovered entity which General Fletcher, as you may recall, suspects to be of terrestrial origin and on our side. In time, perhaps we can better understand the 'possible' alien cause of the atmospheric energy flux that has hindered most space communications and, as we suspect, destroyed the Santa Marsia, just after yesterday's lift off. To restore the relative balance for which we have striven, I urge you to exercise <u>extreme</u> tact when you establish actual dialogue with this 'incredible' one as we believe that you are the only person capable of such a feat. Remember, you are representing <u>more</u> than just the United States. In fact, <u>you</u>, Xavier, represent the <u>entire</u> world community! And therefore…" While she certainly was about to become long-winded, the holographic image broke up into a scrambled cylinder and the audio became, most thankfully to Xavier, too distorted to understand.

"And blah-blah-blah, yeah well, <u>thanks</u> for the history lesson, Teach!" Xavier scoffed as Andrewska fussed with the controls in a futile attempt to recapture the signal. "Give it up, Andy," Xavier chided. "It's the spreading interference, man. It'll be hittin' <u>all</u> the waves in time! Hit <u>us</u> just in the nick of time…I mean, can you believe that lady? Slippin' in that <u>load</u> of partisan <u>bullshit</u> when it was just a 'fad' that got a little out of hand. Dangerous rhetoric that amounts to nothing but stagnating friction, just like the past three years…"

His criticism drew Jeanine to his side to chastise his remarks, hitting too close to home. "Come on, Xavier—you, ingrate! <u>That</u> lady was the only viable candidate back then, and I'm not just defending her because she's a very strong and accomplished woman, but…of course, she <u>is</u> a fellow Bostonian. My hometown, in case you forgot!" she lashed with a backhand to his chest, exhibiting the re-emergence of her spunky demeanor. "She's like a female J.F.K. and I think she's doing quite well, considering the 'for crap' situation that was thrown onto her lap—and hey! I thought you said you voted for her, and not that <u>unscrupulous</u>, psychopathic snake! So, just be honored that she wasn't just acknowledging your unique role in this thing, but actually spoke to you with <u>such</u> reverence. I admit, I'm still pretty confused by all this, and you're gonna <u>have</u> to give me some time to digest what seems <u>far</u> beyond reality…even so, I know one thing—I'm <u>very</u> proud of you, Xavier." She put her arms around him with his sweet reply, but then backed away, disturbed by his unfinished bashing of the President's reputation as he drifted back into his ole cynical, college debate mode.

"Well, it's true…I did half-heartedly vote for her, but only because I was and <u>still</u> am, whole-heartedly in love with you…the <u>things</u> we do for <u>love</u>—right?" he professed, with a corny 'heart' gesture towards her, then continued. "It's just that I wish I could have given 'Madam' President a piece of my mind. Sure, she speaks beautifully, articulately and looks <u>great</u>…for her age, but everyone knows she was just a <u>slick</u> prop for the Republicans to 'seem' progressive. And while she goes around, spouting her <u>philosophical</u>

crap, you've got more and more people retreating to their homes. With work, shopping, education and communication, in general, all rounded out by the <u>goddamn</u> social-media, 'zombifying' internet, there's your life…and you <u>never</u> have to go outside to the ever-spreading crime. Even with the legalization of pot, the drug lords and the cartels <u>still</u> haven't felt the pinch. Running the underground along with <u>everything</u> else under the sun, they rule the flourishing metropolises all across the nation. And <u>what</u> is the government's insightful response? More satellites, street cameras and internet-censorship…uh, what other surveillance? Oh…the <u>spy</u> drones! Getting tinier and tinier—shit! <u>Forget</u> our rights to privacy! <u>God</u>, what a 'Hell on Earth' mess we're in!

"Thankfully however, the time has <u>finally</u> come, as you will see, for a <u>real</u> change," he declared with a brave-fist salute in the air and a firm hand to his chest as the ultimate visionary. "This 'whole thing' is <u>our</u> destiny. The proverbial kick in the ass that this 'oh so <u>fucked</u> up' society and, what the hell, whole goddamn 'sum of humanity' so desperately needs. Now, <u>that's</u> what makes me proud…is playing center stage to something <u>so</u> profound, <u>so</u> vital! The 'shock wave' reality check—just what the 'celestial' doctor ordered!"

"So, you suppose that if a <u>man</u> were in office, this proverbial 'kick in the butt' would be less necessary?" the riled Sandos insinuated, her eyebrow raised as if to challenge him. "Besides your being crudely cynical and impetuous, noted by simple unbiased observation, that is…do you, Xavier, suggest here before your 'significant' other that, among other things, the problems of today lie in our leader's gender?"

Totally game on, Xavier approached her with his back then to Andrewska, head-shaking with disapproval, and the eye-rolling Jeanine still bubbling from his profoundly stimulating zeal. There before her where they could not see, he captured Sandos' undivided attention. Surfacing from within him, the vampiric alien possession injected by the mind-meld began to introduce itself, if only to one. "Oh, Sandy, you wouldn't think me a 'misogynist,' toxically masculine sexist or whatever, <u>would</u> you?" he challenged with a lustful stare, as she perceived, from which she could not turn away. "You <u>sure</u> wouldn't think so, if you saw me a little earlier—which I <u>bet</u> you and Andy did! On this very table, in <u>full</u> submission to this <u>domineering</u> vixen." While Jeanine merely smirked in embarrassment and Andrewska distressingly looked out the window, only Sandos witnessed Xavier's eyes in transformation to red with black slit pupils.

Thus, she panicked and pleaded, "Mister Branion, you <u>must</u> fight this…<u>parasitic</u> 'entity'—own yourself!" Her futile words fell on deaf ears, as the others took no notice.

To follow the bizarre soul-draining effect, time seemed to stand still for her as his canine teeth curved outward in rattlesnake projection and a black-forked tongue poked through his demonic smile. From there, his waving tongue shot out of his mouth like a bug-catching frog and probingly licked past her resistant lips to plunge into her throat. She gagged by its burrowing expansion. Yet, in panicked desperation, Sandos was able to pull the slippery member out of her violated orifice before choking to death. The viperous tongue immediately retreated into Xavier's mouth while his face returned to normal. With a coughing huff, she looked to Andrewska and Jeanine after the horrific incident and was astonished by their lack of concern.

"Didn't you <u>see</u> what he did to me!" she screamed at the top of her lungs, with tears streaming down her face and her hand locked in the crossing gesture of the crucifix. "He's <u>El Diablo</u>, and he was <u>inside</u> me!" She continued her accusation of the cloaked intrusion that not even Xavier was aware. "You're all lookin' at me like I'm <u>crazy</u>! I <u>know</u> what happened! And I <u>must</u> see my priest…I <u>cannot</u> stay on with this messenger of Satan!"

Innocently to her outburst, Xavier attempted to console Sandos with a shoulder pat. Yet, that only sickened and set her off to respond in a Spanish tirade, with a solid kick to his stomach. *"Para Criste— te mato, Diablo! Te mato!"* she shouted, holding her gold crucifix towards him as if to stave off his evil presence. With a pitying sigh, Xavier backed away with his hands up in surrender, and sat in the cabin's most distant seat while she only braced herself against the window and whimpered, her face scrunched in hysterical anguish. "When the <u>hell</u> are we gonna land? I mean—<u>fuck</u> this! I've <u>got</u> to see my priest, or I am damned…"

Unable to bear the apparent breakdown of the poor woman, Jeanine approached her with a warm smile and was able to gain her confidence, guiding her aft toward the lavatory. "What have we got, guys? An hour…maybe two, you know—till we land?" Jeanine asked, somewhat miffed, mostly by Andrewska's lack of compassion for his partner. "She asked the question for a reason, like she's totally lost track of time because of this, whatever? So, as if you even care—just tell her how much longer!"

"A little over an hour," Andrewska answered in a rather unfazed manner. "These things are to be expected in this line of work, so I suggest you give her some oxygen. It'll take the claustrophobic edge off." After the women went into the washroom, the male bonding resumed with a regretful twist.

"I swear, Andy, I didn't do anything besides make a little joke and then see her eyes nearly pop out of her head," Xavier defended in a barking whisper as he sat next to Andrewska who stroked his chin, compiling a double-tiered theory. "She just lost it, right there. Well, I understand that, like you said, in your line of work it's not all that uncommon."

"Yes, it's true that just being psychologist types…we are, paradoxically, most on the edge. And when you add to that our knowledge of the paranormal, there's a resulting struggle between what shouldn't be and the ignorant bliss which you so begin to miss," he explained quietly, with his hand to his forehead in a depressed pose. "Now in Sando's case, I was stunned because she was always so professional, and kept her personal beliefs just that. Yet, when she lapsed into Spanish and held that crucifix, it was like she reverted to the Phoenix barrio where she grew up. I got the distinct impression that she thought you were the Anti-Christ, specifically revealing himself to suck her into his wicked fold.

"In light of that, she probably had such a struggle between her religious beliefs and your mysterious creation that blaming 'demonic forces' qualified the dilemma in tolerably simplistic terms. So, there you go, instant psychosis: I won't be the devil's helper, so I'll go 'religiosity' nuts and diffuse the internal conflict, etcetera…However, when you look at the other side of the coin…is it so crazy to suggest that, in your haste, you projected this thing into her mind like you did the 'attitude adjustment' for your girlfriend. You <u>did</u> seem a little contemptible toward Sandos and her 'adversarial side' in your jest."

Instantly triggered, Xavier grabbed Andrewska violently by the collar and pressed the big man against his seat with near bone-crushing force. "That simply is <u>not</u> true! And <u>that</u> is the <u>last</u> mention of such accusations—understood?" he demanded in a roaring whisper while releasing his grip then tapping his pointed finger against Andrewska's chest. "Now, please, <u>don't</u> get me goin'. Just face it—Sandos flipped-out! And now she's doing the right thing and dropping out…so, Jeanine takes her place. Case closed."

Just seconds later, the women came back from the restroom, chatting nicely, while Andrewska led on to none of what transpired.

Fortunately, Sandos seemed put at ease in Jeanine's care. And though feeling a bit disgraced, she was immeasurably glad to be relieved of duty from the 'Xavier induced' hellish mission. During the remaining hour of flight, very little was said. Then to quickly follow their somewhat bumpy landing, she was escorted by two of the flight Marines to an awaiting, much smaller private jet for her Phoenix-bound transport at the Cache Crown Airport northeast of Vancouver, British Columbia. A Spartan place of giant gray hangars, sprawling office structures and runways, Andrewska led the two of them further down the stretch while only Jeanine, with sympathetic tears, watched the ejected Sandos board her flight back home. Thus, down to three and standing before a nearby double-propped helicopter of camouflage green, they were awed by the sight of the largest aircraft in the Royal Canadian fleet, which was ready to go. So then hosting the Canadian leg of the investigation, there he stood, at the top of its entry ramp, one of the pilot witnesses from the 'space plane grounding' incident, waiting to greet them.

"Hello, and welcome aboard!" the dark haired, freckled man of about thirty-five shouted as they boarded the craft with its massive blades producing a wind tunnel roar. "Agent Andrewska, I'm so pleased you could join us…I'm Captain John Tooley, the pilot who first spotted the flying creature the second time. I <u>must</u> say it was the most fantastic sight of my life, but I can tell you about that on the way. I'm <u>so</u> sorry about your partner's sudden resignation, so be sure to let her know we wish her all the best—oh! And you must be the 'notorious' Xavier Branion, the superhuman psychic link, accompanied by his special civilian guest. Well, you <u>look</u> normal enough…Now then, let me show ya some of the maps where we've pinpointed the likely refuge of the beast."

"<u>Jeanine</u>, the name is Jeanine Vercelli!" she hollered into his ear, making a point against his anonymous reference.

"Yes, of course, Miss Vercelli," he blushed to her insistence, a reaction which caused Xavier to laugh. "I meant no disrespect. I was only commenting on the misappropriation. But considering the situation, I'm <u>sure</u> the regulations will be falling, one by one." The crew of a couple dozen military pilots, navigators and research personnel seemed to share Captain Tooley's loose attitude. They made the three of them feel quite welcomed in their high-tech electronics lab located in the rear of the bulky two-hundred-foot vessel, which lumbered into the northwest cirrus sky toward the mountains.

"When it came down from the upper atmosphere, we picked it up on the radar during our regular seven-corners-drill," Captain Tooley described with green eyes of intrigue as the American trio, soon well situated, listened intently. "We tried to intercept what, at first sighting, appeared to be a space plane with a grayish tan mass upon it. But its dead-weight drop accelerated downward at such an incredible rate, we couldn't reach it unless <u>one</u> of us was <u>foolish</u> enough to energize a laser, or worse, fire a missile. While the itchy trigger finger shall remain nameless, he did seem to prompt its disengaging at terra impact because right before the missile hit, the blurry earthtone thing slid off and blended into the ground. Anyway, it's <u>so</u> strange that it swooped down and carefully placed the plane on the ground, fully intact, <u>just</u> to be blown to bits. And, of course, we'll never know if there were 'any living' aboard of whom would otherwise have been spared.

"So, while it seemed to disappear into the earth, I had a hunch that we'd see our friend resurface eventually and, sure enough, after about ten-minutes over an area quite a distance into BC, I saw the winged beast suddenly reappear, weaving through some ravines on a westward path," the captain continued. "Then, the chase was on, with 'yours truly' leading the pack to then come up on its red-tipped tail feathers which were only a fraction of its plumage. I mean, upon closer inspection, the thing had a flowing headdress of dull blue and, I don't know…yellow? And its wings were tawny, maybe with red-tipped feathers? I'm just saying that it was actually quite colorful but in a dark-dingey tone, once you got up close…and if you could have seen its face—Jesus Christ! It was like a mask etched in sandstone by the gods. So anyway, when the big guy turned his head with red eyes aglow, he seemed very pissed! But later on, you could see that he had a sense of humor.

"Making absolute fools of us in our top-notch fighter jets, he instantly flipped over in an impossible maneuver, going the opposite direction beneath our puzzled sights. As if he were doing the back float, the creature mockingly waved at us with his rusty gray hands, with arms and a torso so human. At the time, wanting to cheer for him seemed the 'order of the day,' and so he topped it off at an amazing speed, disappearing behind us in ricochet fashion. It was a remarkable experience to see one so menacing, yet so strangely unthreatening. Oh, and one other thing that caught my eye was the blue ball lodged in his chest. Unfortunately, even though I saw all of this as did the others with absolute clarity, the flight-cam-footage revealed only a phantom-like image that was too indistinct to justify reviewing. However, if you really want to…" Captain Tooley trailed off.

"Yes, we do," Andrewska insisted to Captain Tooley's shoulder shrug of half-hearted compliance. "Nothing's too indistinct when it comes to the 'extra-sensed.' Where we see shadows, Xavier might see full exposure!"

They viewed the video sequence on one of the many monitors and, throughout the show, Xavier smiled with wide eyes while the others squinted, disappointed. "You missed his five-pronged talons, Tooley…they were waving, too!" he laughed with pride for his 'connected' one of such agility whose acrobatics were preserved, even if only for his eyes alone. "You're right, Andy, I can see him clear as day, but all I can tell from this is that he loved giving you guys the slip, nothing more—hey! Whoa, I'm getting something, very strong…down there!" he shouted, pointing toward a deep chasm of sheer-faced cliffs, which they had just passed over. "The energy's erupting out of that gorge like a geyser, there's <u>no</u> question. I've <u>got</u> to go down there!"

"It's rather southwest of our prescribed coordinates, but <u>you're</u> the boss," Captain Tooley said to then accommodate Xavier's request over the loudspeaker microphone. "Come about to a backtrack! We've got a 'live wire' on that inlet we just passed. <u>Repeat</u>, come about and retrace to that last chasm, uh, 'Daredevils Gorge,' that is. Probing team to disembark!" The operating pilot took the giant chopper around to the deep mountainside gash of Tooley's direction, hovered a couple hundred feet over it and rolled a hundred feet of flexible ladder from its spool, extending from an underbelly chute.

"Ever use a jet pack?" Captain Tooley inquired as two of the crew came up to them with the compact flying devices and the heat-resistant jump suits to wear over their clothes. "Not that there's any experience really that necessary with these…I mean, self-balancing, lightweight and with independent double thrusters? <u>Man</u>, with the double joy sticks and the trigger throttles, it's easy. To dump it, you'd have to <u>really</u> be trying!"

After Xavier and Andrewska slipped eagerly into their 'road worker' bright green jump suits and were harnessed with a pair of the comfortably light jet packs, Xavier alone was also fitted with a cam-cord helmet which would monitor his findings. "Yeah, now I remember…for ranger rescue training in Wisconsin I used one, but it wasn't nearly as nice as these," he approved with a thumbs-up gesture. "I can't <u>believe</u> how light it is! Oh, my God! I can see his impression on the side of the cliff right there, facing due east, maybe. That's where he crossed over into the ocean!" No one else could see the markings to which he referred, yet his 'tactile' investigation down there was encouraged with cables on their harnesses for safety's sake.

"Be careful and <u>don't</u> try to show off too much," the sweetly bossy Jeanine warned and wished him well, with an affectionate kiss on the lips. "I'll be watching your every move—so <u>do</u> us proud!" Followed by Andrewska, Xavier went through the shoot, climbed down the ladder and started the surprisingly quiet thrusters before the gaping gash of towering rock. With his feet still on the ladder's bottom slats, he leaned back, sampled the controls and was soon comfortable enough to release the training brace.

Initially, his flight was wobbly, but as Andrewska hovered nearby with steady control, Xavier emulated the expert and quickly mastered the power pack control levers in relation to the updraft spouting from the gorge. They drifted downward beneath its rim, a couple hundred feet to the center of the west wall visage of his privy reception. Then, clinging to the minor protrusions on the face of the cliff, Xavier began to have a vision at the key location where he would soon discover another of his unusual capabilities.

"I can see a control room of some sort with counters, consoles and strange instrumentation, surrounded by walls at a weird angle and there's some kind of commotion in the background—Jesus! Look at my hands!" he touted, surprised that his bare hands were seeping into the rock. "Can you see that! The sleeves won't go in, but I bet, if I were naked…okay, back to this room, and there's definite activity in the back by an oval eye tunnel, silver and black. That's better—I'm moving toward it for a closer look and there are little gray figures…Owlmen! Owlmen? Why did I say that? Well, anyway, they're floating into their silver ship and, instantly—it's disappeared down the tunnel. I can't let them get away! I'm going full speed through the tunnel, and it's curving down…down very deep! Ah, I've got them in my sights and I'm gaining on 'em! Uh-oh, hittin' the water, and wow! What a splash, but I'm still gaining on 'em, ultra-fast, and now the tunnel's opening up to the 'awesome' vastness, in like infra-red vision, just above the dark ocean bed."

"Grays…he's after the Grays!" Andrewska proclaimed, clinging beside him, as he was sure of his interpretation yet worried about Xavier's deep enthrallment. "Xavier, why don't you take a little break…uh, Xavier?"

"Finally, I've got their ship and now…I'll take their minds!" he told in a deep trance of celebrated conviction until the mood became suddenly that of dread. "This isn't right…they'd rather die!" Andrewska reached out to steady Xavier as he seemed distressed and detached, yet he missed apprehending him due to a sudden back-flip reaction that hurled him downward, full throttle. The abrupt motion yanked on the slack cable and snapped it, sending him twirling down into the gorge in a state of unconsciousness.

"Ease off the <u>goddamn</u> thrusters, Xavier!" Andrewska shouted into the communicator as he unhooked his cable and took a controlled plummet, though much too far behind to intercept the falling comrade. "You've <u>got</u> to let go of the sticks to level it! <u>Whew</u>, thank God!" Awakening from the haze of his 'visionary' shocked mind, Xavier narrowly escaped collision with the jagged rocks, two thousand feet below the tension-ridden chopper. Thrilled rather than shaken, he ventured upward to meet Andrewska, feeling ever more resilient. Though his death-defying confidence was further fueled, Xavier expressed his gratitude as they ascended to the hovering air base, inside where all awaited in relief.

"Thanks, Andy," he said in an unexpectedly humble tone. "I could almost <u>taste</u> that fast-approaching bed of boulders; that is, until I came out of it, and took your advice to let go. Man! But luckily, I also had the state of mind to give it full throttle when I leveled out because I had <u>so</u> much momentum. Anyway, you got my attention just in the nick of time and I <u>really</u> appreciate it." They rejoined the ladder and were glad to once again have solid footing.

After climbing through the chute back into the lab, Captain Tooley awaited to show a replay of Xavier's helmet-cam experience while Jeanine smothered him with life-preserving kisses. "Oh, wow! Did you ever give <u>me</u> a scare!" she professed with a hug that seemed to never want to let go. "My heart almost jumped out of my <u>throat</u> after you! Well, thank God, you're safe. Now, would you care to explain this 'sticking your hands into the solid rock' like that?"

"Yes, we're all <u>so</u> relieved that you miraculously came out of that tumble, but I think your hand-in-rock-trick is overshadowing that as the crew is absolutely abuzz about it," Captain Tooley added to lighten the situation, following Jeanine's lead. "While one of the men goes down to mark your point of contact for further study, let us take a gander at your helmet cam debut, which was <u>quite</u> an ear full. I only wish it had a 'visual loop' going through your mind at the same time."

They viewed the video and Xavier was stunned by his telling through the eyes of another. "I remember the strange control room and the explosion that knocked me off my ass, but the stuff in-between <u>isn't</u> me," he said, bothered by the power over him which he feared would only be continually intensified to the point of full possession. "All <u>I</u> know is that Andy here is <u>convinced</u> about the correlation between the Owlmen and the Grays which, as we all know, are the most commonly reported extra-terrestrials. I suppose you would have this mean that my mythological brother is in the ocean, looking for these Grays in retribution… assuming, of course, that he wasn't destroyed by their ship bomb, but that couldn't be," he laughed, "<u>since</u> he had to meet up with the 'white whale' after that. Well, on the serious side, I <u>knew</u> he wasn't pissed at us, but, as I told 'em back in DC, were still gonna be <u>trapped</u> in the war zone."

"Well, folks, next stop is a pre-emptive intercept course in the South Pacific, where <u>all</u> our bets are on the 'Dragon's Triangle' hot spot as being his ultimate destination to which your alien-tracker perceptions nearly confirm and our loose itinerary had already anticipated," Andrewska announced with a supportive nod from Xavier, and a gleam of adulation by Jeanine who was still clinging to him. "The U.S.S. Ronald Reagan, one of the <u>finest</u> aircraft carriers in the world awaits us, a few hundred miles south of Japan. This is <u>all</u> beginning to make sense and with your invaluable connection, Xavier, I think ocean exploration is about to take a 'profound leap' into the unknown." Leaving a black outline of a human silhouette like murder scene body tape, the mark would precisely indicate the point at which Xavier perched for the second research team that had been contacted to resume testing of the area.

From the Cache Crown Airport, where an efficient runway relay was implemented, Xavier, Jeanine and Andrewska were promptly flown to Hickem Air Force Base in Honolulu for a scaled-down, carrier-runway-capable jet transport onto the U.S.S. Ronald Reagan. There in the triangle's north-central portion, the carrier was penetrating the target area in calm seas amidst warm temperatures and clear skies. However, the ideal conditions would soon hold a mysterious splashdown site, waiting there with a drastic change halfway into the afternoon, rendering them unprepared for the inevitable.

CHAPTER XVII

The Beasts beyond
the Bay

WHILE TEMPORARILY DOCILE, THE young whale suddenly backed away from Lone Hawk. Then, erupting with misdirected anger and contempt, it readied to attack in a striking posture. With explosive tail fin propulsion, its anticipated charge was surprisingly swift and at first amusing to him. Like a seasoned matador to a frustrated bull, Lone Hawk dodged every lunging attempt. Yet, the fun quickly subsided when the relentless 'ocean rhino' managed to ram its blunt-bottled nose into his side.

Though the hit did not hurt, Lone Hawk became quite annoyed with the tenacious little beast. "Oh, calm yourself, kid…of all this hostility," he ordered kindly as he cloaked and restrained its thrashing body via arms and wings. "How do I reach you, poor refugee, through your incoherent tizzy? The killer whales are long gone, and I healed your wound. Of course, the whalers anger you, but there is something more, tragically more."

To initiate a communion for vital interaction, Lone Hawk created innately a telepathic pool around the fifty-foot cetacean's mind, hence enabling a free-flow of communication. As a sense of trust was established in the process, he released the inquisitive juvenile which stayed close, unafraid.

"What <u>are</u> you, kind beast?" the ivory whale asked with astonished curiosity in its eyes. "I have <u>never</u> seen or learned of one so big and strange as you. Are you from beyond the bay, or some <u>other</u> world?"

"<u>What</u> I am is strange indeed, and even somewhat of a mystery to me," Lone Hawk, a bit evasive, answered while amazed by the clarity of words he converted from mere clicks and squeaks. "And where I'm from is of <u>this</u> same world, but beyond the bay as <u>your</u> reversed reference would suggest. However, there was another place of 'great effect' where I stayed for a long time. Oh, but it's all <u>too</u> complicated!

"Now, <u>enough</u> of myself! What's important to know is what happened to you…<u>because</u> I'm sure I can help. I feel your hatred for those predators from which you fled. And, I do <u>not</u> mean the killer whales, but rather the small ones with the great vessels and flying hooks of <u>painful</u> death. You were fortunate to have escaped and <u>especially</u> so to cross my path. So, tell me the rest: <u>Was</u> there another? <u>One</u> so dear?"

The whale's initial response was of silent hesitation and a mournful drift to the choppy surface. Then after taking a deep breath of air, he began to weep, quickly choking the emotion in embarrassment. Still, his anguish was too painful to suppress and an opportunity to unload awaited below him as the door was open to a kindly soul in Lone Hawk. Thus, he returned to reveal the torturous details of the recent past.

"Yes," he admitted candidly, with waving flipper-gestures; "there <u>was</u> another one, my mother. She <u>knew</u> they were stalking us as we fled, but the ship was fast. Even when we went <u>deep</u> underneath in a different direction, it always followed the same. Then when it was closing near to where we needed to come up for air, she told me, "The beasts beyond the bay will have me, but you can save yourself, my 'little Iceberg.' Swim away as <u>fast</u> as you can! You are well weaned; you <u>will</u> survive…now, go!"

"Of course, I didn't leave her immediately because I was <u>always</u> with her. Yet, when we surfaced and she took some loud hooks in her side, I began to listen to her advice in my fear. She pleaded again as her <u>life's</u> last wish for <u>me</u> to be free of the beasts, and so

I abandoned her. Though, <u>not</u> before a booming hook got me. It hurt <u>so</u> much and even more when I broke away with all my power. Then, with the many hunting whales soon to follow, I thought I would <u>surely</u> rejoin my mother as the dead.

"Then I was even <u>more</u> afraid when <u>you</u> came along. 'A <u>monster</u> from the Xenos?', I thought…but now, I know better. <u>You</u> are a <u>good</u> thing!"

Lone Hawk fell prey to his undying compassion and as a result, he pondered for a solution to this one's plight that would need his most thoughtful approach. He could not leave the whale and resume his quest, with so many open wounds of the bloodless kind left behind. "So, you're named after the <u>Iceberg</u>, a big chunk of ice clumsily floating and crashing wherever it may," he acknowledged, disapproving, then reverting to the old Native American way of renaming. "You are far too nimble for <u>that</u>! And with your white plumage, you should <u>reach</u> for the sky. <u>Nimbus</u>! That is so <u>regal</u> and fitting for you. Do you like it?"

"Like a cloud that watches over <u>everything</u>," he approved, cheerfully twitching about. "I thank you, good stranger, <u>but</u> with no name for yourself?"

While already scheming Nimbus' restitution, Lone Hawk kept their trust at an even scale. "<u>I</u> am Lone Hawk; a name which you may not understand, so I will explain," he reasoned from their separate origins to then broaden the naive one's horizon. "The hawk is the <u>fiercest</u> bird of prey from beyond the bay. I only say <u>that</u> because…so very long ago, I raised an orphan of such to maturity. His loyalty was boundless and like an aerial brave of the 'highest order,' he died for me. That <u>wonderful</u> bird of whom I affectionately called 'Screecher,' he became my inspiration and, somehow, I believe his relentless spirit lives on in me. <u>Nimbus</u>, in honor of his fearless example—you <u>must</u> face your enemy! And do this <u>not</u> to avenge your mother's slaughter, but to <u>heal</u> yourself and be <u>free</u> of this sense of enraged failure. Are you agreeable to this, good Nimbus?"

"And <u>you</u> will come along, Lone Hawk?" Nimbus asked, with enthusiasm brewing in his soul. "If so, I'll be like your brave hawk, Screecher, and do my <u>very</u> best."

277

Lone Hawk was thoroughly pleased by his positive effect on the young aqua-brave, as they were still shallowly submerged in the green sunlight of the North Pacific's vast water world. "Of course, I will be with you, brave Nimbus," he reassured, patting the end of his bottled nose. "Let's retrace your path and find these killers. Though I <u>cannot</u> bring your mother back…I can, with your direction, bring them to justice and spare any other potential victims. So, my new friend, lead the way and your <u>true</u> enemies we shall find!"

They swam side-by-side at a good rate in a westward direction. While they blazed an invisible trail through the ocean's well-lit portion near the surface, the abundant aquatic life instinctively cleared their path. Even though the natural forces seemed to comply to their forge, the limited pace preyed on Lone Hawk's patience and spurred him to speed up the operation. So, in reference to a very proud memory of Xavier's past, he tucked Nimbus under his arm like a football. Then as if he were going for the winning score in the semifinals game, he plunged forward, increasing their velocity ten-fold.

"My idea, as you will see, was inspired by an old story about a <u>great</u> white whale called 'Moby Dick,' much like a full-grown version of yourself. Anyway, he was pursued by the <u>vengeful</u> human beast, Captain Ahab, who wanted to kill him more than anything," Lone Hawk told the adulated Nimbus who could barely direct their path at such a brisk pace. "While Ahab, a whaler from long ago, wanted the great Moby Dick as his prize of revenge for the injuries he got, trying to kill him before…he only ended up being Moby Dick's prize, instead, killed by his own tethered hooks. You see, Nimbus…using revenge to justify killing doesn't end well. But teaching your enemies a hard lesson they will <u>never</u> forget, and that <u>forces</u> them to change for the good, you will find, is <u>much</u> better. However today, not even the <u>mighty</u> Moby Dick would be a match for the 'killer humans' you encountered—but <u>I</u> am! So, <u>here's</u> the plan:

"After we find their mighty vessel and I sink it, they will wade helplessly at the surface. So then, you can go ahead and do your part, administering a good <u>strong</u> dosage of fright into them," Lone Hawk encouraged, then cautioned; "but remember, you're merely to scare them—<u>not</u> kill them! Even though, I understand how temptation might warrant it, but—<u>don't</u>! And when their spare rescue craft appears, nudge them toward it. From your higher example, the 'beasts beyond the bay' will hopefully learn to change for the better.

"Nimbus, you and your kind will <u>get</u> the respect you deserve. I promise that, among many other changes, these slaughters shall <u>never</u> happen again," he vowed valiantly while slowing and releasing Nimbus, who only basically understood his conditions. "Ah, could <u>this</u> be the one we seek?" Just at the horizon to the west, Lone Hawk spied a huge tan colored trawler with its slaughter deck in full operation.

"I don't see it, but it <u>sounds</u> the same," Nimbus said, blind to the distance yet bearing an auditory sense so acute. "<u>That's</u> the one … <u>yes</u>, go ahead and <u>sink</u> it, Lone Hawk!"

And so, they closed into a distance where Nimbus could visually detect his transgressors' hull for final confirmation. While he was then without doubt, an over eagerness was building within him as well. "Absolutely, for sure! I can <u>even</u> smell my <u>mother's</u> blood!" he reaffirmed most contemptuously. "Hurry, Lone Hawk—<u>spill</u> them into <u>my</u> world!"

With a moment's hesitation, Lone Hawk grew concerned by the fanatical avenger spirit welling in one so innocent. In his efforts to help a very different species with this very human approach, was he spawning their own corruption? Since advising the young whale's temperament, he denied the possibility. And, with a second reminder, he convinced himself of infallibility for this timing of such righteousness. "All right, it will be done," he agreed, though while demanding his attention with a firm grasp of his shoulder; "but remember what I said before … <u>scare</u>, don't kill. You will <u>not</u> disappoint me … <u>understood?</u>"

Though in agreement, Nimbus still held an impish aura about him as Lone Hawk bolted toward the doomed vessel. Thus, once he crept into the plane of execution like a shark, his lone witness was most certainly without dismay as his hero made the target look so small, with his use of the ever-abundant water. By creating a sudden upheaval directly below the human beasts' mobile factory, a bursting spout brought the entire vessel to an incredible height. Lifting its lengthy heft over a hundred feet, Lone Hawk then buffered its downward plunge and, with a sporting tip of the bow, shot it cleanly into the imploding waters. Totally submerged, the ship and its whale parts drifted below the surface where he made sure that all the brown-clad poachers had escaped the hazardous depths.

According to plan, no one was killed or seriously injured. Yet understandably, the survivors cursed and complained in their native Russian tongue about the lousy stroke of misfortune. While their crew gradually swam together as an instinctual circle of wading defense, Lone Hawk was bumped by Nimbus then carrying his mother's nose-severed head, awkwardly, in a gaping bite to show him the familial evidence of their atrocities. Thus, with a ferocious rumble from his blowhole, he ditched the surfaced remains and almost sealed a travesty of trust down his gullet.

In turn, breaking their circle by lifting his head just below them, the infuriated Nimbus took one of the poachers' double-dozen into his mouth. The terrified little man cried, trying to pry himself from Nimbus' snugly clenched teeth while enduring a violent thrashing. As no joy could be found in the violent aggression for the young whale, he let the 'thankfully still alive' individual go. Lone Hawk's approval became the most important concept in his life, something for which to strive in hopes of better things to come. As a result, he was able to back away from those he so wanted to extinguish and allow them to climb aboard their lifeboats, which Lone Hawk salvaged from their ship. And luckily for them, they were able to start the well-equipped, electric emergency craft in an instant, despite their complete submersion.

"I wanted to _tear_ them to pieces, just like they did my mother, but _then_ I remembered what you said," Nimbus admitted, relieved he resisted the temptation while rejoining Lone Hawk in the depths below the thankful humans who started back toward their east Russian mainland, several miles away. "Looking at their pathetic little faces only made me feel sorry for them. I could _not_ kill them, Lone Hawk, even though they were _so_ bad and did not deserve to live. _What_ does that mean?"

"It _means_ that you are of the _highest_ good, Nimbus," Lone Hawk complimented with his beholding outstretched arms, further convinced that he had created a mind of human-whale fusion. "You could have _very_ easily, with such a clear advantage, taken the _whole_ lot under, but your forgiving nature told you that more hurt only makes it worse. You have done well, Nimbus…very well!"

After his new mentor's expressed approval, Nimbus suddenly burst into an upward course and flung himself with the agility of a dolphin high above the waves. Proudly, he caught a glimpse of his heavenly namesakes streaming through the sky and began to wonder how he could repay Lone Hawk. Then crashing with a spectacular white-water splash, he vowed to return the favor. Yet, he could not even begin to imagine what special value his 'simple being' could have for one so great. "Now that I feel so much better, let us do what you need to do, Lone Hawk," Nimbus suggested, hoping to learn more about his quietly contemplating hero. "Maybe I can help somehow, or even just keep you company…do you want me to show you the big squid? I know where the best place to find them is, but it's very far away."

"I admit, Nimbus, I am somewhat lost, but I have a feeling that you can help me find the way," Lone Hawk told while recalling a curious term he used when they first met, alluding to 'him' with a sense of awed fear. "Tell me, what is this Xenos place?"

"Xenos Abyss? It's probably the best but worst place in the world! The 'far away' place I was talking about," Nimbus spouted as if only the most ignorant would not know of it. "Down near the bottom in the big squids' realm…deep below where the light cannot reach, the horrible Xenos-creatures live there as well. While there is said to be many kinds, most of them look like giant manta rays with many shiny eyes. And the reason they are so feared is because nothing can escape them. Even the human beasts and their largest vessels have been captured and taken down to the Xenos. Even so, we dare to risk it only because of the great squid-hunting, but I doubt that's what you want…So, do you still want to go there, Lone Hawk—do you?!"

Barely containing his exploding intrigue while rubbing his hands together, Lone Hawk was enthralled by the 'matter of fact' attitude of fair Nimbus and the luck that this 'Xenos Abyss' must be the place. Compelling like nothing he had heard before, the draw of it became an instant obsession. However, the location was less than certain. "What you describe, Nimbus, could very well be my destination," Lone Hawk speculated, retaining his ever-present mystery. "Bring me to the closest point above this Xenos Abyss where you'd safely dare go, alone…or better <u>yet</u>, let's try a quicker route…"

In his haste so fearing the scope of time closing, Lone Hawk set forth his accelerated plan. With careful consideration of Nimbus' generous size as compared to Xavier, he implemented the mind meld, downplaying the possibility of any serious side effects. As well, his sense of direction was so intolerably jumbled in this prominent 'water world,' he deemed his actions justified, practical and well worth the risk.

"Let us commune now, Nimbus, in the <u>purest</u> form," Lone Hawk persuaded, with no fair warning of possible dangers which could befall his proposal. "Only then can we become Earth Force brothers, you know, 'just like family.' And, in addition to this sacred bond, the contribution of your so-underrated-wisdom will honor and revere the 'Nimbus name' <u>forever!</u>"

As Nimbus was eagerly agreeable, he flapped his flippers excitedly, and nodded in a strangely personified manner. "Earth Force <u>brothers</u>? I think I <u>like</u> that!" he oozed with enthusiasm while his pinkish brown eyes gleamed through the lime green strands of mid-morn sunlight. "Okay, just tell me what I must do for this, Lone Hawk."

"We only need to exchange stern stares and let our eyes combine their means with the power of the Earth Force," Lone Hawk stated, cleverly allowing a third party to seem the actual inducer while he prayed that no harm would come to the preciously willing one. "It will then be done in a moment's blast of light. Afterwards, we shall have a much better understanding of the world and, therefore, the better good we can do in the future.

"So then, hold steady Nimbus…yes, <u>that</u> is perfect! <u>Now</u>, let us begin…" As a precaution, Lone Hawk eased the process upon Nimbus by starting with a lower intensity level than Xavier's transfer. Soft, translucent rays like tiny rainbows arched from his slightly distanced eyes of gold around his 'future' whale brother's head in a funnel formation. Gradually, he increased the intensity to a full encasement that grew into a swirling-red storm cloud, reflecting his piercing optical source. The effect proved much too frightening for Nimbus, whose animal instinct set him off. Thus, he fled the danger and defied the magnetic pull of the meld.

While Nimbus bolted away from Lone Hawk at a rate much greater than his escape from the killer whales, it was obvious that his physical abilities were enhanced. 'But, what of his mind?' Lone Hawk wondered anxiously as he immediately launched himself into a coordinating westbound flight, barely clearing the moderate waves. Soon, when he gained on the startled Nimbus surging forward with the velocity of a marine missile, he dove back into the sea, readily adapting to the element as if native born.

"It _is_ complete, Nimbus. There's nothing more to fear," Lone Hawk assured as his restraining hand slipped off Nimbus' spurred shoulder hump; yet magnificently, he was able to retain his grasp by creating a green, black-tipped dorsal fin in its place. 'Hmm, sharp-looking fin—_this_ should cheer him up,' he surmised of the regal addition in his solid hold; but then the trick was to convince his 'freaked out' pal. "I _sure_ appreciate the good water sense you've given me, Nimbus, as I'm sure you're enjoying the lightning swiftness I've sown into you…well, since you're heading towards the dreaded Xenos Abyss, anyway…you don't object to my dragging along on your _mighty_ new fin, _do_ you?"

Nimbus consciously ignored him. And with his eyes nearly thrice the size as before, they stared stubbornly affixed forward when he took an abrupt northward turn, just to spite Lone Hawk's levity. Though as expected, the rebellious action causing him to lose his grip, spinning off to the side had consequences. Thus, the wayward whale suddenly found himself crashing out of the water into mid-air suspension.

"Nimbus, what in the _world_ were you thinking?" Lone Hawk demanded, wading and pointing at him, while also discovering to his surprise that his telekinetic ability could so easily support the whale's sizable, blanched mass in aerial confinement. "Your anger has returned, and _I_ want to know _why!_"

"You denied me my revenge while you seek the same—_hypocrite!_ Now _bring_ me down! On my honor, I will not go," Nimbus insisted with newborn sharpness in his enlarged eyes then set in a shorter, more streamlined snout that made him look almost cute. "Alas, you do need direction, but as well you must explain <u>yourself</u>!"

Lone Hawk, though weary of potential side effects, was shocked by Nimbus' adversarial attitude, yet conceited to the request in so lowering him back into his oceanic abode. "Tell me, Nimbus, how much <u>do</u> you know?" he asked with an air of dread at reaping the bittersweet consequences. "What <u>horrible</u> thing have I given you?"

"<u>You</u> are supposed to be <u>dead</u>, Lone Hawk." Nimbus spoke as the enemy, re-submerged and then circling to Lone Hawk's guarded pirouette. "A <u>freak</u> beyond nature…<u>selfishly</u> holding faithful prisoners toward an empty quest. Yes! That sums you up <u>quite</u> well now, in the light of truth.

"You plan to destroy those of the Xenos only because they killed your pet hawk, and rendered <u>you</u> insane. <u>That</u> is all! <u>Why</u> do you blind yourself to the fact that it was your 'own kind' who ultimately did away with you. The human beast <u>shuns</u> the strange as a <u>threat</u> to either conquer, abolish or, as a curiosity, to serve for their amusement. <u>When</u> will your stubborn mind realize who the <u>true</u> enemy is? It is in your roots to sustain hope for them, but it is now time to sever those ties."

"<u>Stop</u> with this nonsense, Nimbus!" Lone Hawk rebutted. "Your views are <u>far</u> too narrow to know the sanctity and diversity of human life. Did <u>I</u> somehow make <u>you</u> of the Evil One? And, what about <u>these</u> prisoners? I've <u>not</u> felt their presence…they were lost in the crossing, I was sure!"

Fearing that he did transfer something planted by his arch enemy, Lone Hawk found himself uncomfortably on the defensive. And though he was so ever appreciative for the finely tuned aquatic sense bestowed him and needed for his directive, the overtness of his 'inherited' dark side through Nimbus, turning against him almost became a stifling aversion.

"They are certainly trapped within you, Lone Hawk. Yet, most surprisingly they hold no animosity toward <u>you</u>, their captor," Nimbus revealed as quite plausible to which Lone Hawk, steeped in regret, buckled under and heard him out. "But actually, they put up with it <u>only</u> because they've been assured that their 'freedom' will be granted once you reach your destiny. These prisoners don't care about <u>you</u> and your 'silly' quest. They just want to rejoin the living, and get <u>away</u> from you!

"Go ahead, all powerful Lone Hawk! You <u>have</u> what you want from me. So, <u>go</u> to the Xenos and discover your <u>galling</u> ignorance and 'twisted' faith, trying to save a world that <u>only</u> turns against you. Ha-ha, <u>be</u> the <u>fool</u>, Lone Hawk, as you were <u>always</u> meant to be!"

While excusing Nimbus of the 'accidental' possession from his own, Lone Hawk felt he had been challenged to a debate as such and so, he defended his quest with soulful vigor: "Poor Nimbus, I'm sorry you've been rendered but a pawn of the dark force within me; though unfair as it seems, you have been nonetheless dubbed the chosen one to discourage me or, at the very least, test my will. However, I remain resolute in my invasion and eradication of this evil spawning ground to which you have so profoundly directed me…

"If Black Moon and the others truly <u>are</u> within my being, I will <u>not</u> interfere with their 'quest for freedom.' Because, to stay on as my ally through to the end would have to be <u>strictly</u> of their own choice. Finally, it is now no secret that…despite my appearance, I am, in essence a—'beast beyond the bay' human! So, <u>deal</u> with it! My loyalties lie with them, good or bad…the helpful little strangers who save you when you're beached and the <u>vile</u> ones who kill you when you're free. Yes, opposing forces which I believe favor the good and <u>will</u> for evermore…That is, once I have finished destroying the Xeno's Keeper and all its domain."

Nimbus' provocatively negative attitude seemed effectively neutralized, as Lone Hawk thought, by his poignant rebuttal. Yet, his calmness was a result of the steely hand of death pulling him downward. In urgent response, Lone Hawk propped his cold body up to the surface for air. While he desperately shook him in hopes of revival, the dying whale's words evoked intense communal pain: "I cannot see anymore, Lone Hawk. Am I going to the Evermore of your dark loneliness and raging anger? Or will I join my mother in heaven? Do <u>not</u> answer! I am the 'Aqua-brave' and I will face it as one should, but…Lone Hawk, I'm <u>so</u> scared…"

The life force was gone from the whale he sacrificed, yet Lone Hawk tried to imagine Nimbus as the vibrant and curious one of before. However, in this case, wishful thinking did not produce the intended results. Nimbus' body lay in his arms like a carcass ready for the whaler's butchers' deck.

"No! <u>Not</u> Nimbus!" Lone Hawk cried in shocked disbelief. "He was the <u>balance</u> for me, and I <u>killed</u> him!"

Back and forth he swam cradling the body, chanting, "Nimbus, come back!" Then, when it seemed he would be a shark's city of feasting, Lone Hawk called out to 'the One' of his last hopes: "Earth Force, save this <u>good</u> creature from the death abode…It was <u>my</u> fault but yours as well to allow one of the 'already endangered' to die for this mission he did not even understand," he pleaded, awaiting a miracle while bowing his face upon Nimbus' surfaced corpse. "Bring him back—<u>untainted</u> by our <u>righteous</u> treachery!"

After a moment's calm, Lone Hawk began to accept the sacrifice of his new friend as a tragic yet unavoidable necessity. Though, with slight delay just as he was about to mournfully proceed to the Xenos Abyss, a wondrous reprieve began to unfold. Thankfully, the Earth Force was in sympathetic concurrence, for the sphere nestled in his chest cast forth amber fingers of light which swirled about the white carcass. Like an angelic fog of life, the death-defying force created the stir of a warm heartbeat, awakening an innocently groggy Nimbus. "Sorry, I think I fell asleep! Hey, Lone Hawk…are you <u>still</u> going to the Xeno?"

Lone Hawk, though incredibly overjoyed, maintained a cool disposition. "I think I must have fallen asleep, too…uh, Nimbus…did you say something else?"

To that, Nimbus bumped his sporty new nose against Lone Hawk's chest as an affectionate wake-up call. "Lone Hawk! You <u>cannot</u> fall asleep! <u>You</u> are supposed to be the leader!" he scolded while wiggling in disappointment and still using the 'singular' name for the abyss. "Once again, are you <u>still</u> going to the Xeno? And, before you answer, I wanted you to know that, if you are, I feel brave enough to be your first warrior, like the Screecher. I also feel <u>very</u> strong, so I <u>know</u> I can help you find this mysterious enemy!" With the revived Nimbus' up-beat demeanor so fresh and inspiring, Lone Hawk, then knowing the course, tucked Nimbus under his arm and took him on an amazing trip into the southwest sky over the ocean. During their nearly six-thousand-mile blurred flight, which landed them to splashdown right above the Xeno, Lone Hawk again envisioned Xavier's touchdown run but in 'full effect' with the delightful 'short-shorts' cheerleaders, dancing and waving their pom-poms toward the endzone for the score.

"Wow, Lone Hawk—that was the <u>best</u> ride I could ever imagine!" Nimbus raved, wanting more, though he was about to be snubbed by his idol from any action below. "And <u>here</u> we are, with the Xeno just <u>waiting</u> down there…for <u>us</u> to start some trouble— so come on!"

Unwilling to subject Nimbus to another premature bout with death, Lone Hawk craftily denied his proposal. "Nimbus, just as Screecher used to be my eyes in the sky, you must monitor here, at the surface," he transposed their relationship softly, without suggesting any lesser role. "You have described the…'<u>Xeno</u>' as a vacuum of such, but I believe that we will find it much the reverse with my presence. So, by containing this back flush and keeping its order as all things rise to the surface, you need just report all your findings to me and then your mission will be done, good Nimbus, <u>proud</u> Aqua brave of the Seven Seas…understood?"

Even though he felt robbed of his chance for further adventure, Nimbus swam a few circles, disappointed, but then complied. "As you wish, Lone Hawk, but if too much time passes, you <u>know</u> that <u>I</u> will go down there looking for <u>you</u>!" he expressed most vehemently, with the all-too-eager eyes of before. "I know a <u>lot</u> more than you think I do, Lone Hawk. Do <u>not</u> desert me; I <u>am</u> on your side, but I'm <u>not</u> stupid anymore!" Lone Hawk was speechless to the sharp-witted transversion of his super whale companion.

"Oh, Lone Hawk, <u>worry</u> not! I merely await and expect something great…so, be gone with you!"

Perceiving another down-right brazen Nimbus who seemed so pompous and cavalier as to repel, Lone Hawk started to fade away toward the about-to-be-de-fabled Xenos Abyss, fittingly nestled within the infamous 'Dragon's Triangle.' There, in the extraordinary depths a few hundred-miles south of Japan, he submerged with a brave-fist salute toward a suspiciously confident Nimbus who waved his flippers in a 'please proceed' manner. Yet, to his utter surprise, the super 'smart' whale called out with 'poetic' words of inspiration. "Uphold your rightful stance, Lone Hawk, for <u>they</u> are the ones to fear and pity. <u>Yours</u> is the superior force as all absolutes will become clear, down there in Xeno City!"

To such a 'weird' send off, Lone Hawk gave Nimbus a nod of appreciation then vanished into the depths below the sunlit reaches. Finally, he was gratefully free of distractions and could follow his acquired directive and avenging rage toward a, so far, intangible adversary.

CHAPTER XVIII
Xeno's Keeper

FURTHER PLUNGING INTO THE darkness, Lone Hawk encountered a few giant squid that fled like russet torpedoes at an impressive length equal to his own height. `Ah, the favorite food of Nimbus' kind,' he noted while he continued miles below the watery surface to where his infrared vision revealed the oceanic basin. In all its majesty, the deeply submerged world of towering peaks and intricate ravines exuded molten warmth, though it lay in eerie calm. Amidst the splendid scenery, his attention was drawn irresistibly towards a gaping, well-sunken chasm, prompting his entry into its two-mile width. As he descended a mile upon an oval-shaped pit at the bottom-center of the canyon, Lone Hawk's adulation brimmed, convinced that the Xeno's doorway bowed before him.

Through its jagged mouth of a quarter-mile's gauge, he observed a contrasting interior, boasting synthetically smooth walls and introducing him to an abyss of perfect design. Proceeding further downward, he noticed an array of luminescent geometric symbols sporadically decorating either side of the enormous tunnel it had become. While just a passing curiosity, they seemed to lead the way to a great wall of limited entry. Like a mammoth electrical socket with a seven-inlet configuration, the break of passageways offered a natural choice. While there were three tunnels in triangular formation on each side of one much larger in the center, he selected, by prominence, the more generous middle throughway.

As it took a few curves and leveled off, Lone Hawk traveled a relatively short distance and once again faced a seven-socket wall identical to the first, yet smaller in scale. Following the same logic, he entered the prominent center and was suddenly greeted by a flood of bright violet illumination. While it filled the rounded path with a gradual upward curve, he was sure he had been acknowledged. They were very near and so he exploded full force to his long-awaited destination.

Then, during his surging ascent through the violet-burst waterway, Lone Hawk began to hear ominous laughter, spurring his memory of the Toltec on the Big River. Their cruel taunts, so perfectly reproduced, sent him back to the slaying of his beloved uncle, Wonders Eye. In turn, his concentration began to wane as he was angrily distracted. Once the disturbance faded, he thought the bout with trickery was won. However, repeating from meek whispers to intense annunciations of song was a simple message building with voices of unmistakable familiarity: *"Hail, Lone Hawk, Champion of the Earth…come forward!"* the obnoxious chorus saturated his audio sense without mercy. *"The 'Giving One' invites you to celebrate your glorious return! Please, come forward!"*

With careful deciphering of the vocal ensemble, Lone Hawk identified Wonders Eye, his parents, Rainbow, and the unique graveled bellow of her father, the Chief. Additionally, recognized were Night Owl's most suitably cast sensual tones and Screecher's well-timed shrieks and calls, which created a very strange melody underneath the lyrical content. Effectively entranced by the musical chant, he sank momentarily into an embrace of the past yet soon, his stronger self then shook free of it with suspicious contempt. Thus, he was refocused to course and repossessed his fiery esteem when he met the end of the Xeno's waterway and crashed out of its pond like a geyser.

When he splashed beyond the insanity of the cacophonous tunnel, there was a dead silence in a fantastic underworld where Lone Hawk observed the redundancy of the six-and-one theme in grand form. As a colossal infrastructure of Gothic-Roman detail, the desolate sub-oceanic city was a marvelous sight, with six arched hallways leading to lesser ponds. And while there was much more expanse to explore, his concentration remained toward the center and above. Then upward, he rose through its inner tower with a spiraling balcony to a white-lit dome. Nearing it, he cautiously slowed his levitation, well suspecting treachery awaiting in the abandoned hollow oozing with synthetic mastery.

At a quarter of a mile above the central pool, Lone Hawk stalled right beneath the cloud-like dome which mushroomed to a three-hundred-foot width. Upon the gray-stone intro-scape, it emanated like a bright overcast sky. The attraction of the light only seemed to dare and invite. Teetering on foolishness and forcefulness, Lone Hawk merely touched the non-intimidating source of luminescence when an invisible force grabbed his hand. Suddenly, his thoughts, once firmly in control, regressed to terror as he was pulled inside the hellish place on the other side.

In abrupt contrast to the serenity of the Xeno's city, the environment above it consisted of one churning vortex of a volcanic orange and yellow swirl which captured Lone Hawk. His violent resistance proved futile against the molten whirlpool. After it dragged him into its twirling current, he rode toward the center through its ever-tightening curves, soon to reveal a black eye. And so, he was carried on the winding path to the dark hole which sucked him inside, leaving all else to fade.

Complete darkness surrounded him as a disheartening end to a marvelous fantasy. Just like his pitiful beginnings in the Evermore, he had gone full circle back to nothingness. Was it possibly a dream of impossible proportions, meaning he never left his dark little corner of the alter-universe? He suspected the worst. Yet, after a moment's wallowing in apathy, anger once again manifested itself; his true nature grew to frustrated rage.

"I could <u>never</u> be so easily baited and neutralized," Lone Hawk, seething, told himself; "I am the chosen one, the Earth Force Son. <u>This</u> is to be my <u>victory</u> and all the world's. You <u>know</u> this to be true…Faith…I <u>must</u> have faith. Evil One, you only delay 'my wrath.' The passing of time only holds <u>more</u> pain for yours to suffer and <u>mine</u> to savor. Soon, I shall <u>damn</u> you to this hell!"

During Lone Hawk's barrage of threats and infernal curses toward the evil force he blamed for his encapsulation, a distress signal was sent unbeknownst to himself. For high above the torture chamber, his Earth Force brother awaited to receive the transmission, also quite unaware yet profoundly responsive.

Well situated on the USS Reagan aircraft carrier after a smooth flight and landing from Honolulu, Xavier and Jeanine were hanging out on the forward flight deck near the starboard side railing, waiting for Agent Andrewska. Gesturing wildly, he stood further mid-ship grouped with the pilots and some Top Navy Brass that had stepped out onto the platform amid a dozen jets parked in rows of three. With the high sun beating down on them where seagulls were flying and squawking about, Jeanine put her arm around a moody and distant Xavier who shielded his eyes while staring into the point of interest's rolling waves. There, as the carrier circled the splashdown site clockwise at a ten-knots crawl, Jeanine playfully backhand-patted him on the side of the face and got his somber-smiling attention. Concerned, she tried to cheer him up with her cute, spirited voice.

"I know the whole thing's been <u>totally</u> nerve-racking for you, Xavier, but I've come to accept, or rather, be honored by whatever role I might be of value, here…" Jeanine encouraged, leaning close; but then, without fetching the desired response, she spoke in a more genuine tone. "And I am <u>so</u> proud of you, being chosen for what is quite possibly the most <u>important</u> mission in human history! I <u>suppose</u> you're going to have a 'world-saving' epiphany at any moment, and <u>I</u> was there…Oh, and too bad about Sandos—when they went forward to the main cabin, she must have told Andrewska <u>much</u> more than all that hysterical stuff we <u>all</u> witnessed! But he's been as tight-lipped as ever, barely even talking to us…" Xavier shook his head, tight and fast like he got a chill, to then only respond in his defense.

"Yeah, sorry, I was just waiting for a psychic message, signal—or <u>something</u>! And, about Sandos…she just stared at me, freaking out like on a bad acid trip…and then, she <u>kicks</u> me?" Hardly listening, Jeanine's frightful attention was stolen by an ominous change in the sky. "Xavier, look at those <u>weird</u> dark clouds, coming our way so fast," she warned, cradling his arm. "It's like they're covering the entire western horizon…and <u>now</u>, in layers south and north too, going around in opposite directions—<u>God</u>, how <u>creepy</u>!"

"Oh, shit! And from the east, just the same—holy <u>fuck</u>!" Xavier shouted, appearing much more panicked than as if it were an approaching typhoon. "From <u>every</u> direction, like the Mars rocket before it got destroyed, but <u>so</u> much bigger—Jeanine? I think it's starting…" Wrought with imploding forces, Xavier suddenly keeled over and clasped his forehead while drawing Jeanine's undivided heart-sinking attention away from the hypnotizing, surreal storm clouds rapidly closing. Soon, she realized that he had gone into a psychic-related seizure. Then with scaley gray rashes breaking out on his arms and face, he stumbled away from her towards the runway's bow and stopped in his tracks, wincing and grunting in pain. Soppy-eyed, Jeanine rushed over to him. But right when her hand touched his shaking shoulder to help, she was jolted and repelled in a trail of lime-green sparks.

Feeling the post-electrocution effects, Jeanine hit the gray-painted concrete deck and, in her numbed panic, pulled herself up by the railing and twisted around, disoriented and terrified. To her shocked witness, she winced to the torturous sight of Xavier, then convulsing and devolving on the unforgiving deck. When in just seconds, he so quickly morphed into a greenish-gray reptilian version of himself, the dark thundering clouds formed a shrinking circle of blue sky and blocked out the sun as Jeanine noticed an invisible force, dragging and then propping him up against the railing. Elevated to sheer panic, she hollered over to Andrewska who was pointing at the sky along with the Top Navy Brass while also glaring at her from near deck-center.

"Hey! Agent Andrewska—<u>hurry</u>! It's dragging him off, into the ocean!" Jeanine waved and yelled as loud as she could, jumping up-and-down while jab-pointing at Xavier being targeted by the supernatural phenomenon; outraged, she then sassed, "come on, <u>damn</u> it—<u>move</u> your ass!" Responding with a delayed sense of urgency, Andrewska and some crew members power-walked toward them, but they would arrive too late as Xavier was hanging outside the railing and holding on with his body in a horizontal flutter. Then, in a 'seeming divine' synchronicity, the blackened clouds closed and collided with a thunderous crackling roar, casting a twelve-foot-thick spiraling shaft of lightening that struck straight down to the ocean just fifty-feet from the deck before them. There, at its impact point, a luminous whirlpool developed and started drawing on Xavier's legs and stretched them into light fragments. Aware of his forceful calling, the grimacing lizard-eyed Xavier spoke his apparent last words to her in a strange double-octave voice before having to let go and be devoured by the fluorescent aquamarine vortex.

"Sorry, Jeanine…maybe <u>this</u> is how Sandos saw me—<u>gross!</u>" he forced a sense of humor, but then rasped out an amorous goodbye. "Anyway, just remember me before all of this, when we were 'in love' and free of <u>such</u> heavy things…well, <u>is</u> what it is…so just know <u>this</u>, Jeanine, that I will <u>love</u>, love-love you always, and forever more…" Thus, blowing her a kiss then releasing his hand while giving her the 'peace sign' with a shark-toothed smile, Xavier snapped backward and blurred into the glowing spiraled void.

Criss-crossing, twirling streams of multi-colored light immediately formed beneath him like trail blazers in a downward path to the bottom of the abyss. Inside the high-pressure resistant tube, an elated Xavier rode it like a waterpark ride yet encountered quite a scare when a giant orange squid tried to intercept him. Between the tenacious beast's tentacles and snapping beak, it failed to penetrate his travel tube and thus retreated. At the opened end near the ocean floor, he then jettisoned toward a glistening wall with the seven tunnels in diamond formation, same as Lone Hawk's course just hours earlier. Drawn into the entrance of the larger, center portal, he was pulled upward through a channel of hyper-dimension in an array of tangerine lit symbols so otherworldly. Soon afterward, he broke the water's surface into a gigantic hollow. Out of the circular pool like a spouting gusher, he ascended through the 'Xeno City' inner-tower's dome to the glowing blue sphere of the Earth

Force. However, with his Devils Lake midnight patrol contact, the humongous birdman's frightening form around it, Xavier went into a state of shock. Meantime, Lone Hawk with his red-lit watchtower eyes on alert only glared on from above, without taking notice.

Then vacuumed inside his half-concealed orb were eleven strangers of Native American features huddled before the other side of it, looking outward. Among the ten orb-entranced men, the only woman there, of whom he thought quite pretty, broke away from the rest and approached him with a golden spear for his taking; she greeted him as well, with the utmost exuberance. "Hello, Xavier Branion! <u>Oh</u>, and of the 'serpent' no less!" Black Moon noted as she stood close, putting the weapon's shaft near his hand and adding, "<u>now</u>, I see that <u>this</u> was meant for you and so, the balance shall go <u>our</u> way!"

As Xavier took the spear, the shaft blazed with a fiery hue which he held to his chest. And in an instant, he returned to his human form like an 'unclean spirit' had been extracted from him. With stares abounding by those who knew him as intimately as himself, only Black Moon gained his initial trust. "Well, thanks for the magic spear, Lady—<u>wow</u>! It really helped me out of my funk," he elated, directing his much-improved attention toward her in a comfortable tone. "And now that I'm back to normal, relatively speaking, I have a <u>million</u> questions, but I'll settle for answers to <u>just</u> a few. Who <u>are</u> you, and these other 'ghostly' people in what look to be Native American costumes? <u>What</u> is that big, bluish orbital window you're all huddled around? And <u>finally</u>, with the spears and all…are we going to war in this other dimension or <u>wherever</u> we are? I mean, My God! <u>This</u> sure as hell's no dream!" he raised his voice with a titter, then eased his tone as a flood of experiences from Lone Hawk's bartered life surfaced in his consciousness. "<u>Wait</u> a minute, I know <u>what</u> this is…the Earth Force sphere! It <u>chose</u> me in my past life, and I was re-incarnated to fulfill the 'sacred mission' to destroy the Grays, the <u>Owlmen</u>…at the gorge—<u>that's</u> why I said that! This is <u>great</u>! You must be here to brief me, before we head into battle."

"Oh Xavier, you are <u>so</u> as I imagined, at ease in such a strange place," she told in a loud whisper while the others concentrated on the sphere. "I am Black Moon. We were summoned from the past by the Earth Force as well, to save your, _our_ world from the domination of evil intruders. And, I understand your confusion. However, you were _not_ re-incarnated, for we now await within Lone Hawk, the very large one you just saw again who, upon his emergence, copied your mind to know the present. In turn, you were given his life experience, just as the rest of us, to cherish and believe in his quest. While he's become ever more powerful, Lone Hawk would _not_ have gotten far without having your familiarity with the new Earth. So, enough of that. _All_ you need to know is 'ready your spear' and join us in communion with the sphere before us. We _must_ help Lone Hawk _break_ this spell of darkness for our passage to be granted."

Still mystified, Xavier accepted his role as what he considered a 'come to life' comic book character, playing the 'mystic warrior.' He found sanity in the removed approach, like an acting debut. So, when they joined the rest in a most direct form of prayer, he knelt between Black Moon and Spirit Slayer as a throneless standout. Indeed, he seemed a misfit and a pretender. Yet, his addition did seem to provide the spark that fed Lone Hawk some much-needed inspiration.

"_Perhaps_ the 'possessed' Nimbus was telling the truth about Black Moon and the others, making the journey within me," Lone Hawk reassessed, abandoning his wasteful growls of anger and redirecting his attention to the orb in his chest. "If so, I _definitely_ cannot fail! I _promised_ them glorious victory and _must_ deliver—_think_!"

Continuing to watch the sphere, Lone Hawk realigned his demeanor to a calmed invincibility as it burned, a bright crimson beacon. "_If_ this is merely a 'masterful illusion' able to confine me as a specter to myself," he reasoned most confidently; "so shall _I_ counter this 'tawdry,' most impressionable spell with my _own_ vivid imagination, so now _hear_ me: _Bow_ to your master, oh wicked shroud of night! _To_ the Fire God, your cleanser to the light!"

Immediately upon his command, a blue blow-torch flame blasting from the sphere was invited by the surrounding darkness to ignite itself into a barn-burning roar as, layer-by-layer, it was unveiled to translucence, a cubed enclosure that had held him.

When the last layer was incinerated, its charred fragments melted into a smooth floor of marble which stretched across a vast oval plane. Above, a star-lit sky with a full moon shone down upon rows of inclined seating beyond the perimeter of the main floor. It was a packed house that night and Lone Hawk was center stage. Then, to no surprise of his own, the entire audience was of the opposing team.

In an almost cartoon setting, throngs of Owlmen Grays sat, numbering in the thousands, on big steps etched like stairways beside smooth aisles, creating six sections. Their attire reflected their spartan auras as each wore a long white tunic bearing the same red, seven-dot insignias worn on their silver suits, nine-centuries before. While they coldly affixed their 'purely pupil' bug eyes upon him, Lone Hawk leered back with his of inferno hue. He felt a mere spectacle supplanted to this 'Xenorena' for their amusement, complete with synthetic crowd noise brewing. Yet curiously, even being put on the spot as such, he held no malice toward the neutral onlookers. Because when it came down to it, there was just 'One' he wished to topple.

"Behold! Lone Hawk, the 'Earth Force Son,' has arrived!" a husky, all-encompassing voice announced in a congratulatory manner, but then went on into a lengthy monologue of clarification and so much more. "How _very_ long it has been since we met in the cave, and _so_ sadly you misunderstood. Your rites of passage _were_ so very painful when my loyal ones finalized our souls' fusion. Yet, it was the _enemy_ of your own kind that managed to temporarily silence us with death, but we were _too_ strong. Our partnership grew because we were _never_ alone and had a purpose. Now, returning to the source in 'magnificent form,' you have come 'full circle' as heir to the Earth Force.

"_Yes_, it is _I_, my son, and so _very_ proud you have made me…I knew you were special from the start! Emanating so high a 'energy force' of your own, you were _no_ random choice; you were _destined_ to be the chosen one. First, to boldly cross the barrier of death and dimension, then, to defy the black box…_most_ remarkable!

"To offer the scale of your accomplishment, be aware, Lone Hawk, that along with many otherworldly invaders, there was an indigenous force, a fallen one considered the 'absolute power of terror' yet who failed the box miserably. Here, in this very arena, the powerful-though-primordial being appeared to me as a rather impressive seven-headed serpent. Bluffing, he threatened punishment if our loyalties were not declared upon his <u>immediate</u> demand. As the upstart clearly underestimated the vast superiority of the Earth Force, I became most annoyed. So, I put this <u>vulgar</u> entity, heralding himself as the Light Bearer Lucifer, into the black box.

"Powerless and cowering within its darkness, it pleaded and promised me a billion souls for his release. And though I waived such an offer as meaningless, I <u>mercifully</u> allowed the box to dissolve, only to reveal a scrawny goat-headed man with black, blood-sweating eyes. Even in his <u>sorriest</u> state, the little beast then proposed an allegiance against the 'most arrogant' God of the Christ! So insulted was I by such a presumption, I melded its surprisingly gifted and diverse mind to well know my enemy, as you would have as well, I am sure. So, as it was done, I flushed the remaining lying spawn of 'divergent human' manifestation into the Earth's core, extinguishing its flame with my ultimate power base. However, that one was only a reflection of the source…which dwells above and who <u>must</u> be averted from destroying our beloved planet.

"As you now can see, Lone Hawk, the enemy is the untethered human race which has grown far more powerful than we can safely trust. Already, the 'loyal ones' have neutralized all of their nuclear arsenals, yet there is <u>so</u> much more to be done. Yes, you <u>are</u> the 'Chosen One,' the <u>catalyst</u> to implement the final 'World Order' which, after some vital training in the ways of omnipotence, shall save the Earth. In turn, Lone Hawk, your rewards will be endless while your dreams of being the Warbird Chief are finally answered, only <u>now</u>…they encompass the entire world. Lone Hawk, the **Earth Chief**! So regal and lofty a title, yet so true…and once you accept, <u>most</u> worthy one—<u>so</u> will it be you!

"I understand that your 'incredible journey' may have rendered you into a state of speechless exhaustion, and that the news of your godly status has you <u>immeasurably</u> overwhelmed. But <u>please</u>, if you will, Lone Hawk, now give us an affirmative nod to seal our trust.

Think of our loyal ones who serve us so well, as they have gathered here <u>specifically</u> to witness this momentous event…Lone Hawk?"

In a noncommittal cross-armed stance, Lone Hawk merely looked up and about in distrustful silence, trying to pinpoint the source of the booming voice. Unfortunately, his sensors had judged it as an even flow from every direction.

"All right then, prepare as you will," the voice boomed again. "<u>Ours</u> is to patiently await your word…"

Upon further investigation, Lone Hawk took to flight and found that the Xenorena had no exterior. The clear night sky, he surmised naturally as another illusion, surrounded the place like a glass lid on a brimming black hole. After a few passes around the Keeper's impressive cosmic fabrication, he swooped very near the Owlmen for a lap, inciting nothing but turning heads. Resisting the urge to take out a row or two of them, he returned to center stage with a brutal response readied for delivery. "Your presumptions only insult <u>me</u> as the Lucifer's did <u>you</u>, oh clever Keeper!" Lone Hawk shouted in a fierce grumble of purposeful irreverence. "<u>You</u> are no more the Earth Force than <u>I</u> am the Christ! And you have the <u>audacity</u> to judge me as the <u>fool</u> to perform your dirty deeds like these <u>soulless</u> Owlmen!

"You so <u>arrogantly</u> misunderstand my motives. And I am <u>not</u> here to ally…I'm here to lift the curse, as the good chief told. The prophecy will now be fulfilled and, in turn, quell my <u>infernal</u> hatred which only persists because of your <u>unforgivable</u> violations toward 'dear Screecher' and myself in the past, and all those in the present. With the righteous power of the <u>true</u> Earth Force, your destruction lies only moments away…so, now <u>show</u> yourself, cowardly keeper…<u>here</u>, in this alter-world of trickery, and meet your <u>inevitable</u> demise!"

His bold and challenging words echoed to only fade into the seemingly boundless reaches of the ominously tranquil setting. Still and quietly tittering like a laugh track, the gaping audience again tested his primordial aggressions to lash out upon them. For as his quandary thickened, he had little else to do. Contrary to his expectations of a glorious battle, imprisoned release to abandonment by his nemesis seemed the present course until a rectangular slot opened before him from the edge of the main floor. Thus, from the shadows within the lone entryway, six human figures and another emerged with heartfelt familiarity.

While they stood there in rowed assemblage, Lone Hawk glared in disbelief, yet then warmed to experience the well of loving emotions from a long-lost past. In waiting were Rainbow, the Chief, his parents and Wonders Eye, arm-in-arm with Night Owl. Even good ole Screecher was there, circling above them. While he wanted to reach out and greet them, Lone Hawk felt quite odd as his great size now dwarfed these precious people, like the figurines he used to whittle in the days of old. However, when he reasoned that their presence in the future could be writhe with treachery, his warm demeanor was cooled by his well-earned suspicion.

"Now, <u>what</u> is <u>this</u>? You've <u>wakened</u> them from their 'Evermore slumber' to be taken as hostages, tools of <u>your</u> coercion?" Lone Hawk called out, raising his fist in disgust of the presumed tactic, as a reassuring gesture for his 'strangely inanimate' loved ones. "<u>Denied</u>, Evil One! I will <u>not</u> bargain for the dead!" Then to his loving ties from the ancient, he added, "<u>Don't</u> worry, my good people. Once I defeat your keeper, I will <u>free</u> your souls."

"No, no, <u>no</u>—Lone Hawk! Please, do <u>not</u> reject the Earth Force's welcome!" the Chief bellowed as he leaned into a determined pace and stopped within proximity, leaving the rest of them to meekly lag behind. Even in his relative-miniature form, Rainbow's chiefly father still emanated an aura demanding respect and so, was well received in his fearless stance. "There is a misunderstanding, to be sure. We are <u>not</u> hostages. Our summons was a request to share in this celebration, honoring you. The good Earth Force has freed us from the spirit realm as an act of compassion.

"Since all that you knew and loved from 'the old' was taken away so abruptly, the Giving One happily rejoins us. You will have <u>everything</u>, Lone Hawk: The 'Great Reformer of the Earth,' its glorious rule in the 'Utopian New Age' and <u>all</u> this, with your loved ones by your side, forevermore. In fact, from this point on, I will call <u>you</u> the Chief while you may <u>now</u> refer to me as Big Oak, the name I proudly held as a young brave. Come, everyone…let us show Lone Hawk, the future 'Chief of the Earth,' our congratulations!"

First among the others to greet him was Screecher who frantically called out to him like a 'tell all' as he, the relative size of a wasp, perched on his index finger.

"Oh, Screecher, it's <u>so</u> good to see you again, my loyal friend," he raved, rather convinced of Big Oak's sincerity, along with the realism they portrayed. However, he still was not comfortable with the strange turn of events.

"This unexpected reunion is <u>most</u> wonderful, Big Oak, but the 'Earth Force' prophecy of my quest to destroy an evil presence now seems a travesty. To believe that <u>I</u> was summoned to <u>lord</u> over humanity like a tyrant seems unfathomable. <u>All</u> my expectations have been twisted and deranged. <u>Please</u>, make some <u>sense</u> of this!"

"Of course, I understand your reluctance as your preconceptions do not jibe with the realities at hand," Big Oak explained with effective persuasion while the rest began to saunter towards him. "This here is the Earth Force's magical domain…<u>that</u> of the 'Giving One' who just spoke, <u>and</u> of the sphere in your chest that has guided you, home. As you've come to learn the nature of this 'new' future world, you <u>must</u> now know that the <u>true</u> 'evil presence' flourishes above in vast numbers.

"White devils from the east, yellow devils from the west and all the others who have mercilessly raped and pillaged our planet, they are the evil plague which you have been summoned to contain. It is <u>time</u> to <u>avenge</u> the past as they nearly wiped out our people and, likewise, other aboriginal societies who <u>lacked</u> the military power, yet <u>respected</u> the land as its own. Though today, they may <u>claim</u> that social equality has been achieved, they exploit our descendants as novelty and suppress them as the lowest of the low.

"This <u>cannot</u> continue," Big Oak forbade, then wrapped up his shouted spiel with zeal. "We <u>must</u> restore our <u>pride</u>! You <u>know</u> what you must do. You are the spearhead, Lone Hawk 'Great Earth Chief,' to <u>take</u> it back and <u>put</u> the world on its proper course!"

Lone Hawk stroked his beaked chin as a wise old scholar his beard, thoughtfully analyzing every angle of the debate. "Of course, I do agree with much of what you say, Big Oak, but your tone so <u>disturbingly</u> reeks with a thirst for bloodshed," he respectfully cautioned. "<u>True</u>, humanity has evolved into a widespread caste system of <u>gluttonous</u> materialism favoring the 'privileged' few while the vast majority suffers. Sure, this fact angers me considerably. <u>Yet</u>, whatever means I would use to correct the situation, they'd be peaceful. In contrast, you almost seem to suggest <u>genocide</u> as a solution. I <u>hope</u> that's not the case!

"Also, the Earth Force's black box test, the talk of this Lucifer, and the entire manner of speech was too peculiar. And these <u>Owlmen</u>! They are <u>extraterrestrial beings</u> called the 'Grays', that is, according to popular belief in this technologically advanced society. <u>What</u> is supposed to lead me to believe <u>otherwise</u>?"

Big Oak responded right off without a word, but a worshipping grin. And though not of the Warbird tribe, he brave-fist saluted to which Lone Hawk automatically complied by completing the brave-bonding tap with his middle finger. While Screecher promptly migrated to his other hand in response to the sudden motion, the others came forward at full stride. It was as though the gesture dissolved their fears, signaling perhaps the frightening monstrosity and Lone Hawk were one and the same.

"Yes, Lone Hawk, the Chief you <u>certainly</u> are…so thorough and <u>much</u> wiser," Big Oak fawned accommodation, supplying what seemed a plausible explanation; "I am so…<u>still</u> of the old ways, <u>behind</u> the times, ha-ha—seeking revenge and such! Your approach, to the contrary, is that of a god's patient foresight combined with 'human altruism.' While you have <u>both</u> these wonderful qualities, the Earth Force is lacking in the latter, and so, needs <u>you</u> to fill this void.

"As for the loyal ones you call the Owlmen, they were created 'long ago' by the Earth Force as its eyes and ears. Like monitoring spirits, they have proved most vital for investigating surface activities and, most importantly, preparing the 'chosen one' for his cocoon. They have performed most adequately in their covert function, but theirs will be retiring to another. For now, the time has come for the Earth Force's will to be known in overt fashion through a true and mighty figurehead…And so, it is <u>you</u>, Lone Hawk. <u>Prophecy</u> fulfilled!"

Mildly content with Big Oak's clarification and charmed by his praise, Lone Hawk grew tired of such serious discussion. In turn, he also became especially distracted when his gaze had affixed itself to the beautifully delicate Rainbow, who cracked a hopeful smile. "When once again the Earth Force speaks, I will begin negotiations to form an agreeable agenda," he complied, casually putting his opened hand before Rainbow's bare feet as an invitation. "In the meantime, let's visit for a while. I have endured <u>so</u> much and wasted, it seems, an immeasurable amount of anger. I <u>deserve</u> a moment's rest!

"Please, <u>Rainbow</u>, and once the 'Sky Goddess'? Hmm … whatever, come aboard! <u>Don't</u> be shy. <u>All</u> of you, relax and talk to me. Though I am physically distorted and much larger than life, I'm still the 'good old' Lone Hawk, you used to know!"

Without hesitation Rainbow hopped gleefully onto his hand and knelt there, caressing his expansive palm in a state of awed exploration. "Even behind the beaked, sandstone mask and beautiful eyes of opaline caverns, I can now tell that it truly <u>is</u> you, Lone," she said with welling eyes while she draped her arms around his thumb in a warm embrace, like it was he. "I missed you <u>so</u> much when you were gone, but I never lost faith. My love for you kept me strong … and then, there was that <u>dream</u> in the Evermore sky we shared. But look at us now, <u>here</u> with the Earth Force's blessing to start again."

"Oh, so <u>that's</u> what that was—ha-ha! A shared dream? I'm sure there was more to it, but I'll let it slide … my <u>dear</u> sweet Rainbow, how could I ever doubt you? Well, you <u>must</u> know by now that I never stopped loving you," he gushed as he raised her to his face. "In fact, to your short yet passionate memory I owe so much for my survival there in the dark, and especially when I dreamed of you as the Sky Goddess to break the spell …"

"Lone Hawk! Do you <u>not</u> remember us, your family and <u>talented</u> Night Owl, my soul mate?" Wonders Eye shouted, with his hand obscenely groping up-and-down around Night Owl's waist while the others waved for their attention's due. "I must say, my spirit watched <u>proudly</u> as you slaughtered that second pair of Toltec and took the trouble to haul my body to Big River City. But you <u>certainly</u> reaped your rewards with <u>this</u> one!"

"Yes, I prepared him <u>well</u> for the Princess," Night Owl added with a naughty grin. "Would you not agree, Rainbow?"

"Indeed!" she lit up, in her most sultry voice, still clinging to his thumb. "To 'perfection,' as I most <u>fondly</u> recall."

"Enough of the sexual allusions, ladies; he is now a god!" Timbers Earth, the serious father, called out to tame the escalating levity. "Please excuse them, my son. Just let it be known that we are <u>all</u> so very proud of you. How this surpasses your earlier aspirations to be the Warbird chief! Simply <u>phenomenal!</u>"

"From rambunctious little Bobcat to the Earth Chief," Solarain endearingly commented with a maternal smile; "oh, my dear Lone Hawk, 'no mother' could <u>possibly</u> be more pleased with her son than I!"

Amidst the wave of fawning admiration, Rainbow's actions awakened his carnal urges while thoroughly captivating his fancy. "I hope the Earth Force will grant you that 'fine body' of your <u>manhood</u> to use again," she tempted with a lick of his 'phallic' thumb while she rubbed her flimsily concealed crotch and breasts against it. "Then, perhaps after you complete your mission above, we could celebrate with a <u>glorious</u> 're-consummation' of our marriage."

"Even if this were impossible, I vow to create the possibility and be <u>that</u> man again!" Lone Hawk declared, impassioned by the slit-eyed Rainbow who intensified her writhing into a rhythmic dance. "As well as the Earth's rule, I will have you, my Love, satisfied in <u>every</u> way, forever!"

As pained witness with an air of jealousy, Black Moon glared helplessly through the sphere in urgent disbelief at Lone Hawk's gullibility, with the cross-armed Xavier shaking his head in concurrence. "Really?" he scoffed as he raised his eyebrow to her, expecting a proactive response. "I know, how could he fall prey to such a charade?" she asked, anxious and disappointed, as she noticed that the sexiness of the synthetic Rainbow had caused a stir among the other braves. "Can't you fools tell that this is a trick? You are just as blinded by your male lust as he! We <u>must</u> alert Lone Hawk to this blatant snare of reminiscence!" Unknowing to what contacting Lone Hawk might trigger, Black Moon persisted while it loomed, so nearby.

CHAPTER XIX
The Vipersphere

Despite the mesmerizing effect of the 'resurrected' Princess Rainbow's pole-dancing-like technique in raunchy demonstration outside the sphere's window, only the sole shaman could defy so tempting a view. And though his attention was torn away for merely but a moment, he did acknowledge her concern. "You are <u>quite</u> sure that they are a mere fabrication?" Spirit Slayer wished to reconfirm, though he and the others remained entranced, peering up with delight at the erotic display. "She, the hawk and the others appear even <u>more</u> real than us. How can you be so sure, Black Moon?"

"Their timing is too perfect, their overall behavior is ludicrous and there is no time for a deposition," she insisted while pacing back and forth in front of the window, trying to pull their attention away from the deceptive view. "You <u>must</u> trust my intuition here. I am <u>perfectly</u> convinced that these are manifestations of the enemy. Oh, <u>forget</u> the lot of you!"

"Earth Force, please let my voice be heard in <u>all</u> its clarity to <u>free</u> him of this misgiven trust!" she begged while kneeling with her arms raised to the good orb as only the 'not fooled' Xavier stood by her, his hand on her shoulder in spiritual support. "Lone Hawk! Those are <u>not</u> your people! They are <u>puppets</u> of the Evil One who spoke through the 'false' Chief to trick you!"

"Black Moon?" Lone Hawk acknowledged her faint cries and paused for a new perspective. "Puppets?"

———

305

Encouraged by his response, she started to repeat the message. However, her voice suddenly became muted by the shock of a most hideous face that quickly dominated the window's view in protrusion. With its long crocodile-toothed snout poking through the sphere's curvature, a dark green, red-eyed pterodactyl-dragon beast made its presence known. Then causing the floor to rise behind them, it fused with their thrones and formed gray-ribbed wings to gather them. Before any of the braves could effectively respond to the creature's abrupt attack, they were confined to its inner wings by cable-like vines which simultaneously sprouted.

Fortunately, though, one of them was free in a stumbling Xavier who fell backward, tripping over the rising floor. "Goddamn it! What the hell?" he yelled in utter dread while eying the beast, focusing on him with a blindingly bright emerald orb in the front of its bazooka-like crest. And while the situation reminded him of his first encounter with Lone Hawk when he froze in fear, Xavier intended to redeem himself and thus faced the intruder as a true brave ready to attack. "Let 'em go...you, ptero-demonic fuck! Or, now yer gonna git it...grr!"

The growling Xavier cocked his spear yet a weird green haze filled the air, so he could not launch it with any accuracy. Hence, he was caught off guard and his feet were dragged out from beneath him by the lunging, snapping snout of the reptilian avian terror. As it prepared to gobble down his carcass, he hung upside down with his legs in its jaws and caught a glimpse of Black Moon entwined pathetically to its breastplate with the others, five-rowed inside each spread wing. Wincing to the pitiful sight, Xavier seethed with rage. Then in violent reaction, he swung his body upward and around with a daring move.

"Now, here's an 'eyeful' for ya!" the 'joker' hero that he was boasted with a toothy grin while he stabbed the spear as deeply as he could into its eye. Firmly entrenched with its jaws' release, he hoisted himself atop its shoulder and stirred the skull's contents well, causing the hideous monster to shriek with earsplitting intensity. And though he had been shaken off and dropped, Xavier clutched the weapon's shaft for a moment's suspension by the spear still lodged in the tortured beast's eye. Maintaining his grip, he swayed with the last few shakes of its hammer-head which soon led to the creature's fading and near complete disappearance. After he was grounded by its physical depletion, Black Moon gave him a hero's embrace.

"Xavier, the Dragon Slayer!" she raved, with a leaping kiss on his cheek in thanks. "Brave Sir Branion—Quest Saver Extraordinaire!" While her flattery was appreciated, it was no time to celebrate since the crest's blaring orb had survived. Thus, out of the floor, it rose and hovered above them as if gloating. Then after casting a shower of sharp green sparks upon them, the streaming orb dove out of the Earth Force sphere while pulling Rainbow, Screecher and the other replicas to disappear into its tail-like vapors.

"Look at that! I think it has something much worse planned for Lone Hawk, now!" Red Bear warned astutely with a slap of his forehead, pointing his spear at the ominous pyramid of violet gas growing before them from the Xenorena floor where the emerald orb had seeded itself. "I hope the Earth Force releases us soon. We saw the power of just one spear and now there are twelve, free of surprise. Hurry, good Earth Force, please grant our passage before it becomes too powerful!"

Without delay, the figure began to spin and whip into an inverted tornado with Jupiter-like stripes of red, purple and green. As its rotation accelerated, it developed a mirrored image atop, creating an hourglass design which increased the colorfully cumulus whirlwind to a height twice that of Lone Hawk's. Then growing no larger, the revolving slowed and a frighteningly tangible image started to unfold.

Thankfully, Black Moon had reached Lone Hawk in the last sliver of time, so that his sensibility could return. With his trusting complacency of near doom vanquished, his raging spirit of awareness came back ever rejuvenated. Thus, he soared into a state of exuberance by the suspenseful treat of seeing his opponent take form.

"Finally, then, show your wicked self!" Lone Hawk commanded with terse conviction while impatiently he rubbed his hands together, barely containing himself. "Dredging up my past was very clever. Those re-creations almost tempted me away from the truth.

But fortunately, <u>I</u> have <u>real</u> friends who have <u>rejected</u> you from my being. You now hold nothing to challenge me."

Immediately after his daring words of challenge and proclaimed invincibility, the twirling ceased with a deafening crash and revealed a mountainous snake of red and purple zigzag coils. Through bright blue, diamond-shaped eyes, the wickedly beautiful viper peered down on Lone Hawk. As it smiled with an almost human quality, a pink forked tongue poked out of its relatively small, white-fanged mouth. With full pouty, glossy red lips in near kissing form, its flailing tongue suggestively waved at him.

Lone Hawk merely disregarded the mocking gesture and began to slowly hover around the magnificent serpent. Undaunted by his scouting, it turned its head, still grinning in silence. Once journeying halfway around its coiled wall, he met the tail's end and, much to his surprise, it sported a hissing head of a viper. But unlike the mother's above, the other end had bigger fangs and a dead black stare. And though much smaller, this one was far more menacing than the 'deemed' mother atop. And so, moving on and clearing the lessor's view, Lone Hawk was thoroughly relieved to be past such a disturbing encounter.

However, while he was refocused on the prominent 'mother' Keeper, peeking from above as if it were a game, the tail-viper below its majesty latched onto his wing and suddenly flung him around to where he had been. To that entertaining start, the entire congregation of Owlmen stood and raised their hands with fabricated applauds abounding while Lone Hawk, quite shaken, maintained his distance to further analyze the situation. Then, with his attention affixed to the orbicular jewel in its triple-crown, he began to formulate a strategy against the alien viper by the entrancing object's searing emerald glow.

"Tsk, tsk, I'm <u>so</u> sorry that our union has been dissolved, my precious Lone Hawk," the Xeno's Keeper, now the viperous monstrosity before him, started in a tenor range of demeaned poignancy. *"It would have been so perfect. A world empire to <u>bedazzle</u> the universe is what you could have had. The realization and utilization of your power's full potential, which you have barely scratched, would also have been at your disposal. Unfortunately, this fabulous opportunity has been*

whisked away by your 'so called' friends. Hence, you can thank that <u>*relict*</u> *bitch and contemporary clown for your ruination.*

"Oh, and what a shame indeed. You will never know the pleasures of which the shape-shift transformation process would have brought to you. Your lust really began to flare when my 'alluring' Rainbow was on display, but you could only watch in frustration. Over nine long centuries without probing that warm and slippery paradise which you so enjoyed... how utterly <u>*horny*</u> *you must be!"* The Keeper laughed, clanging and clattering its numerous metallic scales like thousands of shaking tambourines. *"And wow! Remember when she first revealed herself to you—yum!"* To further the insult, the viperous being then temporarily transformed the center of its triangular face into a wispy image of her finely formed nether region. *"Ah, the carnal delights, as well, never to be fulfilled. Well, I hope you enjoyed your brief little escapade because this time, the void awaiting you* <u>*is*</u> *eternal.*

"But, before I put you away with my other disappointments, I will allow you to marvel at this, your last visual sensation and my personal favorite. The fabled feather snake of Native Central American lore, known by many names, yet, as I rise from the ruins of Teotihuacan, restored to the beauty of their glory age, I will merely be known as 'God' thereafter. A far more refined grand entrance, you <u>*must*</u> *agree, than your explosion of* <u>*mud*</u> *at that obscure bird mound."* The great entity chuckled again; yet, for special effect, it sprayed mud from its mouth like a geyser amid more canned laughter emanating from the Owlmen fans, an assault Lone Hawk deflected gracefully with his wings. *"But what is a feather snake without feathers?* <u>*I*</u> *know! In your honor, Lone Hawk, and as my better half, nonetheless, happily ever after, our union lives on for the world to see and worship!"*

Re-modified to his mirror image and triple down-sized to fit, the former tail-viper beast swung forward and was replaced by Lone Hawk's fused legs, torso with well-muscled arms, sabered wings and his stone-faced feathered head. The trunk-bound duplicate was the final blow to his pride and self-restraint as it was made to brave-fist salute him, and turn its head toward its gloating viperous master for approval. To see himself, a fawning sidekick to the one he so infernally hated spurred his most responsive course of action since he had emerged.

Within an instant, following a miraculously swift and accurate catapult upon the Keeper's face, Lone Hawk's prying hands were cradled around the emerald sphere, he deemed its power source. Anchored by his wings, he began to extract the jewel from its crown like a giant third eye from its socket. As he pulled it to his chest, he was sure that the Earth Force sphere would help him crush and destroy it. "By the power of the Earth Force, Evil Keeper, my vengeance will now reap justice as your patience goes unrewarded, and your <u>wicked</u> dreams unfulfilled. <u>The</u> End!"

Suddenly, in slick denial of his threat, the electric green orb turned to a greased, supple consistency and squirted out of his clutches, snapping back into its crested socket. The crowned face followed suit as it became concave and closed to a pinch around Lone Hawk's head. In the vice's grip, the Keeper's powerful eyes were directly next to his while his limp body lay draped upon the alien viper's pointed snout.

"That was <u>impressively</u> daring, Lone Hawk! But, without the power to match, it only serves as amusement, and I have <u>had</u> my fill of <u>you</u>," the thoroughly dominant entity explained in its flaunted arrogance with optic intimidation of the absolute extreme. *"I will put you into your misery now, impetuous fool! So, give my regards to the 'Dark' Light Bearer Lucifer… The two of you should make an 'interesting' pair!"*

Upon his release, Lone Hawk was repulsed even further when the Keeper's wet lips covered his entire face with an unexpected, sumptuous kiss. Immediately following the heinous act that left his face dripping with saliva, it pulled away from him and struck with a whip-lashing head-butt far too rapid for any reaction. While he expected to be thrown some distance by the great impact accompanied by roaring applauds that quickly faded, the force merely transposed his being to ride once again in the lava vortex toward the black hole. Most curiously, however, he lay naught a struggle and was neither discouraged nor resentful.

"Bravo, Feather Snake hopeful!" Lone Hawk cheered, clapping his hands with fervent delight. "That was <u>stupendous</u>! As have been <u>all</u> your feats of 'vile creation,' savor them well, falling Keeper…for your last trick turns back to you with your <u>worst</u> regrets!" Lone Hawk then became positively disimpassioned to an invincible state of nirvana that was mediated by the Earth Force sphere, and shared by his disciples within. Freed from the emotions which were essential for the entity's unfair advantage, he rose from the molten swirl. Intuitively then, he forged his way to the Xenorena's floor with undeniable passage. Solidly crashing through its stony lid, he sent the rubble to splatter in all directions. Yet, just before the deadly barrage reached the astonished alien assemblage, he swept his wings forward and, in reversal, gathered the debris to whence it came. There, the massive hole of his surprise re-entry was filled promptly so restoring the Xenorena stage to its smooth perfection, clearing the path for the 'grandest of entrances.'

For as Lone Hawk stood before his viperous foe, hypnotized like a charmed cobra, he spread his arms and wings to their fullest extent while soft, blue sloping waves streamed down from his gushing chest-bound sphere and surrounded the base of the ever-lofty opponent. Then, with their captivity finally at its end, the 'Earth Force' dozen, spears in hand, rode the magical waterfall to come around the enemy on both sides to meet the 'false' Lone Hawk at its tail end. Immediate to follow, they evenly skewered the bottom coil with strong, short-range throws. But a disruption occurred when Lone Hawk's 'lesser twin' swiped Red Bear's spear.

"<u>No</u>! You will <u>not</u> deny Red Bear his moment of glory, Anchor of Doom!"

Red Bear was not about to lose his treasured spear. And so, driven by a warrior's rage that could not accept defeat, he pounced upward and towards the feisty one, cradling the stolen spear. Displaying amazing physical ability which they all soon would find they shared, he crashed high above the floor right into its chest. Shrilling like a hawk, it then tried to jab him with his own spear, but he wrestled it away, climbed up and stabbed its throat while having no effect. Thus, climbing further, he spiked its stone-piercing tip deep into the miniature Lone Hawk's face, right between the eyes. The tail-spawn's form then reverted back to that of the lessor viper's and soon collapsed. After Red Bear was thrown down to where he was before by the sudden drop, he handed off his spear to better positioned Spirit Slayer who had been transformed by the crossing into a young man with a full head of hair.

By circumstance, the Earth Force shaman would hold the highest honor. And so, aiming with so little time at the 'Vipersphere' centered in the Keeper's tripled crown, he three-step lunged and catapulted the spiraling shaft with all his might only to achieve a wobbly, widely off-the-mark throw. Then 'upon a miracle' as Spirit Slayer roared and cursed in shame, the 'Hawk Spirit' Screecher's translucent raptor soul darted out of the Earth Force sphere at a blinding speed. Thus, to the rescue, he successfully intercepted the ill-fated spear and corrected its course straight into the Keeper's emerald orb. Upon completion, the ghostly hawk simply shrieked with joy and vanished into the darkness of the artificial night's sky.

Their eminent duties fulfilled with special thanks to the Hawk Spirit, they backed away to witness the final phase of the mission as Lone Hawk took over. Starting it off, thick blue bolts of light emanated from his palms and became the igniter that sparked each shaft with the necessary charge. The mystically neutralized Keeper was then encapsulated by a frenzied array of lightning and vibrated to a rumble. Soon, it disintegrated coil by coil, pounding as a percussive nightmare. Thankfully, the sonic attack merely echoed for a moment and quickly gave way to silence, with the entity gone without a trace.

In turn, they all looked around at the Owlmen Grays in the stands for a reaction, which amounted to nothing. Yet, subtle shock in defeat could be surmised by their sudden stillness. For the moment, they began to regroup with sighs of relief, as the scene took a temporary turn to peacefulness. Short lived, their eagerness to expose the aliens rendered 'void of a protector' was about to follow. Unfortunately, there was only a fleeting reprieve when a hopeful sign, on the Owlmens' part, had them standing. With their hands held high, the ominous multiple-sets of blackly hopeful eyes peered up to the quasi-night sky. As giddy as they could be in their stoic-ness, the audience knew there would be a second round. Henceforth, the Keeper's fiery green Vipersphere re-appeared in its bodyless form high above the Xenorena bowl. Lighting up the entire sky, it then thrived and descended with a pulsating hum that intensified. Peering upward, Lone Hawk cast his piercing red, flood-light eyes upon the spheroid and quickly levitated until he was right beneath it. Just out of his grasp with the blue beams, once again, emanating from his palms, they were repelled and fired back at him, causing his spiraling mass to crash onto the unforgiving floor.

As the fabricated applauds roared and filled the stadium once again, Lone Hawk began to gather himself to his knees while the activity in the artificial sky's shallows grew evermore threatening. Sparks began to shower upon him from the Vipersphere's electrical field, grinding around it with an increasing rhythmic tempo that signaled the moment of destruction was just seconds away. Then back on his talon-feet, Lone Hawk held his forehead slow to refocus and in obvious need of a morale boost, which Black Moon provided. With a brave-fist salute and her fervent shouting of the most effective ancient chant she could think of, a catchy bit created by some adolescent boys at his charisma-packed tribal address nine-centuries-before. "Lone Hawk, Earth Force Son—Owlmen, your days are done! Lone Hawk, Earth Force Son…" Thus, with the others joining in and repeating the chant over-and-over, the reinvigorated 'Son of the Earth Force' stood tall and set his crimson laser sights on the 'critical mass' vibrating Vipersphere, just as it released its lavish destruction.

In the form of red and purple, expanding and thumping rings like Saturn's but spaced widely and compressed, curving bands were expelled from the raging Vipersphere into six-massive bursts of smooth circular waves in all, to fill the transforming sky. However impressive, the last and the brightest was so devasting that strange bellowing voices boomed out in sensor-round while the Owlmen Grays' crowd noise sounded like crying and growling wounded animals at the same time. Soon after the final and most disturbing dose of artificial audio anomalies faded with the sixth-power surge's delayed release, the very real sounds of the Earth's pained moaning and groaning were heard world-wide with their deepest fears a brewing. Yet to the wicked Keeper's Vipersphere, the reaction was of absolute delight, as it released a jolly bit of laughter while jettisoning upward and out of sight.

Nonetheless, with a jabbing brave-fist and a champion's nod to Black Moon and the gang doing the same, Lone Hawk took off in pursuit of the fleeing saboteur at full-speed. And once he pierced through the oceanic crust and rocketed from the curving wall of a tidal wave, he calmed it in passing and forged on. As every major fault-line had been triggered by the trilled energy bursts, he was well aware of the wide-spread quakes to be yet another challenge, piling onto his all to burdened conscience while continuing the chase. Thus, he focused even more intently on the capture of the retreating Vipersphere that sparked the same rings above throughout the stratospheric grid as it did below. While gaining on the electric-green orb, beginning to lose its luster more-and-more into Earth's ionosphere and magnetosphere, Lone Hawk, closing in, trailed it by only a thousand-feet. Coming up fast, he shouted his last words of advice as the deposed Keeper's Vipersphere proved most clever and resilient, knowing how to play him to the bitter end.

"You are <u>much</u> too depleted to keep this pace, so <u>give</u> it up, Fallen Keeper—I have 'clearly' won!" Lone Hawk brimmed with confidence of near triumph; yet he was all too self-absorbed in the vengeful side of his quest to consider the immediate urgency of the second set of discharge blasts released in the upper atmosphere. Though more than happy to clarify its advantage, the Vipersphere ignored his victorious declaration and brought the situation to light in a dark, whimsical manner that included a full symphony orchestra, playing classical theme music conjured by the sound effects master. *Alas, the slow-witted Lone Hawk wondered in his quandary, 'hmm, do I forever chase my creator, the Giving One, who bestowed me the power of omnipotence, or do I save the remaining human race from extinction?'... You, big <u>hideous</u> freak, even with your limited intelligence, now my knowing as such—of <u>course</u> you will return to them!*" the sputtering orb mocked and went on while spewing exploding red, purple and green sparks into its comet-like tail that crashed against Lone Hawk's face yet did not thwart his gain on it, then only a hundred feet away. "*Serve, save and protect, hmm, sure—<u>knock</u> yourself out! And spoil them <u>rotten</u>, as you languish in your loneliness, unappreciated and <u>always</u> the fool!*" Lone Hawk slowed his pursuit to reconsider as the Keeper's taunts turned to his last laugh, and a cryptic warning to follow. *"Well, if you don't hurry back, Feather Brain, and continue the futile chase, they <u>will</u> burn—I assure you! Oh, and for your information, my precious Lone Hawk, I <u>will</u> be returning to you, to them because, in part, I've never really left the place—you'll see! Tee, hee-hee…"* Thus, zipping off and away from the tongue-tied stalling Lone Hawk, the Keeper's Vipersphere blended into the bright light of the moon and left him with no choice but to quickly turn back.

Leaving a u-shaped stardust impression in his trail, Lone Hawk raced against time to save the upper atmosphere, clearly fragmented by the sabotage compounding below. During his searingly anxious return, he assessed the scattered gaps in the failing sky's matrix and spied a tiny gold figure spreading its healing light into the web, gradually connecting and repairing it though at too slow a pace. Then upon his closer approach, he saw the gleaming figure as that of a splendidly naked woman, his 'real' wife of the ancient, Rainbow the 'Sky Goddess' calling out to him in a distorted voice as his perspective transformed strangely to being within the sphere. Though glowing a bright pale blue, Lone Hawk was pleased to be back into his virile human form and thus inspected his nakedness with nodding approval to a possible invitation. Intrigued, he looked up to watch her stunning beauty grow evermore distinct in closing as her sweet voice became audibly clear. "Hurry, Lone Hawk—we <u>must</u> save them!" the same 'golden sun' Rainbow from his quest's start shouted with the utmost urgency, then demanded with opened arms what he had hoped. "We must merge right now—immediately! Or <u>all</u> is lost!"

Seconds later, Rainbow absorbed herself into the sphere with an embrace so lovingly familiar, it was like their last was only yesterday. Then while they shared a deep probing kiss, Lone Hawk ever-so-meekly expressed his desire as to what she had meant. "Ah, so nice to be with you again, my 'sweetest' Rainbow, so <u>you</u> mean 'we' can fix this by…" he implied with a knowing smirk while welling in arousal to the delight of further approval. "<u>Yes</u>, my dear Lone, the purest and <u>deepest</u> expression of 'our love,' right here and now…yet <u>this</u> time, with the Earth Force's blessing! So, without <u>further</u> delay…" As limber as ever, the ambient Rainbow pulled her knee to her shoulder, like the last night they had together, allowing a more accessible angle as he eased himself inside her wonderful warmth with ecstatic sighs just beginning. In rapturous flux, their wavering bodies' gold and blue light swirled around them and all about. Then in response to every thrust, their magically distinct colors combined to form a lime green shroud that burst into the grid, brighter and stronger, until it filled all-the-skies around the globe. Soon after they reach the absolute height of their ethereal lovemaking, their gasping mutual climaxes caused the auroras borealis and australis to stretch and intertwine with each other, their multi-colored fingers caressing in kind.

Following with frenzied facial kisses of the most loving nature, Lone Hawk and Rainbow as man and wife, together once again, paused forehead-to-forehead and laughed in relief that they were not too late. Then splashing into some good-humored pillow-talk like they used to way-back-when, Lone Hawk trilled his fingers along her firmly curved backside and spoke soothingly while palming the side of her angelic face. "Oh, how beautifully a glow you are … and this time, quite literally," he joked, lamely adding a mock-spoken laugh. "Hah, ha-ha, sorry about that … well anyway, I must confess that the Keeper's sexy-dancing replica of you made me 'strangely' primed for this, like a 'gift of appeasement' … um, I don't know—coincidence?" She tilted her head and gazed at him, smirking with a nice retort then leading to an unexpected request. "Yes, maybe, but that's quite alright because it doesn't matter where you whetted your appetite, just as long as you eat at home … or something like that—ha-ha! But on a serious note, this 'joining' of ours truly was the only way, and 'more wonderful' than I could ever have imagined. Yet, there is someone else who needs you right now, more than ever … We had our time and this 'rekindling' as well, but as I exist no more a sky spirit, she is a 'real woman,' once again, and with real needs—so go to her! Our paths will cross again someday, I am sure … however, the here-and-now is with her …"

Lone Hawk was stunned by her fervent endorsement of the 'other woman' yet could not argue her point. "Alright then, but I just can't see myself loving anyone as much as I do you … Oh, but when I thought I would never be with you again, well … Black Moon, she's very special to me, and <u>such</u> a leader…hmm. So, we'll see. If only I could morph myself like <u>this</u> but rather, my natural color…huh, who am I kidding?" Lone Hawk scoffed, getting discouraged yet then he perked up to their world-saving team effort. "Anyway, hey-hey! Hurray for **'Earth'**—we <u>really</u> did it!" His spirited rebound had her soaring as well with a leap of faith toward his 'moving on' with the most-worthy Black Moon. "We <u>sure</u> did and trust me, the two of you will figure it out…"

Leaving with an adoring smile, Rainbow backed away out of the sphere, blew him a kiss then mouthed 'I love you' to his welling eyes and heart, pounding in joyous appreciation for such a sweet and enlightening moment bestowed him as she faded back into the sky's matrix. Thus, with mixed emotions returning with his human form seeping out of the sphere back into his colossus birdman being, he nonetheless revised his priorities to Rainbow's wise encouraging advice. And so, he carried on with a steep, hyper-sonic dive into the late afternoon troposphere with a smoky deep-crimson sun, hanging and blurring amid endarkened cumulus a swirl. There, on one of the western Volcanic Islands a couple hundred-miles-or-so northeast of the splashdown site earlier that day, Lone Hawk spied an aircraft carrier with planes sloppily strapped to its deck wedged into a mountainside, a few miles below him.

Then focused on the ship's runway with people scrambling about, he sustained a controlled drop over it where volcanic ash was swirling from every direction with the abounding scent of smoke-laden death, overwhelming Lone Hawk's acute olfactory sense. As he veered from a steep plunge to just a mile above the disabled vessel, he could hear a woman's voice, so familiar, screaming for help. Recognizing her upon arrival, he grabbed a hold of the giant ship's bow and gingerly freed it from the mudslide into the ocean. Sea-worthy in the choppy waters, the mighty aircraft carrier, U.S.S. Reagan was, once again, afloat. On its deck, however, Agent Andrewska, dozens of sailors and others scurried to hide except for one brave lady—the 'faithful' Jeanine, clinging to the railing near him and in a state of shock.

To re-assure her, Lone Hawk stared into her eyes while his were glowing forth, so invitingly, in a tranquil sky-blue hue. "Worry not, 'brave heart' Jeanine, he awaits you below…with <u>all</u> his love," he comforted, soft of voice. "<u>Come</u>, I'll bring you there…" With a nervous smile, she nodded while waving in peace and walked out onto the palm of his out-stretched hand. There then a stumble, she fainted and collapsed into a deep sleep. Curling her to his chest, he then cradled her gently into the safety of the Earth Force sphere and shoved the ship further offshore to avoid its re-grounding. Waving in appreciation, the other survivors on board crept out of their hiding places while he and Jeanine continued back into the watery deep.

Lone Hawk proceeded through the ocean floor in 'spirit transition' form, and zeroed in on the Xenorena coordinates. Awaiting were Black Moon, Xavier and the rest of the Earth Force contingent, main floor center, all eager to learn of the outcome. However, his somber entrance from above was news enough, well shy of glorious. And to concern him even further, the thousands of Owlmen once there were unexpectedly absent.

"The Vipersphere of the Keeper has fled," he reported, disappointed and depressed, as they looked up to him with apathetic sighs. "It left me with a choice between 'revenge or rescue.' I chose the latter, of course. At least, it <u>is</u> weakened and gone for now, but we <u>must</u> fortify this Earth since that <u>wicked</u> orb still has the <u>gall</u> to assume its ownership. It even claimed to have <u>not</u> gone away from here…at least, not 'entirely' and, in so many words, <u>swore</u> to reclaim it! Now, with <u>that</u> food for thought, did <u>any</u> of you notice that the Owlmen have vacated this mystic bowl?"

Though his tone being obnoxious, Lone Hawk trusted that there was a reasonable explanation. Thus, Black Moon stepped forward with open arms, set to work her charms. "They communicated with us telepathically and made clear their intentions to repair the systems that their former 'master' had sabotaged," she assured with a warm smile. "Their loyalties now lie with you, Lone Hawk, and I'm <u>sure</u> they will prove most valuable for the rebuilding yet to come. And <u>now</u>, congratulations are in order…for you, Lone Hawk, are finally and undeniably so, the **Earth Chief**!" Amidst heartfelt, brave fisting applauds led by Xavier and Red Bear, Black Moon approved with a beaming smile and flinging hands, beholding them all.

"That's right!" she shouted, with the Xenorena echo on 'their side' for a change. "Let us celebrate this 'for the most part' <u>victorious</u> moment!"

Lone Hawk reflected on the concept with up-lifting pride and, as the tectonic plates were pacified to a halt, his optimism returned.

CHAPTER XX

Unisons

RETURNING THROUGH ONE OF the dimly lit, concealed hallways at the edge of the Xenorena, six Owlmen approached the center in the floating gate, Lone Hawk so well remembered. As a gesture of surrender, adaptation and congratulations, they stood before him and raised their four-digit spindly hands, with pivotal-long pinkies of thumbing capacity that began to stammer.

'*You have returned the victor, just as your loyal one, Black Moon, had predicted,*' they communicated with worshipping black eyes, beaming as simultaneous telepaths; hence, they were an audibly silent coterie, due to the absence of vocal cords. '*We are the Six Elders and now exist to serve you, the new leader who shall guide our course. For our first report, full control of atmospheric core systems, which were damaged by our former master and mostly repaired by your efforts, has been nearly restored to optimum capacity. Upon your inspection, would the new master delight in a full-scale demonstration of its abilities?*' Although declaring their loyalty, the Elders, awaiting Lone Hawk's decision, would unknowingly make the ultimate sacrifice.

As with Xavier and Nimbus, his natural demand for knowledge would result with the dangerous mind-melding process; only, this time was to be the first for multiple recipients. While the opportunity to absorb the secrets of the Keeper 'directly' had slipped away, the Owlmen Elders would be the alternative supply, a vast library of new information. Also, as time was most precious, considering the mass destruction of the planet, complete and immediate awareness was needed to spare himself and the others of any more unforeseen obstacles.

To the sight of Lone Hawk's eyes, transformed from opalescent to churning red and white, the Six Elders dropped their tiny jaws with bug-eyes a bulge and minute mouths agape, all too humanly personifying the expression of terror. Then as they began to somewhat sadly accept their fate, the presence of these Owlmen Grays was far different from his first encounter when they were the superior aggressors, and he was the ambushed victim. The proverbial tables were turned, yet necessity rather than revenge motivated his actions as he felt sorry for his former enemy.

Alas, Lone Hawk proceeded as before and released sweeping vectors of multi-hued light in a plane to the level of the Elders' eyes. Upon contact, their heads then became encapsulated by glowing spheres of rust and violet oscillation that lifted them to temporary suspension at a meager height. After a short moment's chemo-electro feasting, he dropped the six alien bodies to impact while falling forward and convulsing, their white tunics flopping on the cool gray swirl of the Xenorena floor like dirty snow angels. Seconds later, they were motionless. And so, the dead Elders shed their mind-meld spheres that evaporated back into Lone Hawk's eyes.

"They have gone off to an 'Evermore' of their own," he said with mournful, deep blue eyes while his disciples watched in awe. "They could <u>not</u> survive the meld…probably because they were so <u>very</u> old. Over <u>five-hundred</u> years each of virtually <u>ceaseless</u>, toiling tedium for the now fleeing Keeper. Yet, the fruits of their routine efforts would culminate the 'most dedicated' human scientist's dream, considering what they were about to unveil. A technologically 'perfected and controlled' world solely prepared for their god, the Keeper, to bolster his overt claim and rule of it. Hence forth, my fellow Earth Force chosen, <u>this</u> is what we have <u>successfully</u> averted.

"Might I also share, without taking too long, that the Keeper's an alien spheroid much like the Earth Force, but from another planet and much more powerful. And though it may not have always been evil, such a nature would <u>definitely</u> have been enhanced by the melding of the 'Lucifer' entity. But without getting into all that, it obviously had <u>some</u> compassion, as it <u>did</u> save the Owlmen species…by guiding their 'chosen armada' through a worm hole to Earth, <u>barely</u> escaping their six-mooned, purple paradise that fell prey to a super nova. Then, soon after they had settled in this buried Xeno's realm, the first Owlmen pioneers were advised by the Keeper to remain here until it had deemed the surface fit for their habitation. However, these clever creatures commenced their 'human abductions' program devoid any disobedience…since <u>none</u> of them was aboard. Hmm, though disturbing, I feel that I must show you their first victims, a group of Native Americans from six millennium ago." Astutely, the twelve gathered before him like intrigued monks to a new 'Buddha' monument, even though a hidden communal reluctance toward the viewing of such atrocities was their actual sentiment. Then after pondering their underlying dread, Lone Hawk's own apprehension nearly made him reconsider until, with a sharpening stroke of his beak, he reaffirmed his decision. Their inclusion to the truth, however painful, was vital to sustaining their trust. Thus, making it so, the documentary was displayed in the sphere like visions in a soothsayer's magic ball.

While their eyes lit up to the visuals of the first nocturnal hunt logged by the Owlmens' low-flying robot craft, Lone Hawk provided some pre-capture narration. "After crossing the Asian, European continents and the North Atlantic Ocean, this high-capacity drone followed the seaway to the North American Great Lakes, which would accommodate their wishes quite well as you can see…"

The archived action scenes played on: Well past dusk, the probe was following a big river's outlet to the ancient shoreline of present-day Lake Ontario, which glistened by a high new moon in its southwest course. Dotting the great lake's divided edge, the bonfires of the Stone Age Native Americans could be seen in surprising concentrations, discouraging any immediate abductions. But further on, the grounded flames began to thin soon after the waters widened to an ocean-like vastness where a fair distance down the south shore, the perfect victims awaited. There, the stealthy capture-probe swooped upon the isolated, unsuspecting lot huddled next to their beachside fire, faces ablaze in fear. Then, hanging in a tight circle of low-level entrapment, the robot ship's scooping mechanism was extended like an escalating ramp. Combined with the engaged vacuum, ten of thirty were gobbled up.

"Like a great bird of prey <u>snatching</u> up a pack of mice…how <u>undignified</u>, how sad," Thunderhead commented, echoing all their pitying sentiments.

"Yes, good Thunderhead, how deplorably sad," Lone Hawk acknowledged, with the visuals in rapid-terrain sequence. "But how pleased the Owlmen would be with the gender ratio. Seven-to-three, wombed-to-fertilizing—the <u>way</u> they think! And of such heartiness, 'what a <u>fine</u> first batch of human specimens,' the project leaders thought, remotely viewing while the 'sample set' was rushed with a sense of urgency to the Xeno. <u>Now</u>…as much as it pains you, watch how they're disgraced before the massive congregation, standing pondside to see the prized 'human' earth dwellers in the flesh." Lone Hawk's voice became disturbed and so he paused again to allow the sphere to reveal the first captives' nightmare.

First to be shown was their expulsion from the ships chamber, forcing them out with a microburst and reversing the ramp's ridged belt. Staggering in confusion, the startled longhaired humans had nowhere to go as the hatch closed behind them. Dressed in simple deerskins with shells, teeth and feathers, they were not so unlike the ancient Warbirds, thus captivating Lone Hawk's 'flock' even further. For soon, the three men arose to a defensive posture, with their backs against the women who were facing each other in a circle. Then shouting mysterious chants to the Keeper's dome, they had mistaken it as a porthole to the natural sky. As they seemed pacified by the hope from above, the Six Elders of the time approached the close-knit-group when the men drew their sharpened stone knives, slashing out at them in bluffing intimidation while they still kept glancing up to the dome.

"They were not disgraced; they were <u>braves</u> to the end— <u>see</u>!" Badger shouted to save their honor. Yet, with an obscure, unfounded faith, the apathetic natives then seemed to give up and expect nothing more than a magical rescue from the sky above. But nothing was coming, and the Owlmen were losing patience.

Through with the amusement had by the primitives' erratic behavior, a nerve wave interrupter was activated from the ship that made the ten unfortunates collapse into a helpless yet conscious heap. From there, they were transported on floatation stretchers and paraded by the gawking multitudes to their giant laboratory, situated just beyond the outer rim of the main floor. They were laid on husky examiner's tables of a cold stone-like metal and were immediately stripped by teams of four-per-subject. Once naked, a well-lit station of various probes, injectors and extractors descended above each table to the terrified eyes of the immobilized humans. While two would work on either end of the body, concentrating mostly on the head and pelvic region, every orifice was delved, including the navel and the eye sockets, a cruel demonstration that caused the twelve of them to wince at the subjects' coursing agony. Even more unbearable was the sphere's view of the Owlmens' celebrated extraction of three fetuses in midterm development, drawing extreme objection by the most deeply affected Black Moon.

"Stop this, Lone Hawk!" she protested, her eyes welling in sorrow while her forbidding hands waved affront her own face. "I know it took place very long ago, but we do not need to see any more of these atrocities!" The Earth Force Sphere faded to green and blue swirls, prompting Black Moon to fold her hands and bow in pity for the poor savages. Following her lead, the others did the same, awaiting his response.

Feeling the pressure, Lone Hawk, though not at fault, was touched by her sensitivity. "I am sorry, Black Moon, but these images tend to flow with a life of their own," he defended but with some regret as gently, he stroked the draped locks from her face, reaping at least half a smile. But then, he became aware of the current abductee situation, with a heightened sense of urgency.

"Oh, no … and there are many abduction victims, right here—to this day!" His voice began to rumble with his 'signature' angered shade of red, brewing in his eyes. "I must release them from this heinous detention, at once!" With a timely appearance, six Owlmen, looking just like the first set, entered the Xenorena, herding six self-levitating stretchers before them. To task, they parked them beside the forgotten corpses of their predecessors and rolled the bodies onto the white rectangular skids with the six-and-one insignia. Thus, like riding on magic carpets, the 'stretchered retirees' floated off autonomously into the corridor beneath the stands.

Then accommodating the current situation, the Six 'replacement' Elders brought him 'news of pre-fulfillment' to his anticipated command. *'New Master, we have been monitoring your discussion and acknowledge your disapproval of the human captivity,'* they informed, hands raised to eye level in their meek approach while Black Moon and the others cleared to the sides. *'All two-hundred-eighty-three, total living, have been released and shall soon arrive for your full inspection prior to transport. Will you also require our execution like the Six Elders before us for further punishment? If it must be so, we will send for the third set.'* Everyone looked eagerly to Lone Hawk, for his reaction to such a stunning report.

"Very good, I look forward to meeting them," he encouraged while calming to an agreeable tone that was leading to yet another re-naming idea. "And as for you and your species, there will be no more mind-melds and, therefore, no more sacrifices of Owlmen life. 'Owlmen', my first primitive impression of your kind…that quite simply will <u>not</u> do! And for the Keeper, the 'Loyal Ones'? So dryly demeaning! Then, there is your 'six-and-one' theme of your destroyed home planet and its moons…an identity, but mere numbers—that will do you <u>no</u> honor here! So, since I will labor on this no more, I shall respectfully call your kind the 'Unisons', as it describes you best. You are the <u>epitome</u> of efficiency and cooperation. Pure action in accord toward a common goal…you are the 'envy' of what human industry and development had ever hoped to achieve.

"Now then, Six Elders of 'the Unisons,' I have one more request: Prepare for a global broadcast of my state of the planet address, so I can explain the situation to as many humans as possible, all at once. And by this, I mean reaching the masses, <u>free</u> of 'big government' and 'big media' intervention…that is all."

Backing away as they bowed, the newly proclaimed Unisons acknowledged Lone Hawk's encouraging words. *'Thank you for your confidence and the noble name you have bestowed us,'* the Elders said as they stopped at the edge of the main floor. *'Arrangements for your global transmission will begin immediately.*' Disappearing into the corridor from whence they came, the Unisons left a treachery-free, positive aura in their trail as ever-trusting allies. Thus, with the 'abductee release' mission underway, Lone Hawk directed his attention to Xavier, unable to wait any longer to spring the 'Jeanine' surprise on him.

"Xavier, you have some…personal concerns which you would like to voice?" Lone Hawk baited, waving his precious 'modern day' warrior in his tattered military attire forward to speak. In turn, the 'love sick' Xavier obliged his motion with a barrage of questions.

"Yes, Lone Hawk, uh, Sir Earth Chief…as you can 'probably' read my mind, you <u>must</u> know that I'm worried to death about Jeanine who lastly, as I recall, was with me on the 'Reagan' jet carrier. Did she survive? Also, what about my family near Chicago? I may have been out of touch with them, but <u>goddamn</u>, what if?" Xavier queried in a strained raspy tone while he looked to Lone Hawk and the others with a sense of belonging. "As much as I'm honored to be a part of all this glory beyond my <u>wildest</u> dreams…to find out that they didn't make it would <u>kill</u> me! <u>What</u> is the extent of the damage? How many dead?" He stood cross-armed and stared, unflinching, into Lone Hawk's eyes which flared with oscillating shades of green and blue.

"You have grown <u>quite</u> bold since our first meeting, Xavier my brother," Lone Hawk admired with a quick brave's fist salute to his new 'Earth Age' recruit. "I hail you for your enlightenment of these times. I would have been blind to this future world without your knowledge…and <u>all</u> of us <u>doomed</u>, if not for your response to the Earth Force summons. <u>You</u> were the vital link, connecting with timely perfection. I thank you as do the rest, I'm sure. But—I <u>am</u> sorry that I can tell you nothing of 'all' your loved ones and how they fared in the disaster. So many have suddenly joined the ranks of the dead that to single out an individual, a vessel or an area is not yet available to me this instant, however…" The Earth Force sphere began to stir as a wonder-eyed Jeanine emerged from its soft-churning watery light.

"I just woke up…then, I saw you through this round window-doorway to…<u>wherever</u> here is? It's so <u>beautiful</u>…yet so weird—ha-ha!" she elated, looking all about and absorbing the surreal environment as she baby-stepped down Lone Hawk's carefully placed forearm like a ramp. "Your 'kindred spirit' here, made a 'snatch and stash' move on me from the ship and, I guess, it scared me so much I fainted." Xavier, caught off guard, shouted awkwardly out to her with an exaggerated echo effect, which Lone Hawk had amplified for them both as a fun-filled splash of drama for 'their' moment. "Wow, just…oh, wow—hey! you're okay! I was so damn afraid you didn't make it, but here you are!" he rejoiced, hands pressed together as his prayers were answered, then he added, "I guess…against all odds, this makes us 'an item' again?"

With 'puppy dog' eyes, he extended his hands forward and clumsily formed the 'heart' sign to her. Thus, scoring 'big time' for love, he had the dreamy-eyed Jeanine frozen in her tracks, more smitten than ever. So, in the spirit of the moment, she shook her head with an adoring smile and said so cleverly, "you had me at 'well, I think I'll go reptilian now and jump in the ocean!'." Impressed, Xavier laughed and waved her over. "Good one! Now, get over here before everyone gags on this cutesy 'cringe fest' here…" Amidst applauds and giggles, she trotted over to him and planted a lunging kiss on his lips. While not 'Frenching' too deeply, they engaged in a quick, legs-spinning hug then just held hands, redirecting their full attention with nods of heartfelt gratitude towards Lone Hawk.

"Sorry for the delay, Xavier, but after all that Jeanine had been through…your 'brave heart' love just needed a little more rest," he said, beholding his well-flung hand to them and their blissful reunion. "How so very fortunate, or rather—wonderful for the two of you! Now," Lone Hawk swept his hand out to include them all, for another request; "before you are all transported to your destinations of choice, you will need to stand as visible witness to the global address I'll soon present—which is sure to reveal much more than we already know—and here we go! Elders—have you no sense?!"

Led to him like a parade, a 'naked human' ensemble of abductees was brought and presented to Lone Hawk by the Unison Elders, shocking everyone to their forced immodesty. Approximately two to one, women to men of varied races and cultures, they huddled together with neutralized mind-sets, due to the Unisons' sensory sweeps. However, the effect was clearly wearing off as they became frightened and embarrassed, with their meek glances up to Lone Hawk, as 'scary looking' as he was, registering into their all-new twisted reality. As well, their suffering was painfully apparent as many of them began to stammer and weep.

"You <u>poor</u> people, don't worry—these Unisons just don't know any better…I, <u>too</u>, endured their tortures but long ago. However, <u>now</u> they serve <u>us.</u> And soon, they'll bring you home," Lone Hawk reassured in a soothing syrupy tone, yet to their ever-heightening cries. "In the meantime, though…I think some clothing will make you feel more secure and, perhaps, a little more 'the brave' to my <u>monstrous</u> presence in this strange, mystical place." With a sweep of his hand, their quivering nakedness was well adorned with custom-fit US military attire just like Xavier's, with his restored to new condition as well. Hence, with their 'birthday suits' covered, the behavior of this 'unlikely flock' took a drastic turn for the better, evolving to a relaxed bit of mingling among themselves.

And to the ensuing social mood, Xavier, with Jeanine proudly looking around, took it upon himself to embrace the crowd while finding that at least half of them spoke English. "Y'all are <u>very</u> lucky, despite what you've been through…since the damage to the planet's surface caused by the vanquished 'alien leader' who created this place—<u>must</u> have <u>killed</u> millions!" Xavier shouted to the people who looked trustingly to him with nods of hope. "I witnessed the <u>blasting</u> circular waves of destruction that it released, just before this 'great one' here, Lone Hawk, quick-chased it off into the sky and saved the Earth from oblivion. And, in case you don't believe what he said about these Grays, uh, now called the Unisons, serving us…well, it's totally true! They're going to take us centuries into the future with their <u>awesome</u> technology! But, by no means am I making light of your <u>dreadful</u> experiences…"

"<u>We</u>…are <u>actually</u> going to ally with those 'horrible creatures' that used me like a breeding machine?" a tall blonde woman of early middle age called out, with sheer disgust in her Australian accent. "They <u>think</u> they can use us and <u>wipe</u> out our memories! But I've been through the regressive-hypnotherapy, and I know <u>damn</u> well what they've been doing!"

"Yeah, to <u>hell</u> with forgive and forget! These atrocities <u>must</u> go to an international war trial!" another outspoken one, a young Amer-Asian man of conviction, then took the floor and hollered with a jabbing fist of protest raised toward the Unison Elders, standing nearby. "<u>This</u> is <u>no</u> different from the Nazis of World War Two. I'm <u>sure</u> that you're going find that, for <u>every</u> one of us, there are many more who have been killed by them! We're just 'lab critters' to these freaks! <u>Sure</u>, get the benefits of their technology, but <u>then</u> you've <u>got</u> to rid the Earth of these goddamn 'Grays'—you were right the first time, <u>buddy</u>!"

The crowd began to grow comfortable in their complaints while Xavier tried to calm them, leaving Lone Hawk to stand merely as a landmark amongst the others. But when the unrest escalated into a distempered uproar with the angry victims closing in on the circle-formed Elders, Lone Hawk brought it to an abrupt end.

"There will be <u>no</u> backlash, like this! They are…through their 'robotic ignorance,' innocent to the evil that was done!" he bellowed to the stalking multitudes that were hindered suddenly by a force field, which he created for the Elders' much appreciated protection. "The <u>one</u> responsible for those 'unforgivable' evil deeds, has fled. And with that, besides their own naiveté, the <u>vile</u> influence that they could not defy, no longer takes hold. As with their name, the Unisons <u>have</u> changed for the good—<u>completely</u>! I can see that it's going to take a lot more than I had thought, to see humankind to such a graduation. So, <u>hey</u>! No pressure, 'really'…but I <u>won't</u> be discouraged." The angry crowd shuffled away from the impenetrable Elders, disappointed, and regrouped to whispers away from the others, in a block at the Xenorena main floor's furthest end.

While Xavier, Jeanine, Black Moon and the youthful Spirit Slayer left the fold to offer counseling to the freed abductees in their brooding denial stage, a host of red, basketball-sized optic spheres floated into the Xenorena from the corridors. As the spheres of three dozen hovered and positioned for an elaborate audio-visual transmission, Lone Hawk thought their means inadequate. Though the Unisons' sky matrix would out-perform any number of conventional satellites, receiver controllers in the 'legacy' Media would have an unfair advantage. And so, while thinking back to the Evermore when he projected his life's story into the sky, he started to brain-storm. For during that presentation, his disciples could more than merely see and hear it like a movie, but feel and mindfully absorb its full sensory array. Thus, the ever-inspired Lone Hawk devised a new plan. To achieve overall fairness, he was determined that his delivery of this 'most important message ever told' would, in its fullest effect, reach everyone on the planet at once, no matter where they were.

CHAPTER XXI
Earth Age Dawn

T O LAUNCH HIS ALL-ENCOMPASSING communiqué, Lone Hawk accessed the Unisons' vast network by utilizing one of their optic spheres. In the form of a tiny blue ember flashed from his eyes, he became another who could easily venture into the spherical receptor towards its power source. As a continuous being of pure energy, he found himself surging from the Earth's core where he absorbed momentous power reserves. By the time he reached the ocean's surface out of the Dragon's Triangle's point central, he had developed into a glowing, quarter-mile shaft of varying hues which resembled an electrically charged mushroom cloud spouting into the overcast, late afternoon sky.

When his core-anchored trunk reached the artificial grid, it spread ever-directionally as a curious flux of multi-colored checkers, traveling a hundred-miles-per-second at a constant altitude on the smooth, curving plane. In effect, he dissipated the clouds, volcanic ash and air pollution to perform a filtration sweep while major fires and lava fields were extinguished and cooled by telekinetically rerouting the flood waters effectively in every which way. Within minutes, his cleansing shroud narrowed to a close on the opposite end above the South Atlantic Ocean near Brazil where he reversed the shaft phenomenon, back to the Earth's core. As he joined his beginning point, he formed an axis and had gone full circle in a magical journey leading back to himself. Lone Hawk had become the entire 'core-to-sky' matrix system, observing all the world. And in simultaneous existence, he was still the staunch, benevolent birdman watching wondrously, the peculiar mix of humanity the Xenorena had come to hold.

Atop the world, Lone Hawk's alter-ego assessed the horrible destruction, with a full-scale view of his global perspective. He estimated that at least a quarter of the total population had met their deaths, including the wild and domestic animals also suffering astounding mortality figures. The new face of the Earth was a mapmaker's dream as North America had been altered the most. While the east and west coasts were fragmented deeply into several new islands, its sunken mid-west was filled with a huge gulf fed by a massive extension of the Pacific Ocean, replacing Central America and southern Mexico. The Hawaiian Islands were totally submerged, leaving relatively few survivors in boats and planes. Additionally enlarged was the gap between Africa, Europe and the Middle East, as the Mediterranean Sea became an oceanic thoroughfare from the Atlantic to the Indian Ocean, with most of Spain, Italy, Egypt and Saudi Arabia taken out by a major crustal tear. With the highest population concentrations, India, Malaysia and Indonesia and all the destructed land masses to the south experienced the most casualties, due to widespread flooding and earthquakes. Drownings, burnings and crushing were generally the cause of demise for most of Earth's dearly departed. They were the sacrifice forced by the Keeper's hand, but Lone Hawk felt at least partially responsible for their lives' abrupt end. Thus, he would mourn and pay homage to them first in his global message.

As the entire Earth's sky glowed a deep, royal blue creating a black light effect, Lone Hawk injected winding streams of gold, turquoise and violet shades from its poles. Sharply resolute, they reached their fingers across the globe and met like two spidery hands, merging as an exaggerated aurora borealis and australis in effect. The stage was well set for his carefully prescribed audio-visual, telepathically enhanced address which would deny neither the deaf nor the blind among the survivors, of its full impact.

Since he still wished to maintain an air of mystery, his use of pseudo-hypnotic flashes of actual imagery from the Xenorena would replace continuous full-motion visuals to sporadically emphasize, point-by-point. Amidst the light show beheld into the surreal sky and their borrowed minds, this announcement of the most radical dawning of a new age would be the first to include the entirety of humanity in simultaneous commune of the same miraculous experience.

"Survivors of the Earth, you are the 'fortunate ones' of a <u>new</u> era," Lone Hawk started and would finish his address in his normal 'tenor-relatable' voice, but with the audio enhancements of a song vocalist. "And for the many dead who've moved on among you, ours is to grieve their loss as well, and to honor their sacrifice as it was <u>not</u> in vain. Fortunately, though, the destruction that took them has now been halted while additional medical and reconstructive assistance is being implemented for the areas, most in need. Oh, and just so you know, I, 'Lone Hawk' was once a mortal man … as human as you, but that life was lived nine centuries ago. So, as I've been harkened back for this 'pivotal day,' I am <u>now</u> something <u>much</u> more, chosen to champion for the 'Earth Force' … the conscience, life source and ever-caring soul of this great 'Planet Earth,' on which you call home.

"Resist whatever fallacies your legacy media has formed in its ignorance and deception as to my purposeful emergence. Since the dawning of your civilizations, there has been an alien presence monitoring your advancement. They <u>almost</u> successfully launched a worldwide siege under the rule of an evil one <u>much</u> too powerful for <u>you</u> and your obsolete military to subdue. I have expelled this one, as my sacred quest required, yet … our foe did <u>not</u> go quietly. It used its remaining powers to sabotage and almost terminally disrupt the planet's equilibrium. Then to my good fortune and with some 'spirited' help, I was able to chase the 'depleted' evil entity off into space, and restore the atmospheric overhead while the Unisons retained control of the Earth's core.

"The <u>Unisons</u>, as you may wonder, were the 'programmed' followers of this fallen threat," he explained while visual flashes of the Six Elders sequentially accompanied their mention, following those of himself at the introduction. "Hold no animosity toward them, for they were virtual slaves to their 'underworld' Keeper. But now, their loyalties lie with you and me while providing some major accommodations to start. Soon, they will arrive at various locations around the world in their silent silver ships of 'saucer and cigar' shaped designs to perform their first good will mission of delivering 'just recently discovered' abductees back or close to their homelands. If you happen to see them, I'm sure you won't be surprised as their physical appearance is that of the stereotypical 'Gray Alien' type, with bubbled heads and big black eyes. The Unisons are a very odd species, indeed! But even so, they actually are 'true earthlings.' However, their ancestors were from 'another world'…destroyed by a super nova over six millennia ago.

"Though I understand your skepticism, try to welcome these 'reformed Grays' turned Unisons. Their technological abilities, soon to be revealed, will fascinate the world and provide the basis for solutions to many of society's problems…especially with their 'Unison' clean energy utilization and atmospheric control. That's right, 'free' clean energy for all—just for starters! From there, availability of resources will be widespread and abundant. Hoarding will only prove futile as the gap between unfair advantages and disadvantages will shrink. Enlightenment rather than greed will serve as your primary inspiration while you still enjoy the competition and challenges that so fuel your inner drive.

"Now then, to officially negotiate, organize and secure this transition, an envoy representing the Earth Force, 'Black Moon' will soon be delivered," he continued, with the image of Black Moon transfixed to everyone's mind as the one to recognize. "This appointment of her through me shall, for the 'first time' in human civilization, truly be the voice of your host, 'the Great Earth,' in a government capacity. Thus, as a sovereign nation, the lands of western Wisconsin and Illinois that hold our ancient roots have been annexed to form the new 'Earth Force Nation.' Let us hope for maximum cooperation towards this change between the former host of these lands, the United States, and our most welcoming 'freedom loving' country that will take the lead as the testing ground for these exciting new technologies while distributing them accordingly. This is not a precursor to 'me nor the Earth Force,' throwing our weight around like an 'authoritarian ogre' with his godly crystal ball taking charge, and all. But…we certainly will persist and persuade towards a worldwide balance, in which we <u>all</u> can live and thrive…

"Finally, as for these 'abductees,' I mentioned, who were likely presumed dead or missing…they have now assembled as they wished, and so I am <u>most</u> honored to present them…" His words reflected a strobing flash scan of the congregation of 'said people,' cheering and waving as if appearing on a baseball game's jumbotron video screen; and from there, he switched to a minute's rotation of the Earth's new face. Then in closing, he signed off to a fond farewell. "And so, the healing begins. The <u>true</u> 'Earth Age' has dawned, my good people. May it bring you peace, prosperity and a renewed love for life."

Lone Hawk wished to say much more, but to maintain the elaborate effect became exhausting. Thus, he retreated from the grid at the equator to the poles, leaving the skies behind in their natural state. The axis faded into the oceans and the energy was returned to the core, with Lone Hawk's alter-conscience sent to rest. He then informed the Unison Elders to commence transport of Black Moon and the 'fondly freed' abductees to their appropriate destinations. As for Xavier and Jeanine, Spirit Slayer, Red Bear and the other Earth Force braves, all were content to go back to where it all started. To be re-grounded with the familiarity, Devils Lake's south shore was where they chose since, fortunately, the park suffered no further damage.

However, in sharp contrast to the joyous 'send-off' mood of the brave-fist saluting disciples, Lone Hawk was strangely somber and started to sink into the floor with somewhat lackluster words in the aftermath. "You have done well, my good…brave Earth Force brothers," he said softly, saluting half-heartedly back at them; "please, <u>do</u> wish your sister well as our representative to these governments…which may harbor 'resentment' towards her…so <u>suddenly</u>, being put in place for such a change. I hope you didn't find this appointment too presumptuous, Black Moon, but you <u>must</u> have known you were the only one…" he paused, already chest deep in the floor, as Red Bear sneered at her, so jealous; "for <u>that</u> position, of course—oh! Red Bear, <u>don't</u> worry…I am <u>sure</u> that you'll find much to satisfy your ambition, playing the 'key administrative role' in the forming this new Earth Force Nation. And beyond that, the world is your oyster! But <u>don't</u> forget! Though you may not notice, ha-ha, I'll be keeping an eye on you…along with <u>everyone</u> else."

"<u>Where</u> are you going, Lone Hawk?" Black Moon cried, her eyes welling while only his face and fist still showed above the Xenorena floor. "What will you do, besides <u>watch</u>? Come on—we are <u>not</u> done here! Come back!"

"Please don't cry, Black Moon," he begged to her silent tears; "I only need to figure out some other things. Once I do, I <u>will</u> contact you." He disappeared under the Xenorena 'battle' stage and plummeted straight into the eye of the churning vortex from where he had arisen. Passing through the dark zone, he had no fear because it was now his to rule. All the Keeper's creations remained intact, even though its 'Vipersphere' wizardry had gone. And so, accepting the spoils, Lone Hawk began to find his way as he exited the eye of a duplicate vortex, facing the opposite direction. He descended to its end where a white circular plane of familiar dimensions awaited his third exit. "The <u>dome</u>! And the <u>big</u> pond below it, no doubt," he correctly identified, soon crossing the curious divider to the inner tower, continuing his descending pattern. When he reached the pond, the emotionally-strained Lone Hawk perched at its edge and looked up to the dome with thoughts of the magical playground he had coincidentally inherited.

"Of course! I could redesign this place to be a 'fantasyland' for the public to vacation. With men, women and children bustling about, <u>this</u> wouldn't be <u>so</u> depressing," he pondered a loud, mildly serious until he looked at his reflection in the water. "Yes, and <u>I</u> would be the <u>main</u> attraction, the <u>colossal</u> oddity! 'See the Birdman Like a Mountain!' the advertisement would say—<u>what</u> a flyin' <u>freak</u> show! Oh, what's the use…" His brooding, so unbecoming to his greatness, continued; yet, a thoroughly plausible question would then baffle him: "<u>How</u> is it that I can blanket the 'entire Earth' with my being, but cannot even recreate my old virile self, so I can <u>really</u> be with her?" his whiney human voice rang out to fading echoes in the vast hollow. "Unlike <u>all</u> my other manifestations…when I try to envision and project <u>him</u>, humanly free of <u>this</u> beast I am, it reaps nothing. I <u>must</u> know the Keeper's shape-shift secret, or

I will <u>never</u> be content! Though, how can I complain? No one is more discontent right now than the millions, billions of freshly dead overflowing in the Evermore, so becoming an utter hell—I <u>cannot</u> shut out their tortured cries!"

The burden of his dissevered reception from the 'extreme concentration' of wailing souls who had plunged into a session of unbridled 'fear and contempt' became louder and more distinct. They were locked in an 'Evermore void' of complete darkness, and thus, were huddled together in a fright-feeding frenzy. While Lone Hawk had endured his time there in relative peace, they were in a self-destructive loop of chaos. Involving so many, he had to try 'something' to fix it, if only for his own sanity's sake.

With his most willful effort and genuine expression, he hoped that he was also a transmitter. "Locked in your fear, you are blind and cannot be seen," he told in a soothing advisory tone; and like his global message, it came complete with tranquil imagery and a hopeful future. "Abandon these wasteful emotions that doom you and separate into the vast 'Lake of Hope' which you now become. The lake then empties into the 'Destiny River' and from there, you flow to the 'Rainbow Mountains,' glistening on the horizon. <u>That</u> is the edge of 'Paradise' where your 'loved ones' passed before await to greet you. Let go, flow and allow yourselves this passage to a heaven that welcomes you all…Mm, hmm—<u>that's</u> it! <u>Very</u> good!"

As the tormented voices thinned and soon faded to silence, Lone Hawk was convinced that he had created the greatest illusion of all. Nonetheless, he sincerely hoped and prayed that it would sustain itself or that possibly another force would adopt his good deed. He imagined so serenely their teardrop souls transforming, one by one, into beautiful creatures of light that soared into the colorful mountains at the end of the river. His thoughts of their joyful exploration would have brought a smile upon his face, if it was not a rigid mask. Yet, he was temporarily content in his well-earned solitude.

However, not long after his rapturous 'spiritual achievement,' the Unison Elders graced him with their unwelcomed presence and interrupted his sweet dream. *Maximum assistance has been implemented on the surface in cooperation with existing emergency aid units. Early estimates place human loss at two-point-sixty-one billion of the previous nine-point-thirteen,'* they coldly informed, standing in a perfect row beside him with their hands folded. *'All systems are repaired, and the transports have begun. Have you any further requests, oh Great Earth Chief?'*

Lone Hawk was blatant in his displeasure as he dropped his forearm in front of them, and leaned toward them with his eyes ablaze. "Earth Chief? <u>No</u>, I don't <u>think</u> so! A monster of 'Japanese film' lore? A huge, <u>comical</u> thing…perhaps? But, <u>Earth</u> who? My, oh my…woe's me, is <u>right</u>—ha-ha!" he lightened up a bit, but continued, depressed. "And so, it seems…the Keeper has cursed me to <u>never</u> reach the shape-shift level—forever, trapped in this 'vile form'…"

Seeming to appear out of nowhere, Black Moon shook her head in disappointment and, with her hands on her hips, became stern in her conviction. "The Keeper only wins when you wallow in self-pity and doubt, like <u>that</u>. At <u>least</u> have the courtesy to look at me when I speak!" she demanded, glaring, as Lone Hawk begrudgingly complied. "<u>Rid</u> yourself of these Keeper residuals. They <u>still</u> seem to thrive in you like a virus, but only because you <u>allow</u> their consumption. Let them go, Lone Hawk! Free yourself, and only then, am I sure that this shape-shift mystery will unfold for you <u>quite</u> naturally," she lovingly advised, then softened her voice and posture to sit beside him with her feet in the water and her hand on his talon.

"When you first woke me in the Evermore, I thought you were nothing more than a demon of sly ways and impressive trickery. Then, when you held me there in outer space, I grew rather fond of you. But later, especially right after your 'life experience' extravaganza, I became more and more frightened of you. Well, of course, we <u>all</u> know the rest…and so, in meeting the Earth Force, I understood and respected you truly as 'The One.' You are an angel, Lone Hawk, and you gave me a second chance at life. With the honor of your trust in me to serve as the Earth Force representative, I have even more reason to give you my undying gratitude.

"<u>Please</u>, let's not ruin this. Forget the Keeper and be involved in the 'New Age' of your promise. Also, as I intended to comment before, don't punish the Unisons with such harshness. If they could only begin to know returned kindness, they wouldn't be so cold. Anyway, you still languish about something else, but I can't read something that's <u>so</u> buried. Need you be so <u>bashful</u>, Lone Hawk?" As Black Moon could sense his smitten emotions toward her, she was immeasurably charmed, even though she had to pry the words from him like an adolescent's first love.

"Black Moon, when we first met, almost <u>any</u> woman would have captured my lusting heart, but you were <u>much</u> more," Lone Hawk gushed with reminiscing affection while daring to stroke her softly curved side. "I believe that my attraction was rather obvious. Especially so, with my first creation being the cloud that mirrored your beauty. But when we were high above the changing Earth, those feelings grew—like crazy! I wanted to give you <u>all</u> the world, just to let you know how I felt…and then I began to change into <u>this</u>. I became unworthy and unable to be one of that capacity to you. However, I <u>cannot</u> stop hoping.

"As we speak, I look at you and see the beautiful, sensitive and brilliant woman I've grown to love and respect with such an intensity that it hurts. I <u>so</u> long to kiss your lips and feel your body next to mine, so I can hear your sighs of pleasure when I come into you…as only a <u>man</u> can do. The frustration is <u>absolutely</u> unbearable, all these things being impossible because I'm <u>trapped</u> in here. That's why I'm so obsessed with this shape-shifting thing; I can <u>never</u> be happy until I can <u>really</u> be with you."

Enamored but separated by the distance between their eyes, she gazed up to his, staring down to hers with pink, yellow and purple swirls of passion. They felt awkwardly regretful in their beauty-beast predicament. Thus, Black Moon drew her eyes away from his in a saddened downward stare, but when suddenly, she noticed something peculiar inside the Earth Force sphere. To her astonishment, there was a ghostly image of Lone Hawk, the man, in his naked unmutilated form swimming like a fish in a fishbowl. Upon closer examination, she could see that he was calling out to her while waving his hands with wanting eyes and a joyful smile. Becoming fully visible to her in his complete natural form of tan skin rather than the blue of before, he scratched inside the pinkish aquamarine orb, but to no avail.

"Earth Force, I beg you—set him free!" she pleaded while climbing up his forearm which he had positioned like a bridge to his ecstatic open-armed self, behind the chest-bound window. "Come to me, Lone Hawk. You are unlocking the secret…keep trying!" When it seemed that their physical union was just about to be fulfilled, a most disruptive, up-surging splash burst from the pond and to her dismay, the image faded away. It was Nimbus with a most inopportune surprise appearance that also sprayed water all over them as he landed, plopping on his side then going under. When he re-emerged, his ability to sustain a tail fin stand exhibited his boastful super-whale strength, besides the fact that he had withstood the crushing water pressure to get there. "Oh, Lone Hawk, and we were so close," Black Moon despaired as she stood in his uplifted hand and leaned against the sphere, finding her urges temporarily denied. "You must find a way to occupy this Nimbus, so we can resume. I just can't wait much longer!" In swift response, Lone Hawk summoned the Elders to soon substitute for his attentions.

"Lone Hawk! I told you I would come after you, and so, I present to you the 'Mighty Nimbus,' Savior of the Deep!" Nimbus bragged in a more-than-telepathic 'teenage boy' voiced introduction that brought about a wide-eyed smirk from Black Moon, who listened with intense fascination. "I proclaim myself as such only because…I saved a massive cruise-ship-full of people. Going totally 'Poseidon,' I gave it a ride on top of a tidal wave that otherwise would've crushed it. When the entire ocean began to rumble and 'wave up' like that, it's a miracle how I was able to lift the thing and surf it into safe waters—without them ever even seeing me! But then I realized that I am an Earth Force brother and there's nothing I can't do! So, after your 'beautiful' sky message, I knew that I must go to the Xeno and see it, along with the Unisons that you had found down here. They're the same as the Owlmen of old, right?"

"Yes, of course, and you would know that…" Lone Hawk answered, juggling many thoughts, with the impassioned Black Moon as his priority; however, even when he was on the brink of fulfilling such pent-up desires, he did manage to tap into Nimbus' high seas adventure and with his rescue efforts deemed credible, he would need to reward him later. "You've done very well, 'hero'

Nimbus…but, as you probably know, I must deliver our 'Earth Force' representative to her duty abroad. Ah, and here come the Elders to entertain you until my return…"

"Oh…then, very well!" Nimbus emphasized his point with marked displeasure, thoroughly aware that he had been given the proverbial brush off. "By all means, good Sir, deliver 'the Queen'…hah!" he then blurted, in a 'mock' British accent. "And these 'funny-looking' Unisons, my god, they're even more puny and frail than the humans, but…they are much smarter. Hmm, this should be interesting." The 'pompously abrasive' Nimbus followed with a swim over to the awaiting Elders and began to unload his arsenal of questions while Black Moon quietly commented, "I thought he was cute, at first. But then, with such a tongue…I think you may have created a monster."

"This monster, you can thank for 'your freedom,' lady…as I am the one who steered him to his destiny, down here," Nimbus interrupted with a 'smirk' if he could, delivering his piercing rebuttal to her overheard critique.

Lone Hawk laughed, with a comment of his own. "The spoiling of the 'human touch' in grand, adolescent form is all we have here. This phase will pass…" Then, when he could see her again just outside the sphere's window from his human perspective, he paused in frustration. He could not penetrate the concave, glass-like barrier that separated them, but he could attempt the reverse. "Black Moon, I can only go so far, but there is another way…" Lone Hawk promised with all his will, praying to allow her through, and thus it was granted. She fell into the sphere as the seal was broken, and there, Lone Hawk caught her by the hips in a room of opalescent clouds. In their sweet embrace, Black Moon found that she had been 'so magically' rendered naked by a 'very functional' Lone Hawk, the man. Thus, he stroked her flexing backside cheeks, up and along her slender waist to her firming breasts, with circular motions, and kissed her lips, long and deeply. There and finally, they gazed into each other's eyes for 'humanly' real. And oozing with desire, they made themselves at home in a *cradle de cumulous.*

"It seemed…that my only choice was to bring you inside, instead," he said, with tender disclosure; "Black Moon, I—" She put her hand over his mouth and, with caressing fingers, held his readied staff with the other. "Shh, now I bring you inside," she whispered as she guided him into her long-dormant, luscious warmth and began the unleashing of what seemed an eternity of pent-up, erotic passion. While he pulled her close by the hips with thrusting penetration, Lone Hawk then buried his face between her wavering breasts, as she held onto his neck and crossed her ankles behind him. It was all she could do to keep them together, since they kept floating and bouncing off clouds. Thus, amid take-off, they ascended through the dome, the double vortex and the Xenorena by his encapsulating self with a wonderous porthole view. Yet, they were too involved to even take notice.

With probing lunges and frenzied tactile exploration, the varied positioning of their weightless communion transposed many stages through the Earth's crust, ocean, sky and, finally, outer space. Climaxing in a glistening pool of silver streaks which spiraled their bodies with carnal energy, their libidos were immediately recharged, even though they had just achieved the utmost level of harmonious bliss. In celebration, Lone Hawk most playfully spun Black Moon, like a cartwheel, on his relentless spindle as they laughed with fulfilling delight. Then after their lovemaking continued for a moment with the same intense vigor, the merging concluded with their second climaxes pulsating gently amid soft facial kisses and affectionate hugs that wished they would never part. Though to her pleasant surprise during their 'special' moment within, Lone Hawk had craftily navigated his vessel-like being to a familiar spot of noted change.

"The last time you brought me here, the colors were so morbid and askew," the glowing Black Moon said in a giddy-girlish voice, smiling and giggling as they marveled through the sphere upon the new Earth, three-hundred-miles above Devils Lake. "And now, the colors are vibrant and alive…but the land has retreated and the water reigns, hugely, and so close…down by the 'ole Wise Crow.' And where your Big River City used to be, it's been engulfed by the new ocean. But, how lucky could we get? Our birthplace hasn't even been touched! You're not taking me there, first…are you?" she posed in jest, well knowing her actual destination could not wait.

"Don't be silly, girl! This is the 'sentimental leg' of our journey, with no stop-offs," he told, sounding a bit regimented, yet still cuddling her with warmth. "I just wanted to be here…while we were on better terms with each other, for a moment's glimpse at the new Earth Force Nation you will proudly represent. Let's savor this just a little more…but then, my young, incredibly sexy lady—you've got a serious assignment! Just waiting there across the ocean, it's come time for you to know this modern world by your own memories, with real interactions. Already, you are the 'most popular' face in the world, and so, you'll have 'celebrity and power' to withstand and uphold. Yours will be of 'excitement and glamour,' yet the demands will be great and times of privacy few. However, when it becomes too much, you can always just call my name…and I'll take you away on a 'fantasy holiday,' if you so desire…"

"Mm, oh yeah—absolutely! As soon as I'm situated, and negotiations are reasonably complete, but wait a minute…just let me say this before I forget: I bet these 'ever-corrupt' world leaders' wicked black hearts sank to their 'reptilian toes' when you mentioned 'free' clean energy for all—hurray! So smug they were and now, hah-hah, so 'utterly disempowered' with no leverage against the 'good people' who no longer need bow to their self-serving elitist whims!" Black Moon, seething, went off to Lone Hawk's sympathetic nodding, but then she backtracked to their tender moment. "Uh, sorry, it just makes me so sad and angry yet 'giddy,' ha-ha—weird! Anyway, back to us…to such an invitation, of course, sooner than you think, Lone Hawk…you will surely hear my sweet, longing voice calling to you, dear lover," she tempted enthusiastically while lacing her words with kisses on his ear and cheek. "But please tell me, what will you be doing? I do wish to inform them of your future intentions, point by point, to ease their fears…No doubt, you just want to be the 'mysterious superhero,' emerging for dramatic rescues with elaborate displays of your powers to spice up the mundane. Yet, for the most part, I see you watching and planning from your hideout in the Xeno…and, of course, making sure the Keeper never returns. So, am I pretty much on to you, my 'Earth Chief' lover?"

"Well, yes…maybe, but most importantly to your point, uh, once you do finally take them down on the world stage, exposing them for what they really are ... just remember, I've got you covered. And that's <u>all</u> the leverage you will <u>ever</u> need. Plus, may I add on a personal note that I <u>do</u> plan to raise Nimbus in a proper, well-adjusted environment. <u>That</u> alone should consume quite a bit of my time!" Lone Hawk laughed, drawing a giggle from Black Moon who could see that they were already halfway across the Atlantic Ocean, nearing her new home-away-from-home. "But, on a serious, um, 'spiritual' note, I did something <u>quite</u> remarkable, before you found me down at the pond. With their cries driving me crazy, I took care of the hellish mass of freshly compacted souls, you know, overwhelming the Evermore ... and I did it by creating a 'pseudo heaven.' Ha-ha, so <u>full</u> of myself, but I <u>do</u> honestly believe that they were drawn there and, through my suggestion, are now in a synthetic paradise."

"<u>I</u> think you 'unveiled' a wonderful place that had always been there; and through your loving, ever-wise perception, you sparked their awareness, as you did mine," she added, the eternal optimist. "You have, and always will have that effect on people ... <u>wherever</u> they may be—and <u>I</u> should know!" Her inspirational magic impressed Lone Hawk far more than any of his supernatural feats. He treasured her even more as the 'sacred one' who kept his demons at bay. However, they had crossed the North Atlantic and were quickly descending into the thick cloud cover above Brussels Square.

Already missing her, Lone Hawk began to choke with emotion, as they were about to separate again. "Too soon we must part, so there," he said, tears rolling down his cheeks, as he swept his hand across her naked body, restoring the colorfully beaded, deerskin vest-skirt and her custom 'Black Moon' necklace that she was wearing before. Then, as a surprise addition, he adorned her feet with of a stylish pair of multi-strapped, olive-hued sandals that she utterly adored. "I think 'they' will be more respectful, if you are 'nicely' clothed. Otherwise, I have no advice for you ... because you <u>already</u> know the Earth Force's will, like it was your own. Therefore, I only leave you with my trust ... and my love." Lone Hawk, the man, said in farewell as he kissed her lips and began to fade.

"Remember to listen for my call, Lone Hawk," she called, with her eyes about to flood; yet she held back her tears while caressing her 'black orb-centered' turquoise amulet like a sacred rosary, and said with a flutter, "I love you…"

Melting to her sentiments, Lone Hawk nodded in common with a somber smile, holding forth the 'heart' gesture to hers in smiling reciprocation. Too soon, he disappeared and rejoined his mythical form. Then with their longings satisfied, they refocused to task as he spun out of the overcast sky, appearing as a gray-ribbed, tan, red and white-feathered monolith while cloaked behind his wings. Hence, the multitudes spread out to the surrounding structures of the Belgian capital's square, but lingered nearby to bear witness. Landing three-pronged, talons and tail-feathers, squatting at center, Lone Hawk cracked his wings just a sliver, before the sphere. In a thin blue beam projected down to the concrete from the breach, Black Moon glided to the square's surface as a two-dimensional image but retained her depth once upon impact. The people began to crowd her where the Brussels police and a host of many dignitaries paved her way graciously to the fleet of Mercedes Benz limousines. Quickly, she was ushered inside the lead limo to take her to the United Nations Headquarters where introductions would be made for her, the first globally known Earth Force representative in human history. Mission completed, Lone Hawk reversed his entrance, plunging back into the grayness above.

He soared in an arching path through the stratosphere and submerged back into the Dragon's Triangle, eager to make up for his earlier inattentiveness toward Nimbus. In so doing, he followed his initial route through Xeno's ocean-floor doorway to add an element of surprise. He darted through the main tunnel and lit them blue and gold in passing. When he rose from the pond, Nimbus was still in the same spot, before the Unison Elders at the water's edge. While the 'white whale' wonder was enthralled by them in earnest, he consciously ignored Lone Hawk who then quietly perched a quarter round of the pool away.

"I admire your patience, Nimbus. But still set right there as you were, it's as though I had never gone," Lone Hawk praised while trying to be amiable, but with no response. "Nimbus, uh, want to go…" Suddenly, with a sideways slap of his tail fin, Nimbus sent a flagrant fouling splash of water upon Lone Hawk and laughed. Lone Hawk, instantly red-eyed, was not amused. He pounced on Nimbus with his wings and arms around him in a vice-like grip. The sorry whale was shocked into submission.

"Why this blatant insolence, Nimbus? You know I would never tolerate such treatment! Are you so jealous of Black Moon?" he demanded, possibly a little too harshly, he thought as Nimbus fled upon releasing his full body pinch. "Nimbus, come back!" Before Lone Hawk started after the speedy whale, fearfully escaping further scolding toward the open sea, the Elders stood as they were, but with looks of silent disapproval.

He acknowledged their sentiments. "Worry not, good Elders," he said, aware of their fondness for Nimbus and concern about his tendency toward mood swings of abrupt anger. "I will be kind and gentle to your star pupil. I'll just let him know we both need to exercise a little more self-control…I also have an idea that'll give him the importance he so desperately needs. This, I will let him tell…and show you—later!" His trek through the Xeno's main passageway was much swifter than Nimbus', for he caught up to him at the bottom of the Abyss. He swam alongside the bolting aqua-brave-gone-scared with a generous buffer zone out of the darkness into an upward, lightening path. They soon reached the sunlit layer of the ocean where fish of all shapes, colors and sizes abounded, and surprisingly, did not fear them.

"Hey! Where ya off to, Nimbus?…wherever I am not?" he called out in a rather 'Xavier style' of speech; the perfect charm it was, nonetheless, to produce a slowing and calmer Nimbus who actually began looking at him again, void the attitude. "Come on…I just snapped because I was afraid you lost all respect for me." Lone Hawk positioned himself ahead of, and facing him. "I'm sorry about that thing back there…it'll never happen again—I promise! Let's just remember to be more civil to each other, all right?"

With his attention fully captured, Nimbus realized Lone Hawk's sincerity and was put at ease. "Yes, that's a 'for sure' but—hey!" Nimbus bubbled as he began to loosen up. "I started it, being so insulting…and I'm sorry too." He tempered their pace to a gradual float to the surface and added, "I now know that, even though you seemed like you wished I hadn't even found you, you <u>really</u> only needed to get intimate with, uh, what's-her-name you so fancy." Lone Hawk was taken aback by his insightful comment but showed no reaction and continued to listen. "So, don't worry, I'll be a good Aqua Brave from now on…"

"Aqua Brave! No, no, <u>no</u>! That will <u>never</u> do!" Lone Hawk hollered in a jolly tone, ready to spring a most welcomed honor upon him. "For saving the 'giant ship' from the tidal wave, I now dub thee 'Nimbus the Sea Chief,' Master of the Waterways. And, to start you off, I will <u>gladly</u> serve as your proud and loyal subject. Do you accept the challenge, great Sea Chief?" Nimbus was so ecstatic, he could only nod and flap his flippers in approval. "Then, it is done. Though as a distinction to this, you need something more than just that mighty dorsal fin…oh, yes! I know <u>just</u> the thing…"

Lone Hawk patted Nimbus' chin and donned it with a bright gold hawk's beak of custom-form fit. "Very distinguished and regal. Very <u>chiefly</u>, indeed!" he praised in fascination of his work.

"Well, I know you put something shiny on my chin, but what is it?" Nimbus asked, in notice only of its strong light reflection since he was unable to see it from the angle of his eye-set. To help, Lone Hawk put his hand on his eye for a visual transfer. "See that? It's a hawk beak like mine, but <u>yours</u> is a brilliant gold," he touted while showing him various angles. "Do you like it?"

"It's beautiful, Lone Hawk! But somehow, I feel like I'm becoming your 'new' Screecher," he approved, but then added with a dash of humor, "when do I get my wings?"

"Nah, you don't want to look so much 'the freak,' like me." Lone Hawk laughed to change the subject. "So, uh, I just happened to notice that you and the Elders have taken to each other <u>quite</u> well. And I was wondering…what kind of stuff do you talk about?"

"Oh, lots of things…they know <u>so</u> much, and I like them a lot. So, we talked about this-and-that, but mostly about <u>you</u>," Nimbus told, almost as a proud son. "They worship you as a god, Lone Hawk…and <u>why</u> shouldn't they?"

"A God? Hah! A timely anomaly, yes, but I won't argue," he said, with a little levity while maintaining an air of humility. "Well, what do <u>you</u> think I am, Nimbus?"

Without hesitation, he fervently replied, "You are the Earth Force's 'Chosen Son,' and for good reason. You are the <u>balance</u> of all that is the Earth, and more. While you are also the 'miraculous being' of its self-defense, which has proved so responsive…you are the perfect instrument of its life-sustaining presence. <u>That</u> is what <u>you</u> are, Lone Hawk, the 'all-in-one'!"

"The Elders sure have made you smarter, 'Sea Chief' genius," Lone Hawk delighted for a dual compliment while bathing near the sun-drenched surface, eyes ablaze with golden exuberance. Meantime, Nimbus looked puzzled, twitching his right fin as though he wished to scratch his head. "Lone Hawk, why are we talking like this? Like old friends, maybe…anyway, we're just so <u>different</u> from before."

"It's because <u>we've</u> come a <u>long</u> way, and now, we're <u>finally</u> comfortable with where we are…and, most importantly, <u>who</u> we have become," he explained, with a gentle hand to his shoulder blade. "We're at home in 'every way,' and it's <u>wonderful</u>…Now, with all those other distressed vessels out there, haven't we <u>dawdled</u> here enough, good Sea Chief?"

With renewed enthusiasm, Nimbus agreed and gladly accommodated his wishes, waving and pointing his over-grown flippers as he motioned westward: "Just follow me, good Earth Chief…forward, towards the sun," he invited, most graciously, with a hearty burst of salty mist from his blow hole. "Let's <u>get</u> this thing started, Lone Hawk, the 'Earth Force' way!"

"Right on, Nimbus ma boy, ha-ha…I'm with <u>you</u>!" Lone Hawk spread his wings and raised his brave-fist salute to the glistening 'sun-halo-donned' Nimbus who then led the way, embarking on his second humanitarian quest as proudly as the first. And though he possessed phenomenally more knowledge and power than anyone else on the planet, 'Lone Hawk the Earth Chief,' as he came to be known was quite content to venture off with the 'super whale' Sea Chief, scouting and rescuing as the Nimbus-cutely-coined, 'Saviors of the Deep'. Unstressed in reminiscence, the companionship reminded him of the treasured times of the ancient with Screecher, the winged 'clutch appearance' warrior who would always stay alive in his soul. At this juncture in time, love and friendship had shone through in all their glory, 'the absolutes' for his appreciation of life.

348

Yet, time was waiting for no one. So, on stellar pace, the needs of Earth's remaining inhabitants were met, and then far exceeded expectations, upon which, the proud Earth Force disciples were suitably rewarded with their independence in whatever endeavors they chose. However, for his vital link to the future, Lone Hawk's gratitude dwarfed the rest. In the form of a dreamland Martian outpost near Olympus Mons, Xavier and Jeanine came to be among the first pioneers on the re-awakened world, with a very special flight-capable gift parked outside and the beginnings of a family in tow.

During a video recording, Jeanine strutted by their sparkling new, purple sports sedan like the one taken over the Capitol on 'the Day,' and patted the gaudy orange-flamed 'hawk spirit' emblem on its hood. Then continuing onward, she sauntered towards their recently formed painted-desert lake that had a vast, curving palm-tree-laced shoreline. There, she noticed off in the distance, a couple of prong-horned antelopes drinking from it. But as a roadrunner in hot pursuit of a rattlesnake darted across her path, she paused for a moment until it seized the viper, whipping about in a nearby cactus patch. She then quickly reached the beach. Wearing a turquoise bikini and her engagement ring again, Jeanine dipped her foot in the water, looked back and smiled, sporting a half-term pregnant belly which she began to stroke. To the adorable sight, Xavier laughed from behind the hovering camera, an optic-sphere with a crystal-clear panoramic view, and mercilessly teased.

"Hey lady, <u>nice</u> beer belly!" he yelled to her in the distance as she sipped her non-alcoholic beer in synch to his unflattering comment and, so appropriately, smirked while flipping him 'the bird.'

"Baby belly—you, <u>big</u> baboon!" the finger-wagging Jeanine playfully retorted as Xavier came into view with exaggerated theatrics, pleading and flinging his out-stretched hands towards her in hopes of redemption.

"Just kidding, okay? Cause you're <u>still</u> pretty hot…even 'preggo' style," he smoothed over to then praise, "and <u>what</u> a lucky girl!

To have a mom, <u>so</u> 'beautiful and wonderful' in every which way." Adoringly shaking her head, Jeanine waved him over. "Awe," she gushed, "<u>get</u> over here, <u>you</u>...ma 'sappy ole' Martian man!"

Before joining her, Xavier raised his finger for a moment's narration to entertain their family and friends on Earth. "Well, people at home...not to blow you off, but while Jeanine and I go for a romantic swim, I'll just program the sphere to take you on a brief tour of the town back there and return, so we can chat..." he told of his 'thoughtfully arranged' plan while tapping on his phone. But then, he remembered to bring up a very precious event, awaiting them just months away. "Oh, and by the way, the baby's due right around my birthday in early May. And all I can say is...a better present, I couldn't <u>possibly</u> imagine! So, see you all in a bit..." Thus, Xavier turned away, skipped over to the beach like a goof ball and engaged Jeanine's loving embrace. Kissing along the way, he carried her from the virgin shore into its tranquil watery zone upon which their homestead-view camera show moved on to complete the 'pretty picture' of their new settlement, with a pink-and-blue-swirled haze softening the sun in the Martian sky.

Meanwhile, back on Earth, Lone Hawk's torrid love affair with the ever-so-busy Black Moon stayed fresh. Through countless escapades in his virtual fortress, the ever-changing view in the sphere's window took them anywhere around the world, the moon and, some day, beyond. Yet still, only she could leave the confines. And while the other Earth Force braves were also very busy moving forward with no pressing needs for his assistance, contacts with them faded to moderation. In time, Lone Hawk's heavy work was done, and thus allowed him to slide back into a deep, longing in reminiscence.

With such a lull of demand, he turned to his own inner space on the other side where he had preserved the past. In the perpetual realm, they awaited and prayed for his visitation. Thus, he announced his plans, to which he had long promised: *At last! The time is right, my good people—I will be there soon, <u>very</u> soon!*

The all-enticing void to an Evermore he thought he could control had come, his absence sparking a rebirth from afar.

About the Author

G ROWING UP IN THE suburban flatlands of Chicago, family vacations to the mountains and the oceans gave young James Thulin a great, refreshing appreciation for nature. Included along the way were visits to Native American tourist spots. During one of these trips, a most memorable visit to the Great Smokey Mountains' Cherokee Valley, back in the summer of '69, piqued his curiosity and thus, an interest in America's aboriginals took hold. Then, a decade later amid an extended 'beer run' into Wisconsin, James hit the motherlode of enduring inspiration when he first discovered the beautiful Devils Lake State Park.

Amidst formidable cliffs and bluffs towering above its picturesque lake, he marveled summer-after-summer at its marque effigy, the 'Bird Mound,' and knew—"There's a story here!". Already lyrically inclined, his first story's expression was in the form of a pop song about a party of ancient spirits in the burial bird mound combining and uniting as the one, all-powerful savior of our future, imperiled world entitled "Earth Chief." So inspiring was this 'early recordings' favorite, the catchy tune sparked a series of brain-storm sessions, ultimately creating the foundation for something much more profound.

In turn, James spent most of his free time, impassioned, writing this 'tour de force' that eventually evolved into a spiritual journey of discovery, with a visually 'specific,' new superhero in mind. Then, also carrying the EARTH CHIEF title, the epic novel unfolded and evolved into a complex story of extremes which, thanks to his

90s women-friends, also included a prevalent 'romance novel' angle completing the formula. Hence, while using such a fusion of genres to effectively honor the long-lost people living there at the time, James envisioned their ancient experiences then brought them to life in his first fully-formed version of the sci-fi thriller. Featuring their Earth Force's chosen son, Lone Hawk, who re-emerges far in the future firstly as a global threat, the 'Earth Chief' he has become quickly turns humanity's attention towards the true danger, surrounding the entire planet and possessing its core. Thus, the 1999 publication went into print, which then eventually and most notably led to the far more spectacular 2024 Silver Edition, a carefully crafted revision that secures the story's relevance in these rapidly changing times.

Also worthy of mention: While finalizing the original EARTH CHIEF book, James found the time to satisfy his cryptozoological interests by writing the 'Bigfoot-based' short story, PURGE @ 8000, which features a dejected mountain man and a most heinous sasquatch encounter. Abruptly turning his sad, solitary existence upside-down, this shocking dark comedy turns a tall tale like no other. In addition to such 'outside' projects, James got back on track with a natural inclination toward the movies, and tried his hand at screenplay writing. As a result, he churned out two, elaborately descriptive EARTH CHIEF film adaptations, separately depicting the ancient and future portions of the novel. These then proved greatly influential in developing this 'timeless' enhanced version of the original book, written for a new age.

On a career note, James worked 27 years at an R&D facility for a major building materials company, formulating performance surface applications for various substrates. In 2011, he was issued on a U.S. patent for a melamine-formaldehyde-free back coating, supporting sustainable ceiling systems. Long gone from the industry, James, better known as Jim, now enjoys retirement through his writing, song-smithing and visual arts, designing potential 'Earth Chief' merchandise. While his ongoing writing agenda includes completing the EARTH CHIEF book sequel and its coordinated screenplay, he's also in process promoting an EC theme song, with many other original recordings to follow. And for the outer-fringe fans, Jim's next major writing project is based on his ten-years' plethora of paranormal experiences.

EARTH CHIEF

A Native American brave follows his ambitions to a cave that was rumored to harbor a powerful magical sphere…

"Bring that back to the valley and you, Chief Lone Hawk, have the beginnings of an empire!"

Guided there by the beautiful princess of a mysterious tribe, the brazen young Lone Hawk then finds he has inherited much more than he bartered for:

BESTOWAL	DENIAL	ABDUCTION	REVENGE
"I had no control while it chanted into my head!"	"The Earth Force Son? This is crazy!"	"…a strange, spirit-like breed of men who made the 'Big Sleep' to capture me!"	"Bide your time, Evil One, for when I wake, the dawn of your destruction will be at hand!"

Thus, far in the future, his alter-being rocks planet Earth and captures its soul, in the ultimate thrill ride to seek and destroy the evil below.